ALEX HAWKE is

". . . everything we want in an action hero."—*Booklist*

". . . a secret agent who takes you into the danger zone with a ballsy wit that had me hooked."—Vince Flynn

He's a razor-sharp new thriller hero—a James Bond for the 21st century!

ACCLAIM FOR THE ALEX HAWKE THRILLERS BY

NEW YORK TIMES **BESTSELLING AUTHOR TED BELL**

SPY

"A great beach read that will not disappoint."
—*Richmond Times-Dispatch* (VA)

"Think Tom Clancy and Robert Ludlum meet Stephen King. . . . *Spy* is THE book of the summer!"
—*Glenn Beck, CNN Headline Prime* and author of *An Inconvenient Book*

"Outstanding."

—Lou Dobbs, CNN

PIRATE

"*Pirate* is a heck of a good ride."

—*Houston Chronicle*

"A rollicking tale ripped from the disturbing headlines of our dangerous times. . . . [Bell is] an author who has clearly mastered his trade. The ingenious subplots gel seamlessly."

—NewsMax.com

"Contains more action and interesting characters than most books do in three. . . . Bell easily could be considered the rightful heir to the throne of Robert Ludlum. . . . *Pirate* and its predecessors are unbeatable."

—Bookreporter.com

ASSASSIN
Also available as an eBook!

"Fast and furious. . . . Readers will be caught in the whirlwind of action and find themselves having a grand old time."

—*Publishers Weekly*

"Fascinating characters, a hairpin plot, and wonderfully talented writing. *Assassin* is what you get when you pair a great story with a great writer."

—Brian Haig

"Readers will be enthralled."

—*Booklist*

"I love authors like Clancy, Ludlum, and Flynn. Ted Bell is in that league. His research is so amazing you'd swear the events in the book actually took place. And here's the scary part—they could."

—Glenn Beck

"*Assassin* is the most highly imaginative thriller to come along in a long while."

—James Patterson

HAWKE
One of *Library Journal*'s Best First Novels of 2003

"A fiery tale of power and privilege, lusty and sinister intrigue, *Hawke* is a fast-paced adventure . . . truly an exciting read!"

—Nelson DeMille

"Rich, spellbinding, and absorbing. . . . Packed with surprises . . . great fun."

—Clive Cussler

"A perfect summertime thriller."

—*Dallas Morning News*

"Outstanding . . . [A] rip-roaring tale with a grand hero. . . . A commercial blockbuster packed with pleasure."

—*Library Journal*

"Ted is my favorite author. . . . If it were up to me, he'd get the Pulitzer Prize!"

—Lilly Pulitzer

"Not-so-secret agent Alexander Hawke makes James Bond look like a slovenly, dull-witted clockpuncher."

—*Kirkus Reviews*

"Nautical, rugged, and sophisticated."

—*American Way*

"[A] thundering debut."

—*Sun Sentinel* (Ft. Lauderdale, FL)

ASSASSIN

TED BELL

POCKET STAR BOOKS
New York London Toronto Sydney

Pocket Star Books
A Division of Simon & Schuster, Inc.
1230 Avenue of the Americas
New York, NY 10020

This Pocket Star Books premium edition June 2008

POCKET STAR and colophon are registered trademarks of Simon & Schuster, Inc.

For information about special discounts for bulk purchases, please contact Simon & Schuster Special Sales at 1-800-456-6798 or business@simonandschuster.com.

Cover art: Bridge: SIME s.a.s./estock Photo; Explosion: Daron Cooke

Manufactured in the United States of America

10 9 8 7 6 5

ISBN-13: 978-1-4165-8712-5
ISBN-10:   1-4165-8712-8

This book is respectfully dedicated to Captain Theodore A. Bell Jr., U.S. Army Air Corps, Ret. In June 1942, Captain Bell's 77th Bomber Squadron, 11th Air Force, began combat operations against invading Japanese carriers and battle groups in southern Alaska. In October 1943, his squadron participated in a raid on the main Japanese Navy base at Paramisha, Japan, destroying that base as an effective offensive unit. For his actions, Captain Bell was awarded the Distinguished Flying Cross.

He is my father.

He was my first hero.

ACKNOWLEDGMENTS

I would like to offer my thanks to several people who have given so generously of their time and talents in support of this book. First, at Atria, the talented Paolo Pepe and Sarah Branham, of the unflagging cheer and patience. I thank my dear friend Wiley Reynolds for his meticulously informed observations on all things aeronautical. Captain George C. Fogwell, who circles the globe in the big 777s for Delta Airlines, and who read me loud and clear all the way across the Pacific. Mary Anne Page for her keen eye and perfect pitch. And the Hon. Robert Lloyd George for valiantly striving to keep my Anglo-American sensitivies somewhat attuned.

Also at Atria, my deepest thanks to Judith Curr, and at Pocket, Louise Burke. And, of course, to my editor, Emily Bestler, for her unstinting aid and comfort, sage advice, and encouragement. I couldn't ask for more.

I owe a huge debt of gratitude to my agent of many years, Peter Lampack. He is astute, a friend, and a gentleman.

Lastly, but most especially, I wish to thank my wife, Page Lee Hufty. Her contributions to this work are too numerous to mention; but this book is immeasurably better because of her timely flashes of creative inspiration.

Cry "Havoc!" . . . and let slip the dogs of war.
—JULIUS CAESAR, ACT III, SCENE I

PROLOGUE

Venice

The late afternoon sun slanted through the tall windows opening onto the Grand Canal. There were silken peacocks in the velvet draperies and they stirred in the salty Adriatic breeze. These warm evening zephyrs sent sunstruck motes of dust swirling indolently upward toward the vaulted and gilded ceiling.

Naked, lying atop the brocade coverlet of the grand canopied bed, the Honorable Simon Clarkson Stanfield rolled over and impatiently stubbed out his cigarette in the heavy crystal ashtray beside his bed. He lifted his keen grey eyes to the windows and gazed intently at the scene beyond them. The timeless and ceaseless navigation of Venetians had never lost its fascination for him.

At this moment, however, the *vaporetti*, water taxis, and produce-laden gondolas plying their way past the Gritti Palace were not the focus of his attention. Nor were the fairy-tale Byzantine and Baroque *palazzi* lining the opposite side of the canal, shimmering in the waning golden light. His attention was directed toward a sleek mahogany motorboat that was just now working its way through the traffic. The beautiful *Riva* seemed to be heading for the Gritti's floating dock.

Finally.

He swung his long legs over the side of the bed and stood, sucking in the beginnings of an unfortunate gut reflected from far too many angles in the mirrored panels between each of the windows. He'd recently turned fifty, but he worked hard at staying in shape. Too much good wine and pasta, he thought patting his belly. How the hell did these local Romeos stay so thin? He was sliding across the polished parquet floors in his leather slippers, headed for the large open balcony when the telephone jangled.

"Yes?"

"*Signore, prego,*" the concierge said, "you asked to be called, *subito,* the moment *la Signorina* arrived from the *aeroporto.* The Marco Polo taxi is coming. Almost to the dock now."

"*Grazie mille,* Luciano," Stanfield said. "*Sì,* I can see her. Send her up, *per favore.*"

"*Va bene, Signore Stanfield.*"

Luciano Pirandello, the Gritti's ancient majordomo, was an old and trusted friend, long accustomed to the American's habits and eccentricities. *Signore* never used the hotel's entrance, for instance. He always came and went through the kitchen, and he always took the service elevator to the same second floor suite. He took most of his meals in his rooms and, save a few late night forays to that American mecca known as Harry's Bar, that's where he stayed.

Now that he was such a well-known personage in Italy, *il Signore*'s visits to Venice had become shorter and less frequent. But Luciano's palm had been graced by even more generous contributions. After all, the great man's privacy and discretion had to be ensured. Not to mention many visiting "friends" who had, over the years, included a great number of the world's most beautiful women, some of them royalty, some of them film stars, many of them inconveniently married to other men.

Shouldering into a long robe of navy silk, Stanfield moved out under the awning of the balcony to watch Francesca disembark. Luciano stood in his starched white jacket at the end of the dock, bowing and scraping, extending his hand to *la Signorina* as she managed to step deftly ashore without incident despite the choppy water and the bobbing Riva. *Sprezzatura*, Francesca called it. The art of making the difficult look easy. She always behaved as if she were being watched, and of course she always was.

Not only Stanfield watched from the shadows of his balcony, but also everyone sipping aperitifs or *aqua minerale* and munching *antipasti* on the Gritti's floating terrace stared at the famous face and figure of the extravagantly beautiful blonde film star in the yellow linen suit.

Luciano, smiling, offered to take her single bag, a large fire-engine-red Hermès pouch that hung from her shoulder by a strap, but she refused, pushing his hand away abruptly and snapping at him. *Odd*, Stanfield thought. He'd never seen Francesca snap at anyone, especially Luciano, the soul of beneficent charm. Foul humor? She was six hours late. Hell, six hours of sitting on your backside at Rome Fiumicino Airport would be enough to put anyone in a bad mood.

Stanfield watched the top of Francesca's blonde

head disappear beneath his balcony balustrade and took a deep breath, inhaling both the scent of damp marble within the room and the smell of springtime marsh that came in off the canal. Soon, his room would be filled with the scent of Chanel Number 19. He had known she would not dare look up and catch his eye and he had not been disappointed. He smiled. He was still smiling, thinking of Francesca's backside, when there came a soft knocking at the heavy wooden door.

"*Caro,*" she said as he pulled it open to admit her. "I'm so sorry, darling. *Scusa?*"

Stanfield's reply was to gather her up into his arms, inhale her, and waltz her across the floor. There was a champagne bucket full of mostly melted ice, two upside down glasses, and a half-empty bottle of Pol Roger Winston Churchill standing by the window. Putting her down, he plucked a single flute from the bucket and handed it to her, then filled the glass with the foaming amber liquid.

She downed it in one draught and held the glass out for more.

"Thirsty, darling?" Stanfield asked, refilling her glass and pouring one for himself.

"It was, what do you call it, a fucking nightmare."

"*Sì, un fottuto disastro,*" Stanfield said with a smile. "All part of the glamour of the tryst, the illicit liaison, my dear Francesca. The endless obstacles the gods delight in placing between the two venal lovers. Traffic jams, rotten weather, the suspicious spouse, the vagaries of Italian airlines—what happened to you, anyway? You were invited for lunch."

"*Caro,* don't be angry with me. It was not my fault.

The stupid director, Vittorio, he would not let me leave the set for two hours past the time he promised. And, then it was a vagary with the stupid Alitalia. And then—"

"Shh," Stanfield said, putting a finger to her infinitely desirable red lips. He pulled a small gilded chair away from the window, sat, and said, "Turn around. Let me look at your backside."

Francesca obeyed and stood quietly with her back to him, sipping her third glass of champagne. The dying rays of light off the canal played with the taut curve of her hips and the cleft of her celebrated buttocks.

"*Bella, bella, bella,*" Stanfield whispered. He emptied the balance of the cold wine into his glass and, without taking his eyes off of the woman, picked up the phone and ordered another bottle.

"*Caro?*" the woman asked after the click of the receiver in its cradle had punctuated what became a few long moments of silence.

"Tiptoes," he said, and watched the fetching rise of her calf muscles as she giggled and complied. He had taught her the word *tiptoes* soon after they'd met and it had become one of her favorite words. She flung her blond hair around, twisting her head and gazing down at him over her shoulder with those enormous brown doe eyes. Eyes which, up on the silver screen, had reduced men the world over into quivering masses of helpless, dumbstruck protoplasm.

"I have to pee," she announced. "Like a racecourse."

"Horse," Stanfield said, "racehorse." He smiled and nodded his head and Francesca walked across to the bathroom, pulling the door closed behind her.

"Christ," Stanfield said to himself. He got to his

feet and walked out onto the balcony and into the gathering twilight. He found himself breathing rapidly and willed his heartbeat to slow. He saw this emotion for exactly what it was. Unfamiliar, yes, but still recognizable.

He might actually be falling in love with this one.

A phrase from his plebe year at Annapolis floated into his mind as he stared at the familiar but still heartbreaking beauty of the Grand Canal at dusk. An expression that the pimply cadet from Alabama had used to describe the path of his alcoholic father's personal ride to ruin.

My daddy, he was in a hot rod to Hell with the top down.

She could bring it all tumbling down, this one could, like one of those devastating Sicilian earthquakes. His thirty-year-old marriage, his hard-fought place on the world's political stage, his—

"*Caro? Prego?*"

The Campanile bell tower in the nearby Piazza San Marco tolled seven times before he turned and went to her.

Pale blue moonlight poured through the windows. Francesca feigned sleep as her lover slipped from the bed and went toward the dim yellow light of the bathroom. He left the door slightly ajar and she watched him perform his usual rituals. First he brushed his teeth. Then he ran two military brushes through his silver hair until it swept back in perfect matching waves from his high forehead. She admired his naked back and the muscles bunched at his shoulders as he leaned forward to inspect his teeth in the mirror.

He then pulled the door softly shut. She couldn't

see him but she knew precisely what he was doing. He'd be lifting the seat to urinate, then putting it back down. Then he'd take a hand towel and wash himself, down there. His grey trousers, white silk shirt and cashmere blazer were all hanging on the back of the door. Reaching for them, he—

It would all take five minutes, easily. More than enough time to do what she had to do.

She'd deliberately left her shoulder bag on the floor just under her side of the bed, shoving it there with her foot while he was admitting the room service waiter. She rolled over onto her stomach and reached for it, pulling the drawstrings apart. She reached into the bag, slipping two fingers inside a small interior pouch. She found the tiny disc and withdrew it. She then back-handed the heavy bag under the bed again so that he wouldn't step on it when, as was his custom, he bent to kiss her before slipping out for his traditional solo nightcap.

She rolled over to his side of the bed and reached for the alligator billfold on his bedside table. She held it above her face, opened it, and ran her index finger lightly over the gold monogrammed letters S.C.S. Then she carefully slipped the encrypted micro-thin disc into one of the unused pouches on the left side, opposite the credit cards and a thick fold of lire on the right. The thin disc was made of flexible material. The odds of his discovering it were nil. She put the wallet back on the bedside table, exactly as he'd left it, then rolled over onto her back.

A soft shaft of yellow light expanded on the ceiling as the bathroom door was opened and Simon padded quietly around the foot of the bed. Eyes closed, her bosom rising and falling rhythmically, Francesca listened to Stanfield slip his cigarette case, billfold, and some loose change into the pockets of the beautiful black cashmere blazer she'd bought for him in Florence.

He came around to her side of the bed and stood silently for a moment before bending to kiss her forehead.

"Just going over to Harry's for my nightcap, darling. I won't be long, I promise. One and done."

"*Ti amo,*" Francesca whispered sleepily. "This is for you, *caro,*" she said, handing him a small red rosebud she'd plucked from the vase on her bedside table. "For your lapel, *così non lo dimenticherete,* so you won't forget me."

"*Ti amo,* too," he said, and, after inserting the stem of the rose into the buttonhole in his lapel and stroking a wing of her hair away from her forehead, he left her side. "*Ciao.*"

"*Ritorno-me, caro mio,*" she said.

A moment later, the bedroom door closed softly behind him and Francesca whispered in the dark. "*Arrivederci, caro.*"

Stanfield took the service elevator down to the ground floor, turned to his right and proceeded down the short hallway that led to the kitchen. *Il facchino,* the ancient hall porter named Paolo, was dozing with his chair tilted back against the tiled wall. Stanfield placed the tasseled key to his suite on the folded newspaper in the old fellow's lap.

"*La chiave, Paolo,*" he whispered.

"*Con piacere. Buona sera, signore,*" he said as Stanfield passed. *He's been through this routine so often he now says it in his sleep,* Stanfield thought.

Stepping through the kitchen's service door and out into the empty Campo Santa Maria del Giglio, a smile of pleasure played across Stanfield's features. It was his favorite time of night. Very few people about, the enchanted city now turned many shades of milky blue and white. He started walking across the plaza, the recent memories of Francesca still blooming in his mind like hothouse flowers, the lush scent of her still lingering on his fingers.

Yes. Her ivory skin, whiter in those places where the most delicate articulations of the joints showed through; and her lily fingers which danced upon his body still, to some mystic memory of music.

And now, the small perfection of a quiet stroll over to Harry's for a large whiskey, straight up, an appropriate cigar, the Romeo y Julieta, and some time to reflect on his incredible good fortune. He'd always enjoyed wealth, been born with it. But he'd played his cards right and now he'd reached the point where it was time to see what serious power felt like. Now he knew. A thoroughbred pawing the turf in the starting gate.

And, he's off! called the announcer in his mind, and indeed he was.

He turned right on the Calle del Piovan, then crossed the little bridge over the Rio dell'Albero. It was only a quarter of a mile to Harry's, but the twisting and turning of the narrow streets made it—

Jesus Christ.

What the living hell?

There was a strange, high-pitched chirping sound behind him. He turned and looked over his shoulder and literally could not believe his eyes. Something, he could not imagine what, was flying straight towards him! A tiny red eye blinking, blinking faster as whatever the thing was headed rapidly for him, and he realized that if he just stood there it would, what, hit him? Knock him down? Blow him up? Breaking into an instant sweat, he turned and started running like a madman.

Insanity. No longer out for an evening stroll, Simon Stanfield was now running for his life.

Feeling the surge of adrenaline, he sprinted down the Calle Larga XXII Marza, dodging passersby, flying past the darkened shops, headed for the Piazza San Marco where maybe he might just lose this apparition. A quiet drink at Harry's would just have to wait. He'd shake off this thing somehow, and what a story he'd have to tell Mario when he got there! No one would believe it. Hell, he himself still couldn't believe it.

Stanfield was a man who took care of himself. He was, at fifty, in impeccable physical condition. But this thing matched his every move, never losing nor gaining ground, just hurtling after him turn for turn. He raced over another tiny arched bridge and dodged left into the Campo San Moise. The few people he passed stopped and stared after him, open-mouthed. The chirping, blinking thing streaking after a running man was so absurd it made people shake their heads in bewilderment. It had to be a movie scene. But where were the cameras and crew? Who was the star?

"Aiuto! Aiuto!" the man shouted at them, screaming now for help, calling for the police. *"Chiamate una polizia! Subito! Subito!"*

There were always a few *carabinieri* hanging about St. Mark's Square, Stanfield thought feverishly. He'd just have to find one to get this goddamned thing off his back. But what could they do? Shoot it down? He was getting winded now, he realized, looking over his shoulder at that horrible flashing red eye as he raced into the nearly empty *piazza*. Very few people around, and no one at the distant café tables lining the square paid much attention to the screaming man since they could see no one chasing him. A drunk. A loco.

What the fuck am I going to do? Simon Stanfield thought feverishly. *I'm fast running out of gas here. And options.* The familiar shapes of the Basilica of St. Mark and the Doge's Palace loomed up before him. Can't run much farther. Nowhere to run to, baby, nowhere to hide. His only hope was the goddamned thing hadn't yet closed the gap. If it were meant to take him out, surely it could have easily done so already.

Maybe this was just a really God-awful nightmare. Or this little flying horror was someone's incredibly elaborate idea of a practical joke. Or maybe he had acquired his own personal smart bomb. He was not only running out of gas, but ideas as well. And then he had a good one.

He angled right and made straight for the tall tower of the Campanile, swung hard right into the *piazzetta* leading to the canal. Pumping his knees now, Stanfield passed through the columns of San Marco and San Teodoro and kept on going. The thing was getting closer now, louder, and the chirps had solidified into a single keening note. He couldn't see it, but he guessed the red eye wasn't blinking anymore either.

The Grand Canal was maybe twenty yards away.

He might make it.

He put his head down and barreled forward, just

like the old days, an enraged bull of a Navy fullback bound for the end zone, no defenders, nothing standing between him and glory. He reached the edge, filled his lungs with air, and dove, flew into the Grand Canal.

He clawed his way down through the cold murky water, and then he stopped, hung there a moment treading water. He opened his eyes and looked up. He couldn't believe it.

The little red-eyed bastard had stopped too.

It was hovering just above him, a glowing red oval contracting and expanding on the undulating surface of the water.

Gotcha, Stanfield thought, relief flooding him along with the realization that he'd finally managed to outwit the goddamn thing. That's when he saw the red eye nose over and break the surface, then streak downward through the shadows towards him, growing larger and larger until it obliterated everything.

Few people actually witnessed the strange death of Simon Clarkson Stanfield, and those who did, did so from too far away to be able to tell exactly what they'd seen.

There were a number of gondoliers ferrying a group of late night revelers from late supper at the Hotel Cipriani back to the Danieli. Singing and laughing, few even heard the muffled explosion in the dark waters just off Venezia's most famous plaza. One alert gondolier, Giovanni Cavalli, not only heard it, but saw the water erupt into a frothy pinkish mushroom about fifty yards from his passing gondola.

But, Giovanni was in the midst of a full-throated rendition of "Santa Lucia" as he poled by; his clients were enraptured, and the gondolier made no move to pole over and take a closer look. Whatever he'd seen had looked so unpleasant as to surely dampen the Americans' generosity of spirit and perhaps seal their pockets as well. Minutes later, as his gondola slid to a stop at the Hotel Danieli's dock, he ended the solo with his famous *tremolo obbligato,* bowing deeply to the vigorous applause, sweeping his straw hat low before him like a matador.

Early next morning in the Campo San Barnaba, the gondolier Giovanni Cavalli and his mother were inspecting the ripe tomatoes on the vegetable barge moored along the seawall of the plaza. Giovanni noticed the owner, his friend Marco, wrap some newly purchased *fagiolini* in the front page of today's *Il Giornale* and hand them to an old woman.

"Scusi," Giovanni said, taking the bundle of green beans from the startled woman and unwrapping it. He dumped her carefully selected vegetables, just weighed and paid for, back on the heaping mound of *fagiolini.*

"Ma che diavolo vuole?" the woman shrieked, asking him what the devil he wanted as he turned his back on her and spread the front page out over Marco's beautiful vegetables. There was a picture of a very handsome silver-haired man with a huge headline that screamed: *Murder In Piazza San Marco!*

"Momento, eh?" Giovanni said to the outraged woman, *"Scusi, scusi."* Ignoring the woman's flailing fists, which felt like small birds crashing blindly against his back, Giovanni devoured every word. There had indeed been a most bizarre murder in the *piazza* last night. An American had died under the most curious

of circumstances. Witnesses said the apparently deranged man dove into the Grand Canal and simply exploded. Police were initially convinced the man had been a terrorist wearing a bomb belt who had somehow run amok. Later, when they learned the identity of the victim, a shockwave rippled throughout Italy and down the long corridors of power in Washington, D.C. The dead man was Simon Clarkson Stanfield.

The recently appointed American Ambassador to Italy.

CHAPTER ONE

The Cotswolds

The gods would never have the nerve to rain on his wedding. Or, so Commander Alexander Hawke told himself. The BBC weather forecast for the Cotswolds region of England had called for light rain Saturday evening through Sunday. But Hawke, standing on the church steps of St. John's, basking in the May sunshine, had known better.

Hawke's best man, Ambrose Congreve, had also decided today, Sunday, would be a perfect day. Simple deduction, really, the detective had concluded. Half the people would say that it was too hot, while the other half would say that it was too cold. Ergo, perfect. Still, he had brought along a large umbrella.

"Not a cloud in the sky, Constable," Hawke pointed out, his cool, penetrating blue eyes fixed on Congreve. "I told you we wouldn't need that bloody umbrella."

Hawke was standing stiffly in his Royal Navy ceremonial uniform, tall and slender as a lance. Marshal Ney's ornamental sword, a gift from his late grandfather, now polished to gleaming perfection, hung from his hip. His unruly hair, pitch-black and curly, was slicked back from his high forehead, every strand in place.

If the groom looked too good to be true, Ambrose

Congreve would assure you that this, indeed, was the case.

Hawke's mood had been uncharacteristically prickly all morning long. There was a definite tightness in his voice and, were Ambrose to be perfectly honest, he'd been rather snappish. Curt. Impatient.

Where, Congreve wondered, was the easygoing, carefree bachelor, the blasé youth of yore? All morning long the best man had been giving this storybook groom a decidedly wide berth.

Heaving one of his more ill-disguised sighs, Ambrose peered hopefully up into the now cloudless sky. It wasn't as though Ambrose actually *wished* for rain on this radiant wedding day. It was just that he so despised, detested really, being wrong. "Ah. You never do know, do you?" he said to his young friend.

"Yes, you do," Hawke said, "Sometimes you actually do know, Constable. You've got the ring, I daresay?"

"Unless it has mysteriously teleported itself from my waistcoat pocket to a parallel universe in the five minutes since your last enquiry, yes, I imagine it's still there."

"Very funny. You must amuse yourself no end. And, why are we so bloody early? All this lollygagging about. Even the vicar isn't here yet."

The Scotland Yard man gave his friend a narrow look and, after a moment's hesitation, pulled a small silver shooter's flask from inside his morning coat. He unscrewed the cap and offered the flagon to the groom, who clearly was in need of fortification.

Rising early that morning, a cheery Congreve had breakfasted alone in the butler's pantry and then hurried out into the Hawkesmoor gardens to paint. It was delightful sitting there beside the limpid stream. Lilacs were in bud and an unseasonably late snowfall had all but melted away. The light haze of spring green in the treetops had recently solidified. Beside the old dry-stone wall meandering through the orchard, a profusion of daffodils thick as weeds.

He'd been sitting at his easel, slaving over what he judged to be one of his better watercolour efforts to date, when the memory of Hawke's earlier remark stung him like a bee. Hawke had made the comment to the aged retainer, Pelham, but Ambrose, lingering at the half-opened Dutch door leading to the garden, had overheard.

I think Ambrose's paintings are not nearly as bad as they look, don't you agree, Pelham?

Of course, Hawke, his oldest and dearest friend, had meant the jibe to be witty and amusing, but, still—that's when a solitary raindrop spattered his picture and interrupted his revery.

He looked up. A substantial pile of gravid purple clouds was building in the west. More rain today, of all days? Ah, well, he sighed. The fat raindrop's effect on his picture was not altogether unpleasant. Gave it a bit of cheek, he thought, and decided the painting was at last finished. This lily study was to be his gift for the bride. The title, whilst obvious to some, had for the artist a certain poetic ring. He called it *The Wedding Lilies.*

Packing up his folding stool, his papers, paints, pots and brushes, he looked again at the purple clouds. The best man had decided on the spot that, while an umbrella may or may not come in handy on Alexander Hawke's wedding day, the brandy flask was a must. Grooms, in his experience, traditionally needed a bracer when the hour was at hand.

Hawke tilted back a quick swig.

When Ambrose recapped the flask and slipped it back inside his black cutaway without taking a bracer for himself, Hawke shot him a surprised look.

"Not even joining the groom in a prenuptial?" Hawke demanded of his companion. "What on earth is the world coming to?"

"I can't drink, I'm on duty," Congreve said, suddenly busy with his calabash pipe, tamping some of Peterson's Irish Blend into the bowl. "Sorry, but there it is."

"Duty? Not in any official sense."

"No, just common sense. I'm responsible for delivering you to the altar, dear boy, and I fully intend to discharge my duties properly."

Ambrose Congreve tried to appear stern. To his lifelong chagrin, achieving that cast of expression had never been easy. He had the bright blue eyes of a healthy baby, set in a keen but, some might say, sensitive face. His complexion, even at fifty, had the permanent pinkish pigmentation of a man who'd once had freckles lightly sprinkled across his nose.

For all that, he was a lifelong copper who took his duties extremely seriously.

Having gained an upper rung at the Metropolitan Police, he had had a distinguished career at New Scotland Yard, retiring four years earlier as Chief of the Criminal Investigation Department. But the Yard's current Commissioner, Sir John Stevens, unable to fill Congreve's shoes at CID, still retained his services from time to time. Sir John was even kind enough to let him keep the use of a small office in the old Special Branch building in Whitehall Street. In the event, however, Congreve spent precious little time in that cold, damp chamber.

Numerous globe-trotting escapades with the fidgety groom now standing beside him on the church steps had mercifully kept the famous criminalist away from his humble office and hot on the trail of various villains and scoundrels these last five years or so. Their last adventure had been a somewhat heated affair involving some rather unsavory Cuban military chaps down in the Caribbean.

Now, on this bright morning in May, on the steps of this small "chapel of ease" in the picturesque if unfortunately named village of Upper Slaughter, the groom was giving a first-rate impression of a lamb on his way to the slaughter. Hawke's glacial blue eyes, normally indomitable, finally wandered from the study of a lark singing in a nearby laurel to rest uneasily upon Congreve's bemused face. Hawke's gaze, Congreve often noted, had weight.

"Interesting. Since I was a child, I've always wondered why they call this place a 'chapel of ease,'" Hawke remarked.

"Any sense of 'ease' being notable by its current absence?"

"Precisely."

"These small chapels were originally built to ease the overflowing congregations at the main churches."

"Ah. That explains it. Well. My own personal demon of deduction strikes again. I'll have another nip of that brandy if you don't mind. Cough it up."

Congreve, a shortish, round figure of a man, removed his black silk top hat and ran his fingers through his disorderly thatch of chestnut brown hair. Alex had nowhere near the tolerance for alcohol he himself possessed, even at his somewhat advanced age;

and so he hesitated, stalling, pinching the upturned points of his waxed moustache.

"And, of course," Congreve said, with a sweeping gesture that included a good deal of Gloucestershire, "every one of those yew trees you see growing in this and every other churchyard were ordered planted there by King Edward I in the fourteenth century."

"Really? Why on earth should young Eddie have gone to all that bother in the first place?"

"Provide his troops with a plentiful supply of proper wood for longbows." Congreve had removed the flask but hesitated in the uncorking of it. "You know, dear boy, it was King Edward who—"

"Good lord," Hawke said, exasperated.

"What?"

"I want brandy, not arboreal folklore for God's sake, Ambrose. Fork it over."

"Ah. Smell that air."

"What about it?"

"Sweet. Mulchy."

"Ambrose!"

"Alex, it's only natural for the groom to experience certain feelings of—anxiety—at a time like this, but I really think . . . ah, well, here comes the wedding party." Ambrose quickly slipped the flask back into his inside pocket.

A procession of automobiles was winding its way up the twisting lane, bounded on either side by the hawthorn hedges, leading to the little church of St. John's. It was a beautiful chapel really, nestled in a small valley of yews, pear trees, laurel, and rhododendron, many just now coming into full pink and white bloom, the trees filtering light onto dappled grass. The surrounding hillsides were green with leafy old forests, towering oaks, elms, and gnarled Spanish chestnuts many hundreds of years old.

The little Norman church was built of the mellow golden limestone so familiar here in Gloucestershire. St. John's had been the scene of countless Hawke family weddings, christenings, and funerals. Alexander Hawke himself, red-faced with rage, age two, had been christened in the baptismal font just inside the entrance. Only a mile or so from this wooded glen, stood Hawke's ancestral country home.

Hawkesmoor still held a prominent place in Alex's heart and he visited his country house as frequently as possible. The foundation of the centuries old house, which overlooked a vast parkland, was built in 1150, with additions dating from the fourteenth century to the end of the reign of Elizabeth I. The roofline was a fine mix of distinctive gables and elaborate chimneys. Alex had long found great peace there, wandering about a rolling landscape laid out centuries earlier by Capability Brown.

At the head of the parade of automobiles was Alex's gunmetal grey 1939 Bentley Saloon. Behind the wheel, Alex could see the massive figure and smiling face of Stokely Jones, former U.S. Navy SEAL and NYPD copper and a founding member of Alexander Hawke's merry band of warriors. Sitting up front with Stokely was Pelham Grenville, the stalwart octogenarian and family retainer who had helped to raise young Alex following the tragic murder of the boy's parents. After the subsequent death of Alex's grandfather, Pelham and a number of uniformly disappointed headmasters had assumed sole responsibility for the boy's upbringing.

"Let's duck inside, Ambrose," Alex said, with the first hint of a smile. "Vicky and her father are in one of those cars. Apparently, it's unlucky for the groom to see the bride prior to the ceremony."

Congreve's eyebrows shot straight up.

"Yes, I believe I mentioned that custom to you any number of times at the reception last evening. At any rate, we're supposed to have a final rendezvous with the vicar in his offices prior to the ceremony. He is here, actually, I saw his bicycle propped by the vicarage doorway as we drove up."

"Quickly, Constable, I think I see their car."

Congreve breathed a brief sigh of relief that Hawke had not bolted on him, and then followed his friend through the graceful Norman arch into the cool darkness of the little church. Now the event itself was inescapably set in motion, Alex seemed to be shaking off his case of the heebie-jeebies. Here was a man who wouldn't blink in the face of a cocked gun. Amazing what a wedding could do to a chap, Ambrose thought, glad he'd so far managed to avoid the experience.

The church could not have looked lovelier, Ambrose observed as they approached the rear door leading to the vicar's office. Because of the narrow leaded glass windows, candles were needed even at this time of day and the churchwarden had lit them all. Their waxy scent mixed with the lily of the valley on the altar caused a rising tide of emotions within Ambrose's heart. Not mixed emotions exactly, but something akin.

He adored Vicky, everyone did. She was not only a great beauty, but also a dedicated child neurologist who had recently won acclaim for her series of children's books. Alex had met Dr. Victoria Sweet at a dinner party thrown in her honor at the American ambassador's residence in Regent's Park, Winfield House. Her father, the retired United States senator from Louisiana, was an old family friend of the current ambassador to the Court of St. James, Patrick Brickhouse Kelly.

Kelly, a former U.S. Army tank commander, had come across Hawke during the first Gulf War. Hawke and "Brick," as he called the tall, redheaded man, had remained close friends since the war. The soft-spoken American ambassador, whom Congreve now glimpsed sprinting up a side pathway to the chapel, had saved Hawke's life in the closing days of the conflict. Now, Hawke's chief usher was late.

Congreve had goaded Alex into asking the beautiful American author to dance at Brick Kelly's home in Regent's Park that night. The two of them had been inseparable ever since that fateful first waltz. Vicky had, that very evening, effectively put an end to Alex's legendary status as one of Britain's most eligible bachelors. No, it was not Victoria's future Congreve was so much concerned about, but rather the long-term prognosis of his dearest friend Alex.

Alexander Hawke led, to put it mildly, an adventurous life.

Having been thrice decorated for bravery flying Royal Navy Harriers over Iraq in the Gulf War, Hawke had subsequently joined the most elite of the British fighting forces, the Special Boat Squadron. There they'd taught him how to kill with his bare hands, jump out of airplanes, swim unseen for miles underwater, and blow all manner of things to kingdom come.

Having acquired these basic skills, he'd then gone

into finance in the City. His first order of business was to resurrect the somnolent giant known around the world as Hawke Industries. After his grandfather retreated from the boardroom, he reluctantly relinquished command to young Alex. Hawke had no great love of business; still, he never dared disappoint his grandfather and so, a decade later, the already substantial family interests flourished once more.

Some called his series of brilliant but hostile takeovers around the world piratical and there was some truth to that. Alex was a direct descendant of the infamous eighteenth-century pirate, Blackhawke, and he was fond of warning friend and foe alike there was indeed a bloodthirsty hawk perched atop his family tree. With his black hair, his prominent, determined features, and his piercing blue eyes, a black eyepatch and solitary gold earring would not have looked even remotely ridiculous on him.

As Alex had told Congreve after one particularly fierce takeover battle, pools of blood still much in evidence on the boardroom floors, "I can't help myself, Constable, I've got the pirate blood in me."

As the man who presided over the sprawling Hawke Industries, Hawke had friends at the highest levels of the world's major corporations and governments. Because of those contacts he was frequently asked to engage in discreet missions for both the British and American intelligence communities.

Highly dangerous missions, and that's what concerned Congreve. Alex Hawke put his life on the line constantly. If he and Vicky were fortunate enough to have children, well, Ambrose hated to think what would happen to the brood if—

Congreve realized he'd been daydreaming as the plump little vicar droned on and Alex, who had his own private views on religion, did his best to appear both compliant and reverential. By the rising hum of conversation now emanating from the direction of the chapel, Congreve could tell the pews were filling with ladies in shades of lilac and rose and big brimmed hats and men all in morning clothes. He could hear the level of keen anticipation growing for what was, after all, the biggest small wedding of the year in England.

Or, the smallest big wedding, depending on your tabloid of choice. Although Alex had tried desperately to keep the wedding secret, weeks ago someone had leaked the details to *The Sun*, sending the rest of the tabloid press into a feeding frenzy.

Security in the Cotswolds had never been tighter. In addition to members of H.M. Government, the British prime minister, and the American secretary of state and ambassador, all close friends of the groom's, there were a number of foreign dignitaries and heads of state seated amongst a select group of Alex and Vicky's friends and family. Alex, dogged in his determination to keep the affair small, had deliberately chosen his family's rustic chapel. The press was barred entirely, although they were certainly manning the police barricades at every obscure little lane leading to the tiny village.

A suspicious helicopter circling above the church at dawn had been quickly escorted out of the area by two RAF fighters and—

"Well, your Lordship, I think it's high time we got you married," the vicar said to Hawke with a smile. "The good Lord knows you've broken quite enough hearts for one lifetime."

Alex's eyes narrowed, wondering if the vicar was having him on.

"Indeed," Alex finally replied, stifling whatever riposte was surely forming in his mind, and he and Ambrose followed the old fellow into the chapel itself and took their assigned places before the altar. The church was full, a sea of familiar faces, some bathed in shafts of soft sunlight streaming through the tall eastern windows.

Hawke couldn't wait to get the whole bloody thing over with. It had nothing to do with misgivings or second thoughts. He had felt nothing but spontaneous and unstinting love for Vicky since the first second he'd seen her. It was just that he hated ceremony of any kind, had no patience with it at all. If not for Vicky and her father, this wedding would have been taking place in some ratty little civil service office in Paris or even—

The organ boomed its triumphal first notes. Victoria appeared in the sun-filled chapel doorway on the arm of her beaming father. All eyes were on the bride as she made her way slowly up the aisle. Standing before the altar with a trembling heart, Alex Hawke had but one thought: *By God I am a lucky man.*

She had never looked more beautiful. Her lustrous auburn hair was swept back into a chignon held by ivory combs that also held the veils that fell to the floor behind her. Her white satin dress had been her mother's; the bodice was festooned with swirling patterns of pearls which, as she moved through gold bars of sunlight, cast a soft glow upwards, lighting her face and her smiling eyes.

The groom would remember little of the ceremony.

His heart was now pounding so rapidly there was an overpowering roar of blood in his ears. He knew the vicar was speaking, having begun his intonations in a slow, deep register, and he was aware he himself was saying things in rote reply. The vicar kept upping the oratorical ante and, at some point, near the end of the thing, Vicky had squeezed his hand, hard. She looked up into his eyes and, somehow, he actually heard her speaking to him.

"I, Victoria, take thee Alexander to my wedded husband, to have and to hold from this day forward, for better, for worse, for richer, for poorer, in sickness and in health, to love and to cherish till death us do part, according to God's holy ordinance, and thereto I give thee my troth."

There was the exchange of rings and suddenly the organ pipes filled the church with what could only be called the sounds of heaven and he was somehow aware that he was lifting Vicky's veil to kiss her; that Congreve, having delivered the ring, stood now with eyes full of tears, and then he heard the vicar's final volley of oratory thunder.

"Those whom God hath joined together, let no man put asunder!"

He embraced his bride, actually lifting her off her feet, to the delight of all assembled, and then he was hurrying her down the aisle festooned with white satin and lilies, through all the applause and smiling faces of their friends and towards the sunshine which filled the doorway and the future. Outside the entrance, his uniformed comrades formed two opposing lines. On the command, "Draw swords!" steel was raised, forming an arch, cutting edge facing up.

He'd meant for the two of them to quickly duck

through the gleaming silver arch created by his Royal Navy Guard of Honor and race for the Bentley, but the overflow of well-wishers had spilled out onto the steps and he and Vicky were forced to stop to receive the hugs and kisses everyone seemed determined to bestow upon them amidst the clouds of white blossoms filling the air.

Out of the corner of his eye, Alex saw Vicky bend to kiss the cheek of the pretty little flower girl and he turned away from her for a moment to embrace her beaming father. Vicky was rising from the kiss, smiling up at him, extending her arms towards him, clearly wanting as much as he did to escape to the back seat of the waiting Bentley.

It was just then, when he was bending to embrace his bride, that the unthinkable happened.

Suddenly Vicky was not leaning into him, she was falling away with a breathless sigh, white petals whirling from the folds of her veil. There was a bright flower of red blooming amongst the snow-white pearls of her satin bodice. Shocked, staggered by what he saw, Alex grabbed her shoulders and pulled her towards him. He was screaming now, as he saw her gaze go distant and glaze over, feeling the gush of warm blood flowing straight from her heart. Victoria's blood soaked through his shirtfront, and it broke his own heart into infinitely small pieces as he stared into her lifeless eyes.

CHAPTER TWO

Stokely Jones was standing on the church steps with Brick Kelly and Texas Patterson, the three of them maybe four feet away from Alex Hawke when it happened. Stokely thought he'd caught the wink of a muzzle flash. It had been high and on the outside, straight down the third baseline and up in the tree line, near the left crest of that hillside, just opposite the front of the church.

Vicky was dead. That much was for damn sure.

Only took one glance at the girl and he'd known the wound was crosshairs mortal. Then, looking at Alex, still holding his bride in his arms, his anguished face buried in her hair, Stokely heard American and British security forces inside the church shouting at everyone to get down, hit the deck. Heavily armed and flak-jacketed personnel immediately formed themselves a cordon around those standing outside on the steps, telling them to get their asses down as well.

Inside the church, everybody had heard Alex's scream. There was screaming and confusion in there, too. Hell, man, you had the British prime minister in there, you had lots of royal folks, and you had the damn American ambassador and secretary of state.

Not to mention all kinds of other foreign dignitaries and some famous Hollywood people. Lots of likely targets in the little church. But the sniper, he shot the bride.

"Get a doctor here for God's sakes," he heard Alex cry again and again in a broken voice. "She needs a doctor right now!"

Stokely saw the look on Alex's face when he spoke and then he just took off running for the hills, knowing there was nothing he or anybody else could do for Vicky, but thinking there was something he could goddamn well do for Alex.

"Saw a muzzle flash," he shouted ahead to the group of British special forces and plainclothes guys, bristling with weapons. They were forming up into a perimeter along the stone wall surrounding the churchyard. "Shooter's up there in the trees on that hill!" The old wall was over four feet high but Stokely, still in his morning clothes, vaulted it in mid-stride and kept running. "You guys, you not too busy, you might want to give me a hand up there," he shouted back over his shoulder. If the Brits had any brains they'd come with him. If not, he'd go catch the son of a bitch all by himself.

And when he did—

He'd entered the dark woods, the mossy ground spotted with sunlight but dark now even though it was mid-morning, and was scrambling over the roots of some of the biggest trees he'd ever laid eyes on. He saw old stone tablets sticking out of the ground at odd angles and realized he was running through a graveyard, now overgrown with underbrush. The slope of the hill angled sharply upwards and he was having a tough time keeping his footing in the fancy-ass new shoes he was wearing.

That must have been why the young plainclothes guy had been able to catch up with him, and, shit, run right alongside of him for a minute. Stoke was the fastest guy he ever knew and here was this blond-haired, freckle-faced kid matching him stride for stride. Maximum speed of a normal human being, in a short sprint, was about fifteen miles an hour. Stoke had been clocked at a shade under twenty, and this kid was pulling away. Looking at him kind of sideways, too. Hell, six-foot-six black guy in striped pants, a black cut-away and top hat probably not all that common a sight in this neck of the woods.

"Who the bloody hell are you?" the English guy said, not even breathing hard.

"Friend of the groom," Stokely said, as the two of them leapt over a heap of fallen trees. "Who the bloody hell are you?"

"MI5. Security. Assigned to the prime minister."

"Good. Shooter was at the top of one of those trees. Just up there on that overhanging cliff . . . if you—"

The guy sprinted ahead so fast that Stoke didn't even bother to finish his sentence. For a white guy, the kid was quick. And, if they managed to get lucky, two guns were always better than one. Stoke ripped the top hat off his head and flung it away, picking up his pace and closing the distance between them. Still it was tough to run in a pair of shiny sissy shoes, especially when you had to keep your eyes looking up all the time. Chances were, the shooter had split, but he also could be sitting up there somewhere in the treetops just waiting to pick off somebody like Stoke or the plainclothes kid. Tough call.

Kind of guy who would shoot a bride just coming out of the church? Flat-ass crazy.

He looked down for a split second, having seen or sensed something, all those years in Nam kicking in, and that's when he saw the trip wire. He managed to clear it by maybe half an inch.

Christ, Stoke thought, *the asshole has mined the god-damn woods!*

"Stop!" he screamed at the kid up ahead. "Mines! Fucking land mines! Stop right now!"

The kid was wide-eyed, looking back over his shoulder at Stoke when he tripped the wire.

"Aw, Jesus," Stoke said as he watched the kid go up in a fiery reddish burst of blood and bones and smoke. "Jesus, goddamn Christ!"

The kid still had his eyes open when Stokely reached him. The big man dropped to his knees on the ground beside the boy and cradled what was left of him in his arms. Blood was pouring out of his mouth, but the kid was trying to talk.

"Tell . . . tell me mum that . . . tell her that . . ."

"Hey. Listen up, 'cause this is important. Ain't nobody but *you* gonna tell your mum anything, son. You going to be okay, you hear me? You just take it easy, now, and old Stoke, he's going to stay right with you till the medics get here, all right? They going to fix your ass right up, understand? Good as new. You going to make it, kid, I'm going to personally see to that."

He sat there, waiting for the boy to die, eyes scanning the treetops, using his handkerchief to catch the blood coming out of the kid's mouth, and suddenly he was back in the Mekong, middle of a firefight, holding on tight to his troops, tears running down his face, so many of his good friends and best asshole buddies blown all to shit by Charlie's AK-47s and land mines and RPGs, all of them talking about they mamas at the end.

He looked down at the kid and saw him die.

"You was fast, son," Stokely said to him, still stroking his head. "You the only person on this earth ever to out-run old Stoke, and, man, that's truly saying something. You was a brave kid, I could see it in your eyes just in the short time I met you. You going to a better place now. You be all right."

Stoke heard noises below him and looked up to see three commandos in black coming up over a small rise, gunsights already on him.

"Stop!" he screamed. "Stop right there! Land mines all over the goddamned place!"

They did what he said and one of them called up to him. "We heard the explosion. What's his status?"

"His status?" Stoke called back. "His status is over."

After they'd taken the kid away, Stokely led a team of the Brits up to the place where he thought he'd seen the muzzle flash. Stoke was out in front, picking his way over the tripwires and calling out their locations when he came across the tree with the cable hanging down.

There was a loop in the bottom of the thick wire cable and, higher up on the stainless steel cable, a small electrical-type box with a black button and a red button.

Stoke, not worried about prints because he was still wearing his wedding gloves, grabbed hold of the cable, stuck one foot in the loop and pressed the button on

top, the black one. It was like being in an elevator without the elevator. He was instantly flying up through the
trees, at least fifty to sixty feet in less than five seconds.
When he got near to the top, he saw the big electric
motor mounted on the tree trunk with four heavy
bolts. Electric? Up in a tree? Had to be battery powered.

But the motorized cable wasn't the amazing thing.

The amazing thing was the shooter had left his gun
in the tree.

It was right there, stuck in the crotch at the top of
the tree. Stoke had removed his blood-soaked gloves
and now used the wedding program to try and remove
the weapon without messing up any prints. Wouldn't
budge. He hit the butt sharply with his hand and the
thing didn't move an inch. No wonder the guy had left
it up here. Need a goddamn crowbar to get it out, way
he'd managed to wedge it in there.

Stoke instantly recognized the kind of sniper rifle it
was, even though he hadn't seen one since the seventies.
It was a Russian-made Dragunov SVD. A Snayperskaya
Vintovka Dragunova to be exact. Amazing. How many
times you go to a crime scene and find the perp's left his
goddamn weapon stuck right there in your face?

One thing was for damn sure, evidence or no evidence.

Guy who murdered Vicky and the English kid, he
was long gone.

CHAPTER THREE

River Road, Louisiana

After the funeral, Alex said good-bye to Vicky's father, got into his hired car, and drove down the River Road, following the Mississippi south towards New Orleans. The sun was a big blood-red orange hanging out the open window on his right, except for the times when the road dropped down behind the levee.

His mother had grown up on this river; her early life had been shaped by it, and Alex had heard stories about the river from her until she was murdered the day after his seventh birthday. One day he'd found her tattered copy of *Huckleberry Finn* where it had slipped behind his bookcase. She always said it was the truest book about the river ever written, and maybe the truest, best book ever written about anything. She was reading it to him every night in those last days they had together. Huck and Tom and Nigger Jim were every bit as real for Alex as any of the boys at his school, and certainly a lot more interesting way for a boy to learn about life.

Listen to me, Alex Hawke, she'd said one day when he'd come home all scratched and bloody, having brought home a foundling cat, *a boy carrying a cat home by the tail is learning something he can learn no other way.*

He was ten or eleven years old when he finally read the book for himself. The story of Huck Finn filled in a lot of the holes created when his mother's own life story ended so abruptly. His father was English and so was he, but he'd had an American mother and the book had helped the boy feel a connection to his mother, to see her America, feel it the way she did, even though it was a story from a time long ago. He was thinking about his mother now, Hawke realized, because thinking about anyone else was unbearable. His idea was to try and find the house where she'd grown up, find her childhood room on the top floor, and look out her window at the river.

See what she'd seen with his own eyes.

The real estate agent in Baton Rouge had told him the house was still standing. The Louisiana Historical Society protected it, although some developer was trying very hard to change that. According to the agent, the house, called Twelvetrees, was Italianate style, completed in 1859 by a Mr. John Randolph of Virginia. It was now owned by a family named Longstreet, but had stood unused and unoccupied for decades.

Alex had been driving for some time before he saw the flashing blue lights coming up fast in his rearview mirror and realized he was going well over a hundred and ten miles an hour. Fast, but well below escape velocity. You can't outrun this one anyway, Alex, not this time, he told himself. Not ever. He slowed down and pulled off the side of the road, waiting for the police to pull up behind him, run his plate through the computer, approach him with their hands on their hip holsters, ask him what the hell the big hurry was, Mister.

The blue lights went screaming by him, siren wailing. The vehicle with the flashers wasn't a police car, it was an EMS van and it raced past him and disappeared around a bend in the road. Five minutes later he saw the ambulances and the fire engine and the fiery accident itself up on the side of the levee. He knew instantly it was bad and averted his eyes, kept them on the road ahead, sped up again. He punched some buttons on the radio, looking for Louis Armstrong.

He finally caught Satchmo singing "Do You Know What It Means To Miss New Orleans?" It helped a little bit. *Laissez les bon temps rouler.* That's what his mother had always said, her favorite expression. Let the good times roll. Bloody hell. You couldn't cry anymore so you had to laugh. After half an hour or so, he saw a Louisiana Historical Site sign. "Twelvetrees Plantation." He turned into the drive. Satchmo was singing "When It's Sleepy Time Down South."

He could see the house standing at the end of the long *allée* of oak trees. The oaks formed a solid canopy above him, turning the entire drive into a green tunnel. The sun was low enough in the west now, hovering just above the levee, to flood the entire length of the drive with rusty light. As he got closer, he began to sense the enormity of the old house.

He parked the car under a big oak and got out. His shirt was drenched with sweat and clung to his back. The heat and humidity were part of the place. The mosquitoes and the music, the bugs and the blues. And the moss, he thought, taking a fistful from a low branch and turning the matted greyish-green filaments in his hand. Tentacles of moss dripped from all the branches of all the oaks around him. It was pretty, but there was something decadent about it as well, something that sent a graveyard chill up his spine.

Spanish moss, Hawke said to himself, suddenly remembering the name. He walked out from under the low-hanging branches and looked up at what was left of the house where his mother had been born. He was glad he'd come. It occurred to him that he'd needed to do this for a long, long time.

Make a connection.

It was a stunningly handsome work of architecture. Four graceful stories rising up above the trees, each one with a verandah, massive Corinthian columns now shrouded in the heavy green vines which had almost overtaken the entire house. He climbed the steps leading to the front entrance and paused when he reached the top. He saw the doors were missing, and twisting vines had worked their way through the open portal and into the interior of the house.

There were some faded beer cans and old newspapers littering the steps and the sagging floorboards of the front portico. It was irrational, he knew—he wasn't the proprietor after all—but all this refuse made him not just sad, but angry. The trash and debris were just a natural accumulation, the commonplace detritus of years of human neglect. Still, it felt to Alex Hawke like a sacrilege, a desecration. He brushed away veils of drooping cobwebs and ducked into the musty coolness of the reception hall.

The staircase. That was the thing which helped him get beyond all the ugliness at his feet. It soared upwards to the very top of the house in two gently curving sets of stairs which intersected to form landings at every floor, then bowed out once again and

ascended higher only to join once more. It was perhaps the most beautiful thing Hawke had ever seen. At
once delicate and strong, it was the work of an artist
commissioned by someone, this John Randolph apparently, who clearly wanted to make the most functional
fixture in the house also the most beautiful.

The stairway reminded him of something, Alex
thought, mounting the stairs and climbing upwards.
Something in nature. What was it? Damn it, he
couldn't remember anything lately.

Alex reached the top floor, paused on the top step,
and pulled the old postcard out of his jacket pocket. On
the faded front was a Mississippi steamboat, white bil-
lows of steam floating from her big black stacks, coming round a wide bend in the river. On the other side
was a little note from his mother. He'd read the thing a
thousand times, but now, standing in her house, he
found himself reading it aloud. Not whispering either.
He pronounced each word in a loud, clear tone, as if he
were addressing an invisible audience gathered below.

"My darling Alexander," he began. "Mummy and
Daddy have finally reached New Orleans and what
fun we are having! Last night, Daddy took me to hear
a famous trumpet player down in the French Quarter
named Satchmo. Isn't that a funny name? He toots
like an angel, though, and I adored him! This morning
we drove up the River Road looking for Mummy's old
house. I was amazed to see it still standing! It looks
dreadful to be sure, falling down, but I took your
father up to the very top floor and showed him my
room when I was your age. It's a very silly little room,
but you would love it. It has a big round window that
opens and you can sit and watch the river go by all day

if you want to! Rivers go on forever just like my love for you. I miss you, my darling, and Daddy and I send you all our love and oodles of kisses, Mummy."

The sound of his voice was still reverberating throughout the empty house as Alex returned the postcard to his pocket. He walked to the banister, which seemed solid enough, gripped it and leaned over, looking down through the intertwining stairs to the ground floor hall far below.

"Hello," he cried, listening for the echo. "Anybody here? I'm home!"

He turned and walked along the hall until he came to the center door. It was slightly ajar and he pushed it open, surprised by the flood of sunlight still streaming in. It was coming through a large round opening in the opposite wall. The opening was in an alcove formed by the pitch of a gable. Going to it, he saw the window itself was long gone and all that remained was the empty hole. Shielding his eyes from the glare of the setting sun, he went to it and rested both hands in the curvature of the sill.

Her room was filled with light every evening. This is where she would have had her bed. She would have read her books here, listening to the sonata of a songbird, the sweet scent of magnolia floating up from the gardens. During the day, she could watch the boats out on the river, looking up from her book whenever she heard one hooting, coming around the wide bend. At night, pulling her covers up, she would lay her head down on the pillow and see the broad avenue of trees which led all the way out to the stars over the river and sometimes to the moon.

There was a rickety old straight-backed chair tilted

against one wall, and Alex pulled it over to the window. He sat there, seeing the world through her eyes, until the sun had finally set behind the levee and all the stars he could see from his mother's window had been born.

Finally, he stood up and turned to go. He was walking across the dusty floorboards when it came to him. What the lovely spiral staircases of Twelvetrees had reminded him of. That thing in nature they had so closely resembled.

"It's DNA," Alex said softly to himself and then he pulled his mother's door shut behind him.

CHAPTER FOUR

Venice

Francesca stood alone, drinking champagne and looking out at the hazy lights along the Grand Canal. A slightly swampy evening breeze off the water carried a fog and blew the blonde curls back from her forehead. She allowed herself a smile, standing there at the railing of the terrace balcony of the suite at the Gritti Palace. The last of the Italian detectives and American diplomatic security agents had all come and gone. Each group had visited the suite at least three times during the week following the bizarre death of the new American ambassador to Italy. They had, they claimed, all they wanted from her. A lie.

She'd allowed herself the smile at this lie because no man on earth had ever had all he wanted from her.

The three Italian detectives had left the hotel, each one clutching her glossy autographed eight by ten. The two handsome American agents from the State Department had, after their third visit, departed the Gritti with only one burning memory: three exquisite inches of pale white thigh and pink garter above the tops of her sheer black stockings visible as she rose from the deep cushioned chair to say good-bye.

One of them, Agent Sandy Davidson, had, she felt, a certain boyish charm.

"*Sfumato!*" she had exclaimed on his last visit, tears welling in those enormous brown eyes. "*Sì!* Up in smoke! Poof! That's what they tell me has happened to him, Sandy! Horrible, no? *Ma Donna!*"

The American DSS agent in charge thanked the world-famous movie star profusely for her time and apologized for asking so many delicate questions at such a horrendous time. He was sure they would soon catch the terrorist group behind the gruesome murder of Simon Clarkson Stanfield. Any threats? he asked, putting on his raincoat. There had been, she said, certain threats, *si*, as recently as the preceding week. Her lover had said he was tired of always looking over his shoulder. An American expression, no? What she didn't tell them, what they certainly had not needed to know, was precisely why her lover had actually been looking over his shoulder that warm summer night one week earlier.

Two minutes after Stanfield had left her alone in the bed that night, Francesca had poured herself a glass of Pol Roger and walked naked out onto the very balcony where she now stood.

Her little silver bird had flown. The red bag hanging from her bare shoulder was much lighter now, without the slender missile. She drew a deep breath and composed herself. A few quiet moments to reflect before she opened the red leather bag again.

Certo, she'd made only one real mistake. She'd stupidly snapped at Luciano out on the dock when he tried to help her with her bag. Surely the target had been watching, seen that behavioral misstep. She couldn't fly to Venezia; she'd had to take the train because of the contents of the bag. The long ride was tiresome and boring, what with all the begging for autographs. No excuse. She'd lost it down there on the dock, momentarily, and surely the target had seen her step out of character.

She was only lucky he hadn't asked to see what was in her bag that was so important, no? *Stupido!* Only the stupid could allow themselves the luxury of luck!

She removed two items from the red leather bag. A Sony Watchman television with a tiny dish antenna affixed. And a very sophisticated satellite telephone to which she had attached a scrambling device of her own design.

First, she switched on the palm-sized television and adjusted the antenna. The image broadcast from the nose-mounted camera of the tiny missile was riveting.

The target was twenty feet ahead, bobbing and weaving and continually looking back over his shoulder. His face, so handsome in repose, was a mask of raw fear. He was just leaving the *Alla Napoleonica* and entering the central *Piazza*. Not taking her eyes off the screen she speed-dialed a number on the scrambled satphone. Snay bin Wazir, otherwise known as the Pasha, picked up on the second ring.

"Pasha?"

"My little Rose," the soft male voice said in classical Arabic, but with a distinct English lilt to it.

"*Sì,* Pasha."

The Pasha had long ago decided to call all of the female *hashishiyyun* in his seraglio of death his *"petites fleurs de mal."* His little flowers of evil. Each of his small army of seductive assassins was entitled to her own flower name and, since Francesca had some seniority, she'd quickly chosen her favorite, Rose.

The best name was long taken, chosen years ago by one who was the envy of them all, a great beauty descended from one of France's oldest aristocratic families. She was the very first assassin recruited to do the Pasha's bidding when his movements were restricted by the Emir. A recluse now, she lived in splendor in a large house on the Ile de la Cité. No one save the Pasha ever saw or spoke to her. She was known only as Aubergine. And called only by her chosen name, Deadly Nightshade.

"Are you watching this, my Pasha?" Francesca asked in English.

"*Wallah,*" the Pasha said. "Incredible. Dr. Soong's remarkable silver arrow flies straight and true."

"Is it not all we hoped for?"

"The Emir is sure to be pleased, little flower. I am certain when he sees this he will— Wait! What is he going to do?"

"Dive into the canal, I would guess? That's what I would do. Look! He's—"

"*Jara!*" Pasha said. "Shit!"

Ever since he'd left England and returned to the high mountains of his native land, the Pasha sprinkled his English with Arabic and his Arabic with English.

"Don't blink or you'll miss the good part, Pasha."

"Astounding! How does it—poise—in mid-air?"

"This is why I am so in love with this new weapon, Pasha. The thrusters, they angle in every direction. Dr. Soong, he explain to me it is like a, what, English Hurrier jet? Yes. Same principle, just smaller."

"They call it the Harrier, little Rose."

"Yes, but 'Hurrier' it is more funny, no?"

"And, it goes under the water?"

"Of course, Pasha!"

"Yes! Yes! It's going under the water . . . it's . . ."

The video transmission abruptly ended in a silent blast of static.

"Allah akbar!" the Pasha shouted. "You shall be richly rewarded in the Emir's Temple of Paradise, little Rose."

"Allah akbar," Francesca replied after the Pasha had disconnected the call. The marvelous weapon had worked flawlessly. This Dr. Soong, whom she had met at an arms bazaar in Kurdistan, deserved his reputation as a true genius with weapons. Biological, chemical, or nuclear. He'd first made his name with poison gases, so, although the doctor's name was I.V. Soong, he was commonly known amongst the cognoscenti as Poison Ivy.

The Venetian moon slipped from behind a cloud and bathed the terrace in pale blue light.

"One down," Francesca whispered to herself, smiling.

The Pasha, born Snay bin Wazir, fifth son of Machmud, replaced the solid gold receiver and took another bite of his chocolate chip cookie. Famous Amos. The recipe anyway. Couldn't buy them anymore, so bin Wazir's pastry chefs made them by the dozens. He hit the intercom button and told the projectionist to take down the screening room lights. To witness the death of the American in real time had been most satisfying. Almost as satisfying as the cookies.

"Roll it again!" the Pasha commanded.

Snay bin Wazir clapped his hands twice. It was a signal to the two concubines beneath his vast embroidered silk robes to return to their ministrations. "Death in Venice!" he'd roar each time the dramatic scene ended. "Run it again!" He'd recorded it for the Emir's collection of such tapes and made the projectionist play the tape over and over.

Finally, he had his surfeit of the thing. "Out! Out!" the Pasha said, and the two naked courtesans emerged, giggling and tinkling with bangles and rings, running for the exit. Snay bin Wazir clapped four more times, a sign to his four personal bodyguards that he was ready to move.

Although the screening room had plenty of plush velvet seats, over a hundred, the Pasha wasn't sitting in any of them. He traveled about his palace in an elaborately carved eighteenth century Italian sedan chair. Sad, but true. He had grown to such a magnitude he preferred the chair to his own two feet. As his weight now hovered around four hundred pounds, the palace doctors were concerned about his sixty-year-old heart. He kept telling them this was not a problem.

He had no fucking heart.

His four principal guards appeared, grunted and squatted, each grabbing one of the four posts of the sedan chair and lifting it easily. Lifting the Pasha and his gilded chair was no effort at all, because Snay bin Wazir had chosen as his closest, most personal guards perhaps the four greatest Japanese sumo wrestlers of the last century.

Ichi, Kato, Toshio, Hiro.

Snay bin Wazir, the notorious sultan of Africa, now known throughout the Emirate as the Pasha, had traveled to Japan to make his selection. He watched and studied the sumo world for months, attending bouts in Tokyo and Honshu, Yokohama and Kyoto, before making his decision. Four men were ultimately kidnapped. Captured, drugged, and smuggled out of Japan aboard the Pasha's private 747, they were brought up into the high mountains by camel caravan. The sumos had been installed in Snay bin Wazir's palatial fortress four years earlier. If there was small chance of escape then, there was none at all now.

The furor all this caused in Japan was immense. But no one knew where the *rikishi* were, and, over time, the country's economic woes eclipsed the story.

The Pasha clapped once, and the four guards took off at a stately pace, the sedan chair headed down a series of marble halls, the only sounds the music of the crystal jets in the many splashing fountains. From far away floated the notes of a Persian flute and the distant jingle of tambourines. In one of the great arched halls, a number of the Pasha's concubines were dancing for their own entertainment.

The sumos carried the Pasha past endless doors plated with beaten gold and inset with jeweled hyacinths and chrysolites. Their bare feet padded silently over silken rugs embroidered with silver stars and crescent moons. A tapestry depicted fleets of golden dhows with silvered lateen sails ghosting upon the mirrored Nile. Brilliantly colored songbirds flew freely about in the many vast courts of the Blue Palace, held captive only by the thin-meshed golden nets hanging high above.

Finally, the regal party arrived in the small gardens strictly reserved for the Pasha's principal wife, Yasmin.

The four sumos carefully lowered the sedan chair and, after bowing deeply to the Pasha, retired discreetly to enjoy a few hours of free time in their private suite of rooms.

They were no longer kept chained like disorderly slaves or the political prisoners down in the catacombs. The Pasha had enslaved them by creating a sumo paradise within the walls of the palace: he paid them in gold and diamonds, made them wealthy beyond measure, he had given them their pick of the most beautiful women in the seraglio, put legions of servants at their command.

Still, Snay bin Wazir saw the sumos were not happy. Being a keen observer of human nature, the Pasha quickly surmised the source of their unhappiness. They missed the fame and adulation accorded them in the streets and sumo shrines of their homeland.

So the Pasha had constructed a great hall in the manner of the most magnificent sumo shrines of the Nara Period of the eighth century. It was a soaring affair, with gilded sandalwood beams rising high above the *dohyo,* the Ring. There were bouts every week, and enthusiastic attendance was mandatory. Everyone from the captain of the imperial house guards to the lowliest minion was obliged to attend, and every seat was always full.

The Pasha took great delight in the emotion on the faces in the crowd. Some were faking, he knew exactly who, and made a mental note, but most were honestly enthralled when each of the wrestlers, with great dignity, performed the opening *dohyo-iri* ceremony. First, the clapping of hands to attract the attention of the gods. Then the upward turning of the palms to show the absence of weapons. And finally, the climactic act of bringing each foot down with a resounding blow to drive all evil from the *dohyo*.

In time, the sumos each acquired a devoted following and were treated with great respect and even reverence inside the walls. They had become celebrities within the Pasha's great mountain sanctuary. That the Pasha allowed any but his own radiance to shine was a source of great puzzlement and gossip in the barracks, where the guards lived, and amongst the women in the seraglio.

Although they would never dare say it, most thought this diverting chapter in the Pasha's life could only end in tragedy. Lights that burned too brightly within this palace tended to get snuffed out. There was but one sun permitted in this solar system.

In addition to defending the Pasha at the cost of their own lives, if necessary, and bearing him about daily in his chair, the four sumos had been schooling their new master in the fifteen-hundred-year-old sumo arts. Snay bin Wazir, heartless, powerful, and full of guile, was a willing and able student. Kato himself said that bin Wazir had already achieved such a level of proficiency as to make him competitive against the top ranks of *rikishi* in Japan. He had only to refine his techniques and one day he might rival them in grace and skill and artistry.

Snay had made it plain to the four *rikishi* that if he were ever able to defeat any one of them, the penalty was instant banishment from the palace. It was a fate only Ichi desired. No amount of wealth or women could salve Ichi's broken heart. Night and day he longed for Michiko, an angel who'd come to earth to bless him with peace just before his abduction. While his honor forbade deliberate loss in the *dohyo,* in sumo parlance a feigned *Tsuki dashi,* it did not, he'd come to feel, forbid the death of a master who held him captive and whom he did not honor.

And so, every morning when the sun rose over the high palace walls, and the thin mountain air was crystalline with light made radiant by the snowy mountain peaks looming above him, Ichi would walk alone in the gardens, consult his heart, and listen carefully to the song of the splashing fountains. He waited for the pure and innocent voice of Michiko. Surely one day the waters might whisper the secret way in which Ichi might escape his prison and find his way back to her heart. And so return to the source of the sun.

CHAPTER FIVE

London

"Another pint of stout, then, Chief?" Detective Inspector Ross Sutherland asked Congreve above the hubbub at the bar. The two men had dashed out of the Prince Edward Theatre, escaping before the final curtain had even touched the boards. They then made their way through a cold, drenching rain to the nearest pub in Old Compton Street. Ducking inside the Crown and Anchor, they were now more or less comfortably situated at the bar.

"No thank you. I really should be pushing off, Inspector," Congreve told his companion, glancing at his watch. "Time to knit up the raveled sleeve of care, I believe."

"Not your brand of poison, that musical, was it, Chief?"

Someone, Ambrose Congreve couldn't for the life of him remember who—his pal, Fruity Metcalfe, perhaps—had recently told him he would enjoy an enormously popular musical entertainment called *Mamma Mia*.

He hadn't.

"I'm aware that many actually enjoy the sort of thing we've just had the misfortune to witness. A blatant, sugar-coated confection, cynically calculated to appeal to the LCD."

"LCD?"

"Lowest common denominator."

"Shoe fits, I suppose. I rather enjoyed it, myself."

"Rubbish! It was about a *wedding,* for God's sakes, Sutherland. A wedding! How could anyone, now that I think about it, I think it was Sticky Rowland, suggest something about a bloody wedding? Confound it, man! Is there not an ounce of, of, what's the word, left in this world?"

"Propriety?" the junior New Scotland Yard man said, not quite sure it was the word Congreve had been searching for.

"Propriety, exactly. Decency! It's been only what, two weeks since the—since Victoria's—wedding. Well. What's a chap to do but turn to drink? I will have another pint if you don't mind."

Sutherland caught the eye of the Crown and Anchor's portly barman. "Half of bitter, please, and another pint here," he said, looking at Congreve out of the corner of his eye. The old boy was positively morose, he thought, putting another fiver down. Having caught his own reflection in the smoky mirror above the bar, Sutherland was startled to see how weary he himself appeared.

Inspector Sutherland, a man in his early thirties, was, like his companion, on semipermanent loan from the Yard to Alex Hawke. Ross Sutherland, a Scot from the Highlands north of Inverness, stood somewhere just short of six feet. He had a lean, lanky frame, with a healthy, ruddy complexion, a pair of keen grey eyes, and straw-colored hair kept close-cropped like his brush-cut American cousins at the CIA. Were it not for his broad Highland accent, and an occasional fondness for loose tweed jackets, the former Royal Navy flying officer turned Scotland Yard inspector might easily be mistaken for an American.

But the face he now saw reflected looked gaunt, even haggard. Hell, they'd all been through it. The horror of Vicky's death, the outrageousness of it, had taken an enormous toll on anyone and everyone who cared for Alex Hawke.

Other than Hawke himself, Congreve seemed the hardest hit, both personally and professionally. MI5, MI6, and the Yard were all over it and doing all they could. To Congreve's great chagrin, however, they had rebuffed his every effort to get involved.

"What exactly am I supposed to do about this, Sutherland," Ambrose said now, ignoring his freshly arrived pint. "Sit on my bloody hands and do nothing? Good Lord!"

"Aye. It's frustrating."

"It's a bleeding outrage, is what it is," Congreve said, properly browned off now. "We both still work for Scotland Yard, unless I'm very much mistaken. Has someone from Victoria Street told you differently?"

Sutherland stared morosely into his half bitter, feeling every bit as frustrated as his superior. "Hmm. It would seem that we are surplus to the Yard's requirements, Chief."

Ross and Alex Hawke had a long history together. During the Gulf War, when Alex was flying sorties for the Royal Navy, Ross had been right behind him in the after cockpit, serving as Commander Hawke's Navigation and Fire Control Officer. Kept the boss from getting lost in the desert and lit up the juiciest targets, basically.

Near the end of that conflict, after a particularly nasty skirmish in the skies over Baghdad, they'd been brought down by a SAM-7. Both men had ejected from the burning fighter, landing in open desert about thirty miles south of Saddam's capital. Captured and imprisoned, they'd barely survived their treatment at the hands of the Iraqi guards. Sutherland, more than any other prisoner, had been beaten senseless during daily "interrogations." Hawke, seeing his friend near death, saw no hope but escape from the makeshift hellhole.

That night, Hawke had killed a number of guards with his bare hands. They'd fled south across the desert, navigating by the stars, searching for the British or American lines. For days and nights on end, Hawke had carried Sutherland on his back. They were wandering in circles, staggering blindly over the sand-blasted dunes, when an American tank unit under the command of U.S. Army Captain Patrick "Brick" Kelly had finally spotted them.

The same Brick Kelly who was now U.S. Ambassador to the Court of St. James.

Sutherland sipped his half-pint and considered Congreve's question. Why *had* they been rebuffed by the Yard at every turn? As one of Hawke's inner circle, he wanted immediate action and he'd seen precious little.

"They won't let us near it," Ross finally said with a gallows grin, "because they think we're too close to it."

"Too close? Too bloody *au fait?*"

"Let me rephrase it, sir. They imagine our emotions might cloud our judgment."

Ambrose Congreve scoffed at the very notion, picked up his pint and drank deeply. He looked past the patrons of this somewhat grim establishment to the sheeting rain swirling about the streetlamps and clawing at the windows.

"Not even allowed to inspect the crime scene? Turned back at the very edge of the woods where Stokely discovered the shooter's lair?" he asked the air. "Me? Ambrose Congreve? Words fail me."

"Aggro?"

"Beyond aggravation, Sutherland. Well and far beyond. Do you suppose the scene tape is down at this point?"

"We're two weeks in."

"Tape is down, then. Forensics and scene-of-crime officers will be long gone."

"What are you thinking, sir?"

"I'll bloody well tell you what I'm thinking. Are we all even here?"

"Surely you don't intend to—"

"Pay a little nocturnal visit to the crime scene? That's exactly what I intend, Sutherland."

"You can't be serious. In this weather? At this hour of the night?"

Congreve drained his pint, slipped off the barstool, gathered himself up, and leaned into Sutherland's face, his eyes alight with something akin to, if not merriment, then certainly mischief. It would not have surprised Ross to see him actually twirl the tips of his waxed moustache.

"Good God, he's serious," Sutherland said.

"Never more so. The rain seems to have let up nicely. We'd best be pushing off. We'll just nip round to your flat and pick up your Mini. Oh, and your murder bag, of course."

"Nip round?" Sutherland said, glancing over his shoulder at the rainlashed windows of The Crown and Anchor.

It was well after midnight when Sutherland whipped the racing green Cooper Mini S through a roundabout, did a racing change down into second, and then accelerated into a narrow lane leading to the tiny village of Upper Slaughter. Curtains of rain and standing water on these country roads made driving a bit of a challenge, but Ross had every confidence in his car, having raced it successfully at Goodwood and other venues in far worse conditions. A crack of lightning illuminated a road sign as he roared past. Three miles to the village proper, meaning the church would be coming up on his left any moment now. The hedgerows were high and solid on both sides of the lane and Sutherland leaned forward in his seat, looking for some familiar landmark.

"I'm well aware of the fact that you think we're chasing wild geese, Sutherland," Congreve said, breaking his silence and peering through the bleared windscreen. "But, now that we appear to be gaining on them, could you ease off the throttle a bit?"

"Sorry. Force of habit."

Sutherland slowed and Congreve sat back in his seat. He looked over at Ross and smiled. "Sporting of you to do this, actually."

"Not at all, sir," Sutherland said, downshifting as they went into a tight right-hander. "You were right about this trip. I feel better about the thing already. No matter what we find or don't find. Thing is, I keep asking myself, why Vicky? Alex has no end of enemies. But, Vicky? Ach! It's right senseless then, isn't it?"

Ambrose Congreve said, "She was shot through the heart with a sniper rifle. At a range where the power of the scope used made the margin of error minuscule. Vicky was the target. It was deliberate and it was meant to hurt Alex as much as humanly possible. I've made a list of every single person or entity with reason to inflict such agony on Alex Hawke. You and I are going to go through that list one by one until we find—hold on, here's your turning just ahead on the left."

Ten minutes later they were slogging up the muddy hillside in their green gumboots and yellow macs, the beams from their powerful flashlights stabbing through dense veils of rain. Forward visibility was less than five feet and the storm seemed to be gaining in intensity.

"Bloody weather front seems to have beat us up here," Congreve cried, the two of them having to shout to be heard above the downpour and constant rumble of thunderclaps.

"We're almost there. It's up on the brow of the hill, just beyond this graveyard," Ross shouted back.

An arc of lightning momentarily lit up the little cemetery with stark white light and Congreve managed to avoid a substantial headstone which would have sent him sprawling. The ground angled fairly sharply upwards now, and Congreve's torch caught the fluorescent yellow crime scene tape the SOCO chaps had strung from tree to tree. The footing in this porridgy muck was treacherous and it was all a man could do just to stay on his feet.

"I'm sure scene-of-crime officers have cleared away all the land mines," Ambrose shouted ahead to Sutherland who was leading the way now, almost to the tapes. He was not at all sure. He'd only just recalled that this entire area had been chockablock with antipersonnel land mines the day of the murder. He guessed they'd all been removed; still the thing was a bit dicey.

"Only one way to find out," Sutherland said. He ducked under the tape, waiting on the other side for Congreve.

"Bugger it," Ambrose muttered to himself and, slipping and sliding, made his way up to Sutherland who held the tape up for him. He ducked under, having retained all four limbs, and was surprised to find the rain considerably diminished. Looking skyward, he saw the dense canopy of trees overhead and was thankful for the respite. He swung his light in an arc, looking for one particular tree.

"It's over there, sir!"

"One thing we needn't worry about," Ambrose said, picking his way carefully through the gloom of the sodden forest, "is mucking up the crime scene. This one is already about as mucky as one could ask for."

"Yes, I believe this is our tree here," Sutherland said, moving towards the base of a massive oak, his light playing about the trunk. Congreve was running his fingers over the rough surface of the bark.

"Spikes," he said, his eyes tracking the beam of his torch into the uppermost branches of the three-hundred-year-old tree. "The kind British Telecom linemen and tree surgeons wear. See the trail of small punctures leading up? You can still see the freshly punctured bark."

He turned from the tree and looked at Sutherland. There was that familiar glistening in the eyes, a slight flaring of the nostrils, and Ross knew the boss had picked up the scent.

"Question. When were the roads into the village sealed, Superintendent?" he asked Sutherland, eyeing the soggy, leafy ground around the base of the tree.

"Twelve noon Friday, the day before the wedding. After that, no one except villagers and somebody with good reason to be here got through."

"And the date the church location first leaked to the papers?"

"First Sunday of the month."

"So, he had two weeks to scout the location, pick his spot, rig his mechanism, lay his minefield, and get into position."

"Surely he didn't spend two weeks up a tree."

"What's on the other side of this hill?"

"The village proper."

"He spent the last two weeks in the village. Posing as a tourist with a good reason to be in these woods from time to time. Birdwatcher. Watercolourist. Naturalist or something. He'd have binoculars, a size-able knapsack of some kind. Bring in his gear and explosives one bit at a time. We'll check all local lodging tomorrow, see if anyone remembers a chap like that."

"I keep thinking about that high-speed motor," Ross said. "I mean, why bother with the blooming thing? Why not just spike up and spike down?"

"Speedy getaway, Ross," Congreve said. "Had all the time in the world to get up high enough for a clear shot. But he'd be expecting a rush up the hillside after the shooting. He'd want to get down that tree in an awfully big hurry."

Sutherland nodded his head, wiping rainwater from his eyes. Unlike Congreve, who covered his thinning pate with a hat rain or shine and was now wearing an old wide-brimmed sou'wester, he'd forgotten to grab a lid.

"I think," Sutherland said, "he would have spent that Friday night up there, having hauled the cable up after him. Little chance of accidental detection then, the morning of the wedding."

"Yes," Congreve agreed, "he might just. Minimum he'd have gone up well before daybreak. Long, chilly night up there. He'd have taken food, something hot to drink."

"I know what you're thinking. But it was a very professional hit. He would have been extremely fastidious."

"Still, Ross, gravity is frequently on the side of the law. People drop all manner of things when they're scrubbing the blood out of the bathtub. Chap up a tree all night, well . . ."

"Scene-of-crime officers will have gone over this bit pretty thoroughly."

"Crime scene investigators, Superintendent Sutherland, are not to be confused with Ambrose Congreve."

"Sorry, sir, I only meant—"

"We'll do a three-sixty around the base of the tree," Congreve said, snapping on a pair of latex gloves from Sutherland's murder bag. "Fifteen-foot radius out. You go that way, I'll go anticlockwise. Surplus to requirements, eh? Is that what they think? By God, they've got another think coming, Sutherland!"

Twenty minutes later, their rain gear covered with

mud, twigs, and soggy leaves, the two policemen met on the opposite side of the tree. "Well. Good cursory examination, I daresay. Let's do it again, shall we? I'll take your half," Congreve said. He dropped to his knees and, torch in one hand, began delicately turning over layers of leaves with the other.

Sutherland's heart skipped a beat when, not five minutes later, he heard Congreve exclaim, "A-ha!"

No matter how many times he'd heard Ambrose Congreve say it, he knew an a-ha meant only one thing. A cold trail had just grown considerably warmer.

"What have you got, Chief?" he asked, peering over the older man's shoulder at a soggy blackish object pinched twixt his thumb and forefinger.

"Not sure. Try and keep your light on it, will you? What's it look like to you?"

"No idea. A moldy root of some kind?"

Congreve had his spatula blade out and was levering the thing into a clear plastic evidence bag.

"Looks like, yes, which is why your scene-of-crime chaps missed it, prone as they are to snap judgments. Cigar, actually," he said, holding the transparent bag up to Sutherland's light. "See the teeth marks?"

Ross peered at the thing from the other side.

"Yes," he said. "And, here, looks like a bit of foil from the wrapper embedded in the wrapper leaf. Do you see it?"

CHAPTER SIX

Georgetown

Alex Hawke couldn't sleep. He couldn't stand being alone in his big empty Georgetown house in Washington and he couldn't imagine being back in England drowning in all that bloody tea and sympathy. He rolled over and looked at the clock by the bedside. Midnight. Christ. He flipped the lamp on and picked up his book, a battered first edition of *Pigs Have Wings*.

Wodehouse had been, since childhood, one of the few authors with even the slightest ability to pick him up and drag him, kicking and screaming, into a passably good humor. He must have read this particular novel ten times over and it never lost its capacity to make him laugh out loud. He read for fifteen minutes, sat straight up in bed, and hurled the hardcover across the room.

Even Wodehouse had failed him.

He managed to hit a particularly hideous Waterford crystal table vase someone had sent as a wedding present (why Pelham had unwrapped the ghastly object and left it there was still a mystery), which smashed against the wall with a most satisfying crashing sound. Like glass cymbals struck with a heavy wooden mallet.

There. That's a little better, he thought, eyes darting hungrily round the room seeking something even
more substantial to splinter into a thousand pieces.

He was about to crawl out of bed and pour himself
a stiff brandy prior to putting his fist through a wall
when the telephone jangled.

"Hello!" he snarled, not bothering to disguise his
mood.

"Can't sleep?"

"What?"

"I saw your bedroom light go on."

"Hiya, Conch. How the bloody hell are you?"

"Swell. Cloud Nine. Happier than a pig in—"

"You rang to cheer me up, is that it?"

Consuelo de los Reyes, Conch, was the American
secretary of state. She was rather beautiful and keen-
minded, and she lived just across the road. Hawke's
neighbor for some two years now. She'd also been
Alex's lover. But that was longer ago than either of
them cared to remember. Check that. Conch cared to
remember. And she never let Alex forget it.

"Hey, Mister. Remember me? Your old fishing
buddy?"

"Sorry. I'm in a thoroughly despicable humor."

"Good. Me, too. Let's have a drink."

"Brilliant idea. Your place or mine?"

"Yours. You have a much better wine cellar. Give
me five to throw something on."

The doorbell chimed half an hour later and Hawke
answered it, a bottle of Lafitte '53 in hand. The old
adage "Life is too short to drink cheap wine" had never
seemed more appropriate. Fully aware since childhood
that we're all hanging by a thread every second of our

lives, the savagery on the steps of St. John's had put paid to Hawke's most fragile notion of security.

Hawke pulled the heavy door open.

Conch's eyes glistened, and she wrapped her arms around him, her right hand patting him softly on the shoulder. They stood there in the doorway, silent, just holding on.

Finally, Alex pulled away and looked down at her upturned face, speaking softly.

"Should we skip the wine and go directly to the tequila?" He tried a smile and almost managed it.

"I make a mean margarita, buster."

"The meanest goddamn margarita between Key West and Key Largo."

The two had met down in the Keys. Hawke had been determined to learn how to catch bonefish, and Conch, a Cuban who'd grown up in the Florida archipelago, was the acknowledged master. She was just out of Harvard with a brand-new doctorate in political science the summer they'd met. A free spirit, taking a year off to decide what to do with her life, and meanwhile earning a pretty good living as a bone guide out of Cheeca Lodge on Islamorada.

The Cheeca's bar overlooking the ocean was a favorite watering hole for local captains and bone guides, and Conch had met the tall Englishman with the curly black hair there the afternoon he'd arrived. Unlike most of the tourists, who sported gaily colored tropical fishing shirts, Alex Hawke was wearing a simple navy blue linen shirt, the sleeves rolled up to the elbows over his finely muscled forearms.

"Bartender over there tells me you're headed down to Key West for dinner tonight," the deeply tanned,

deeply beautiful woman had said to him that first afternoon. She was wearing khaki shorts and a coral cotton
shirt that did little to hide her lush figure.

"As a matter of fact, yes I am," Hawke replied, smiling, already hooked, but not in the boat yet.

"Bad idea," she said, shaking her head.

"Really? Why on earth should that be?"

"Crime rate has skyrocketed down there," she
deadpanned. "Chief of police is a good pal of mine.
Just between you and me, he tells me the number of
drive-by spankings has tripled in the last six months."

Hawke, who had some idea of the sexual demo-
graphics of Key West, had laughed out loud.

Within an hour, Conch had a new bonefishing
client. Twelve hours later they were out on the flats,
the sun was shining, the beer was cold, and they were
already making a lot of memories. Alex proved an
adept pupil, though he didn't have the patience
required for the wily Mr. Bone. He'd taken a great
delight in hooking sharks on the light tackle, fighting
them all the way to the flats boat. "Bit more sporting
like this, don't you think?" he'd said with his boyish
grin, his spinning rod bent double by a large shark.

A week of Budweiser, Buffett, and the most beautiful sunsets Hawke had ever seen would spin them
whirling permanently into each other's orbits. Lovers,
friends, lovers, friends. They'd last stopped the wheel
on friends and that's the way it had been ever since.

"Answering his own door," Conch said, trailing
Hawke into the kitchen. She saw a spoon standing
upright in a half-eaten tin of macaroni and cheese.
"Staff has the night off? Where's dear old Pelham?"

"Dear old Pelham is upstairs in his bed. Not feeling

well, I'm afraid. I took some tomato soup and toast up to the old boy and he wouldn't touch it."

"I have to say I'm overwhelmed by the image of your taking a tray up to him."

"Really? Why?"

"I don't know. It's sweet. A girl thing, maybe. Where are the limes? And you better tell me you've got key limes, Sugar."

"In that big fridge over there. I'll fetch the tequila from the drinks table. Back in a tick."

Conch pulled open the stainless steel door and stood staring into the refrigerator, not seeing anything.

God. She was glad to see Alex's stiff upper lip was still intact; and the startlingly blue eyes above his jutting cheekbones were clear. But strangely hollow. Filled with pain and yet so terribly empty. She could see the hurt in them, and it was all she could do to keep the silly smile plastered on her face, keep her hands to herself, keep her mouth shut. She wanted to run to him, hold him, tell him it was going to be all right, tell him a thousand things, the truth about how she still felt, how much it hurt to see him in so much pain.

Since she couldn't, and wouldn't, ever, do any of those things, she took the white porcelain bowl full of limes out of the refrigerator, put the bowl on the counter, found a knife, and began slicing the tiny green limes and squeezing the tart juice into the mixer.

Hers was a dark, secret love. She had learned, somehow, to live with it.

They sat on the floor in the library before the fire Alex had built and they were halfway through the small pitcher of margaritas before either of them could say anything.

"Well, you've still got it, kid," he said to her, staring into the flames. "Just might be the meanest margarita ever created by man or woman."

"Alex?"

"Yes?"

"What are you going to do? I mean—"

"Me? Oh, gosh. I have no immediate plans. Beyond finding the bloody bastard who murdered my wife, I mean. Finding him and ripping his bloody heart out. Beyond that, I—"

"Oh, Alex, I'm so sorry. So—"

"Let's not do this, Conch. I can't talk about me. Let's talk about you. What's going on in the world? I haven't been there much lately. I haven't a clue."

"You really want to know?"

"I do. Really."

"Okay. You asked. As a matter of fact, the world crisis du jour happens to be resting squarely on my frail shoulders."

"Tell me."

"Somebody seems to have decided it's a good idea to pick off a couple of our ambassadors, Alex. Two of them have been assassinated in the last two weeks."

"Christ. I was in Louisiana when I got the news about Stanfield's murder in Venice. Sorry I didn't call you. Quite the lady-killer, old Simon Stanfield was. I shouldn't be surprised if one of them returned the favor. There's been another?"

"Tonight. About six hours ago. Butch McGuire. Our ambassador to Saudi Arabia. You've met him. He was having dinner with his wife, Beth, at their favorite restaurant in Riyadh. According to Beth, he suddenly went very rigid for a moment, looked at her with wide eyes, and then simply keeled over halfway through the meal. No apparent cause of death. He was only forty-five years old, Alex. Excellent health. I've ordered an autopsy."

"An aneurysm. Stroke?"

"Maybe. Two ambassadors in two weeks. I've put the worldwide Diplomatic Security Service on full alert. Could be a coincidence. Or, it could be just the beginning of something worse. Langley and the Bureau are picking up a lot of increasingly interesting cellular traffic. Can't go into any details, but something big is brewing, Alex. Jack Patterson himself is running this show for me."

Alex Hawke looked over at her. "Tex?" he said.

Jack Patterson, the legendary chief of the Texas Rangers, now with State, was one of the finest men Hawke had ever known. Coming from a long line of Texas lawmen, Patterson was a direct descendant of the early Texas Ranger, John "Jack" Patterson. A Comanche Indian who'd switched sides and rode with Patterson in 1840 had given the young Ranger captain the name Brave Too Much.

Bravery was a quality that still ran in the family. Like most everyone in Washington, Alex called the Ranger captain's descendant, the man now in charge of the DSS, "Tex."

"I did a little duet with Tex once. There was that embassy that did not get blown up in Morocco, remember?"

"Right. He still gives you all the credit, Alex."

"Yeah, well, he's still a liar. Splendid guy. Superb criminal intelligence officer," Alex said.

There was light in his eyes. The first light she'd seen

there since she'd seen him standing at the altar two weeks earlier watching his bride-to-be walk down the aisle.

"Tex could use your help again, Alex. He told me so himself. Hell, we all could. The president himself is asking for you. They both also told me not to tell you that. They know you're hurt. What Tex said was, 'I can't call Alex, Conch, that boy, why, he's on the bench.' He also knows you have some huge personal scores to settle."

"Yeah. Spot on, in that regard."

"Alex, I know you must be suffering terribly."

"I'll deal with it."

"I have—a place. Where you could go for a while. In the Keys."

"Go?"

"Be alone. It's not much. Just a glorified fishing shack down on Islamorada. But it's on the water. You could fish. Watch the sunsets. Pull yourself together."

"Very kind. Pull myself together."

"Sorry."

"Not at all. It's me, Conch, not you."

"Alex, we're in grievous trouble. Without compromising my government, I can tell you we're seeing some kind of Armageddon scenario coming together."

Alex and his old friend stared at each other for a few moments. In his eyes, she saw his heart and mind tugging at each other. Saw them going in opposite and equally powerful directions. One way lay vengeance. The other, his highly developed sense of duty.

"Give me a week," he finally said, poking at the fire. "You tell Tex that for me. I'm sick to death moping around feeling sorry for myself. One week. Tell him I'll be off the bloody bench so fast he'll never know I was there."

Conch smiled and reached out to stroke his cheek.

Alex jabbed the logs with the poker again and a shower of sparks rose up the chimney.

He'd avenge Vicky's death somehow. Somebody would pay. Pay dearly, and soon. Like the much-vaunted Royal Navy battleships his ancestors had sailed through two world wars, Hawke's mission in life was to give, not to receive.

For now, duty had won.

CHAPTER SEVEN

Mozambique

Bin Wazir, in the years before he acquired great wealth and notoriety, had fallen deeply in love with one of the world's wealthiest women. Her father, who was known throughout the Middle East simply as the Emir, had vast reserves of oil as well as minerals, uranium, and gold inside the forbidding mountain ranges of his small country. Despite his enormous wealth, the deeply religious Emir lived the life of an ascetic, shunning all accoutrements of luxury. But, when it came to his only daughter's happiness, his generosity knew no bounds.

Snay bin Wazir was just twenty years old and the son of a modestly successful jeweler. He lived where he'd been born, in the village of Ozmir, a lush oasis nestled at the foot of the mountains on the southern coast of the Emirate. He had met the beautiful Yasmin the night before her sixteenth birthday.

Her father had allowed Yasmin, in the company of four heavily veiled maidservants, to visit his father's small shop in the souk. Only the best stones were sold by Machmud and these he proudly showed to Yasmin.

Snay, hiding in the shadows of the storeroom to which he'd been banished by his father, could only

the early eighties, before the ban on ivory trade instituted in 1989 by CITES, the Convention on
International Trade in Endangered Species. Snay bin
Wazir, restless, brilliant, imaginative, and despite some
bizarre eccentricities, supremely practical, had heard
that there were still fortunes to be made in the ivory
trade. The tusk, but also the magic horn of the rhino.

Rhino horn had, for centuries, been much valued in
Arab countries for two reasons. Ground into fine powder and stirred into the juice of the coconut, it made a
most suitable aphrodisiac. Historically, it was also
much prized as a material for the hilt of daggers. A
dead rhino went for ten dollars on the open market in
Mozambique. Snay bin Wazir could sell the ground-up
horn in Yemen, for instance, for $7,000 U.S. per kilo.

It had always been thus. Demand for the much cov-
eted ivory was so great in ancient Arab civilizations,
that by 500 B.C., the vast elephant herds in Syria had
been completely eradicated. What animals the ivory
merchants didn't kill, the Romans imported by the
thousands for the merry slaughter of the Circus
Maximus. When the supply in the Mediterranean was
exhausted, the Arab Islamic dynasties established trade
relations with people south of the Sahara and, later,
along the coasts of Central and West Africa.

If there were many poachers in Mozambique when
young Snay bin Wazir arrived, there were many fewer
when he departed. Bin Wazir could tolerate many
things, and sometimes did, but what he hated most was
competition. Poachers began turning up dead shortly
after his arrival. Strange fates befell them. One hanged
himself by his genitals in a deserted stable and starved
to death. One hurled himself into his cooking fire,

another leapt into a vat of boiling pitch, and yet another impaled himself on a poison-tipped ivory tusk in the bush. Four died when their tusk truck exploded. It was all very mysterious.

There were rumors, naturally, that this spate of bizarre suicides coincided with the arrival of bin Wazir in southwest Africa, but who left among them had the balls to point a finger at him?

After he'd sufficiently discouraged the professional poachers, he went after any villagers still foolish enough to encroach upon his rapidly burgeoning monopoly. His solution was quite cheap and simple. He had instituted incentives, encouraging his agents to go from village to village and cut off the hands, and sometimes the arms, of all the males.

"Shortsleeves or longsleeves?" his men would ask, brandishing their machetes, taunting the poachers they'd run down and captured out in the *bundu*. The answer was always the same, because "longsleeves" meant you lost your hand but got to hold on to your arm.

This method of dealing with competitors, bin Wazir assured his own growing army of poachers, would ensure fulfilling their quotas, not to mention their own life expectancies.

It was a time following a revolution in Mozambique, when the country finally won its independence from Portugal after a bloody ten-year struggle. But the warring factions had inadvertently conspired to present bin Wazir with two great spoils of war: two revolutionary poaching ideas that, combined, would change his fortunes forever.

The helicopter. And the land mine.

Traditionally, African and Asian poachers brought

down elephants with high-powered rifles. You'd shoot an animal, walk up to it, and hack its face off with a machete. You'd locate a herd, get within a reasonable range, and open up. You had to kill them all. No animal was allowed to escape. Even though they were useless, calves and pregnant females were slaughtered. Because of their remarkable memories, any elephant that escaped a massacre and joined another herd would infect the new herd with panic.

The problem with elephant poaching, bin Wazir had soon discovered, was that you had to kill them one at a time.

"Listen, Tippu Tip, carefully," he'd said to his chief that night long ago in Maputo. "You're going to love this idea."

The huge African across the table from him had skin so black it was blue, and possessed large ivory-colored teeth, which, when he smiled, looked like a row of piano keys stained red by the juice of betel nuts. The man was a fierce warrior from the village of Lichinga in the northern province of Nyassa. Besides ruling all bin Wazir's field agents with an iron hand and a steel machete, Tippu had a great head for figures.

The African chieftain was smiling, but not at bin Wazir. They were at a small table near the stage at the Club Xai-Xai, watching the fat strippers grind and sweat in the dense smoky light. One particularly unlovely dancer had been laboring above them for some time now. The grim town of Maputo, squatting on the bluffs overlooking the Indian Ocean, was awash with such women. Most were former sweatshop girls who'd been sitting at their benches doing piecework when they'd finally come to a great realization.

They were sitting on gold mines.

Tippu, staring at the gyrating woman, was gnawing at a hunk of hippo meat he'd purchased earlier in the Zambesi market. Snay tried unsuccessfully to catch his eye.

"Are you listening or watching, Tippu?"

"Ar watching, Bwana."

"Listen."

The great black head swiveled momentarily in Snay's direction. "Ar listen," he said.

"Of late, I've been thinking about something. An idea which runs through my mind with the noblest perfection. I am not a complicated man, Tippu. I am a hungry man. A thirsty man. I thirst for blood and I hunger for gold. Always. The way a pilgrim long lost in the desert might long for water. As of now, this moment, I feel like a pilgrim who has caught a glimpse of a vast oasis, lying just there, beyond that next dune."

Tippu Tip tore himself away from the grunting, gyrating creature above him and turned his blood-red eyes on his employer. Tippu thought the wild-eyed Arab boy was mildly insane, at least deranged, although Tippu had never met a *muzungu*, a white man, who was more ferocious in getting what he wanted. If you had to work for a white man, Bwana bin Wazir was as good as it got. The Sultan, as he was now sometimes called by Tippu, made all of the African's former Portuguese masters, many of whom he himself had killed, look like morons.

"Ar listen, Bwana Sultan," Tippu said loudly, and many heads swiveled in their direction. Tippu Tip's voice had the rumble of distant thunder from a borderless land. He took a deep draught of *chibuku,* the local potion which passed for beer. He said, "What treasure lie in this vast oasis, Sultan?"

"Blood, Tippu. Blood and gold."

"Yes, Bwana. Both good."

"I want to buy helicopters. Two, maybe three to start."

"Helicopters?"

"Helicopters," the Sultan replied, his eyes glittering. "I'm saying to you, Tippu, you are going to be crazy for this idea. Feel free to call me a genius once I have explained it."

"Can you tell it?"

"No. It's a secret. Very hush-hush. I shall demonstrate all, Tippu Tip, but only when everything is in place." Snay licked his fingers noisily, one by one. He was eating fried grasshoppers from a paper sack.

"*Baksheesh, baksheesh!* How much," Tippu wanted to know, "the Sultan pay for these choppers?"

"Sultan will pay however much *baksheesh* necessary."

"Good. Ar know a man up on the coast. Beira. Frenchman. Ar can talk with him."

"See to it."

Tippu Tip nodded his great head and returned his red gaze to the giant naked woman looming above him, pendulous breasts slick with sweat, slapping and swaying together, the drooping lobes of her ears stretched perilously thin by the heavy brass hoops of her earrings.

"Ar lak this one, sah. Not so big."

"Not so big? Her teats alone must weigh twenty stone each." Bin Wazir recalled that Tippu had been married once, to an equally mammoth female, but that one had died long ago of Blackwater Fever.

"Ar lak her, Bwana. She lak like me. See? She lak jig-jig me."

"Ha! She's yours, Tippu! She'll be waiting in your tent when you return from Beira tomorrow evening. With a signed purchase order for three helicopters. You can jig-jig all night."

Tippu smiled briefly, and then his expression settled once more into stony silence. His face, bin Wazir thought, looked at times exactly like the African masks for sale in the dusty jumble of curio shops in the *souks* of Maputo.

That night was the eve of a new era for bin Wazir and Tippu Tip, the ivory traders. Tippu drove his truck up the muddy, rutted coast road to Beira. There, he met a man known as *le Capitain* and he purchased three used French helicopters for one hundred thousand each. The Alouette III transport choppers he bought were some of the first to be sold in Third World countries. Bin Wazir had *le Capitain* import three chopper pilots recently retired from the French *Armée d'Air* and was soon training them in skills he himself was making up as he went along.

One morning, in the baking heat, he summoned Tippu Tip to his tent and said it was time for the explanation of his "oasis" theory. Tippu found Snay sitting at a folding campaign table going over his maps. The visionary was wearing a big ivory-handled Smith & Wesson pistol on each hip and had his rhino hide whip stuck inside his belt. As he spoke, Tippu heard the roar of the three Alouettes descending and landing just outside bin Wazir's tent.

Twenty minutes later they were screaming over the treetops looking for elephants. Bin Wazir sat up front next to the pilot, jumping up and down in his copilot seat like a child. Tippu sat on a jumpseat just behind him in the cargo bay. The pilot and his two passengers were all wearing headphones in order to communicate over the roar. Tippu had never seen the boss so excited.

The three helicopters raced in formation across the vast savanna; they were flying low over pink clouds that were actually vast numbers of flamingos, rising up from the shallows of the soda lakes bordered by the golden mountains. Clouds of dust rose, too, but it was only herds of horned animals: kudu, eland, and impala, no elephant so far.

"There!" bin Wazir shouted. "Allah be praised, there must be three hundred in that herd! François! Get the other two pilots on the radio and give them our coordinates. We are about to make history, my friends. Just you wait!"

He turned in his seat and smiled at Tippu Tip over his shoulder.

"Tippu!"

"Sah!"

"You remembered the camera?"

Tippu patted his large canvas shoulder bag and nodded.

"Video camera, yes sah, two blank tapes, Bwana," he said.

"Most excellent," said bin Wazir, unfastening his harness and squeezing past the pilot towards the rear of the chopper. "Get ready to start shooting, Tippu," he said. Picking up a Russian submachine gun, he began cackling at his own terrible joke.

He slid open the starboard side door, hooked himself into the canvas harness, and sat down in the opening with the machine gun across his lap. The two other choppers appeared; they flew in a wide formation, three abreast, hard on the heels of the now stampeding herd of elephants.

Snay opened fire, shooting over the heads of the elephants. Two of his most trusted poachers, sitting in the open bays of the other two helicopters, starting firing as well. To Snay's delight, the combination of the roaring choppers and the rounds flying over their heads enabled Snay to direct the herd in any direction he wished.

"*Eh bien,* François, let's take them due south!"

The two other pilots heard him and now all three choppers banked hard right, staying just behind the thundering herd. A huge smile broke across Snay's features. The herd had turned south.

"Did I not tell you this was genius, Tippu Tip? Look at them! I could take them to Paris if I wished! Right up the Champs-Elysées!"

"Where you take them, Sultan?"

"You shall see, Tippu! Be patient and you shall see!" Snay was cackling like a *mafisi,* a wild hyena.

The first explosion occurred four minutes later. A female elephant, the matriarch of the herd, had been in the lead and had been first to enter the minefield. Three of her legs were instantly blown off. She went down in a heap. Explosions were coming rapidly now, as three hundred panicked elephants entered the huge minefield. It was a feast of blood, fountains of the stuff, red jets everywhere you looked. It was just the way Snay had imagined it, and his heart sang with the joy of the truly fulfilled.

"François!" he cried. "Right here! Hover over that

big bull . . . I'm going down!" Snay stuck his foot in a wire harness and grabbed the handhold mounted in the open bay.

"But the mines, zey—"

"Do it!"

The chopper leveled off and hovered perhaps twenty feet above the dying elephant. Snay pressed a button that would allow him to descend rapidly. He had his razor-sharp machete in his hand now, and when he got low enough to the bull's head, he slashed the face off. First the right side, then the left. The elephant, like those around him, was still alive. He bellowed in pain as Snay ripped the tusks from his bloody head. There was a small calf lying legless next to the bull, and bin Wazir, in a mad fit of kindness, used one of his .357 magnum six-shooters to put the useless baby animal out of its misery.

Tippu, looking through the lens of his video camera at the scene beneath him, stared in open-mouthed amazement. There were exploding elephants in all directions, as far as you could see. A fine red mist had risen up from the plain. And then there was the Sultan, swinging wildly about at the end of his tether. Tippu couldn't hear him, with the roar of the rotors and the turbocharged engines. But he could see enough of the blood-soaked bin Wazir to know that he was laughing hysterically as he chopped and slashed.

This white man, he is part hyena, Tippu decided in that moment. Half man, half wild dog. A snarling creature who would devour the whole world if he could, eating everything, crushing bones and stones with his teeth, not spitting out a thing.

Snay bin Wazir seemed to have a penchant for collecting nicknames and soubriquets to go with the name he was making for himself in the world. In Africa, he was called the Sultan. Later, in London, he would style himself Pasha. But the name Tippu Tip would give him that day, the day of the first great elephant massacre, would remain with Snay bin Wazir for the balance of his life.

Tippu Tip called him the *Mafisi*.

The world would come to know him as the *Dog*.

CHAPTER EIGHT

Dark Harbor, Maine

Deirdre Slade glanced out her upstairs bedroom window at the sound of an approaching motor. It was too foggy to see anything, even with the floodlights on the rocks and one out at the end of the dock. But she knew by the distinctive putt-putt of the motor that it was Amos McCullough's ancient lobster boat. Nice of him to bring his granddaughter over on a pea-souper night like this. He may not have all his marbles, Deirdre thought, but by God, Amos McCullough still had his good old-fashioned Yankee manners.

She looked at her small diamond evening watch and rushed back into her dressing room, her cheeks expelling a little puff of air. Almost seven. She was going to be late if she didn't get off island by seven-thirty or so. Invitation had said eight sharp and it was a good twenty minutes in the Whaler over to the Dark Harbor Yacht Club docks. Night like this, with the fog really socked in, it could easily take her half an hour.

The Old Guard still took invitations seriously up in this part of Maine. Show up a little late, or a little stewed, or, worse yet, not at all, and you are definitely going to be Topic A at the Beach Club next morning.

Deirdre had, over the years, been guilty of all three transgressions.

Thank God Amos had made sure his granddaughter Millie, the babysitter, was on time. Charlie and Laura, five and six, had had their macaroni and cheese dinner and were already bathed and in their Harry Potter jammies. She and her two children had been having a ball here on Pine Island, the three sole inhabitants of the big old house up on the rocks her parents had bought in the fifties. It was the house she'd grown up in and she adored every musty nook and cranny.

Deirdre added a little gloss to her lipstick and stepped back to look at herself in the full-length mirror. Black Chanel dress. White pearls. Black satin Manolo Blahnik heels. Pretty good for an aging babe, she thought, fooling around with her shoulder-length blonde hair. Certainly good enough for the Maine Historical Society dinner at the Dark Harbor Yacht Club.

She took a quick sip of the glass of grocery store chardonnay sitting on the mirrored top of her dressing table.

God, she hated these things. Especially when she had to go without her husband. Still, it was fun to bring the kids back to Maine for a couple of weeks. It was spring break at their school in Madrid. Evan was of course supposed to be here. But, at the last minute, his job had gotten in the way. He had promised to join them if he could duck out of some urgent Mideast talks in Bahrain a few days early. She wasn't holding her breath. These were tough times for diplomats, and Evan took his job very seriously. He'd plainly been on edge on the phone tonight. Something was bothering him.

Something was going on in sunny Madrid.

He wouldn't, or more than likely *couldn't,* talk about it. What had he said to her when they'd said good-bye in the lounge at the Madrid Barajas airport? *Keep your eyes open, darling. It's going to get much worse before it gets better.* She waited for more, but she could see in his eyes it wasn't coming. Over the years, she'd learned not to ask. They had a good marriage. If there was something that needed saying, and it was something that could be said, it got said.

She'd replaced the receiver and sat on her bedside, staring out into the swirling fog beyond the bedroom windows. *Keep him safe,* she whispered, on the off chance that there really was somebody up there listening. *You keep him safe.*

"Hiya, Amos," Deirdre said, descending the stairway. All she could see at first were his yellow rubber boots and the legs of the foul-weather gear, but she'd know that stance anywhere. The wide-apart stance of an old man who'd spent years on the slippery wet deck of a wildly pitching lobster boat.

"And, hello, Millicent," Deirdre started to say. "It's awfully nice of you to—"

It wasn't Millicent.

"Hi," the girl said, coming towards her with her hand outstretched. She had some flowers rolled up in newspaper. "You're Mrs. Slade. I'm Siri. A good friend of Millie's at school. Here, these are for you."

Deirdre took the flowers, then her hand, and shook it.

"Thank you, these are lovely. Iris. Truly one of my favorite flowers. Sorry, I didn't catch your last name?"

"It's Adjelis. Siri Adjelis. Millie couldn't make it. She

was so sick at her stomach and she was so upset, and, like, you know, worried about canceling at the last minute and everything. So, I was like, hey, why not, I could use the money. I hope it's okay."

"She normally calls if there's a problem," Deirdre said, now looking at Amos. "Is Millie all right, Amos?"

"Oh, she tried," Siri said, interrupting. "Sorry, Mrs. Slade, but your line was tied up and then it was time for me and Mr. McCullough to get in the boat and head over here to the island or we'd be late."

"Very kind of you to help out, Siri," Deirdre said. "Funny. I've never heard Millie mention your name. Have you lived in Dark Harbor long?"

"No, not really, Mrs. Slade. My family just moved up here from New York six months ago. But Millie and I have homeroom together and we just, like, you know, bonded or whatever. We were like instant soul mates. You know?"

Deirdre was looking at Amos, who held his dripping sou'wester in his hands, turning it round and round by the brim, looking cold and soggy in his old blue flannel shirt and yellow foul-weather overalls.

"Amos, you look chilled to the bone. Come out in the kitchen and let me pour you an inside-outer. An old-fashioned stomach-warmer. Siri, the children are upstairs in the playroom. They've already had dinner and bathed. They're allowed story time for exactly one hour. Not a minute longer. I'm halfway through *Black Beauty* and they love it. It's on top of the dresser. Can I bring you up something, Siri? Water? Diet Coke?"

"No, I'm fine, Mrs. Slade. I'll just go up and introduce myself to the kids. Larry and Carla, right?"

"Charles and Laura."

"Oh, right. Sorry. Brain fade. My bad, totally. Millie told me Charlie and Laura. Is five dollars an hour too much?"

"I pay Millie four."

"Four's fine. I just didn't know."

"All right. You go on up and say hello. I'll come up and say good-bye to the kids before I leave."

"Amos," Deirdre said in the kitchen, pouring the old man a tumbler full of Dewar's. "How well do you know this girl?"

She poured a short one for herself even though she'd already had two glasses of chardonnay. The edginess in Evan's voice on the phone had somehow been creeping around the corners of her mind ever since they'd hung up.

"Know her pretty well."

"How?"

"How what, dear?"

"How? How do you know her?"

"Oh, you know. Over to the house all the time. Up in Millie's room. Listenin' to that damn M&M music."

"Have you met her parents?"

"Yup."

"Nice people?"

"Reckon so."

"What does the father do?"

"Some kind of mechanic, I think."

"Oh. Where?"

"Works on airplanes. Over to the airport."

"And the mother?"

"Nurse over to General. Pediatrics."

"Jesus. I'll tell you something, this world is turning

us all a little bit paranoid, Amos. I'm sure she's perfectly nice if she's a friend of your lovely granddaughter's. Please tell Millie I understand and hope she's feeling better in the morning. Well, salut. Bottoms up, you
sweet old soul. I suppose I'd better shove off."

"Thick as chowdah out there tonight, Dee-Dee,"
Amos said, draining his whiskey. "Woman alone out in
that pea souper in that little toy Boston Whaler of
yours. No instruments, a' tall. Easy to lose your bearings in a fog bank that way. Yup. That's what happened
to that Kennedy boy a few summers ago, you may
remembah, over to the Vineyard. Got himself into a fog
bank. My opinion is that poor boy ran out of luck and
experience at about the same time."

"I've been making that crossing twice a day since I
was six years old, Amos, and you know it. Follow your
ears out to that old bell buoy and hang a right. Yacht
Club docks dead ahead. I could do it blindfolded."

She'd found Siri on the floor with the kids, reading
Black Beauty aloud. The light from Laura's spinning
carousel lamp was causing shadowy horses to gallop
around the room. "Mommy," Laura had said with a big
smile. "We like Siri! She's funny! She doesn't speak
Spanish but she speaks another funny language."

"I'm glad you like her, darling. That means you'll
listen to her when she says it's night-night time, right?"
She kissed them both good-bye and said to Siri, "I'll be
home by midnight. You know the rules, I'm sure. No
smoking, no drinking, no boys. Okay?"

"Yes, Mrs. Slade," Siri said smiling. "I know the
rules. Would it be all right if I watch TV after they're
asleep?"

"We don't own a TV, Siri. Sorry. You will find plenty of good books in the library downstairs."

She'd found Amos still on the dock. He insisted she follow his boat over to the club. On his way home, anyway.

"Thanks, Amos," she said, climbing down into the Whaler. "And tell Millie I hope she feels better soon."

"Yup. Ain't like her to come down with a bug. Girl has a cast-iron stomach. Always has. Never sick a day in her life that I can recall."

"I should be home by midnight if you want to pick up the babysitter then, Amos."

"Sure thing. See you then, dear girl."

She followed the halo of the hazy white running light on Amos's stern through the fog, around old Number Nine, clanging mournfully, and fifteen minutes later tied up at the club dock. Eight on the button. She shrugged off her foul-weather gear, shook the beaded moisture off the old yellow jacket, and threw it down across the boat's thwart seat. Her hair was damp and matted, but what the hell. Wasn't like this was some big embassy do where she had to—

"Deirdre, darling," a bourbon-soaked male voice said, emerging from the fog. "Popped out for a quick puff and saw your yacht steaming in."

"Oh, hello, Graham. Fancy meeting you here."

"Well, Michelle's just popped down to New York with the kids for some birthday shopping or something and I'm afraid they've stuck you next to me. Table nine. The two bachelors, as it were."

"No, Graham, you're the bachelor wannabe. I'm the happily married woman. Could you possibly find someone and order me a whiskey?"

"Certainly, my dear. Bit nippy out for early June, this."

She had to smile. She loved Americans who'd lived in London for a few years and came home with the most agonizingly affected British accents. Next thing she knew, he'd be inviting her to "nip round to his flat for a capper." He pulled the club's front door open for her and she waded in, waiting for it, yes, here it came, "After you, luv."

Graham was one of the club's self-proclaimed Wharf Rats. Never took their boats out, would never dare venture out off the perilous rocky coast of Maine. No, they just sat there in their stern chairs and drank, their fancy radars spinning merrily away on the sunniest afternoons. He was insufferable, unctuous was the word, but easy on the eyes in his black tie, and she allowed herself to just float on the buzz of conversation, the bad hors d'oeuvres, the mindless chitchat about children and summer plans.

She'd heard it all a thousand times, the major themes, the minor variations, and, smiling and nodding at appropriate moments, she could get through one of these cocktail buffets in her sleep.

When they were finally seated, Graham was on her right. He kept refilling her wineglass, trying to get her tipsy, and after a while she tired of putting her hand over the top to stop him. The wine was a way to float over the thing, look down upon the actors on the stage, paying just enough attention to be ready for the cue for her next line.

Faye Gilchrist, two seats away on her left, was saying something about children being sent home from school that day. High fevers. Something about tainted flu shots.

"Faye, excuse me for interrupting," Deirdre said. "What did you say about the children being sent home?"

"Well, Dee-Dee, it's just the most horrendous thing, darling. Apparently they've all come down with horrific fevers and stomach cramps. One child went into convulsions and is apparently in critical condition."

"Lord. What happened?" Deirdre asked. "Something bad in the cafeteria food at lunch?"

"Oh, no, my dear. It was in the morning. A nurse in the gym giving flu shots. When the children started getting violently ill, someone called the hospital. Apparently, well, from what I hear, this nurse wasn't even on their records and—well, she's been suspended pending investigation. Isn't it awful? To think that our children—"

"Excuse me," Deirdre said, knocking over a big goblet of red wine as she got to her feet. "Sorry, I'm not feeling well and I must rush off . . . sorry. You must excuse me . . ."

She somehow managed to navigate the crowded dining room and took the shortest route through the club towards the docks, through the kitchen, everyone back there smiling at her and saying good evening, Mrs. Slade. She reached the payphone in the pantry, pulled the door closed and opened her evening bag. No cell phones allowed in the club but she managed to find two quarters at the bottom of the bag and slammed them into the machine.

"Hello, Slade residence."

"Siri, it's Mrs. Slade."

"Oh, hi! What's up?"

"Nothing. I just . . . just wanted to check on . . . to check . . ."

"Mrs. Slade?"

"Check on the children. Are they all right?"

"Oh, yes. Sleeping like two little angels."

"Angels," Deirdre said and was about to hang up.

"Will your husband be coming back with you, Mrs. Slade?"

"My husband? Why do you—"

She burst out the swinging double doors and took a deep breath, willing her heart to slow. It had grown colder, and the swirling fog wrapping itself around her snapped her out of the daze of wine and words, clicking everything back into sharp focus.

Line was tied up. Cast-iron stomach. Never sick a day in her life. Nurse, pediatrics. Nurse suspended pending investigation.

She'd been staring numbly at Faye Gilchrist, her salad fork poised in mid-air, when Siri's breezy lie turned her insides to ice.

No, Siri, the line was most definitely *not* tied up.

There were two lines running under the bay and into the house. The old one they'd had since she was a child. And then a later one Evan had had installed. If the second line rang, it was one of a small number of people they'd given the number to. It was the only line Evan used when he called from Madrid or Washington because he knew she'd pick up. That was the line they'd been on tonight. The only call she'd taken on the old one was when her sister had called from San Obispo around three that afternoon.

Line was tied up. Sorry, Mrs. Slade.

She leapt down into the Whaler and yanked the starter rope. It came to life, thank God, on the first pull. Graham was swaying on the dock above her, sloshing

drink in hand, saying something ridiculous about a
nightcap in his fluty Queen's Guards accent, and she
threw the lines off and twisted the throttle wide open,
up on plane before she was twenty yards from the
dock.

Will your husband be coming back with you, Mrs. Slade?

Fog was even worse but she kept the gas wide open,
straining her ears for the tolling of Number Nine. Her
heart was pounding again and she felt rivulets of moisture running down between her breasts, the fog wrapped
like a cold wet cloak round her shoulders. The blood was
pounding so loudly in her ears now she almost missed it.
There. A muffled clang. Then, another. She waited until
she judged herself to be just abeam of the buoy and then
shoved the tiller hard to starboard. She was trying to
shave it close, maybe gain a few seconds.

She'd shaved it too close. The bow of the little boat
shuddered as it struck and then glanced off the big
buoy. She was thrown forward, into the bottom of the
boat, and the motor sputtered and died. Her shoulder
was screaming with pain, but she climbed back up onto
the wooden bench seat and yanked the cord. Shit. She
tried twice more and the third time it caught. She was
still cursing herself for misjudging the buoy's location
when the hazy yellow lights of the big house up on the
rocks loomed before her.

She ran up the curving rock steps leading to the
house. All the lights were on downstairs and nothing
looked amiss, thank God. Still, she took off her heels
when she got to the wide steps of the verandah. The
front door would be unlocked. You didn't have to lock
doors when you lived on an island. That's why you
lived on an island.

She pushed open the front door and stepped into the foyer. All the lights off upstairs. There was a fire in the library fireplace. She could hear it crackling, the flickering yellow light visible beneath the doors. One of the double mahogany doors was slightly ajar. She crossed quickly and pulled it open.

Siri was on the floor. She was sitting cross-legged on a pillow, staring into the roaring fire, the flames silhouetting her long dark hair and shoulders. Siri didn't turn around at the sound of the door being opened.

"Siri?"

No answer.

"Siri!" She screamed it this time, loud enough to wake the dead.

"My name isn't Siri," the girl said in a flat monotone. She still didn't turn around. "It's Iris, like the flowers I brought you. Siri is just Iris spelled backwards."

"Look at me, goddamn you, whoever you are!" Deirdre felt for the switch on the wall that turned on the big crystal chandelier, but her hand was shaking so badly she couldn't find it. "I said look at me!"

Siri, Iris, whatever, turned around, a white smile in the middle of her dark face. Her face, the whole front of her body looked odd. It was all black and—Deirdre's fingers finally found the switch and flipped the lights on. Suddenly, the black on the girl's face wasn't black anymore; that was just a trick of the firelight making it look black: no, it was bright red. It was red on her arms and hands, too. Red was—

"Oh, my God, what have you done?"

She was staggering backwards against the door. Iris got to her feet, hands behind her back now, and started coming towards her. One hand was coming up and Deirdre didn't wait to see the knife she instinctively knew was in it. But it wasn't a knife. No, it was a . . . what . . . video camera! A blinking red eye! Filming her and—

"Get away from me! Leave me alone! I've got to go up and see my babies!" Deirdre turned in the doorway, stumbling through it.

"I wouldn't go up there, Mrs. Slade. Definitely not a good idea," she heard Iris say behind her.

Deirdre's mind broke apart then. She ran for the stairs.

"Oh, my God! Oh, no! What have you done to—"

She never made it to the top of the stairs. The last thing she heard before she died was someone saying, ". . . like two little angels, I *told* you, Mrs. Slade."

Chief Ellen Ainslie of the Dark Harbor Police Department and her young deputy Nikos Savalas found Mrs. Slade next morning, sprawled halfway up the main staircase, dead of multiple stab wounds. A bunch of long-stemmed blue flowers had been strewn over the corpse. Chief Ainslie bent down and looked closely at the victim's face and the blood-caked handle of a large kitchen knife protruding from under her right shoulder.

"It's Dee-Dee Slade, all right."

"She's got two little ones, doesn't she?" Deputy Savalas said, bending down to get a closer look.

"She did have, anyway, yep," the chief said. "Let's go take a look."

"Her husband's somebody pretty important down in Washington, right?" Savalas asked. "A big-shot senator or something?"

"Ambassador to Spain," the chief said, looking at the baby-faced young deputy with the full black moustache. He'd only been with the force three months and he'd certainly never seen anything remotely as horrific as what he was about to encounter. "Let's go," she said, stepping carefully over Mrs. Slade's body and climbing the stairs up to the second floor, even though it was the very last thing on earth she wanted to do.

CHAPTER NINE

Nantucket Island

One week. That's all Hawke wanted. A week at sea would be best. The tang of salt air and the unceasing roll of the sea had never failed to rejuvenate him. Even as a boy, and now as a man, Alex Hawke was keenly attuned to both his mind and body. It went with the territory. As anyone accustomed to the fine art of living dangerously could tell you: ignore a strong signal from body or mind at your peril. Your next stop could be a backstreet morgue with a tag on your big toe.

Right now, the signals Alex Hawke was receiving were coming in loud and clear.

Listen up, old boy. You're running on empty. Your physical, mental, and emotional systems are seriously depleted, and you damn well better see to yourself before you wander once more into the fray or rejoin any battles. Stow away your old cloak and dagger and get yourself in fighting shape; or the next fight may very well not go your way.

Vicky's tragic death had left him both unnerved and unbalanced. Devastated. He had finally allowed himself to fall in love and had loved her truly and deeply. Her loss was a constant, keening pain; it was as if he'd been split right down the chines.

Give me a week, he'd told Stokely and Ambrose. Same thing as he'd told Conch's head of security, Jack Patterson at DSS. His first thought was to get away somewhere on his boat, *Blackhawke*, all by himself. He'd fleetingly considered Conch's offer of the little fishing cabin in the Keys and rejected it. Didn't want to be beholden. So. A strict regimen of strenuous physical exercise, diet, meditation, and rest ought to do it. But, that very night, when Ambrose Congreve had called with an update from London, the two of them had hatched a much better scheme.

The idea was for Alex to get out of Washington. First he would fly up to Boston's Logan. There, he would meet Ambrose, Stokely, and Sutherland in the first-class lounge when their BA flight from Heathrow landed. The four of them would then make the short hop over to the island of Nantucket. Alex had decided to position *Blackhawke* there for her summer mooring.

Originally, it had been part of his honeymoon plans.

But now the three men could use her as a base of operations, cruising up along the northeast coastline, dipping in and out of interesting ports. Alex could spend the days working out the kinks in the yacht's fitness room, swimming in the ocean, running on the beach (running on soft sand always got him in shape faster than anything else) and reducing his current alcohol intake by at least half. If he could cut it entirely, fine, but Alex believed a couple of glasses of red wine didn't hurt. Helped him sleep, actually, until the nightmares kicked in.

In the evening, they could all gather in the ship's library and sort through the facts of Vicky's case. They could continue the conversation over an early supper and still have Alex in bed by nine each night.

That was the plan anyway.

"We're beginning our final descent into Logan, sir," his captain, Charley Flynn, said over the intercom. "I'll have you on the ground in ten minutes."

"All buckled in, young Pelham?" Alex asked the aged fellow seated just across the aisle. Pelham Grenville, upon learning of Alex's impending voyage, had insisted on tagging along. He said he'd been caring for Alex since the boy had been in diapers and he wasn't about to stop now. What the old family retainer didn't say was that he felt Alex needed looking after more than ever. Vicky's murder had taken a terrible toll.

An hour later, they were all on Nantucket Island, aboard *Blackhawke*. Because of the yacht's enormous size, she was anchored outside the entrance to Nantucket Harbor. The harbor could not safely accommodate her gleaming black, two hundred forty foot–long hull. Unwittingly, Hawke had provided the island with a new tourist attraction. Every few hours, the Steamship Authority's large ferries would arrive from Hyannis and Wood's Hole, loaded to the gunwales with day-trippers. Everyone crowded the upper deck, staring in wonder at the huge yacht now anchored just opposite the harbor mouth.

She was bigger than most ferries.

Having stowed their gear in their respective staterooms, showered and changed, the four friends had all reconvened in the ship's paneled library. By the time they assembled, Congreve had already turned *Blackhawke*'s beautiful library into a veritable War Room.

Ambrose had erected four large wooden easels, two on either side of the fireplace. Each easel held a large pad of blank white paper. Three were blank anyway. Ambrose was now standing before the fourth creating a handwritten list of every one of Hawke's known enemies with a fat black Magic Marker. It was a long list, Alex saw, dismayed but not surprised, as Congreve kept adding names. At this rate he was going to fill up all four pads.

"I say, Constable," Alex said, "your little list there is certainly warming the cockles of my heart. When you've completed this impressive catalogue of 'Fiends and Villains Who Want Hawke Dead,' perhaps we could do one consisting of 'Friends & Acquaintances Who Find Him Rather Chummy.' Just for fun, right, Sniper?"

"Damnifiknow! Hellificare!" the parrot Sniper squawked, somewhat in agreement.

Hawke had cared for the large Black Hyacinth macaw now perched on his shoulder since childhood. Brazilian macaws can live to the ripe old age of 110 years, but Sniper was a vibrant 75. Her plumage, despite her "black" appellation, was still a glossy ultramarine blue. An old Hawke family tradition, allegedly begun by his notorious ancestor, the pirate Blackhawke himself, was to use trained parrots as protection. Any unseen threat, and Sniper would instantly squawk out a warning. She also had a salty vocabulary, courtesy of Hawke's grandfather.

"Friends? Delighted to," Congreve said, scribbling away furiously, his back still turned towards them. *"That* certainly shouldn't take long," he added, earning a chuckle from Stokely and Sutherland.

Alex smiled. It was amazing how many enemies

one could acquire during one brief decade in the service of two rather obvious notions like freedom and democracy.

There were individuals, corporations, and even a section of entire nations on Congreve's burgeoning Enemies Register. Some, Alex found hardly surprising. Algeria, Tunisia, Libya, Somalia, Syria, Yemen, and Kashmir. Okay. But, Canada? Liechtenstein? Sweden? He'd have to ask Congreve about that lot later. At any rate, the idea was to vet out every name on the list and eliminate as many as possible. Those who remained would comprise a new list.

Suspects.

"Very comprehensive list, Constable," Hawke said. "My compliments to the author."

"Thank you, but that would be you, dear boy."

"May I add one?" asked Hawke.

"Certainly."

"Cuba."

"Hmm. Cuba."

"Yes. I left a lot of ruffled feathers down there on my most recent visit. A bloodless *coup d'état* that turned a bit bloody."

"Anybody who was anybody in that rebel army was dead by the time we left," Stokely said. "Still, we might have missed a couple."

"Indeed, Alex," Congreve said, adding the name *Cuba*. "Stupid of me not to think of it."

"Not at all," Hawke said. "Stoke's right. We killed most of the terrorist bastards when we took out that bloody rat's nest at *Telaraña*. Still, a precious few could have escaped. Chaps hoping I've celebrated my last birthday."

"Motive?" Congreve said, asking his favorite question.

"We can safely rule out love or lucre," Hawke said. "That leaves loathing and, of course, lust."

"Yeah. Maybe somebody down there had himself a little crush on Vicky?" Stoke asked, and a silence fell over the room. "You know, when the rebels held her captive?"

"A crime of passion?" Sutherland asked. "A spurned lover?"

"Well," Ambrose said after a few more long moments, "I can see by the expressions on your faces you've all had enough excitement for one evening, gentlemen." He capped the marker. "We shall attack the thing with vigor on the morrow."

"Yes, Constable," Hawke said, rising from his leather armchair. "This little exercise has been most uplifting. At any moment I may burst into song. Do you never tire of all this bloody spadework, Ambrose, beavering away morning, noon, and night?"

"On the contrary," Congreve said. "You remember, to be sure, what Holmes said to Watson in the very first chapter of *The Sign of Four?*"

"Sorry," Hawke replied, "seems to have slipped my mind at the moment. Mind you, keen, alert, and up on my toes as I am, I've not yet got round to memorizing the complete works of Conan Doyle."

He was rewarded with a wan smile from Congreve.

"'The pleasure of finding a field for my peculiar powers is my highest reward,'" Congreve said, relighting his pipe for the umpteenth time, a rather self-satisfied little smile on his lips.

"Ah," Alex said smiling. "My highest reward at this moment would be a medium rare center-cut filet mignon and a single glass of good Napa Valley claret."

"Excellent idea," Ambrose said, expelling a puff of blue-grey smoke. "I do hope no one minds. Since we'll be steaming out of this lovely harbor soon, I've booked reservations ashore at a delightful restaurant I discovered during my wanderings about town. Dinner will be at seven sharp. Shall we all tidy up a bit and meet up on deck at the stern? Fantail Lounge at six? Quick cocktail and then a ten- or fifteen-minute stroll to the restaurant. Jackets and ties would be appropriate, I should think."

Alex had to smile. He loved it when Ambrose took charge of things. He so delighted in doing it and it was amusing to watch the world-famous detective in the role of the mother hen, shepherding the little brood about, clucking about this and that.

Hawke found Nantucket town itself to be completely charming. Sitting under the stars on *Blackhawke*'s uppermost deck during the drinks hour, he had been delighted with the harbor and the picturesque town beyond, especially the many white church spires rising into the deepening indigo of the evening sky.

He imagined all those late eighteenth-century churches filled to bursting every Sunday morning; women and children praying for the great whale fleets to return safely, bearing husbands, fathers, sons, and brothers back from perilous voyages to the South Pacific. Voyages sometimes lasted four or even five years.

Lovely eighteenth- and nineteenth-century architecture lined every street and Alex was pleased to see that, somehow, the island fathers had managed to keep the horrors of modern architecture completely at bay. Real candles were burning in the windows of many houses and you could sense lush rose gardens blooming behind the picket fences and sharply tailored hedgerows. Some streets in the town were gaslit and paved with heavy cobblestones. Stones, Congreve told him, that had once been the ballast in the holds of the first ships bringing settlers across the Atlantic.

"I rather like this island, Ambrose," Hawke remarked, turning up the collar of his yellow slicker as they headed towards the center of town. "Although I seem to like all islands. Something to do with being born on one, I suppose."

A fine spring rain was falling. The brick-paved street glistened with soft yellow light from many windows; hazily lit doorways peeked out here and there from behind thick bowers of white roses. Alex and Ambrose had fallen behind their companions, having lingered to admire en route the forthright simplicity of a particular house or a garden trellis.

"Yes," Congreve said, inhaling the sweet damp air, "it's quite lovely in a haunting way, isn't it? Too much money here now, I'm afraid, but not enough to drive the ghosts away."

"Meaning?"

"Meaning the past is stronger than the present. Here on this island, at least. You see that rather imposing building over there? The Greek Revival temple?"

"I was just admiring it. The public library, isn't it?"

"Indeed. The Athenaeum. I paid them a visit this afternoon. Fascinating. Full of beautiful whaling ship models and scrimshaw and such."

"No books?"

"Of course, books. Melville, you may remember, was a whaler himself. He visited Nantucket with his father-in-law, an itinerant minister. Whilst here, he met with Captain George Pollard of the *Essex*. The tale of the great white whale is based on the true story of the whaler *Essex*. Rammed by a massive leviathan and went down with all hands save a few. Survivors resorted to cannibalism after a month or so drifting on the open seas; drove them all quite mad."

Congreve expelled a billowing trail of smoke and caught his friend's glance, saw his sad eyes return for an instant to the pleats of previous smiles. But Alex looked away, saying nothing. The two had paused on the steps of a lovely church to admire one of the grander captain's houses across the way.

"Listen," Hawke said, peering into the darkened doorway. Inside the candle-lit chapel, a choir was practicing a lovely song of prayer for ancient mariners—

> *Eternal Father, strong to save,*
> *Whose arm does bind the restless wave,*
> *Who bidst the mighty ocean deep,*
> *Its own appointed limits keep,*
>
> *O, hear us when we cry to thee,*
> *For those in peril on the Sea . . .*

"Ghosts," Hawke said, gazing up at the widow's walk atop the captain's house, the words of the choir floating out into the drizzly churchyard. "You're quite right about this place, old thing. Ghosts and angels behind every door."

They turned into Federal Street and arrived at a restaurant that took its name from its address, 21 Federal. It was on the ground floor of an elegant white clapboard building built in the late eighteenth century.

Sutherland and Stokely were waiting just inside, chatting with the amiable host, who introduced himself as Chick Walsh. Once the four men were all seated round a deep red leather banquette just off the bar, Alex looked around approvingly. Dark paneling, brass fixtures, lovely period marine art on the walls. Ambrose had chosen well.

The waiter brought two cocktails, a Diet Coke for Stokely, and a glass of red wine for Alex.

"To the bride," Hawke said quietly, raising his glass and, one by one, looking each one of them in the eye.

"To the bride," they all answered in unison.

There followed a period of silence, not at all uncomfortable. Reflective rather, each man alone with his thoughts and memories of Victoria Sweet.

Ambrose was the first one to break the silence.

"I wonder, Alex," he said, "if you'd be so kind as to fill us all in on this apparently very nasty matter at the U.S. State Department."

"Ah, yes," Alex said, relief on his face. "Conch's crisis du jour. Ratcheted up from 'apparently very nasty' to simply 'very nasty,' I'm afraid. State's DSS fellows have concluded that the death in Venice was an assassination."

"DSS?" Stokely asked. "New one on me. I thought I knew all those spooks."

"Don't get a lot of publicity, Stoke. State Department's Diplomatic Security Service. Responsible for protecting American diplomats and their families at embassies and consulates around the world."

"Rather tall order lately, I'd say," said Sutherland.

The waiter arrived with their food, and all conversation ceased until he left the table.

Congreve asked, "Counterespionage, are they, these DSS boys?"

"Some are," Alex said, "but their primary mission is to act as America's cops overseas. Brilliant track record. It was DSS who finally nabbed Ramzi Yousef, lovely chap responsible for the first Trade Towers bombing back in 1993. Friend of mine, a fellow named Tex Patterson, heads up some 1,200 agents. Tex calls them the best-kept secret in American law enforcement, and he'd like to keep it that way. He lets Langley or the Bureau take all the bows."

"This poor chap in Venice," Ambrose mused. "Their new ambassador. Never did hear a satisfactory explanation of that one."

"Most people never will," Alex said, "Ambassador Simon Stanfield was tracked and killed by a miniature smart bomb."

"Good Lord. You can't be serious," Congreve scoffed.

"Sounds preposterous, I agree. But that's what happened. DSS discovered a tiny encrypted dot, a microchip transmitter planted in Stanfield's billfold. Still broadcasting the GPS coordinates of the dead man's precise location to a satellite."

"A *personal* smart bomb?" Stokely asked. "Man, what the hell is that all about?"

"Divers found fragments of it in the muck at the bottom of the canal. Reconstructing them, it appears to have been a small titanium missile, perhaps twelve inches long. A tiny warhead at the nose, packed with just enough plastic explosive to blow a man to pieces upon impact."

"Astounding," Congreve said, after taking a forkful of

his duck. "And what about this second chap in Riyadh? McGuire."

"Even more bizarre," Hawke continued. "Butch McGuire, U.S. ambassador to Saudi Arabia, keeled over at a table in his favorite restaurant in Riyadh, whilst having dinner with his wife. Looked like natural causes, Patterson said, except the man was in perfect health."

Congreve sat back against the cushions, his interior wheels spinning soundlessly but obviously. He turned his deceptively innocent blue eyes towards Hawke.

"Another splash of wine, Alex? I see they have a good La Tour on the wine list. Excellent vintage."

"Thanks, no," he said, proud of his new regimen, and then he told them all about the strange demise of Butch McGuire.

"So that's it," he concluded a few moments later. "Patterson said that when they opened Butch up on the autopsy table, the entire thoracic and gastrointestinal organs were basically fried."

"Fried?" Stoke asked, taking a big bite of his steak. "What you mean *fried?*"

"Cooked," Hawke said. "Well done. Charred."

"Good Lord," Congreve said. "How on earth did—"

"He swallowed something," Hawke said. "Small enough to go down with food unnoticed. Then, inside the stomach, a microburst of electricity. Either self-detonating or triggered from a remote location."

"Ratchet up the terror level at every American embassy," Ross said, shaking his head. "That's the plan."

"This is bad, Alex," Ambrose said. "Two in two weeks? It's just the beginning."

Alex nodded. "I agree. Question, Constable. Do

you think Vicky was actually first? Or, rather, a botched attempt on me? I have very close ties to the U.S. State Department's counterterrorist operations. If this is some kind of plot to paralyze America's worldwide diplomatic mission, I wouldn't be a bad place to start."

"Not beyond the range of possibilities, Alex. But a separate, personal, and unrelated attack on you is also quite possible, given the chart we just created."

"A target under either scenario, then," Hawke said. "Off the top of your head, Constable. These diplomatic assassinations. Initial reaction? Thoughts?"

"Virulent psychopath with a deep-seated hatred for America. Her ambassadors at any rate. Sadist. Unlimited scientific and economic resources. Enjoys eccentric means to kill."

"Could be just some nutcase genius with a grudge," Stoke said. "Like that crazy Harvard fruitcake."

"Which one?" Congreve asked.

"Unabomber. Kept sending ever more powerful mail bombs to people on his environmental shitlist. Too bad he didn't get a 'return-to-sender' package and forget he had—"

"Mr. Alexander Hawke?" a waiter said.

"I'm Alex Hawke."

"Sorry to disturb you, Mr. Hawke. A gentleman on the phone who'd like to speak with you, sir. Extremely urgent."

"Certainly. What's this gentleman's name?"

"A Mr. Jack Patterson from the State Department, sir."

CHAPTER TEN

London

Snay bin Wazir and his new bride arrived in London in the spring of 1986, bin Wazir's febrile mind brimming with schemes and his coffers bulging with blood money. Elephant blood money to be blunt about it, although that chapter in his life had already been purged from the public record. Throughout the eighties and early nineties Snay bin Wazir would embark on a public relations campaign and a spending spree that eventually had all of London town in an uproar.

At first, putting his toe in the water, he acquired a palatial penthouse flat on Park Lane, with panoramic views of Hyde Park. He hired a staff of three, two maids and a Filipino cook, for his wife, Yasmin. Then he installed Tippu Tip, the former African chieftain, as the highest-paid bodyguard cum driver in London. Tippu in turn hired a houseboy named Kim who was soon lighting the Sultan's trademark Baghdaddy cigarettes with a heavy gold Dunhill. That was Snay's idea of a slow build. There was nowhere to go from there but up.

A Kuwaiti friend recommended a tailor in New Bond Street. Snay had six identical suits made, all black terry cloth. He noticed that people smiled their approval wherever he went. "Where on earth did you get that suit?" people would often ask, and Snay, now a fashion trendsetter of sorts, was happy to direct them to his newly acquired tailor.

After a month or more of prowling the fashionable and not-so-fashionable West End clubs and casinos, he bought Harpo. This trendy, upscale nightspot in Knightsbridge had a huge dance floor on the ground floor and a plush VIP casino upstairs. For a while, Snay himself was on the door every night, ingratiating himself with London's younger upper crust and ogling the Pretty Young Things who shimmered nightly through his increasingly famous portals.

He strode into Jack Barclay's Rolls-Royce emporium on Berkley Square one fine morning and bought his first Roller. A gleaming aluminum-bodied 1926 Silver Ghost with a red leather interior. The vanity plate acquired at a princely sum read *Ivoire*. He outfitted Tippu Tip in pearl grey livery with ivory buttons. Tippu was easily the best dressed, most heavily armed private chauffeur in London.

In one of Snay bin Wazir's more inspired moments, he turned the door at Harpo over to Tippu. The six-foot-six chief outfitted himself in a variety of colorful matching silk turbans and loincloths every night, his massive black chest complemented by a splendid ivory skull necklace of his own design. "Ebony and ivory, Boss," he'd said laughing, "living in perfect harmony."

Almost overnight Snay bin Wazir's rugged, mustachioed face was everywhere; between the covers of magazines and tabloids which covered such things, and smiling at you on a monthly, weekly, and, ultimately, daily basis. He had become, after a fashion, a minor celebrity, and had even earned himself a glamorous nickname, the Pasha of Knightsbridge. He knew he was destined for far greater glory, but, for the present, he was satisfied.

Then there was the night in the late eighties when the world-famous arms dealer Attar al-Nassar himself appeared at his door, a bevy of beauties on each arm. Bin Wazir knew from the moment he first laid eyes on al-Nassar that, somehow, his life was forever changed. He ducked into the cloakroom and rang up his friend, Stilton, a rabid society newshound at the *Sun*. "Al-Nassar's here," he told Stilton. "I'll keep him here as long as I can but you'd better hop to it." Stilton hopped right to it. The Pasha and the reporter had developed a very successful and symbiotic relationship.

Bin Wazir provided the diminutive and somewhat unfortunate-looking *Sun* journalist and his sidekick photographer with women. *The Sun,* which on a good day sells around four million copies, in turn conferred celebrity status of a certain kind upon the arriviste Snay bin Wazir.

That night, bin Wazir showered the world-famous arms dealer with attention, ushering him to the best table on the dance floor and sending over endless bottles of Cristal, compliments of the house. Stilton arrived ten minutes later, his taxi screeching to a halt outside Harpo's crowded entrance. The giant Tippu parted the throngs and personally escorted him inside. The shots of al-Nassar and his bevy on the Harpo dance floor were splashed all over the newsstands next morning.

The end of that splendid evening found Snay and Attar on a first-name basis, huddled in a corner banquette smoking cigars and talking politics, women, religion, and, ultimately, business.

"I take it you're not a religious man, Snay," al-Nassar said mildly.

"On the contrary," Snay smiled. "I am a fanatic. My gods just happen to reside in a vault in Zurich."

Al-Nassar laughed. "Then why do you trifle in nightclubs, my friend?"

"Have you looked carefully at the dance floor tonight, Attar?"

"Ha. Accessories! Baubles and bangles! I will tell you a confidence, Snay. Because I find I like you, and I don't like many people. Today, I sold more than two dozen forty-million-dollar fighter jets to the Peruvian government. Eastern European jets. Highly unreliable design."

"Unreliable fighter jets?"

"Hmm. Every piece that falls off is wildly expensive. The real money will be in keeping them flying."

Snay, smiling, raised his flute of champagne and leaned back against the cushions. It had taken him many long years, but he realized he had finally found a role model.

"Beautiful suit," he told al-Nassar, eyeing the man's exquisitely cut three-piece navy chalkstripe. "May I ask, who is your tailor?"

"Chap at Huntsman, Savile Row," Attar replied. "Fellow named Ronnie Bacon. I'll ring him tomorrow if you'd like."

Snay nodded and said, "I was wondering, Attar . . . I'm sitting on some money."

"Yes?"

"Not a lot. Fifty million or so. English pounds," Snay

said, holding a match to the tip of his monogrammed yellow cigarette.

"Yes?"

"I don't suppose you ever look for investors? At that level, I mean?"

"I don't, to be honest, Mr. bin Wazir," al-Nassar said.

"Sorry. Sorry if my question offended you, Mr. al-Nassar."

"A wise man never regrets the questions he asks. Only the ones he didn't ask."

"This is good advice."

Al-Nassar tapped his temple with his index finger and said, "My gods reside up here, Snay bin Wazir. Right now, my deities have all overindulged themselves. The lowly grape clouds their normally lofty judgment. It's late in the evening. Would you be so kind as to give me a day or so to consider your question?"

"Certainly."

"You're basic raw material, Snay. Good, rough, hard stone. Don't mind getting your hands dirty either, from what I've heard. I like that. A bit of polishing strictly for appearances and I might just be able to use a fellow like you."

"I should be honored, Mr. al-Nassar."

"Good. We'll get you started. Forget ivory. Too visible. Too—messy. I've got one word for you, Snay. Flowers."

"Flowers?"

"Flowers."

"Mr. al-Nassar. Perhaps I don't follow you quite exactly. Could you be, please, more specific?"

"Gladiolas."

"Ah. Of course. Gladiolas."

"Precisely. Just the beginning. You buy day-old glads in South Africa for two dollars a stem and you sell them to rich Russian tourists in Dubai the next day for one hundred dollars a stem. You can carry twenty tons per flight. Better than printing money."

"That sounds good."

"One question, which I shall always regret if I do not ask it," al-Nassar said, fingering the black terry cloth of Snay's lapel.

"Anything, Attar."

"Where on earth did you get that suit?"

CHAPTER ELEVEN

Dark Harbor, Maine

The Packard-Merlin 266 engine sputtered at first, then roared to life. It was the very same engine, circa 1942, that had powered the much-vaunted Supermarine Spitfire Mark XVI, workhorse of the powerful fighter command squadrons that rose up and ultimately triumphed over the Luftwaffe in the skies over Britain. The highly modified Spitfire engine was mounted in the long nose of Hawke's sleek silver seaplane.

It was an aircraft clearly out of her time, and the truth was Alex had designed the plane himself. Completely lacking in any formal aeronautical design skills, he had simply modeled her after one of his favorite boyhood toys. His theory about both airplane and boat design was simple. If it looked good and it looked fast, it probably was both. In a cavernous hold at the stern of *Blackhawke* were many racing machines Alex had collected over the years. There was not one vintage racing car or speedboat that did not look both good and fast.

Especially this little seaplane. She was named *Kittyhawke* in honor of Alex's mother, an American film star before she'd married. One of his mother's more glamourous publicity poses was painted on the port side of the fuselage. Catherine Caldwell had taken the stage name Kitty Hawke when she'd married Alex's father, Lord Alexander Hawke. Kitty Hawke had been a hard-working actress, ultimately nominated for an Academy Award for her performance in the classic Civil War saga, *Southern Belle.* It was to be the last picture she would make.

In the late seventies, Lord and Lady Hawke were murdered in the Exuma Islands. Cuban drug runners boarded their yacht, *Seahawke,* in the middle of the night. There was one eyewitness. Their seven-year-old son, Alex. Hidden by his father in a secret compartment in the yacht's bow, the boy saw the horrific crime. Ultimately, on the island of Cuba, Alex Hawke the man would track down the killers and avenge his parents' deaths; but the boyhood memory of that horrifying night would haunt the man forever.

"All buckled in, Constable?" Hawke asked, putting on his headphones and adjusting his lipmike. He was delighted to be back aboard *Kittyhawke* and was wearing one of his old Royal Navy flying suits, an outfit he favored whenever he took the little plane aloft. The Packard-Merlin Spitfire engine, all fifteen hundred horses, spat fire as he shoved the throttle forward and nosed his plane into the wind.

"No aerial aerobatics on the voyage up, if you don't mind, Captain," Congreve barked in his headset. "I know how you delight in torturing captive passengers."

"Ah. Do I detect a wee touch of the Irish Flu this morning, Ambrose? I did think that third Drambuie at the bar last night was ill-advised. Especially after the vast quantities of Château La Tour. Frankly, I thought you'd sworn off *les vins de France*. Patriotic reasons, and all that."

"Please," Congreve replied, a thick frost coating the word. "Just because you have been the very model of abstemiousness for an entire twenty-four hours, I don't see why I should be subjected to—"

"Sorry, old thing. It is your liver, after all. Not mine."

"God save us," Ambrose sighed and collapsed back in his seat, struggling with the wretched harness which barely accommodated his circumference. He wouldn't admit it, to be sure, but he was actually battling a bit of a morning after. Alex eased the throttle forward, and the seaplane surged across the blue waters of Nantucket Sound and lifted off into the rosy New England dawn.

Over nightcaps in the bar at 21 Federal, Alex Hawke and Ambrose Congreve had decided to fly up to Dark Harbor, Maine, at first light.

"It's bad, Alex," Jack Patterson had said to him on the phone at the restaurant. "I'm on my way up to Dark Harbor right now. Evan Slade's wife and two kids were murdered last night. Butchered. We've got to stop this thing. Fast, before panic sets in. Otherwise, I'm looking at a complete paralysis of America's diplomatic corps. Meltdown, at the worst possible time."

"That's what they want," Alex said. "Panic."

"Yep. That's why we've got to stop it fast."

"I'll be there, Tex. First thing."

"Didn't have the heart to ask. Thanks, Hawkeye. Sorry to interrupt your supper. I know this is a difficult time for you and—"

"See you around eight? I'll fly the seaplane up. What's the mooring situation up there? Any idea?"

"House has a long dock into deep water. Check your charts, buddy. You'll see big old Wood Island just southwest of Dark Harbor. Pine Island lies just east of Wood. Slade family bought the whole rock back in the fifties. Only house on the island. Dock on the south end, according to the local chief of police, woman by the name of Ainslie."

"Cheated death once again, eh, Constable?" Hawke said as they taxied toward the Slade dock. Congreve ignored him.

"I see the local constabulary has turned out to welcome us," Congreve said. A young uniformed officer stood at the end of the dock, a coiled rope in his hand, looking uncertain about precisely what he was supposed to do with it.

"Patterson sent this fellow out to give us a hand, I imagine."

Alex shut down the engine, unbuckled his harness, then opened the cockpit door and climbed down onto the port side pontoon. He waited a few seconds for the chap to toss him the line. "Ahoy," he finally shouted to the young policeman, some twenty feet across the water. "Toss me that line please! She's drifting off! I can't get her in any closer because of the current."

It took Officer Nikos Savalas three tries to finally toss the line within Alex's reach.

"Third time's the charm," Alex shouted at the clearly embarrassed man as he bent and cleated the line off on the pontoon. Once *Kittyhawke* was secure, the two Englishmen climbed a winding staircase carved into the rocks. It led up to the rambling old grey-shingled house, a weathered and many-gabled structure, with a myriad of rooflines dotted with brick chimneys.

"Imagine that," Hawke said, looking back at the Maine cop, still bent over the cleat, tying and retying the line.

"What?"

"Boy grows up in Maine, yet he has no earthly idea how to toss someone a line."

"I noticed that," Congreve said.

"And?"

"He obviously did not grow up in Maine."

"Ah, logic will out," Hawke said, smiling.

They gained the top of the steps and made their way through a thicket of fragrant spruce to open lawn. Hawke saw his old friend Patterson sprawled on the steps of a wide covered verandah. He was smoking a cigarette cupped in his hand against the fresh breeze, talking to a young blonde woman wearing the same uniform as the young salt down on the dock. The badge pinned to her blue blouse told Alex this was Chief Ainslie of the Dark Harbor PD.

"How 'bout that, old Hawkeye himself," Patterson said, getting to his feet and grinning at the tall Englishman. "You're a sight for sore eyes, son."

Ten years earlier, Patterson had been flying a single-engine Cessna that had gone down deep in the Peruvian jungle. Shining Path guerillas had shot everyone who'd survived the crash except Patterson. Alex Hawke and Stokely Jones had finally found him, delirious and barely alive. The guerillas never knew what hit them. Hawke had somehow found a way into the impenetrable rainforest, rescued Patterson, and found a way out.

The grateful Texan had given Alex the nickname Hawkeye, not after the famous television series character as many would later assume, but after the great Indian scout of the same name, the man immortalized as the last of the Mohicans.

Tex Patterson was a big man, a shock of grey hair on his head, but with a youthful linebacker's build under a perfectly tailored navy blue suit. Crisp white shirt, and dark tie knotted at the throat. The standard DSS uniform, slightly modified by the big white Stetson on his head and the shiny black Tony Lama cowboy boots on his feet. And, the small enameled pin on his lapel.

Under his left arm, in a custom leather holster, hung the "Peacemaker," a long-barreled Colt .45 six-shooter, circa 1870. Never without his "shootin' iron," because, as Patterson was fond of reminding you, "God made man; Sam Colt made 'em equal."

"Hi, Tex," Hawke said.

"Howdy, Alex. Awful good to see you again," Patterson said, squeezing his hand. "Can't tell you how much I 'preciate you jumping in on this thing, partner. 'Course, I know Conch leaned on you a bit. She's good at that. This pretty lady right over here is Chief Ellen Ainslie. First officer on the scene. Done a helluva good job keeping a lid on this, so far."

Hawke smiled at the police chief. "Chief Ainslie, how do you do, I'm Alexander Hawke."

Alex shook hands with her and introduced both Patterson and Ainslie to Congreve. The attractive blonde chief of police shook Ambrose's hand, sizing him up, clearly surprised to find the legendary Scotland Yard man up in this remote corner of Maine. There had been any number of surprises in Dark Harbor recently. Alex could see dark blue Suburbans parked along the road, and the house was already crawling with DSS agents.

Patterson placed his hand on Hawke's shoulder.

"There are four big old rocking chairs at the other end of the verandah, overlooking the sound," Patterson said. "Why don't we just let my guys get on with business uninterrupted for a while, then we'll mosey inside. Chief Ainslie was kind enough to bring along a big thermos of hot coffee. Let's jes' go around to those rockers, and she'll fill you in on what we know so far?"

"Sounds good," Alex said.

Once they were settled, the local chief of police did most of the talking. Alex sat back in his rocker, listening to the chief, and admiring the pretty little cove filled with sturdy-looking lobster boats, and small gaff-rigged sloops, and catboats riding at their moorings. The fresh tang of pine and spruce and the iodine smack of salt air filled his nostrils. Most of the early morning fog had burned off, and it occurred to Alex that this beautiful spot was about as unlikely a setting for a grisly murder as one could ask for.

No place is safe anymore. That was his thought when the pretty police chief interrupted his unsettling reverie.

"Should I give them the long version or the short version?" Chief Ainslie asked, looking at Patterson.

"Short," he replied. "You'll find these two gentlemen very adept at asking pertinent questions." She nodded.

"Cause of all three deaths was exsanguination due to

multiple stab wounds. The babysitter did it," Ainslie said, in the most matter-of-fact way she could manage. "Fifteen years old, this kid. She used a butcher knife from the Slades' own kitchen. Killed the two children in their beds, then waited for Mrs. Slade to return from a dinner over to the Yacht Club. Got her on the stairs. Left it, the knife, right under Mrs. Slade's body, didn't even bother to wipe it down."

"Same number of stab wounds to each body?" Congreve asked.

"Yes," Ainslie replied, a look of surprise in her eyes. "How did you know . . . there were fourteen. Does that mean anything?"

"It might, Chief Ainslie. Or, it might not. But everything means something, as you know. Now, Mrs. Slade knew this particular babysitter, did she?" Congreve asked, lighting up his pipe. "Local girl?"

"No. Siri, that is her name, she was substituting for the usual babysitter, who is my niece. A junior at the high school here named Millie. Millicent McCullough."

Ambrose said, "Your niece, the sick girl? What does she have to say about all this?"

"I haven't been able to speak with her, unfortunately. Missing. Last seen in the high school gymnasium. She was injected with a tainted vaccine and was last seen heading for home, ill. High fever, nausea, vomiting. Two children have already died from that vaccine, Inspector Congreve. Many are in the hospital."

"Horrible. Your niece is missing?"

"We have every man we can spare looking for her."

"I see. Who administered this vaccine, Chief?" Alex asked.

"A woman who moved here about six months ago.

Enis Adjelis. She was posing as a nurse from our hospital, Mr. Hawke. The principal immediately called the hospital when the children became ill. Hospital had no record of her. We've learned she was the mother of the girl who murdered the Slade family."

"You have anyone in custody?" asked Ambrose. "Any apprehensions?"

"I wish. They all vanished. The whole Adjelis family. Siri, the babysitter, the mother, and the father, who was a flight mechanic over to the airport. I dispatched Deputy Savalas and two squad cars directly to their apartment after the bodies were discovered. Not a trace of them."

"Who found the bodies?"

"Millie's grandfather, my dad, Amos McCullough. Millie's parents were killed in an automobile accident and she lives with Amos. Most nights Millie babysat the Slade children. Dad would bring her out here to the island in his lobster boat. Then come pick her up at the designated time. He arrived a few minutes after midnight to pick up Millie's friend, Siri. Mrs. Slade's Boston whaler wasn't tied up at the dock like it normally would be. Which was strange since she was never late."

"She was early," Hawke said. "I would imagine."

Congreve nodded and said, "A nurse injecting school children with tainted flu shots would have certainly been a topic of conversation at the supper table. She's got her usual babysitter out of commission and someone completely unknown out there on the island watching her children . . ."

Chief Ainslie nodded and continued. "You're both right, gentlemen. I interviewed all the dinner partners. A Mrs. Gilchrist said she brought up the tainted injections and Deirdre just bolted. Made a pay-phone call, clearly distressed. Hung up, jumped in her Whaler and sped away. Anyway, my dad called me at home at five-thirty yesterday morning and—"

"So Siri used the Slades' Whaler to get off the island after killing Mrs. Slade," Congreve said. "That would have been around ten p.m. Long gone when your father's lobster boat arrived just after midnight."

"Yes. What did your father do between midnight and five-thirty?" Hawke asked.

"Slept. Dad is pushing ninety and not quite with it some of the time. He went down below on his boat to warm up while he waited for Dee-Dee, sorry, Mrs. Slade, to return from the club. Drank a cup of tea laced with rum and fell sound asleep on his bunk. When the sunlight came through the porthole he woke up."

"So they had a good six hours at least to clear out," Patterson said. "Damn. DSS bureau in New York ran down their last known address in New York. Greenpoint section of Brooklyn. Talked to all the neighbors, shopkeepers, et cetera. Totally clean. A model family. Immigrated from Athens four years ago."

"Citizens?" Hawke asked.

"Yep. Newly minted. Red-blooded illegal aliens with phony driver's licenses and Costco cards who'd pledged their goddamn allegiance to our flag."

"Sleepers, Tex," Hawke said, reaching over and laying a hand on his friend's shoulder.

"Yeah," Patterson said. "Van Winkles we call 'em at State. And they've already gone back to bed by now."

"So, your father, Mr. McCullough, found the bodies and called you, is that right, Chief?" Congreve asked.

"Yes," Ainslie said. "He couldn't talk really. He was

crying and mixing everything up. I knew something horrible had happened at the Slade house. My deputy, Nikos Savalas, and I came right out here. You've never seen such savagery, Inspector. Children, for God's sakes!"

"Anything else you think we should know, Chief?" asked Congreve.

"Yes," she said. "There were flowers."

"Flowers?"

"Lying atop each of the bodies. One flower. A single stem iris."

"An iris, you say?" Congreve said. He'd gotten to his feet and was standing at the railing, looking down over the little harbor, puffing on his pipe.

"Yes, an iris," Ainslie replied. "Mean anything to you, Chief Inspector?"

"Doesn't mean anything yet, perhaps," Congreve said thoughtfully, "but perhaps it will. Hmm. Iris is Siri spelled backwards, as you are well aware."

Patterson looked carefully at Ambrose Congreve, then at Hawke, shaking his head.

"I'll be damned," Tex said. Hawke smiled.

"Ambrose is usually roughly three thoughts ahead of the rest of the planet," Alex replied.

After a few moments had passed, each man deep in his own thoughts, Alex spoke. "How's Evan Slade holding up, Texas?"

"Aw, shoot, Hawkeye," Patterson said and just shook his head. "On his way here now. Lands in Portland at three. I'm going down to meet the plane. What the heck do I say to the guy?"

A short time later, Patterson and Alex followed an eager Congreve into the house. As they went through it, starting in the basement, both men were aware of Congreve's photographic mind at work. In the stillness of the dead house, you could almost hear the shutter click of his eyelids as he moved from room to room.

"Never seen this much physical evidence at a crime scene in my life," Patterson said as they mounted the blood-spattered stairway. "Heck, the girl's prints are *everywhere.* The murder weapon, the bathroom mirror, a Coke can in the library. We even found her blood-matted hair in Deirdre Slade's hairbrush. She brushed her hair, Alex. Afterwards."

"She didn't care, Tex," Alex said, "she's been taught since infancy not to bloody care." He turned away and walked into the children's room. Congreve followed him in. Patterson remained out in the hall. He just could not bring himself to go into that godforsaken room again. Ten minutes later, the two Englishmen emerged, ashen-faced and visibly shaken.

"I'm so sorry, Tex," Alex said. "We'll do all we can to help you stop these bloody bastards."

"I found this," Congreve said, showing them a small fragment of cellophane in the palm of his latex-gloved hand.

"What is it?" Patterson asked.

"Easy for your chaps to have missed it first time round," Ambrose said, eyeing the thing more closely. "It was stuck on the underside of the toilet seat in the children's bath. There's printing on it. The letters 'S,' 'O,' 'N,' and below that 'V' and 'H.' She possibly sat on the john, unwrapping a fresh Sony videocassette. Then, when she flushed, she threw the cellophane wrapper in. Static electricity caught this fragment on the underside. So it hasn't been there long."

"Jesus," Jack Patterson whispered as they descended the stairs and returned to the living room. "Where's this going?"

"Videotape is common enough, but not in this house," Ambrose said. "Had to come from the girl, I'm quite sure of it."

"I don't follow you," Patterson said. "From the girl?"

Congreve said, "She videotaped the whole thing. Went in the loo, stuck a new tape in her camera, and then went in and did the children. Telescoping tripod that would hide in her bag, I imagine."

"But, how do you know it was the girl who—"

"Trust him, Tex," Alex said, smiling at Ambrose. "His brain's just getting warmed up. Hell, he's almost tepid."

"Talk to me, Hawkeye."

"I think maybe he's got it, Texas," Alex said. "Videotape? A video camera? In this house? It's the girl. Doesn't make sense otherwise."

"Why not?"

"There's not a single VCR in the entire house," Congreve said. "I looked."

"No VCRs, no televisions," Hawke added.

"Holy God," Patterson said, collapsing into an arm-chair, pressing his fingertips into his eyesockets.

"What is it?" Alex asked.

"The thing in Venice? The miniature smart bomb? Pieces we scooped up sifting through the mud? One of our top forensic guys told me he thought he'd found a piece of a lens from the nose of the thing. Said there had been a nose camera. Chasing Stanfield through Venice and filming the whole damn thing."

"So there you have it," Ambrose Congreve said. "Our killer, whoever he or she may be, has it in for America and likes to watch his victims die. I say, Alex, we know anyone like that?"

Patterson sat back and regarded the two men for a moment. Then he said, "I believe I do know someone who fits both halves of that equation perfectly."

"Who, Tex?" Alex asked.

"They call him the Dog," Patterson said. "He's got a dozen aliases, but 'Dog' describes him perfectly. He's been Number One on the DSS terrorist hit parade for more than a decade. We've come close a couple of times, missed him by minutes."

"Country of origin?" Congreve asked.

"Thin air, far as I can tell," Patterson replied.

CHAPTER TWELVE

London

Attar al-Nassar approached Snay bin Wazir the way a master jeweler at Van Cleef & Arpels might have a go at an uncut twenty-carat diamond. He screwed in his eyepiece and went to work. He paused before each strike, his instrument delicate and poised, and when he struck it was swift, precise, and perfect. Gradually the rough edges became fine under his hand and Attar could begin to see fragments of his own brilliance reflected in his new friend.

If Snay was the uncut diamond, Attar was the diamondback rattler of his era. In the rough-and-tumble world of international arms dealing in the eighties, he struck swiftly and with deadly precision. Having reached a certain age, Attar was, albeit imperceptibly, slowing down. But, no matter, Snay was now fully on board. Having made a fortune in gladiolas, he had moved up to dealing Kalashnikovs, bullets, and helicopter gunships.

Attar gradually displaced some of his more onerous responsibilities onto his new partner's shoulders.

Snay never complained about these duties. His partnership within the vast al-Nassar arms empire had made him rich beyond measure. As an added benefit, he had a keen appetite for some of the more distasteful things which needed doing.

His lust for blood remained undiminished. He found outlets, always discreet and well hidden from both the police and the aristocratic society of London to which he now so desperately sought acceptance. He still enjoyed killing, but now getting away with it was the real thrill. His murders sometimes made the papers, but the police didn't have a clue.

The two men were dining alone this night in one of the smaller restaurants at Beauchamps, in some eyes the most exclusive of London's tiny coterie of truly first-rate hotels. They were enjoying an evening in the Reading Room, breathing the same rarefied air one might find at Claridge's or the Connaught; air consisting of fairly equal proportions of oxygen, nitrogen, and money.

To say the room was grand would be an understatement. Satinwood and burr wood furnishings covered in pale pink and grey brocaded satin filled the room and bronzed statuary stood atop the nickel-plated bar. Above all, a huge chandelier of crystal shimmered within a gilded dome in the ceiling.

Snay cracked open his gold cigarette case and extracted one of his trademark cigarettes. Long, slender, with yellow wrappers, they produced a distinctive odor that some people found distinctly unpleasant. Snay bin Wazir touched his gold Dunhill to the tip and lit up.

"Most unusual, those cigarettes," al-Nassar said, "I've been meaning to ask you; what are they?"

"I buy them from a dealer in Iraq," Snay said, sending a thin stream of smoke upwards. "They're called Baghdaddies."

"Baghdaddies?" al-Nassar said, smiling. "The name, at least, is quite marvelous."

Snay turned to offer a cigarette to the mysterious woman in the veiled magenta chador who accompanied al-Nassar everywhere. They said she was a great beauty, from Paris, but Snay had never seen her face. Nor heard her utter a word.

"She doesn't smoke," al-Nassar said.

"She doesn't speak," Snay replied.

"No."

"What does she do?"

Al-Nassar regarded his friend with a satyr's smile and picked up his wine. "Whatever you wish," he said, caressing her hand.

"What is her name, may I ask?" Snay said.

"Aubergine."

Taking a swig of the '48 Lafite in his goblet, bin Wazir leaned forward in his chair and said to the arms dealer, "My dear Attar, now I must ask you a question. I must say I still don't understand how these bloody Brits get 'Beechums' out of 'Beauchamps.'" In five short years, Snay bin Wazir had managed to acquire a passable British accent and his daily conversation was always liberally salted and peppered with newly acquired turns of phrase.

Bin Wazir had recently learned, painfully, that one never pronounced the name of the hotel "Beauchamps" as "Boshamps." It was always pronounced "Beech-ums."

"I don't know either, to be honest," Attar replied in a rare admission of ignorance, "but you're missing the point entirely. The point is, you *know* that *'Beech-ums'* is how it is properly pronounced."

Eschewing the toast points, Attar spooned some

caviar directly into his mouth and added, "I've told you a thousand times, my friend, there are far more people in this world who get by on style than on substance. Style, not substance, my dear Snay, is your most reliable *passe-partout* into London society."

"You, Attar, have always possessed an abundance of both."

Al-Nassar laughed and took a deep draught of his claret. "You see? This is why I keep you around! Shameless! Absolutely shameless! I have always adored that quality in anyone; man, woman, or child."

Snay, studying his menu, which was printed entirely in French, had been trying unsuccessfully for some minutes to get the headwaiter's attention.

"Who does this little prick think he is, ignoring me? I love this restaurant, but every time I come here that little French poofter over there always acts as if it's the first time he's ever seen me."

"What do you want? I'll get him over here."

"I have a question or two."

"Perhaps I can help. What is it?"

"Pardon my fucking French, but what, exactly, is *Canard du Norfolk Rôti à l'Anglais?*"

"It is Roast Norfolk Duck with some applesauce on the side. Applesauce, according to Escoffier, translates to *à l'Anglais*. Absolutely delicious with a fine Burgundy like the Nuits-Saint-Georges '62."

"I'm thinking of the salmon . . ."

"*Poached*, no doubt?"

They smiled and raised their goblets to each other. It was their private joke.

"Your second question?" al-Nassar asked.

"That one I'd like to ask the little shit personally."

"Watch me closely," al-Nassar said.

He nodded to one of four huge men he had stationed at tables in each corner of the room. When he had the man's attention, he nodded his head in the direction of the headwaiter. His man immediately rose from his seat, walked over to the waiter, bent down and put his lips near to the fellow's ear and had a short, whispered conversation with him. Then he squared his shoulders, turned his great bulk around, and returned to his table.

The headwaiter, looking like a man who was experiencing a most unpleasant coronary event, came immediately to Mr. al-Nassar's table, bowing and scraping when he was still twenty feet away.

"Monsieur al-Nassar," he said, unable to hide the tremor in his voice, "my deepest apologies. I'm so very sorry that I did not see that you required my presence. Oh, *mon Dieu!* Please forgive me. However may I be of service?"

Al-Nassar looked up and favored the man with a dark, heavy-lidded look that would wither kings.

"It seems, monsieur, that my business associate here, Mr. bin Wazir, has a question for you. He has been trying to gain your attention for some time without success. You have caused him some embarrassment."

"*Mais non!* But I did not notice!" the man said, turning and bowing now to Snay. "What can I do for you, sir? Besides beg your forgiveness?"

Snay turned to Attar and said, "I begin to like this groveling little toad, don't you? Even though his words ring false?"

"Apart from this chap's cheap perfume, he's probably a decent enough little frog."

The waiter smiled and bobbed his head, as if

acknowledging the most generous of compliments. "How may I serve you, monsieur?" he asked Snay.

"See that bus stop?" Snay said, pointing at one across the road. "The next bus leaves in ten minutes. Be under it."

"Ah, a most excellent suggestion, monsieur. I will do all within my power to . . . to . . . I'm sorry—"

Snay waved the waiter away with the back of his hand and smiled at al-Nassar. "No style. No substance," he said.

"Shoot him."

"And waste a perfectly good bullet? No, I have a far better idea, with your permission."

"Yes?"

"I've been thinking on this for some time, Attar. I'm going to buy this hotel."

"An interesting notion. To what end?"

"Real estate has been very profitable for me, as you well know, Attar. Every one of my clubs and casinos is posting spectacular numbers. Especially my new hotel, the Bambah in Indonesia. Fabulous resort. But it is time again to expand my holdings. I will create within these walls a sumptuous palace where eminent men of the world like you and I do not have to suffer these miserable insufferables. And this silly English décor."

"It's French, actually. Art Deco. Created by a chap named Basil Ionides sometime in the late twenties."

"All the more reason to fix it up."

And that is precisely what Snay did. He bought the old Victorian brick hotel in the heart of Mayfair. Snay bin Wazir could not know this—his history was too short—but this was not merely a fashionable hotel. It was a cultural icon, one of London's most revered architectural symbols for a century or more. Queen Victoria had visited Empress Eugénie of France when she was in residence here in 1860. The present queen had come here for balls when she was still a princess. Even to this day, the hotel catered to the Royal Family, hosting innumerable teas, state visits, and receptions.

His first move was a summary firing of all the employees. He began with the pompous little head-waiter in the Reading Room, but no one was spared. He fired the doormen in their silk toppers and red frocked coats, the aged valets, dress maids and hall porters, the dining and wait staff in their boiled shirts and cutaways, the *Maître Chef des Cuisines* and all the *sous-chefs,* and, finally, Henri, a confidant of Churchill himself who had presided over the main bar since before the war, and then the general manager himself.

To say this "Bloodbath at Beauchamps," as the tabloids tagged it, had all of London agog would be to put it mildly. There was outrage from every quarter. A spokesman at Buckingham Palace said the queen had no comment other than she was profoundly disgusted. The editorial pages of the *London Times* were spewing vitriol in the direction of the former Pasha of Knightsbridge. It was a lead story on the BBC for weeks. They treated it like a national disaster. It was, as one TV reporter put it, "a cock-up of monumental proportions."

Snay bin Wazir, who happened to be tuned in that night, took this reporter's comment as a compliment and rang up next morning to thank him for being the one newsman in town with the guts to take his side in the matter.

You could have blown up the Tate, the National Gallery, and the British Museum all in a day's work and not had more brimstone rain down on your head than bin Wazir found pouring down upon him in those turbulent times.

But Mr. bin Wazir had been forewarned by al-Nassar to expect this reaction from hidebound Londoners, and so he went about town with his usual aplomb, smiling in the face of the angry stares that met him everywhere, ignoring the shouted insults in the street, acting for all the world as if he were a man who'd found himself in the middle of a summer squall that would soon blow itself out.

The story quickly found its way across the pond where the American newspapers and television networks picked it up. There was a resounding hue and cry from that side of the Atlantic as well. Generations of wealthy Americans had called Beauchamps their "home away from home" and legions of them had grown up knowing the hotel staff by name. Now, the hate mail and death threats were arriving at bin Wazir's door from both sides of the Atlantic.

Unabashed and undeterred, bin Wazir proceeded with his project. It wasn't long before the scaffolding went up and armies of construction workers and demolition squads were hard at work. The windows and doors were all boarded up and the interior and exterior renovation began right on schedule.

It was bin Wazir's fervent belief during this stormy period that he would be redeemed once his new palace reopened and *haute* London got a look at what true grandeur really looked like. He had hired the best architects and interior designers money could buy and given them carte blanche. Within a few guidelines, naturally.

Gone would be the hideous silvered Georges Braque mirrors, the Jazz Age sculpture and paintings, and furniture upholstered in Cubist fabrics so dated as to make one laugh. Bin Wazir told his designers to let their minds venture into a golden future, where computer articulated twenty-four-karat nymphs danced and a ballet of sparkling jets spewed forth in splashing fountains of jeweled marble; and swirling, flashing lasers illuminated multicolored birds singing in massive gilded cages suspended from on high.

He imagined a new skyline for his team of designers as well. Opulently turreted and domed, with pillars and pediments and gables clad in endless mosaics of colored stone; with flags of every nation fluttering from every shimmering bronzed turret top, welcoming the world to bin Wazir's door. Yes, when the world finally came to his sumptuous palace, and gazed upon its many splendors, bin Wazir would find his redemption. And, quite possibly, a knighthood, he sometimes imagined.

His first clue that this fantasy might not come to pass was the day he invited all of London society, all of the press, including his old friend Stilton at the *Sun,* to witness the grand unveiling of the hotel's new marquee. To accentuate the new and dispel the old, it was rumored that bin Wazir had actually changed the two-centuries-old name of the fabled grand dame of Mayfair.

At the stroke of noon, on a hot June day, amidst a

cacophony of shouting reporters and clicking cameras, bin Wazir would pull the silken cord, letting the royal purple velvet drapes festooning the new façade and hiding the new marquee fall to the pavement.

With a great flourish, bin Wazir pulled the cord, the draperies fell away, and a huge gasp arose from all those assembled. The crowd stood in shocked silence, gazing upwards with disbelieving eyes.

There, for all to see, in massive golden letters forming an arch above the hotel's azure-tiled entrance was the new name of London's most magnificent new hotel. And, of course, it was spelled precisely the way bin Wazir thought it should be spelled.

Phonetically.

BEECHUM'S.

CHAPTER THIRTEEN

Nantucket Island

Shortly after *Kittyhawke* took off for Maine, Stokely Jones, Ross Sutherland, and Sergeant Tommy Quick were having breakfast in the gleaming stainless steel galley presided over by *Blackhawke*'s executive chef, Samuel Kennard. Kennard was known by one and all aboard the yacht as Slushy. Since the early eighteenth century, this unsavory moniker had been the nickname commonly given to cooks aboard ships in the British Royal Navy.

"Slushy," Stoke said, swallowing a mouthful of fried grits, "sit your ass down here and eat some breakfast with us. You been on your feet since five this morning."

"Brilliant idea, mate," Slushy said, in his thick cockney accent, and brought a plate piled high with bangers and mash over to the galley staff's main dining table. "Don't mind if I do, thank you very much." Slushy's substantial girth was all the proof you needed of his pudding.

"That's better," Stoke said. "I just can't stomach eating when somebody's standing there cooking. Must have been something in my childhood. Now, Slushy, you got shore leave this morning? Man, you got to see that whaling museum in town. I'm telling you, brother, those old whaling cats were some seriously badass dudes."

"Better trust him on that one, Slushy," Quick said. "Mr. Jones does not use the word *badass* lightly."

Tom Quick, who was always heavily armed despite his crisp white crew attire, reported directly to Sutherland and had total responsibility for the security of the yacht *Blackhawke*. Quick was of medium height, lean, with a shock of sun-whitened hair and frank, inquisitive grey eyes. He had been working for Hawke for more than two years. Alex had met the U.S. Army's number-one sharpshooter at the Sniper School at Fort Hood. Hawke had promised Sergeant Quick an exciting career and he had delivered in spades. Sarge, as he was now called, had helped to salvage Hawke from too many unsalvageable situations to count.

"Says it all the blooming time, though, don't he, Mr. Sutherland? Badass?" Slushy said. Most major yachts of the world boasted chefs lured away from the finest four-star restaurants of Europe. Alex had hired Kennard away from a pub in Clapham Common, which, he argued, had the best food in all of London. Slushy was an innate culinary genius and could cook, literally, anything to perfection. Even the salted shark strips Sutherland was currently chewing on.

"Damn good shark this morning, Slush," Ross said. "C'mon, Stoke. I'm headed for the ship's library. Get a jump on that list we made last night."

"That's good, that's good," Stoke said. "My man Sarge here and I've been doing some checking on that sniper rifle I found up in the tree. I tell you, Quick here is a walking sniper encyclopedia. And I want to hear about you and Ambrose's little midnight visit to the crime scene, too."

"Well, later," Tom Quick said, rising from the table. "Meeting with my team at nine. Good luck, good hunting, guys."

"Sarge," Sutherland said to Quick, "security level aboard is unchanged, correct?"

"Aye, sir. Level Three ever since the boss got the call from the DSS about the incident up in Maine."

"I don't feel good about this, Tommy. Take her to Four." Five was full on, wartime. They'd only been at Five once and that was in the middle of a firefight with Cuban gunboats during a very hairy military takeover down in Cuba.

"Aye, aye, sir," Quick said, "go to Four." He saluted and he was gone. Four meant round-the-clock armed watches and a two-man team manning the video feeds from the underwater cameras night and day. It must be getting very sketchy out there, Quick thought, taking the steps to the upper deck three at a time.

An hour later, Stokely and Sutherland were in the library, hard at it. They had managed to eliminate a few names from the Enemy Register and had created a new chart headed Physical Evidence.

"Trouble with that enemy chart," Stoke said, sitting back in his armchair with his hands laced behind his head, "is that Alex Hawke got a price on his head in half the damn countries on the list."

"Quite right," Ross said, turning from the chart. "But you don't get paid for shooting the bride."

"Yeah, I been thinking about that. Guy who did that to Vicky? He was sending a signal. I can hurt you and I can kill you. But before I kill you, I'm going to put you in a world of hurt."

"Yeah," Ross said. "It's definitely not a standard-fare contract hit. Have to be at least five names up there we might safely eliminate."

"Scratch 'em," Stoke said. "Mr. Congreve wants 'em back up there, he can tell us why when he gets back from Maine."

As Ross drew a red line through some of the names, Stokely got up and went to the evidence chart, a big black Magic Marker in his hand. He wrote the letters SVD at the top of the page.

"Let me tell you a little bit about the sniper rifle this guy managed to leave stuck in the tree," Stoke said. "Gun was a Dragunov SVD. That's short for *Snayperskaya Vintkova Dragunova*. I'm pronouncing that best I can."

"Russian," Sutherland said.

"Bet your ass. Now, here's the weird part. That gun sucks. So out of date, guy might as well used a goddamn flintlock." Stoke wrote the manufacture date, 1972, on the chart, next to SVD.

"Accurate enough, I'd say, assuming the target actually was Vicky and not Alex."

"Oh, it's accurate enough, you got a good enough scope on it. Which it did, by the way. Best goddamn scope money can buy. Now, here's the weird part."

"Yes?"

"I know a lot about this shit, as you know. I don't want to bore anybody."

"Bore me, Stokely, to tears," Ross said. "Make me cry."

"You asked for it, son. Okay. You see, while the SVD

was mass produced in the old USSR in the seventies, they're hard to come by these days. I mean, no serious shooter is going to go out and *look* for one of these things, know what I'm saying?"

Stoke was illustrating his points, getting everything down in writing on the physical evidence chart.

"Wouldn't be professional, is what you're saying," Sutherland said, smiling.

"See? That's why the boss likes you, Ross. You good, my brother. Now. This is the best part. While the gun itself is an antique, the *scope* is definitely not. The scope is a 10X Leupold & Stevens Ultra Mark IV. They don't get much better. Multicoated lenses for superior light transmission and contrast. Bright, distortion-free image in any kind of light. And exposed knobs for easy windage and elevation adjustments. Bored yet?"

"You see any tears?"

"The Ultra Mark IV is brand spanking new. It has a range knob that goes from one hundred yards to one thousand yards with one complete turn of the dial. And that, little buddy, tells you something."

"Namely?"

"That Leupold scope? Total overkill. It's strictly American military or American law enforcement. Joe Public can't buy one for love or money. I called the head tech support guy at Leupold this morning just to make sure. These scopes are locked down tight. Got a big computer with nothing to do all day but keep track of every damn serial number."

"So," Ross said, leaning forward in his chair, "our shooter has to be either a U.S. serviceman or police officer."

"Both possible, but not very damn likely."

"Right. For now, at least. So we've got an outdated Soviet weapon with a brand-new U.S. scope mounted on it. Strange, but I'll go with it."

"I'm saving the very best for last."

"Please."

"This guy Sarge put me onto at Leupold? I talked to the tech guy. Name was Larry. Wouldn't give out his last name. Security. Anyway, he asks me why I'm so curious about this particular scope so I told him the whole story about Vicky, beginning to end. He's listening to me now, 'cause at this point he knows I'm ex-SEAL, ex-NYPD, and shit and the cat *knows* my ass 'cause of reputation or some shit, you know, and the U.S. Navy?"

"U.S. Navy."

"Hell, Ross, Navy's a major contractor with him, do a whole lot of business with his company, dig? Whole damn lot. You *capiche* what I'm saying here?"

"He had a certain incentive to cooperate."

"There you go again, Ross! Shit! Let's just say the boy took a very deep breath and let me into his total utmost confidence."

"What'd he say, Stoke? You're driving me mad here."

"He said, what the boy said was, Stoke, you didn't hear this from me. But. There's one damn scope out there somewhere we just can't account for."

"Christ!"

"That's exactly what I said! Seems like about three months ago, somebody broke into the apartment of a Dade County SWAT team guy down in Miami. Killed him in his bed. M.E. guy on the scene said somebody drove a sharp object through both his eyes. Stole his weapon. Only thing he took."

"Hold on. The SWAT guy had his weapon at home? That's not how it works, Stoke. They lock them down at the HQ after every operation."

"Shit, you think I don't know that, Ross? Wasn't supposed to have his damn sniper rifle in house. 'Course not. Against every SWAT reg in the book, you right. He was a bad boy. Weekends, he took his gun, a .50-caliber Barrett M82A1 rifle by the way, out into the 'glades, did himself a little gator shooting. Somebody watching the boy for a while, knew all his habits."

"Knew weapons and scopes, as well."

"Yeah."

"Where exactly was this apartment?"

"South Beach."

"Question."

"Shoot."

"How come Vicky's shooter puts the new scope on the old rifle? Why not just use the .50-cal Barrett?"

"Thought about that. He's more comfortable with the old SVD. Used it for a long time. The new Barrett is all funked out with new kinds of shit he's not used to. So, he puts the good scope on the old gun."

"You're thinking this shooter is Russian, Stoke?"

"Russian, old Eastern bloc, maybe. Lots of pissed-off Commies running round the planet love to mess with Alex Hawke."

"Chinese. North Koreans . . ."

"Them, too. But the Chinese and NKs, see, they got their own sniper rifles. Wouldn't be messing with some outdated Soviet shit."

"Middle Easterners might—"

At that moment Pelham appeared in the library,

carrying a silver salver with a teapot and tea service for two.

"I daresay I hate to interrupt what is most certainly a most scintillating and fruitful discussion, but I thought that perhaps a cup of good Darjeeling might further stimulate the cerebral cells."

"Pelham," Stoke said, "you something else. You like some whole different species. Ordinary folks never know what the hell you talking about, but it always sound so good."

"Most kind, Mister Jones," Pelham said. "Will you be having tea?"

"I will be having tea," Stoke said, a huge grin on his face. "Pelham, you been with Alex since the day he was born. We sitting here trying to figure out who could have the kind of hatred for Alex that would drive them to murder his bride on the steps of a church. Maybe you could add something. Why don't you sit down there and listen to old Ross talk about his midnight visit to the crime scene?"

"Are you quite serious?"

"I'm quite serious as I ever get."

"Then I should be delighted. My morning was going to be spent sorting through his lordship's jumble of handkerchiefs. The linen and the silk seem to have conjoined. This sounds a much more interesting and worthwhile endeavor."

Pelham lifted the tails of his cutaway and sat in the lovely old Windsor chair Alex had acquired at an estate sale in Kent.

"Good. We need all the help we can get on this. Now, Ross, tell Pelham and me what happened when you and the Constable went up to the church that night?"

"Ah, yes. The proverbial dark and stormy night. It was raining buckets, and my expectations were low. The crime scene had been, by that time, thoroughly investigated. But, the Constable reminded me, mere crime scene investigators are not to be confused with Ambrose Congreve."

Stoke laughed. "Boy is a natural, ain't he? Natural born copper."

"On the assumption the shooter had spent the night or most of it up in the tree, we did a three-sixty around the base of the tree. Twice." Ross reached inside his jacket and removed a small glassine envelope. "The Chief found this the second time round. It's just back from the evidence lab at Victoria Street."

Stoke took the envelope and held it up to the light.

"Don't look like much."

"It's the stump end of a cigar, actually. Both wrapper and filler have been identified as Cuban leaf. There was a bit of foil label embedded in the wrapper. Lab was able to determine the brand. Cohiba."

"So where does that take us? You can buy Cuban cigars anywhere."

"Quite right. But the label indicated this cigar was not made for export. It could only have been purchased in Cuba."

"Well, lots of them Cuban folks down there would like to bust Alex's chops, but we killed most of 'em when we blew the shit out of that rebel submarine base."

"Stoke," Sutherland said, leaning forward, "are you thinking what I'm thinking?"

"Soviet sniper rifle. Got to be hundreds of them lying around in the one Communist country we didn't even mention. Cuba. Russkies left 'em behind when they pulled out of there. Shooter could be Cuban all right. God knows, we pissed a bunch of them off down there and—"

"Cuba," Sutherland interrupted. "The one name Alex asked the Chief Inspector to add to his list."

It was then that Pelham dropped his teacup. It hit the floor with a tinkling crash and shattered, splashing tea on Stokely's trousers.

"Good Lord!" Pelham exclaimed. "I must be losing my mind!"

"Ain't no harm done, Pelham. Here, I can pick it all up and—"

"I've done the most dreadful thing," Pelham said. "Absolutely dreadful. I must be getting perfectly senile."

"What are you talking about, Pelham?" Sutherland asked. "You, dear fellow, are simply incapable of doing anything dreadful."

Pelham took a deep breath and stared at the two men.

"You two are thinking the man who murdered Victoria was possibly Cuban?"

"We currently exploring that possibility, yes."

"This may be completely irrelevant," Pelham said, rubbing his white-gloved hands together anxiously.

"You trying to solve a cold-blooded murder, Pelham, ain't nothing irrelevant," Stokely assured him.

"Well. It was about a week after everyone returned from the Caribbean. After the very successful conclusion of what his lordship humorously called his 'personal Cuban missile crisis.' Vicky was a guest at the house in London, recuperating from the ordeal of her abduction at the hands of the Cuban rebels. Would someone mind pouring me a wee dram of whiskey? I'm feeling a bit off."

"Hell, Pelham," Stokely said, "it's way past nine o'clock in the morning, I'll pour you a glass."

Stokely went to the drinks table and peered at the silver labels hanging from the necks of the various heavy crystal decanters. He'd never had a drop of alcohol in his life and was a bit unsure as to what was whiskey and what was not.

"It's the one on the far left, Stoke," Sutherland said. "Please continue, Pelham."

"Well. At any rate, Vicky and Alex had had a lovely evening at the house in Belgrave Square. They dined alone. After dinner, I took them up and showed them the hidden room where I'd kept all of Alex's childhood toys and mementoes. There was a lovely portrait of Lord and Lady Hawke there. Alex and I somehow managed to get the large picture properly hung above the fireplace in the sitting room. They sat for a long time on the sofa, just staring up at it. Quite an emotional experience for Alex, I must say, finally coming to grips with the death of his parents."

"What happened after that, Pelham?" Stokely asked.

"Well, as I say, there was a beastly storm that night and I had laid a great fire in the hearth. It was a'blazing away and I left them sitting there, cozy and comfortable. I went into the pantry to take up my needlepoint. When I returned some hours later, I discovered they'd fallen asleep. It was about three in the morning and I decided just to put a fur throw over them and go on up to bed. That's when it happened."

"What?" Sutherland said gently, for clearly the old fellow was deeply troubled.

"I was on my way up to my rooms, you see, and I heard someone ringing at the front door."

"At three in the morning?" Sutherland said.

"Yes. Madness, naturally, unless it was some kind of emergency which it wasn't. I went down, turned on the exterior carriage lamps, which I had shut off moments before, and I opened the door. There was a man standing there in the drenching rain. He was wearing a black cloak and holding a large black umbrella. He announced, in an appallingly rude manner, that he was looking for Alexander Hawke.. I informed him that Lord Hawke was hardly receiving at this hour. 'Give him this,' he said, and handed me a small golden medallion. I recognized it as having belonged to his lordship."

"You later gave it to Alex?" Stokely asked.

"No. That's the dreadful thing. I slipped it inside my waistcoat pocket and toddled off to bed, fully intending to give it to his lordship next morning. When I went down to prepare breakfast at seven, I found a note from his lordship saying that he and Vicky had risen at first light and driven down to Hawkesmoor for a few last days in the Cotswolds before she returned to America. I put the medallion in the silver box where he keeps all his medals. And, completely and inexcusably, forgot to ever even mention it to him. Since he never looks at his medals, I'm quite sure that, to this day, he doesn't know a thing about it."

Stokely, looking not at Pelham but at Sutherland, said, "What did that medallion look like?"

"It was a St. George's medal," Pelham said. "It had

his initials on the reverse side. A gift from his mother. I noticed he wasn't wearing it upon his return from Cuba and asked him about it. He told me he'd lost it down there."

"It's the medal Alex was wearing round his neck the night we rescued Vicky, Ross," Stoke said. "One of the guards cut the gold chain and took it away from him. We were so busy trying to get out of there alive, we forgot all about it."

"Pelham, can you give us a physical description of this fellow on the steps?" Ross said, excited.

"Well, I remember he kept the umbrella low, as if to hide his face. But when he turned to go, I caught a glimpse of him in the light of the carriage lamps. Most extraordinary. He had absolutely no color in the pupils of his eyes."

Stokely and Sutherland both got to their feet at the same time.

"This guy," Stoke said, his voice choked with excitement, "he have any kind of accent, Pelham?"

"Yes," Pelham said. "A very distinct accent. Spanish."

"The man with no eyes," Stoke said. "Shit. Alex was right. We should have been looking at Cubans."

"Scissorhands," Sutherland agreed. "That's what Vicky said all the Cuban guards called him. Chap who liked to cut up people with a pair of silver scissors hung round his neck."

Stokely slapped his forehead hard enough to send the average man crashing to the floor.

"Ross? That SWAT guy got whacked down in Miami? Like I was saying, Dade County Medical Examiner said somebody drove a sharp object into his brain. Through his eyes. The M.E. said the object was probably a pair of very sharp scissors."

"Stoke," Ross said, trying to sound calm, "the serial number on the scope in the tree. He'd filed it off, right?"

"I was saving that part for last," Stoke smiled. "No, he didn't. I read that serial number off to my new best friend at Leupold. Identical match. *All* they scopes now officially accounted for."

CHAPTER FOURTEEN

London, December 1999

Twilight on the Thames. It was Alex Hawke's favorite time of day and he stood, hands clasped behind his back, at one of the broad glass windows of his fifteenth-floor office. He was gazing at, mesmerized by would be more accurate, both the river traffic and the motor traffic crisscrossing Waterloo Bridge. There was a fine misty rain falling and it made that late December evening shimmer and glow like one of Turner's luminous paintings of the palaces of Westminster.

Fin de siècle, Hawke thought, last one I'll ever see.

The year was 1999, in the waning days shortly before the turn of the century, and Alex Hawke was thinking at that moment of calling the beautiful woman he'd met at a pre–New Year's fete just the night before. An American doctor named Victoria Sweet who'd written a wonderful children's book called, what was it, *The Whirl-o-Drome.* She was perhaps the loveliest—

There was a quiet knock at his half-opened door.

"Yes?"

"Sorry to disturb you, sir, but Ambassador Kelly is on the line. I thought you might like to speak to him, sir." Alex turned from the window and saw his secretary of many years, the exquisitely formed Sarah Branham, framed in the doorway.

He smiled at her and said, "Yes, Sarah, thank you, I would. Put him through straightaway."

She pulled the door closed and Alex collapsed his lanky frame deep into one of a semicircle of large leather club chairs overlooking the river. He propped his feet on the round table. It was a three-foot-high, six-foot cross section of an ancient, fluted, marble column.

"Hello, Brick," he said, picking up the phone. "Lovely soiree last night. Thanks for including me."

"You certainly seemed taken by the guest of honor."

"She's stunning."

"Why do you think I sat you next to her?" Kelly asked in his soft Virginia accent. "Now, tell me. What lean and hungry young lioness awaits the pleasure of your company at supper this evening?"

"I only wish," Hawke said. "Truth be told, I've asked the lovely Sarah to fetch me up the dreaded *Omelet du jour* from our third-floor eatery. I plan to down it at my desk over the *Times* crossword, actually."

"Horrible idea. Here's an alternative plan of action you might consider. Last minute, but what the hell. Might just lift your spirits. Seeing as how you're the chair and I sit on the admissions committee at Nell's, I couldn't resist calling you."

"You're calling about Nell's? Must be an extremely slow day in diplomatic circles."

Nell's was perhaps the poshest, most glamourous private nightspot in all of London. Dark and clubby, one would imagine it stuffy, but it had retained its alluring aura since the Swinging Sixties. The four imperious and haughty gentlemen in boiled shirts and stiff white ties who guarded the door might give the newcomer the impression of high propriety. But, on the contrary, Nell's snug bar and minuscule disco dance floor had been the scene of some of the wildest nights on record during the booming eighties and, even now, in the late nineties.

It remained a members-only sanctuary where royalty, the aristocracy, and the well-heeled ladies and gentlemen of society could let their hair down, bare their souls, and, rumor had it, sometimes my lady's breasts as well. Unsurprisingly, it had long been one of Alex's favorite haunts, and he'd recently accepted the job of chairing the admissions committee.

"Cough it up, Brick," Hawke said, intrigued. Anything to escape these bloody markets and the dreaded *Omelet du jour.*

"Well, here's the drill, Alex. You probably don't remember Sonny Pendleton?"

"I do. Your second in command in the desert."

"That's him. Anyway, he's ascended to the role of a rather large cheese at the Defense Department now and he's in London on business this week and just called to ask a favor. I was inclined to turn him down, but the more I thought about it, the more amusing I thought it might be. Especially if I could cajole you into joining me."

"Spill the beans, Brick. What's up?"

"See, Hawke? Despite your best efforts, you are gradually picking up the Yank lingo. Anyway, Sonny called to see if I'd have dinner tonight. Meet this guy he's doing some business with who is extremely determined to become a member of Nell's. *Quid pro quo* situation. The guy's putting a lot of pressure on Sonny, who's putting a lot of pressure on me since he knows I'm on the committee."

"I give up. Who's the guy?"

"You're not going to believe it. It's the notorious Mr. bin Wazir, who just reopened Beauchamp's Hotel under a new spelling."

Hawke laughed. "The Pasha of Knightsbridge? You've got to be joking."

"Formerly the Pasha of Knightsbridge," Brick said. "Now, after the Beauchamps fiasco, the Pariah of Knightsbridge."

"Bin Wazir? At Nell's? What's Sonny smoking these days?" Alex asked. "Does he think this lunatic has a snowball's chance in hell of getting past Nell's admissions board after that Beauchamps debacle?"

"I know, I know. Christ. But Mr. bin Wazir, as you well know, is in cahoots with Mr. al-Nassar. And Defense wants very much to lean on al-Nassar. Get to him through bin Wazir. I can't really say any more than that."

"What do I get out of this, Brick?"

"A free dinner at the Connaught Grill with your old buddy Brickhouse, courtesy of the United States State Department. Name a wine."

"Château Margaux. Fifty-four."

"Done."

"You're just lucky I had a date with an omelet instead of the beauteous Dr. Victoria Sweet."

"Luck of the Irish."

"What time?"

"Eight in the p.m."

"Count me in."

Alex Hawke was early, arriving at the Connaught

Bar at seven forty-five. The hotel's quiet, understated lounge was one of his favorite watering holes and, besides, it would give him a chance to catch up with the barman, a thoroughly amusing fellow named Duckworth, an old chum. The small, beautifully paneled bar was empty save an elderly couple seated at a window table, sipping sherry and silently watching the rain spatter against the glass.

"Lord Hawke himself," Duckworth whispered, when Alex Hawke walked in and took a seat at the bar. "Must say I haven't seen much of you lately, sir. On the wagon, m'Lord?"

"I was, Ducky, but we hit a ditch and I was thrown off," Hawke said, smiling at the plump, rosy-cheeked, bespectacled man. "By the time I got up and dusted myself off, the bloody wagon was half a mile down the road."

Duckworth smiled, wiping a goblet, and said, "What will it be, sir? Goslings? The Black Seal, as I recall."

"Yes, thank you. Neat."

As the barman poured his dark Bermudian rum, Alex said, "Awfully quiet tonight, Ducky."

"Indeed, sir. It is Monday. Still. Been a crypt in here all evening. But they're all atwitter over at the Grill Room. Wait staff at any rate."

"Really? What's all the hubbub about?"

"Apparently, the Pasha of Knightsbridge will be dining with us this evening, sir. We're all holding our breath."

"Why?"

"Hoping we're not the next target on his acquisition list."

Alex laughed and nodded at his now empty glass. As Duckworth poured him another, he said, "I shall do all within my power to dissuade him, should that be the case."

"You know this gentleman, m'lord?"

"I will in ten minutes. I'm dining with him."

Duckworth almost dropped his glass.

"You, sir?"

"Don't worry, Ducky. This escapade wasn't my idea. Ambassador Kelly is the man behind this evening's adventure. We'll stop in for a nightcap after dinner, give you a full report."

"Made my day, you have, sir," Duckworth said, smiling.

"Put this on my account, will you? Oh, and by the way, I've just had an idea. Ring the chef and tell him whatever this Pasha orders, burn it beyond recognition. Might cut this dinner short."

Duckworth was still chuckling when Alex Hawke left the bar and ambled over toward the Grill Room. To his surprise, he found himself actually looking forward to the thing.

CHAPTER FIFTEEN

The Emirate

The Emir's stark fortress stood at some twelve thousand feet, nestled between four craggy peaks rising like curved stone incisors at each of the four walled corners of the ancient fortress. Since the Emir himself knew he would never leave his citadel for any destination save Paradise, he didn't care that it was virtually impossible to reach in any season. This was precisely why he'd chosen the inaccessible site in the mountainous heart of the Emirate. He had begun to enlarge and modernize this bastion some thirty years prior.

Remote as it was, security was sophisticated, and pervasive. A large monitor, one of many mounted above the small divan in the Emir's day room, showed a small caravan now making its way upwards through the pass toward his gates, battered by a howling snowstorm. It was the camel train of Snay bin Wazir the infidel, the impious, the indispensable, the son-in-law. Although the Emir despised Snay bin Wazir, his impending arrival met with considerable anticipation.

His Excellency, the Most High, the Emir had but one burning lifelong goal. To establish *Khilafah*. Allah's rule over all the earth. His fiery zealotry was deeply and purely religious. He wanted to purge the planet of every drop of the blood of the infidels, the unbelievers. Only then could humankind live in peace under the One True God.

Truly, a lot of infidel blood had already been shed. But this the Emir considered but a drop in Allah's bucket.

The ice-coated bin Wazir, now making his way up the steep incline, shuddered with cold and anger. His loathing was predicated on far less righteous ideals than those of the noble Emir. Bin Wazir burned with envy. Jealousy. Humiliation. It was a source of great friction between himself and his father-in-law. In the late nineties, the Emir had found Snay bin Wazir's highly publicized love of western luxury and the western mores of London debasing and disgusting.

Then one of the Emir's British agents had sent him a taped BBC segment entitled:

"Beechum's. A First Peek Inside The Pasha's New Palace."

Snay's days as a bon vivant on the London scene were already numbered. This public humiliation of a member of the Emir's household was one thing. But the Emir had heard through the grapevine that his son-in-law had recently attracted the attention of the police. Interpol and the Americans were looking into a series of brutal murders in London. Knowing Snay's bloody proclivities, the Emir knew his guilt in the matter was more than likely. It was only a matter of time before the investigation would lead to the Emir's doorstep. And so he'd had his network of sleeper agents inside Britain kidnap the infidel and his wife, the Emir's beloved daughter Yasmin, fly them out of the country and transport them to his mountain fortress.

In a trial presided over by the Emirate's sole authority, the Emir himself, bin Wazir had been found guilty of endangering the holy cause and bringing great shame on the House of the Emir. He was dragged away in chains, his fate sealed, his wife pleading with her father, to no avail.

On the morning of Snay bin Wazir's scheduled beheading, however, the Emir had second thoughts about his despicable son-in-law. To execute him, however just, would kill his own daughter just as surely. She swore she would follow her husband to Paradise. The Emir could not imagine life on this earth without his precious child, no matter how cruelly she had disappointed him.

He would save two birds with one uncast stone.

His son-in-law was a vicious, vengeful animal with more cunning and raw intelligence than was typical of his low-bred breed. He could, the Emir considered, actually be useful. He could render service to Allah even though he was not remotely a true believer. He could become, with time and training, yet another swift sword in the Emir's hand. He would have to be schooled ruthlessly until he had mastered the Arab warrior's timeless arts of murder. After that, yes, this beast Snay could prove useful.

After some thought, the Emir made another fateful decision. He would re-create an age-old Arabic institution: the *hashishiyyun*. Once a secret sect of medieval Islam, this drug-crazed cadre of exquisitely skilled assassins was originally comprised of both sexes. In the Emir's vision, this murderous clan would be comprised of the deadlier of the species. All seductive females, the better to insinuate themselves more easily into the enemy's hearts and lives. And bin Wazir, who had a certain power over women, would be the ideal chieftain for such a secret army.

The ancient assassins would gladly hurl themselves from the tops of lofty towers at the click of the master's fingers, just to demonstrate their contempt for life and absolute fealty to their lord. The Emir believed Snay could command that kind of loyalty. He had a strange power over women.

So Snay bin Wazir's head, to his amazement and delight, remained affixed to his torso. So long as he trained faithfully, and ruthlessly executed the Emir's evolving strategies for the creation of the new *hashishiyyun,* his existence would be tolerated. He would retire from public life in the West. He and his wife could live as they chose as long as they remained chiefly inside the Emirate's borders. The Emir deposited one hundred million pounds sterling in Yasmin's name in a bank in Zurich. Six months later, Snay and Yasmin began construction on their magnificent new mountain-top residence, the Blue Palace.

There, in splendid isolation, bin Wazir would create this new order of *hashishiyyun.* An army of perfectly trained female killers. Seductive and lethal, they would go out into the world, far beyond the borders of the Emirate, to do the bidding of their immediate master through the orders of Snay's own exalted lord, the Emir.

"Shit!" Snay shouted to his camel boy, wiping a fresh coating of snow from his frozen beard. "How much farther?" His camels stumbled once more and he was nearly thrown from his tossing and pitching sedan.

Camels were for the desert. Normally camels were the transport of choice in these mountains, too. But, ascending icy mountain ranges in a blinding snow-storm was not their strong suit.

The new millennium was already in its fourth year. Riding atop these bloody frostbitten camels was a far cry from gliding around Mayfair in the rear of his gleaming Silver Ghost, sipping a Pimm's Cup with his old friend Attar. Ah, he'd been the toast of London for a while, his handsome face and glitzy lifestyle the stuff of glossy magazines and Sunday supplements.

Then, Beechum's.

He had opened his opulent palace with great expec-tations. It was to be the cornerstone of his expanding personal real estate empire. But, then the disastrous opening and, the morning after, that infamous boldface tabloid headline had appeared. Two bloody words (writ-ten, no doubt, by the treacherous Stilton) were embla-zoned above a close-up picture of Snay at the opening night reception. A full-page, four-color nightmare.

The fatal stab was the headline all London saw that morning. Above the shot of Snay toasting the camera with champagne, the erstwhile Pasha of Knightsbridge read these words:

"YESTERDAY, THE TOAST OF LONDON . . . TODAY, HE'S TOAST!"

Five long years after the fact, bin Wazir, still nursing those old wounds, was riding out another storm. Only now he was slung between two surly camel mounts in a custom cradle of ebony with an ivory rim, richly adorned with gold and jewels. Wind and snow whipped through, lashing the canvas awnings aside as if they were ribbons. Snay's thick moustache was solid ice beneath his nose.

"How long, boy?" he called out.

"Another hour or two, I believe," the boy Harib called back, quaking with fear. *"Inshallah."*

Harib knew his indefinite answer would only serve to anger Snay further. *Inshallah* had many shades of meaning, from "God willing," to "soon," to "don't count on it." But Harib couldn't be more precise because he couldn't see any of his familiar landmarks. The snowstorm wasn't his fault, but Snay didn't care. He'd been screaming at everyone for the better part of the day. Harib had already felt the sting of Snay's rhino-hide whip across his shoulders when one of the camels had stumbled into a deep crevasse hidden by snow, nearly spilling the four-hundred-pound sumo-weight Pasha into a snowbank.

There were, in all, twelve camels in the storm-lashed caravan, the lead six bearing Snay, his four sumo guards, and the African chieftain Tippu Tip at the front of the pack. Six more camels behind them were loaded with supplies, weapons and Snay's mountain fighters. The weaponry was sophisticated in this remote part of the world and included the very latest German machine guns and laser-guided rocket propelled grenades, RPGs.

No sign of trouble yet, fortunately, but there were many ancient warring tribes in these mountains, vicious warriors who bore no allegiance to either Snay or the Emir, and the danger of a surprise attack by these screaming, saber-rattling hordes was ever present.

The wind-whipped snow had been increasing in

intensity. Snay had known he faced a treacherous ascent, even in mild weather. In white-out conditions, as now, it was madness. But what choice did he have?

He'd been summoned by the Emir. And so began the long, dangerous journey which would take him from one mountain peak, his own 18,000-foot Blue Mountain, down and across the Dasht-e Margow, the Desert of Death, that crossroads where three continents meet, and, from the baking desert floor, up again into one of the world's most treacherous mountain ranges.

Ahead, on the so-called trail, Snay bin Wazir could almost distinguish three giant figures atop their struggling mounts. Tippu Tip was leading the two sumos in front of his sedan. Behind were camels bearing the two other sumos. He was well guarded as always, he thought, trying to find some comfort in his situation. But what could protect him from plummeting through a snow-covered crevasse? Or from a rock slide, an avalanche, a murderous horde? These things happened with regularity at this altitude and—

"Pasha! Look!" the camel boy shouted, interrupting his dark musings.

"What?" Snay said, looking everywhere for signs of his imminent demise. As if he didn't have enough on his mind, wondering what the Emir wanted that— "What is it, damn your eyes?"

"There!" the excited boy said, pointing off to the right. "Do you see it? Allah be praised!"

Relief swept over him. No wild devils on horseback were sweeping down on him from the heights. No, what he saw was a massive radar dome. It was just the first of an outlying perimeter of many radar sites leading up to the fortress itself; but it meant the cara-van was much closer to its destination than he'd been told by the witless Harib. First, the radar, and then, climbing higher, the anti-aircraft and surface-to-air emplacements. He was, by all approximations, less than an hour from learning what his future held.

Snay bin Wazir shut his eyes. He knew this next bit well enough. The cages.

Now came the first of many "man cages" erected on either side of the pass. These filthy iron baskets, stretching along either side of the "mile of death" lead-ing to the fortress's massive gates, held men, women, or the remains of either. They were ancient devices, made of thick iron slats, woven into basket shapes. The victim was placed inside, then hoisted high on poles that loomed above the pass, where no friends or rela-tions could pass food, water, or salvation in the form of poison to the condemned. The cages were a sobering reminder of the Emir's absolute power over all his sub-jects and agents; not that bin Wazir, of all people, needed any sober reminding.

"Allah preserve me," Snay croaked, miserably rub-bing away the painful icicles that had formed on his frozen eyelashes.

CHAPTER SIXTEEN

London, December 1999

Three men stood up when Alex approached the corner table, one of only ten tables in the Connaught's celadon green Grill Room. The tall, lean, Jeffersonian figure of Patrick Kelly; a solidly built hardcore Army type Hawke recognized instantly as former First Lieutenant Sonny Pendleton, now with the American Defense Department; and a surprisingly handsome mustachioed gentleman, tall, athletically built, and ruggedly resplendent in a three-piece chalk-stripe that could only have come from Huntsman's.

This bin Wazir was good-looking enough, with a vulpine aspect to his ready grin, and, beneath luxuriant black eyebrows, a startling manic energy in his black eyes that fairly crackled with intensity.

"Why, you must be Lord Hawke," the fellow boomed, sticking out his hand. Heads swiveled. The Connaught's smaller dining room was filled with patrons accustomed to quiet civility and hushed decorum, although, since it had gone nonsmoking, it tended to attract a fair number of Americans. One of the reasons Hawke much preferred it to the stuffier main dining room. He was one of those somewhat rare Englishmen who'd always found the casual bonhomie of Americans refreshing rather than tedious.

Hawke shook hands with all three men. Snay bin Wazir's handshake was surprisingly warm and dry. In Hawke's experience, people in interview situations, which is what this evening basically was about, had very clammy handshakes. "An honor, your lordship," he said.

"Alex Hawke will do," Hawke said, smiling. "Don't use the title, never have. I'm descended from pirates and peasants, you see. A rather churlish lot, but I'm proud of them."

"I see. Well, then." The man seemed at a loss and Hawke covered his obvious embarrassment by making a show of sitting down.

There was the usual small talk as drinks were served. Bin Wazir again surprised Hawke. The man was a brute, there was no disguising it, but someone had sanded off his rough edges. There was keen intelligence in those obsidian eyes, and a ready smile to go with it. Whatever his reputation, here was someone who clearly enjoyed life to the fullest. He was also, by reputation, utterly fearless.

Hawke leaned back and studied bin Wazir while the Arab, Brick Kelly, and the DoD man Pendleton engaged in a discussion in which the name of the arms dealer al-Nassar featured prominently. Here was a chap, this self-styled Pasha, who had just taken a bastion of London society and utterly destroyed it. And subsequently been soundly pilloried for it. If there was even an ounce of remorse over what he'd done to London's most revered hotel, or any sense of social humiliation in the fellow, Hawke couldn't see it.

Fascinating.

Dinner came and went uneventfully, with Pendleton pressing his case against al-Nassar's imminent sale of more fighter jets to Iran and bin Wazir alternating between demurral and assent with Washington's position. It wasn't until coffee and brandy were being served that Brick brought up the subject at hand.

"Alex," Brick said, putting a match to the end of a Griffin cigar, "Mr. bin Wazir here had a most unfortunate experience at Nell's last Thursday evening."

"Really?" Hawke said, looking over at the man. "I'm very sorry to hear that, Mr. bin Wazir. Please tell me what happened."

Bin Wazir laughed and rubbed his big beefy hands together as if relishing the memory. He gave Hawke a look as if to say they were old friends and that this little tale was just idle club gossip amongst gentlemen.

"It was most amusing, actually," Bin Wazir then said, his smile revealing a set of gleaming white teeth beneath the thick black moustache.

"Amusing," Hawke said, giving him a smile of encouragement.

"Quite. You see, I was dining in the neighborhood with a lovely young woman of my acquaintance. After dinner, she asked if I would take her to Nell's for a dance and a drink. Yes, I said, why not, it's right around the corner. We descended the stairway and were met by two gentlemen at the door."

"Yes," Hawke said, "Thursday evening, that would be Mr. Bamford and Mr. Lycett."

"Exactly. Well, they asked if they could help me and I said yes, I'd like to buy the young lady a drink at the bar. Was there a problem? Well, yes, they said, this is a private club. Members only. Not a problem at all, I said, getting out my checkbook. I'll join. How much?"

Bin Wazir laughed again as if at himself, and looked round the table, gathering approval.

"Most amusing," Hawke said, finally.

"I thought so, too," bin Wazir said, now warming to the tale.

"Ah, but Mr. bin Wazir, they said, this is unfortunately not how the club functions. They said I must be proposed by a member, seconded, and have a number of supporting letters. Well, it was a little embarrassing, but, thankfully, my dear friend Sonny here agreed to help me smooth things over."

Smooth things over? Well, Hawke thought, casting a glance at Brick, *well, this certainly could get interesting.*

"Mr. bin Wazir," Brick said, "you certainly took the direct approach, but I'm afraid Mr. Bamford and Mr. Lycett were accurate. You will need to go through the process."

"Surely, you're not serious, Mr. Ambassador," bin Wazir said. "A simple phone call from you would—"

"He is serious, I'm afraid, Mr. bin Wazir," Hawke said, coming to Brick's aid. "I, as it happens, am the current chairman of the admissions committee. I approve all applications and no one is accepted unless they have met all the requirements. Proposer, seconder, and a minimum of five supporting letters. All from members."

"That's right, Mr. bin Wazir," Brick said. "Sorry, but there you have it."

Bin Wazir looked at the two of them as if he could not believe what he was hearing. Finally, he smiled and said, "Fine, you two gentlemen are members. You can propose and second me."

"Unfortunately, we cannot," Hawke said, sipping his brandy. "Membership committee members are not permitted to do that."

"Who says that?" bin Wazir said, the color rising in his cheeks now.

"The club rules say that," Hawke said coolly. "There's actually a whole book of them. Rather thick, to be quite honest."

"I've sent you a book listing the names of the entire membership," Brick said. "It's just a matter of your going through it, calling the members you know, and getting the process started."

"I didn't know any of the fucking members in the book," bin Wazir said, his voice rising. More than a few heads swiveled in his direction at that point and Alex realized he'd have to calm the fellow down and quickly.

"Please," Alex said. "You're taking this personally. It isn't. Everyone at Nell's has gone through the exact same process. Including Ambassador Kelly and myself. You'll just have to be patient and get to know a sufficient number of members, that's all."

The man turned on Alex then and literally snarled. "And, Lord Hawke, how do I get to know the fucking members if I'm not allowed inside the fucking club? Let's cut this bullshit, all right? How much? Give me a goddamn number. I'll write you a fucking check and—"

Barnham, the maître d', had appeared by bin Wazir's side. He bent and looked the man in the eye and said quietly but firmly, "Sir, your behavior is inappropriate in this establishment. Either lower your voice and clean up your language or you will be asked to leave."

"Fuck you," bin Wazir barked at Barnham, and turned away from him. His eyes were blazing and looked back and forth to Hawke and Kelly, who stared back at him implacably.

"You guys think you can fuck with me? Nobody fucks with me. The arrogance of you Americans and Brits! My people were inventing mathematics when you people were still rubbing fucking sticks together. I'll make you bastards pay for this, that I can guarantee you! I will—"

"Mr. bin Wazir," Barnham said, "you are no longer welcome in this establishment. These two gentlemen will escort you to the door." Two burly waiters had arrived and by now all conversation in the room had ceased and all eyes were riveted on the scene at the corner table.

Bin Wazir got to his feet, furiously wiping his mouth with his napkin, which he then threw to the floor. "If they touch me, they're dead," he said, flecks of spittle at the corners of his mouth. And with that he gripped the edge of the table and upended it, sending all the china and silverware flying, and a large snifter full of brandy into Alex Hawke's lap.

Hawke looked at the enraged man evenly and, trying to keep his voice down, said, "I would say the odds of your getting past the Nell's admissions committee at this point are decidedly slim, Mr. bin Wazir."

This brought forth a great deal of chuckling from the surrounding tables. For a moment, Hawke thought the man might actually go for his jugular but he wisely decided to simply turn on his heel and storm out of the Grill Room, pushing and shoving all and sundry out of his path.

The waiters already had the table back in place and were bringing a fresh coffee service and liqueurs. After apologizing profusely to the staff and the other diners, Brick turned to Alex and said, "I'm sorry to have dragged you into this nightmare, Alex. Really, I am."

"Good God," Pendleton said, "I'm the one who should be apologizing. The whole mess is on me. I'll go find the hotel manager and see if I can't clean it up somehow."

"I'm the one who invited Hawke, remember?" Kelly said, as Pendleton got up from the table.

"Don't be ridiculous, old Brick. You either, Sonny. Most fun I've had in months."

Half an hour later, having laughed the whole thing off over a few stiff whiskies courtesy of Duckworth at the bar, Hawke and Kelly went outside, looking for the ambassador's driver. A few taxis stood waiting in Carlos Place, but the embassy car was not there.

"Where in the world's my car?" Brick asked one of the doormen.

"Gentleman came flying out about half hour ago, sir. Quite upset he was, too. Before I could stop him, he climbed into the back of your car, said something to your driver, and off they went. Thought it was a bit odd, but—"

"Unbelievable," Brick said. "Lunacy."

"He pulled a gun on him, Brick," Hawke whispered. "It's the only answer."

"Shall I call a cab for you gentlemen?"

"We'll find one, thank you," Hawke said. It was still spitting rain but he needed a little fresh air.

"I've got to call my DSS guys, Alex," Kelly said as the two men turned into Mount Street. "I think this guy is seriously dangerous."

"Here. Use my mobile."

They hadn't traveled more than halfway up the empty block when a giant black man leaped out of the shadows from behind them. He grabbed a stunned Kelly by the collar of his jacket and ripped the cell phone out of his hand. Brick whirled, his fist already cocked, and threw a vicious roundhouse punch. It was deflected and a head-butt from the giant sent a stunned Kelly sprawling to the pavement. Then the monstrous fellow turned his brutal attentions on Hawke.

"I would say we could go somewhere and discuss this like gentlemen," Hawke said, "but you've made the stupid mistake of attacking a friend of mine."

The thug grunted and made a move towards Hawke. Alex was set, and he stepped inside it. He chopped the flat edge of his right hand across the man's throat and drove the compressed fingers of his left hand up under the sternum. A shockwave rippled up both of Hawke's arms. He might as well have attacked the statue of Roosevelt in nearby Grosvenor Square.

There was iron in the man's bones.

His efforts earned him no more than a grunt from the great box-like man and suddenly he was in a deathly embrace, the huge black arms enfolding him, lifting him. He could feel a hot pain as his ribs were compressed by the two human bands of iron encircling him. His arms pinioned and on fire, his entire upper body useless, Hawke's racing mind surveyed his enemy's anatomy, ticking off the possible vulnerabilities in milliseconds.

Kidneys? Groin? No. He was locked in a death vise which gave his own knees and feet no good angle. He felt the air going out of him. A familiar blackness laced with red was encroaching upon his conscious mind. He'd been in this place many times and knew automatically that he was out of time. It would be a near thing. He felt hot snorts from the giant's nostrils as the man added crushing pressure, preparatory to killing him. Very hot breath against his face? Where? On his forehead. Yes. In a single, violent motion, Hawke whipped his head back, then forward, smashing the top of his skull against the man's nose. There was a satisfying crunch of small bones and Hawke's face was instantly drenched in a spray of the man's hot blood.

The iron grip eased momentarily, and Alex collapsed to the pavement. Shaking his head, panting through clenched teeth, and trying to clear out the black veil, Hawke got to his hands and knees. He was nothing but a furious animal now, unthinking and bent on terrible vengeance. He was getting to his feet, eyeing his adversary through mists of pain, when the vicious blow of a steel-capped shoe caught his ribcage, splintering three ribs and propelling Alex Hawke into the gutter.

"Ar kill you," the giant said, speaking for the first time, his own voice garbled with blood and pain. Alex lifted his head and looked up at the towering figure with the blood pouring from his smashed nose. He struggled to rise, breathing deeply, summoning reserves of strength he knew had to be there. Kelly still wasn't moving. He lay against a lamppost at a grotesque angle. Unconscious, one could only hope.

"On the contrary," Hawke said through gritted teeth, "I read my horoscope this morning. Today's going to be the best day of my life."

Hawke staggered to his feet, ignoring the searing fire in his right side, and charged from a low crouch. He stayed low, feinting left and right before diving, and, then, lunging to his full extent, he hurled himself with all the force left in him directly at the man's knees.

Ligaments tore, cartilage ripped, and the giant bellowed in rage. But he did not go down. His face a mask of bloody fury, his coal eyes suffused with a red glow, he stooped and swung a great looping blow at Hawke's head.

But Alex managed to scramble and roll away and was on his feet again, dodging and feinting, lunging forward to deliver slashing body blows with the edges of his hands, then springing back desperate for another opening. That's when he saw the giant reach into the folds of his robe and withdraw a heavy flat blade from his waistband. Holding the hilt in two hands, the enraged monster advanced towards Alex, swinging his whistling sword like a scythe.

The first thrust flicked Hawke's ribs, drawing blood. The next one Alex almost dodged, but he was a second late. The flat of the blade caught his left temple squarely. He staggered, willing himself to stay on his feet despite the roaring sound of blood pounding inside his head. The giant advanced, the blade poised above him, clearly meaning to split Hawke in half. Alex had other ideas. He managed to get his right hand up just as the stubby machete descended.

Six long weeks worth of recuperation later, Tippu Tip was released from St. Thomas's Hospital. He had suffered a broken nose, a crushed sternum, a splintered clavicle, three fractured fingers, and two broken legs. In addition, his right ear had been torn off, but had been, somewhat successfully, reattached.

And Alex Hawke never did get round to sending him a get-well card.

CHAPTER SEVENTEEN

The Emirate

There were a hundred eyes in the rocky pass, and bin Wazir could feel every one of them. His frozen caravan approached, then finally staggered to a halt at the outer walls of the fortress. The ancient white stone walls, some thirty feet thick, rose to a height of over sixty. Attila had taken this fortress once and was the only one who'd lived to tell the tale.

The White Palace.

Within minutes, the four sumo giants had unlashed and removed the ebony chaise from between the exhausted beasts. As bin Wazir was being lowered to the ground, Tippu went forward to the heavily armed sentries to announce their arrival. Such an announcement of the obvious was ridiculous but customary. When one visited the Emir, one adhered to custom.

The penalties for noncompliance were severe. Eyes gouged out, the living burial, the swift loss of hands and feet—these were only a few of the Emir's ways of keeping order and control within the walls of his fortress and among the ranks of agents and sleepers flung to every corner of the earth. The cage was reserved for more serious breaches of decorum.

Snay bin Wazir would enter the gates in a simple

black lacquer chair. It wouldn't do for the Emir to see his elegant ebony sedan, or even the magnificent robes of snow leopard that bin Wazir now removed to reveal a simple black burnoose. The Emir knew of bin Wazir's sumptuous and exotic tastes, but it would be the height of suicidal stupidity to remind him.

There was a grinding of steel on steel as the massive gates began retracting within the walls. The blizzard had abated somewhat and bin Wazir raised his eyes to the top of the wall, looking up at the sentries looking down at him. They knew who he was but it didn't stop them from training their weapons on him. This was the Emir's standard welcoming committee. Heavily armed men, largely unseen, would be watching every move he made until his caravan was once more outside these walls and the gates closed behind him.

But now they were standing inside one of the most closely guarded, highly fortified, and impenetrable places on earth. The vast white marble and stone complex, regularly swept clean of snow, contained a warren of small roads and paths leading to the various buildings, homes, shops, and military facilities within its walls.

And, buried deep beneath the fortress, a labyrinth of massive, bombproof bunkers. The deepest was said to be impervious to all but a direct nuclear blast.

The four sumos and Tippu Tip were subjected to a total body search. The Japanese had been forewarned and remained sublimely indifferent to what would normally be an intolerable degradation. The Pasha's five men would be led to a garrison where they would be fed and housed for the night. The Pasha would meet alone with the Emir in the residence. A small sleeping chamber would then be provided for him until, hopefully, his party departed at dawn with their heads intact.

The camel drivers and camel boys took the mounts off to be fed and stabled, and bin Wazir found himself alone, ignored, and somewhat wobbly, leaning on his stout walking stick just inside the gates. A minute later, a group of six imperial guards, tall bearded men in identical white robes and turbans, approached him, bowed slightly, then separated to provide a space for him in the center of their formation. They turned and marched him up the main steps of the residence and through the arched entrance, then disappeared.

He stood alone, waiting in a massive empty chamber of pure white marble, keenly aware of the ascetic quality of the Emir's residence. There was no trace of decoration, no hint of luxury within these walls, and bin Wazir knew this was true throughout the entire fortress. It was said the simple purity of the white stone was but a shining outward reflection of the Emir's soul itself.

Musing upon what this surely said about his own soul, he was startled by the appearance of a tiny man wearing the familiar yellow robe and a black turban. This was Benazir, the wizened personal servant of the Emir.

"Allah be praised, you've made it safely," Benazir said, his hands clasped together before his small, wrinkled face. "Follow this way, please. His Eminence the Emir is with his orchids. He has been told of your arrival."

Bin Wazir followed the little elf through endless marble halls and passageways until they came to the gardens. Benazir placed his hand upon a towering wall of glass and it instantly slid down into the floor. The thick air was wet, steamy and so redolent of blooming orchids as to almost stagger the still unthawed Snay bin Wazir.

The Emir's White Palace had nearly two acres under glass.

Snay, who had no knowledge of botany, was passing through some of the most exotic species of flora gathered in one place on the planet. The glass walls and roof were heavily misted and fat drops of moisture splashed down on the plants. The light inside was greenish and unreal, like light filtered through a vast aquarium. Snay did his best to keep up with Benazir, but was continually smacked in the face with sodden leaves.

They found the Emir seated on one of two stone benches in the middle of a small oval space paved with white stone. This small garden was overhung with lovely white blossoms, all seeming to be of the same species of orchid. Songbirds and butterflies flitted about in abundant profusion.

Benazir and the visitor dropped immediately to their knees in deference and bent forward, their foreheads touching the cool white marble, slick with moisture.

"Dendrobians," the Emir said softly in his sing-song voice, delicately stroking a blossom. "You may rise. Be seated and enjoy them in silence for a few moments, Snay. When I have finished conversing with them, you shall have my undivided attention."

Snay gratefully collapsed his huge frame on the bench opposite. He breathed deeply, and took this time to study the Emir, looking for clues as to his present mood and disposition.

The Emir was tall and wraithlike beneath his flowing white robes. His beatific face was framed with curls of snow-white hair and a full white beard lay upon his chest. Snay bin Wazir had never seen such physical grace in another human. His long, delicate white fingers caressing the orchids reminded Snay bin Wazir of those of the harpist he'd hired five years earlier to play in the lobby of Beechum's. But then—

"It has been some time since your last visit," the Emir said, finally turning his powerful dark eyes on bin Wazir. "You have grown most notably of girth."

"I am most sorry, Excellency, but—"

The Emir held up a hand to silence him. Bin Wazir shifted uncomfortably under his gaze. The Emir had hard black eyes and, once he pinned you with them, their force was unshakable.

"It was not a rebuke," the old man said, in his papery whispered voice, "it was a statement of fact. Facts, not feelings, interest the Emir this day. You have brought some with you? Facts?"

"Indeed, Excellency," bin Wazir said. "I have much news that I pray will please you, King who is Most High."

"You are making progress in our Holy War against the infidels? Our assassins have some successes? Speak! I desire every detail. Every word about my beautiful *hashishiyyun*."

The word *assassin* has its origins in the bowl of the hashish pipe. Derived from the ancient Arabian political concept of *hashishiyyun*, originally, the word was derogatory, meaning "hashish taker." Over centuries, it had evolved to connote a captive harem of seductive assassins, kept faithful and ever more dependent by the constant supply of hashish. The sweet scent of the potent hemp, the lush surroundings of the lord's luxuriant gardens, and the lure of willing love slaves all served to keep a ready supply of seductive and resourceful killers on hand. All eager to please their revered provider.

"Yes, Excellency," bin Wazir said, risking a smile for the first time. It looked as if he might keep his head after all. "Your humble servant comes bearing gifts of the *hashishiyyun* that greatly exceed his pitiful powers of description."

"Yes?"

Snay bin Wazir then handed the Emir the leather satchel he'd been carrying inside his robes. The Emir delicately unfastened the silver buckle and eagerly peered inside. When he looked up, he rewarded Snay with a radiant smile. The dangerous journey through the bandit-infested mountains now seemed an infinitely small price to pay.

"Allah be praised," the Emir said. "You were able to obtain the visual records I demanded?"

"The stuff of many ecstatic hours, Most Revered One. I myself have viewed the videos countless times. My engineers have been working to improve the quality of the sound and pictures. Your summons came just as they completed their technical work. I pray you will not be disappointed."

The Emir clapped his hands smartly and Benazir appeared through a tangle of orchids. He took the satchel, bowing deeply.

"I shall watch these immediately following evening prayers. Make sure all is in readiness."

Benazir bowed deeply and disappeared the way he'd arrived, a soundless apparition.

"And your report?" the Emir asked with a level gaze.

"Four of the initial five components of Phase I have been successfully completed by the *hashishiyyun,* Excellency, as you will see with your own eyes this very night. Preparations for the final component of this phase are well under way."

"And, so far, what is the reaction of the Satanists?"

"As you predicted, oh Great Sire and Redeemer. Widespread panic in their diplomatic community. Confusion. Fear reigns where the arrogance of the nonbelievers once held sway."

"The Americans are even weaker than we thought."

"Wickedness breeds weakness, as you have told me many times, Emir."

The Emir's black eyes narrowed then and Snay realized, with a spike of terror, the stupidity of his remark. Wicked and weak. The Emir's precise definition of Snay himself. He had but a split second to recover and his mind was racing.

"You, the exemplar of all that is profane, dare, *dare* speak to me of wickedness and weakness?" the Emir said, and Snay bowed his head.

"I know that you live in a world on a plane far above my own, Most Revered Emir. But my belief in our global Holy War against the infidels gives me strength and faith beyond measure," Snay said.

"Your faith is beyond transparent as well as measure, Snay, son of Machmud. Were it not for my Yasmin's abiding love for you, I should never abide an abomination such as you. Ah, well, it is as it is. We will have our reckoning one day, you and I."

"When my earthly work is done, when my service to the Great Redeemer of our people is complete, then I shall accept my fate with honor, Excellency."

The Emir waved this familiar verbal flatulence away with a sharp gesture of his hand beneath his nose, glaring at the creature who, through some cruel joke, was husband to his cherished Yasmin.

"I will need confirmation from my agents in the field that the first phase has produced the desired effect. If all is as you say it is, and the fifth attack is perfectly executed, I am prepared to move at once to the second phase. Do you have a Phase II target in mind?"

"Most Revered One, I have had this target in mind for many, many years."

"And the *hashishiyyun* who will execute it?"

"She is well beyond sufficient, Excellency."

"Which one? Amaryllis? Aubergine, perhaps?"

"Ah, the Deadly Nightshade. No, sire. It is another, just as good. The Rose."

"Well, see to it. I am eager to move quickly. Tell me. The preparations for staging our ultimate jihad?"

"Well under way, Sire. Most assuredly."

"A suitable staging location is critical. Dr. Soong has precise scientific requirements."

"Indeed, Sire. I own a remote island hotel in Indonesia. Suva Island itself is accessible only by a jungle airstrip controlled by my forces. Soong and I believe it is perfect for our needs. The Angel of Death will fly from Suva Island."

The Emir held a pale pink butterfly up before his eyes and for a moment Snay thought he would pop it into his mouth and eat it, so pleased did he seem by what the Pasha had described.

"America's Day of Judgment," the Emir said. "I see it so very clearly now."

"Yes, Sire, I share your vision."

"Millions will die," the Emir whispered to the flower.

"No, Sire," Snay bin Wazir said softly. "Tens of millions will feel the shadow of the angel."

Without a word, the Emir returned his gaze to his lush white orchids, and Snay bin Wazir realized that he'd been dismissed. He laid a hand to the side of his head to reassure himself that it was still there and then he vanished quickly and silently into the Emir's gardens.

The Emir, alone once more with his beloved orchids, stroked the soft white blossoms and buried his nose amongst them, whispering to the flowers.

"All that is necessary for the triumph of good," he said, laughing softly at the perfect perversion of his own small joke, "is for evil men to do nothing."

CHAPTER EIGHTEEN

Penobscot Bay, Maine

"Good Lord," Alex Hawke heard Congreve say in his headphones, "what was that?" They'd encountered a patch of rough air climbing out and the little seaplane was bucking like a frisky bronco.

"Mere bumps in the road, Constable," Hawke said, grinning.

"Well, I don't see any bloody bumps," Ambrose said, peering down at Penobscot Bay out his starboard window, "and I certainly don't see any roads down there, although I dearly wish I were on one!"

"Nothing to fret about, old thing," Alex said. "It's just that there's more turbulence the closer you are to the surface. It will be smoother once we climb out and gain a little altitude."

"Hmm."

"At any rate, according to my charts here, there are no roads leading from Maine to Nantucket Island."

"It must be great fun to find oneself so amusing."

"It is, actually."

The famous detective closed his eyes, and attempted to lean back in his small seat and compose his hands, interlacing his fingers upon his sizeable belly. He was in heather tweeds, a three-piece suit; but, in a typical display of sartorial indifference, Ambrose was wearing a yellow and white striped shirt from Thomas Pink and an old pinkish-green madras bow tie he'd acquired long ago at Mr. Trimingham's shop on Front Street in Bermuda. All accented with a white silk scarf.

Alex Hawke banked the seaplane, carving a graceful arc into the dome of sky over the dark blue waters of the bay. His flight plan called for climbing initially to five thousand feet. He rechecked his compass and charts and set a southeasterly heading towards Nantucket Island. The sun was taking a peek over the eastern horizon, sending arrows of gold streaking across the dark bay and slanting through the deep Maine forests falling away beneath the silver plane.

Congreve was exhibiting his usual uneasiness with small aircraft. His situation was not helped by the fact that he'd consumed a fair amount of Irish whiskey in the cozy bar of the Dark Harbor Inn the night before. So he was suffering a mild hangover, he'd announced at breakfast that morning, and pointedly informed Alex that he would appreciate a smooth flight back to the island of Nantucket.

As long as Alex had known Congreve, the man would never admit to an actual fear of flying. He simply masked his jangled nerves and discomfort in a cloak of cranky irritability. Alex had long ago concluded that what bothered Ambrose most about going up in the sky with someone else was that it involved the total surrender of control. "I don't enjoy hurtling through space sealed in an aluminum tube," was the oft-heard quote.

"All I'm saying, Alex," Congreve now said, eyes still clenched shut, "is you designed the damn plane yourself. I've mentioned this to you before. I simply don't see why you couldn't have at least added an extra engine."

"Could have done, Constable. But the result would have been a somewhat less airworthy aircraft."

"What?" Congreve sputtered. He sat forward and looked at Alex. "You don't mean to say that an airplane with one engine is safer than one with two! Preposterous."

"I mean almost exactly that," Alex said, smiling over at him. "I know it's counterintuitive but it's true . . . in a way."

"Now I'm going to hear one of your infamously breezy explanations, am I not? I'm quite sure that, should we now be plunging into the sea, I'd be hearing a most complete scientific explanation of the deadly malfunction at fault in my demise."

"Should we lose *Kittyhawke*'s single engine, Constable," Alex said patiently, "we would have the ability to simply glide until we found a suitable landing spot. The plane would respond perfectly normally to all controls."

"Ridiculous," Congreve sniffed, jamming his unlit pipe between his teeth. "If you had a second engine we shouldn't have to 'glide,' as you put it, at all. We should simply keep flying on the second engine until we reached our destination."

"Quite right, except for the fact of torque," Alex said. "A twin-engine craft loses power on one side, and the force of torque produced by the remaining engine wants to flip the plane over on its back. Quite dicey, actually. Responsible for many fatal crashes."

"Can we talk about something else?"

"Certainly. I assumed you were interested in the aeronautics of—"

"Fatal crashes? Please."

"Here's an idea, old thing. Why don't you fly the plane?"

"What?"

"I'm quite serious. I think it would be good for you. Here, I'm turning it over to you. You're flying. You have control."

Alex took his hand off the Y-shaped yoke between them. "Now, you take the stick and say, 'I have control.'"

"Are you mad?"

"Better take the wheel, Constable. Plane will fly itself for a while, but watch what you're doing . . ."

Ambrose regarded him for a long moment and then put his hand gingerly on the yoke.

"You're supposed to say, 'I have the airplane,'" Alex said. "So there's no confusion, you see."

"All right, then, I have the airplane," Ambrose said and hauled back sharply on the yoke. "Let's take her up."

"Easy, watch your airspeed," Hawke said. "You don't want to stall."

"Meaning what?"

"Meaning we lose lift, go into an uncontrolled downward spiral, excessive speed rips the wings off, and we plunge screaming into the ocean. Unless, of course, you use the rudder to stabilize the plane, regain control. Then, we climb once more into the wild blue yonder and live happily ever after."

"What needs to happen now?" Congreve asked, and Alex saw that perhaps he was beginning to enjoy himself.

"Your nose needs to come down before you stall us out."

"Ah. So I just push this thingy forward?"

"Yes. Easy on the thingy, however. These are subtle adjustments, requiring a light touch. Just ease the nose down smoothly. I'll throttle back a bit . . . good . . . right there is quite good. Steady. I'll adjust the elevators and the ailerons for trim. Give me the wheel a tick. Turn left, we bank left, see? So, I correct and level her out. And use the rudder for yaw."

"Rudder? Where the hell's the rudder?"

"Those foot pedals you see in your footwell. I have a set as well. Right and left rudder pedals. I'll deal with those. Okay. She's trimmed. Now, we just use throttle to change altitude. Watch this. Revs up, we go up. Revs down, we go down. Quite simple, this airplane. Just like a see-saw that moves in three axes."

"It is, actually, isn't it?" Congreve said, a broad smile on his face as he toyed gently with the plane's attitude. "I never realized."

Hawke turned and stared at his lifelong friend, a warm smile lighting up his eyes. The man simply never failed to startle and amaze. Despite his little snips and snaps and idiosyncrasies, the man had no end of courage and displayed sangfroid under any circumstance. Like Churchill himself, the man could wander through a hail of bullets with a bemused smile on his face. Hell, Hawke had seen him do it and more than once. Subsequently, he would quote Winston, saying, "Nothing in life is so exhilarating as to be shot at without result."

"Well, Captain Congreve, your copilot is going to take a little nap," Hawke said. "See the horizon line? Just keep our wings level with that. Left and right stick controls the ailerons, remember. Watch your airspeed and the rev counter dials. There, and there. See them?"

"Yes, yes."

"What's our current RPM?" Alex asked, tapping the dial. Congreve leaned forward and squinted at it.

"Two thousand?"

"Good. There's the throttle. Keep it that way. There's the compass. Our course, as you see, is one-two-thirteen. Try to stay on that heading. One final navigation tip: keep the Atlantic on your left and you can't go wrong. Nighty-night. Wake me just before landing. I don't think you're quite ready for that bit yet."

"You're quite serious? Dozing off?"

"No need to worry. In the event of an emergency, the cheeks of your bum will act as a flotation device. G'night, all."

Hawke leaned back and closed his eyes, a broad smile on his face. He should have given this flying lesson years ago. Congreve, despite appearances, had the bottle for just about anything he ultimately had to face head on and he always had. It was the secret of his rise to the very top ranks of Scotland Yard and—

At that moment, the airplane angled down slightly and began a right-hand spiral.

"Alex!" Congreve shouted. "I didn't touch a thing!"

Hawke sat bolt upright, grabbed the wheel and pushed hard left to correct the right-handed spin. The control felt far too loose in his hand. Too much give. Yes. Something definitely wrong with the ailerons, the hinged flaps on the trailing edges of the wings that controlled banking or rolling.

"Problem with the aileron cable," Alex said, mov-

ing the yoke loosely left and right and leaning across
Ambrose's chest to check the starboard aileron.
"Christ, barely responding."

"What did I do?"

"Nothing. Mechanical problem."

"A-ha. One of those. Beastly luck."

"Hold on to your hat, Constable!" he shouted. "I'll
go see what the matter is."

Alex quickly unbuckled his harness, climbed out of
the left-hand seat, and headed aft. The aileron control
cables were just under the metal floor panels stretching
back to the tail. Just here was the connection to the
ailerons—all he had to do was pry up the floor panel and
see what the devil—

Good Christ, this section of cable had parted
almost completely! Only a few strands remained intact.
Bloody thing looked as if it had been cut, sawn
through, leaving just enough intact to make the sabotage unnoticeable until after they were airborne.
Thank God he'd caught it in time. Now, if he could figure a way to jury-rig something, they just might be able
to limp home.

"Everything all right back there?" Ambrose shouted
over his shoulder.

"Wish I could feather-bed you, old thing. But, no,
everything's not quite right back here. Just keep her flying."

Someone was trying to kill him. Someone who had
seen him with Patterson at Dark Harbor. Or, someone
with prior knowledge that he would be there. If
Patterson was right, this could just be the work of the
Dog. But, God knows, there were plenty of suspects
available on Congreve's endless lists.

He kept tools and lengths of cable stowed in a nearby bin. He was reaching for them when the plane's angle of descent increased noticeably. "Ambrose," he shouted over the engine's roar. "Keep her nose up! Only fore and aft movement of the wheel. No ailerons at all until I can jury-rig something up back here!"

"Anything else I can do?" Ambrose shouted back over his shoulder. He'd pulled back on the wheel and they were climbing again.

"Best touch wood, old thing, and quickly."

"I don't see any."

"Your forehead should do it."

"Alex, please."

"Remember the old Yank expression 'a wing and a prayer'?" Alex said, grinning. "I'll work on the wing bit and you work on the prayer!"

Hawke grabbed wire, cable, wrenches and pliers and turned his attention back to the ailerons. At that moment, he was shocked to see the last strands of wound cable part with a loud bang. The plane made a stomach-lurching bank to starboard.

"Bleeding hell, Alex!" he heard Congreve yell, the panic in his voice palpable. "Are we going down?" Congreve turned around in his seat, his face deathly white. As he twisted towards the rear of the plane, he pulled the wheel back with him, holding it in a death grip. *Kittyhawke* angled sharply upwards, sending Alex careening towards the tail.

The little plane shuddered and stalled. The sudden loss of airspeed now sent it rolling down into a violent right-hand spiral. The sickening rate of descent and the degree of spin meant the airplane was now only moments away from being completely out of control.

Any second now, speed could rip the wings from the fuselage. With no time to even scramble forward and take over, Alex instantly realized that Congreve himself would have to do it.

"Ambrose!" he shouted, keeping his voice as level and calm as possible under the circumstances. "Shove the wheel full forward! We need a steep dive to regain airspeed! Get her nose down! All right, good! Now. Those two pedals in your footwell! The rudders! I want you to stamp on the left one just as hard as Billy-be-damned! Do it right bloody now!"

"Aye, aye!" Ambrose shouted, and Alex saw the man lurch forward and left as he shoved the wheel forward and stomped on the left rudder pedal.

Alex half ran and half tumbled forward towards the cockpit, the plane now nosed over into a screaming dive. Full left rudder was all that would save them now. He jumped into the seat, startled by how far and how fast they'd descended. The blue sea was rushing up towards them. At this speed, they had maybe thirty seconds to live.

"I've got the plane," he said to Ambrose, his hand on the wheel and his left foot now nailed to his own left rudder pedal. The plane was responding to full left rudder, the spin had slowed, but they were running out of time and air and all he could see out the cockpit windows was spinning water.

"Good God, we've had it, man," Congreve said, and closed his eyes.

"Not . . . quite . . . yet, we haven't," Hawke said. Playing the two rudder pedals like some master pianist of the air, he neutralized the spin, got his wings level, and, by Christ, he still had a good five hundred feet of air left before they would hit the water at a hundred knots and disintegrate.

"Upsy-daisy," Congreve heard Hawke say cheerfully as he himself braced for his own imminent destruction.

Hawke now pulled back on the wheel in one easy fluid motion. The nose came up, the pontoons skimmed the wave tops of Nantucket Sound, and *Kittyhawke* was once again climbing into the blue.

"You can open your eyes now, Constable," Alex Hawke said, smiling at his mortified friend. "Dodged the bullet yet again, it seems."

CHAPTER NINETEEN

Rome

Francesca, standing in the dim pinkish light of the tiny lavatory, gripped the stainless steel basin and leaned into the mirror, studying the carmine gloss she'd just applied to her lips. There was a swaying motion and screeching sound as the train negotiated a curve. The Paris-Simplon Express was now rolling through Switzerland, high in the Alps, and a beautiful man was waiting for her in the lower berth of the moonlit compartment beyond the door.

She lifted her thin pale arms and ran her fingers through her thick blonde hair, inhaling the scent of Chanel 19 rising from the warmth of the cleft between her uplifted breasts. She was wearing a black negligee, Galliano, and it clung to her like a lover. She smiled at herself and closed her eyes for a moment, her lips parted, her long lashes brushing the swell of her cheeks as she composed herself for the scene she was about to play.

"Caro?" she said softly, pausing in the doorway so that he would see her body backlit by the pale pink light behind her.

"Come here," he said simply, his hoarse whisper barely audible over the metallic chatter of the wheels on the rails.

The small wood-paneled compartment of the Wagons-Lit sleeping car was lit only by the deep violet of the night-light above the door. Nick Hitchcock, her American lover, was lying on his stomach, chin propped in his upraised palms, gazing out the window as the blue moonlit landscape of snow-covered peaks hurried by. He rolled onto his back and stared at the impossibly beautiful figure framed by the doorway.

"Did you miss me, Nicky?"

She ran her hands down over her hips, adjusting the drape of black silk.

"God," he whispered. Even the sound of silk whispering across her body drove him mad.

"Why are you wearing pajamas, Nicky?" Francesca asked.

"I was cold."

"But it's so warm in here."

"It will be," Nick said, pulling back the covers and making room for her.

She padded across the carpeted compartment, taking only three or four small steps before she reached him. She sat on the edge of the fold-down berth and stroked his cheek. In the bluish-purple light, the small crescent of the scar on his cheekbone appeared luminous.

"So many scars, *caro,* for a doctor. Your patients, they cut you, *Dottore?*"

He smiled and stroked one silk covered breast, cupping his hand under it, feeling the weight.

"That's a physician, darling," Nick said. "I'm a physicist. A doctor of physics."

"But you are a spy, too, no?"

"We're both spies. We just don't know yet who's

spying for whom. That's why this honeymoon will be so interesting."

"Nicky, *caro,* is not a honeymoon, this trip. *Non sposato, mi amore,* we're not married."

"We're having the honeymoon first. Much more sensible."

Francesca laughed, leaning over to kiss him on the mouth, her heavy breasts resting softly upon his chest. It was a hard, brief kiss and when she felt his probing tongue she sat upright and turned her gaze to the window.

"You will never marry someone like me. But, *va bene,* it doesn't matter. I love you anyway. And, I love this old train. It doesn't go to the Orient, it's not an express, it doesn't matter. Still they call it the Orient Express."

"A long time ago, it went to Belgrade and Istanbul. It was the fastest way to get there from Paris."

"He knows everything, my darling *dottore pericoloso,*" she said, bending over to kiss him again. "Someday, Doctor Dangerous, when we are old and grey and have made all the love we can make, you will tell me the secrets of the universe?"

"I'll tell you one now," he said smiling up at her. "There's a lot more love out there than we can ever make. But, that doesn't mean we can't try."

His hand moved under the hem of her negligee, tracing his fingers along the warm skin of her inner thigh, desperate to touch her. She caught his wrist in a surprisingly strong grip and pulled his hand away. "No, *caro,* not yet," she said.

He reached up to pull her to him, but she pulled back, laughing. "No, Nicky, you must wait. I want to see all these scars you want to hide from me. I want to kiss every one and learn its secret. Then we make *l'amore*."

She unbuttoned his blue silk pajama top and ran her hands over the thick cords of his heavily muscled chest, her fingers pausing to entwine themselves in the thatch of curly dark hair that began at the base of his throat. Then her hands moved down over his taut belly, quickly undoing the strings and pulling the silk down over his thighs to his knees.

"Now," she said, surveying the pale landscape of skin, "no more secrets, Nicky."

"No secrets," he said as she pressed her lips to the long weal that began at his left shoulder and ended just below his left nipple.

"Tell me about this one," she said, her lips trailing along the length of angry scar.

"Well. That was a bad one, I'll tell you. An arrow got me," Nick Hitchcock said. "Cowboys and Indians, St. Louis, Missouri. Nineteen seventy-five. I was only ten years old when that Apache brave sneaked up and got the drop on me."

"And this one," she said, her lips traveling downwards across his hard, flat belly.

"Self-inflicted. I was up in the attic playing 'Doctor' with my cousin and she bet me I couldn't take out my own appendix."

"Liar," she said. She reached between his legs and gripped him hard in her fist. She bent her head to him and her tongue darted about, causing him to moan and arch upwards involuntarily. "What about this one? Right here on the tip? A naughty old girlfriend bit my Nicky?"

"Cub Scouts," Hitchcock said, his breathing rapid and shallow. "I was late putting on my uniform for a Cub pack meeting and caught myself in my zipper. And that one, darling, is the truth. Now, enough!"

"No, *caro*, not enough. Be still, I must do something."

He saw her hand disappear between her thighs and the breath caught in his throat.

"I have something for you," she said.

"Yes," he said, closing his eyes.

"It is not what you think," she said and he heard a distinct metallic click between her legs. What the—

She held up a small silver switchblade that gleamed in the violet light. "I keep this hidden inside me, Nicky, just for times like this."

"What? This is a joke, right? Some sick game?"

He twisted violently away, but she still had him gripped in the vise of her fist and now she squeezed cruelly enough to make him cry out.

"Nicky?" she said, her voice still warm and seductive.

He felt the cold sharp edge of the blade at the base of his scrotum. She stretched the skin of the sac out even further.

"No secrets, *Caro*," she said, "no more secrets . . ."

"Good God, are you mad? What is this?"

"Have you ever seen a human testicle?" she asked softly. "They pop out very easily, all shiny and pink. Attached by only one thin white tube. One snip of my little *coltello* is really all it takes."

"You are insane! Stop this! What do you want?" Hitchcock cried, his voice thick with fear, choking back the sick tide rising in his throat.

"I've already told you, Nicky. I want no more secrets."

A scream had already wholly formed in his mind and now he opened his mouth wide to give voice to it when she . . .

"Cut! Cut! Cut and print!" Vittorio de Pinta screamed and, leaping down from the boom crane of the big Panavision 35mm motion picture camera, he rushed to embrace her. "Francesca, my angel, this, it was brilliant! This was transcendent! *Magnifico!*"

The director clapped his hands as the sound stage lights came up on the Orient Express set. The entire crew burst into applause as Francesca gave her costar a perfunctory kiss on the forehead and rose to her feet, a broad smile on her beautiful face.

Vittorio, a tall, elegant man with soft brown eyes and shoulder-length white hair, turned to his crew and bowed deeply. The Italian film crew, some of whom had worked with de Pinta in early days, before he went to Hollywood, applauded wildly as the now-famous director spread his arms wide as if to embrace all of them. He began smacking his hands together at arm's length, clapping for his cast and crew. It had been a grueling twelve months. The shoot had taken them to locations around the world; from Washington to the Great Barrier Reef where they'd shot all the shark footage, to Hong Kong, Venice, and the Alps where the second unit had shot all the exteriors for the Orient Express sequence just completed.

And now, this final month at the old *Cinecittà* Studios in Rome shooting interiors for the completion of this latest and perhaps boldest of the Nick Hitchcock spy thrillers, *Body of Lies*. Back on the lot in

Culver City, it was the executive producer's fondest wish that the steamy love interest brought to the screen by this Italian bombshell would lift this pic above the wooden special effects–laden epics of the last few Nick Hitchcock spy thrillers.

It was also Vittorio's fondest wish. His career had been dead in the water ever since his bloated costume drama, *Too Much Too Soon,* had spun wildly out of control, late and over budget, and ended up released as a network Movie of the Week. *Body of Lies,* he knew, was his last shot, his *una ultima probabilità* as Francesca had called it.

"That's a wrap, ladies and gentlemen," Vittorio said, still applauding all the grips and gaffers up amidst the forest of klieg lights mounted high above on the studio catwalks. *"Grazie mille a tutto, mille grazie!"*

A small army of production assistants and caterers appeared, setting up craft services tables full of caviar and crab, carrying trays of glasses and magnums of cold champagne onto the Orient Express set. Vittorio splashed some into a glass, first for Francesca and then one for superstar Ian Flynn, the ruggedly handsome Irish actor who played Nick Hitchcock, currently busy pulling his pajama bottoms up, eager to hide the fact that he had not much to hide.

Raising his own glass to the assembled, the director said, "To the legendary Ian, brilliant as always, for a magnificent performance! And, to our newest Hitchcock girl, the talented and beauteous *Signorina* Francesca d'Agnelli!"

She raised her glass, then tipped it back and downed it quickly. She had a plane to catch.

*   *   *

Some eight hours later, Francesca heard a light tapping on the cabin door. She sat up in bed in the darkness, heard a dull roaring noise and wondered where she was. The door cracked open and she saw a girl framed in the soft light from the corridor. The girl was wearing a snow-white apron over a black dress. The uniform of all the female staff aboard the Pasha's private 747.

"*Signorina* d'Agnelli?" It was the perky English one named Fiona.

"*Sì?*" she said, sitting up and rubbing sleep from her eyes. "*Che cosa,* Fiona?"

"So sorry to disturb you, *Signorina,* but First Officer Adare in the cockpit informs me we will be landing in approximately one hour. I thought perhaps you might like some breakfast? Some time to freshen up?"

"*Sì,* some tea and toast, *e il bagno, per favore.*" The girl pulled the door closed and Francesca lay back against the pillows. A hot bath. Delicious.

The Pasha had been extremely generous, she thought, sending his plane to Rome for her as soon as the production had shut down. It was the first time he'd done it. He was pleased with her. Her last assignment had been carried out flawlessly. Pleased, his generosity knew no bounds. But then, neither did his brutality when you incurred his displeasure.

It was one of the reasons she was so strangely attracted to the man, despite his recent increase in belt size. She'd always had a taste for the unusual.

She rose from her bed and padded across the thick carpet to the marble-clad bathroom. She twisted the gold spigots, and the tub began filling with water. She poured oils and salts and flower petals from the crystal containers and bowls into the steaming water. She smiled. Air Pasha was certainly an upgrade over first class on Alitalia.

Two staff girls appeared with a tea tray and a stack of luxurious white towels.

"Grazie," Francesca said, as the pretty blonde one poured her a cup of herbal tea while the other one tested the water temperature, then turned off the golden spigots. Francesca nodded and smiled, clearly waiting for them to leave. They bowed, and were gone.

Dropping her robe to the floor, she caught herself smiling in the mirror; she was still aglow with champagne from the wrap party and in the limo on the way to the airport. It was an amusing distraction being a movie star. It allowed her to move freely about the globe, come into contact with whomever she wished, exert her will. No one in this world, she'd learned, was fully immune to the star-fucker syndrome.

But this particular star fucked back.

She raised her right foot up onto the wide green marble lip of the deep tub. Using her right hand, she reached into the curly blonde thatch between her legs and removed the porcelain sheath and the dagger it contained. She held it up admiringly. How she would have enjoyed using her *piccolo coltello,* her little knife, on that arrogant Hitchcock. The Irish prick.

An imaginary tabloid headline floated across her mind as she stepped into the steaming hot water.

"Hitchcockless."

CHAPTER TWENTY

Nantucket Island

Some four hours after their brush with death, Hawke and Ambrose were joined by Stokely and Sutherland in *Blackhawke*'s library, a fire going against the late June chill. Hawke was sitting cross-legged on the floor before the fire, his parrot Sniper perched on his shoulder. Feeding the feisty bird pistachio nuts from a bowl he held in his lap, he seemed lost in his thoughts.

Oh nuts! Damright! Sniper shrieked, and Hawke gave the old girl a few more. Congreve was regaling everyone with the tale of the perilous flight, delighted to recount the chilling death spiral, how they'd been near as dammit to crashing into the sea when Ambrose himself had jammed down the left rudder pedal and put the plane into a left-handed nose dive that stabilized the aircraft.

"Quite remarkable, Chief," Sutherland said, "considering your complete lack of flying experience."

"How did Holmes himself put it?" Ambrose asked, puffing away. "'I am the most incurably lazy devil who ever stood in shoe leather, but when the fit is on me, I can be spry enough at times.'" The man was clearly still flying high, even after his near-disastrous flying lesson. Alex smiled at this, but his mind was elsewhere.

His plane had been moored at the end of the Slades' dock in Dark Harbor all night. It had never occurred to Alex to post a guard, so somebody had all the time in the world to hack away at the aileron cable. And there was something else nagging at his memory. He remembered what Chief Ellen Ainslie had said about the murderous babysitter: *"Father's a mechanic . . . over to the airport."*

Texas Patterson needed to know that at least one member of the Adjelis family had stuck around Dark Harbor long enough to sabotage Hawke's airplane. Patterson was catching a ride on a Coast Guard chopper and was scheduled to arrive shortly for a meeting aboard *Blackhawke*. His boss, Secretary of State de los Reyes, had already asked for Alex's help. Now, Tex was coming down to seal the deal.

As always, Alex had told Conch on the phone that morning, he'd do whatever he could. He'd just have to postpone recharging his batteries until the thing was over. Hell, he said, as the old American expression had it, you can sleep when you're dead.

Congreve was quietly bringing Sutherland and Stokely up to speed on the recent events in Maine when Pelham wafted in with the tea service. He set the silver salver down on a velvet ottoman next to Alex. Alex noticed a small black velvet box on the tray beside his china cup.

"This is a bit sudden, isn't it, old boy?" Hawke said to Pelham, picking up the velvet box. "I mean, we hardly know each other."

Pelham smiled, said nothing, and withdrew.

"What on earth's wrong with him?" Alex asked, as Pelham pulled the door closed after him.

"Embarrassed is all. Something the boy meant to give you a long time ago, Boss," Stoke said. "Better open it."

"Really?" Alex said. "How odd."

He opened the box and saw the gold medallion and chain. He lifted it out and dangled it before his eyes. "Unbelievable," Hawke said. "My St. George's medal. Stoke, you remember. That night in Cuba. That guard who—"

"Stuck his knife in your neck and cut the chain. Yeah, I remember that."

"How did Pelham come by it after all these years?"

"Some Spanish-sounding guy apparently showed up with it on your doorstep late one night and told Pelham to give it to you. Boy stuck it somewhere and plain forgot all about it. He feels bad 'cause then you'd have had a heads-up. About somebody being on your case."

"Most unfortunate," Hawke said, examining the medal. "His memory is less than . . ."

"He'll be all right," Stoke said, seeing Hawke's wan expression.

"My mother gave me this," Hawke said, slipping it over his head, "the day before she died." He cut his eyes away, pretending to study a picture on the wall, a small marine painting by James Buttersworth.

"Yeah. That's another reason why Pelham feels bad, boss," Stoke said.

"Your notion that Vicky's murderer may be Cuban was spot on, Alex," Sutherland said. "We have considerable evidence pointing that way."

"Vicky's murderer," Hawke said, getting to his feet. He threw another log on the fire, sending a shower of sparks shooting up the chimney, and then sank into one of the armchairs near the hearth. His face ashen, he looked like someone had just taken a razor to the carefully stitched sutures of his heart. "Tell me," he said. "Tell me what's happened," Hawke said softly.

"Two things, sir," replied Sutherland. "The cigar stub found at the base of the tree was Cuban. Domestic. Never sold for export."

"Bought in Cuba," said Alex. "Go on."

"Two," Sutherland continued. "Stokely determined the murder weapon left at the scene was Russian, but the scope was American. Very limited production. U.S. armed forces and law enforcement account for all of them. One such scope was stolen six weeks ago in Miami."

"Good work, Stoke," Alex said.

"Scope belonged to a murdered Dade County SWAT guy," Stoke said. "Serial number on the stolen scope matches our murder weapon. Last thing, that guy who delivered your medallion? Pelham got a look at his eyes that night. Says he ain't got no color in them."

"Scissorhands," Hawke said, anger flaring up in his eyes. "The bloody bastard in Cuba. The one who interrogated Vicky after she was abducted. What was his name, Stokely?"

"Rodrigo del Rio."

"Del Rio. Right. Castro's former Chief of State Security, until the coup."

"That's the one. The man with no eyes, boss," Stoke said. "Just may be we got our shooter."

"Not yet we don't. But we will."

"I got an idea," Stoke said. "If he's slipped back into

Cuba, I know someone who would just love to tack his testicles to a palm tree. And that someone owes me a favor."

"Who, Stoke?"

"Fidel damn Castro, that's who. The rebel generals was fixing to murder his tired old Communist ass, you remember, and I got him out of there. *El Jefe* himself sent me this goddamn medal round my neck."

"Yes, yes," Hawke said. "The irony of your saving the skin of one of the last great Communist dictators on earth has not been lost upon me."

"Well, hell, Alex, what was I s'posed to do? I know an evil dictator when I see one. But, them drug dealers were going to shoot that sick old fool just lying there in his bed. Cop instinct took over."

"Don't get defensive, Stoke. Terrible as he is, Fidel was far and away the lesser of two evils. The thugs who tried to overthrow him would have made the Saddam-era Baghdad or Kim's Pyongang look like Disneyworld."

"You right, Boss."

"Scissorhands may well be back in Cuba, Stoke," Alex said, "but Cuba's a dangerous place for a high-ranking security officer who went with the losing side. We should start in south Florida, I think. If I were Cuban and on the run, that's where I'd go. Calle Ocho. Little Havana. Great place to hide, Miami."

"And where that gun sight was stolen," Stoke said.

"At the very least, it would be a good place to begin looking for this fellow," Hawke said. "Then, the islands."

"Ain't no place the man can hide from me, Boss," Stoke said. "Look here, you got your hands full with these State Department assassinations. Why don't you just let me and Ross go find this shithead by our own-selves?"

"I don't let other men shoot my foxes, Stoke," Hawke said quietly.

Hawke lowered his head and rubbed both eyes with the tips of his fingers. He was, Stoke knew, torn in half. Vicky was gone and wasn't coming back. Hawke was a man with a vengeful spirit, and the urge to avenge his bride's vicious murder was powerful. Tearing him apart. But so was his urge to do all in his power to help his old friend Conch.

In the end, the professional warrior inside him won. Out there somewhere was the man who had killed his beautiful bride. Perhaps the same man who had also just come very close to killing him. And Congreve. But that was personal. Another psychopath was targeting America's diplomatic corps. And making the world far less stable in the doing. Perhaps the two were one and the same. Perhaps not.

A few moments later, Hawke looked up and stared hard at Stokely, then, finally, fixed his gaze on Sutherland. Ross could see that he'd made a decision.

"There is procedure, isn't there, Ross?"

"Indeed there is, sir."

"Shouldn't you call your superiors at the Yard about this?" Alex asked. "You still officially report there, and they've got jurisdiction in this case." Sutherland looked mutely at Hawke. It was the question he'd expected and one he did not want to answer.

"Galling, isn't it, sir?" Sutherland managed.

"I'll answer that one," Congreve said. "The Yard have told Ross and me to stay completely away from this thing, Alex. Completely." As Sutherland nodded his head in affirmation, Ambrose added, "By all reports, they've not made much headway so far."

"Are you going, Ambrose? To Florida, I mean."

"I'd recommend sending Ross and Stokely, Alex. I might be of more help in this other matter." Hawke nodded assent.

"Good. Go find this son of a bitch, Stoke. You and Ross. Miami, Jamaica, Cuba, wherever the hell he is," Hawke said. "Don't kill him unless you have to. Bring him to me. I'd very much like a word with him before he gets turned over to the Yard. A private word."

"Yeah," Stoke said. "We can do that."

"I'm going up on deck," Hawke said. "I need some bloody air."

CHAPTER TWENTY-ONE

Nantucket Island

Alex Hawke, wearing a faded grey Royal Navy T-shirt and a pair of swimming trunks, was up on deck again in the wee hours, his faithful parrot Sniper riding easily on his left shoulder. He had a pocketful of Cheezbits, one of Sniper's favorite late-night snacks.

He still needed air. Couldn't seem to get enough of the stuff.

A fresh breeze had come up just after midnight and blown most of the fog offshore. A fingernail moon, little more than a sliver of ivory, hung above the horizon in a dark blue sky; there were a few stars, white as bone.

Cheeeez-us! Cheez-us! Sniper squawked, and Hawke popped another tidbit into the air. The parrot snagged it with her sharp beak and fluttered her wings in appreciation.

"Good bird, Sniper," Hawke said. Slushy, the head chef down in the galley, had secretly taught the caviar and cheese–loving bird to say *"Cheez-us"* and Alex had been unable to cure her of the mildly sacrilegious new habit.

The recent cold front that had brought heavy rains to the Cape, Martha's Vineyard, and the island of

Nantucket had now gravitated northeast out over the North Atlantic. In its wake, only wispy remnants of misty vapor snaking through the silent streets of old Nantucket Town and wafting through dark forests of sailboat masts in the dead-quiet harbor.

The remaining heavy air left every surface cool and damp, and the broad teak decks of *Blackhawke* were slippery underfoot. She was anchored out in open water, a good distance from the harbor entrance as a security measure. Tom Quick wanted a lot of empty water around his boat at a time like this. Room to maneuver or get under way if she was threatened in any way. There wasn't another yacht within half a mile of her anchorage out here.

The sharp tang of the breeze coming off the ocean was strong and antiseptic; it felt good as Alex filled his lungs with it. In the owner's stateroom on the deck just below, he had tossed in his bed for hours, but any notion of sleep he'd had this night was clearly just a dream. Padding across the varnished floorboards to the head, he'd opened the medicine chest and reached for the slim orange vial of a small miracle pill called Ambien.

Alex Hawke's personal physician, Dr. Kenneth Beer, had prescribed the sedative when Alex had seen him immediately after Vicky's funeral in Louisiana. He'd been at his wit's end over lack of sleep and had decided not to cure it with spirits as was his old custom. Beer was forever trying to convince him that his lifestyle was hardly befitting his profession. Hawke, of course, had never told Ken what he did for a living, but his doctor had taken enough lead out of him to hazard a guess. Hawke's body was a living testament to Beer's surgical talents.

"Hell, Hawke, you're only as good as your last scar," Ken would say, stitching him up and sending him on his way.

Ten milligrams would put him out, and he'd come to depend on this nightly escape hatch. Beer had assured him it wasn't habit-forming, but Hawke wondered. Freedom from pain of the magnitude he'd been suffering was clearly addictive. He'd replaced the plastic cap without removing a pill, stepped into his still-damp bathing suit and pulled a T-shirt over his head, hoping some fresh air might calm the troubled waters.

He knew he had things to work through. Things that a narcotized brain studiously avoided during sleep state. Vicky was dead. A month later, his grief was still acute. The case had gone cold from lack of attention. The Yard wasn't getting anywhere but, stupidly from his point of view, didn't want any help, either. Stoke and Ross had come up with a plausible suspect. Their case against the Cuban psychopath nicknamed Scissorhands had both motive and opportunity. Hawke at this moment wanted nothing more on earth than to light up his airplane, head down to Miami, and help Stokely and Ross run down the murderous Cuban.

On another, less personal front, there was this bastard they called the Dog. A cunning devil who was, according to reports Conch and Texas Patterson had shared with him, capable of wreaking unspeakable havoc upon a weakened, vulnerable and increasingly isolated America. But no one, it seemed, had even a clue as to his true identity or whereabouts. "Go find this guy, Alex," Conch had said. "And delete him."

Hawke's staunch efforts to keep his personal feelings and his professional obligations separate had not met with much success. But, he'd made his decision to send Stoke out without him and somehow he'd find a way to live with it.

His first stop had been the bridge, where he'd had a brief chat with his ship's captain, Briny Fay, regarding an ongoing problem with the boat's Aegis defense warning systems. The news from Briny was not good. Two of the CPU mainframes that backed up the Aegis had crashed inexplicably, and the techs couldn't figure out why. Now, as he made his way aft along the port side of the bridge deck, Sniper's own less sophisticated but highly effective alarm system went off.

HAWKE! HAWKE! the old parrot screeched. Sniper was trained in the ancient pirate ways, riding the master's shoulder to warn of unseen and unexpected dangers. Like the heavily armed man who now stepped out of the shadows directly in front of him.

"Hullo," Hawke said evenly.

"Sorry, Skipper," Tommy Quick said, lowering his weapon. "Didn't hear you coming."

"Well, I'm barefoot, Tommy," Hawke said, a smile in his voice. "So it's hardly surprising." The young American was in charge of security aboard this boat and he took his job very seriously. Quick, the former sharpshooter, was a stealth warrior who didn't care much for surprises and so very rarely experienced any.

"Still and all, sir," Quick said, looking down at Hawke's bare feet, embarrassed.

"It's quiet out there, Sarge," Hawke said, gliding over the awkward moment by casting a glance seaward. There was a new moon and a few bright stars winking behind high, fast-moving clouds.

Too quiet! Too quiet! Sniper squawked.

"Too quiet, she's right, yes, sir," Quick replied, smiling at the well-worn joke. "The natives are restless."

"To hell with the natives," Hawke said. "What about the bloody tourists?"

Hawke placed one hand on the rail and gazed down into the sea. The water, some twenty feet below the deck where he stood, was brilliantly illuminated, light blue darkening to deep blue, by a security system of underwater floodlights. It attracted all manner of marine life, including not a few of the large local sharks the famous author Peter Benchley, a Nantucketer himself, had made so notorious.

"Mind taking Sniper for a bit, Tommy?"

"Not at all, sir," he said and held out his arm to the bird.

"Thanks. Thinking of going for a quick swim, actually, Sarge," Hawke said, holding out his parrot. The bird flared her wings and alighted on the younger man's forearm.

"Swim, sir?"

"Work a few kinks out."

"Do you think that's a good idea, sir?" His employer's idea of a quick swim might be miles. In open ocean at night with a strong tide running, with possible hostiles in the area, this was definitely not a good idea, at least from a security man's point of view. On the other hand, Hawke was a former SBS commando. Swimming great distances at night in any weather under any conditions came as naturally to him as strolling around the block during a spring shower.

"Why not?"

"Well, security, Skipper. Ship's at full alert. Because the mainframe is down, our Aegis defensive perimeter only extends . . . well, you know our situation, sir," said Quick. "Until we're up and running again, we're pretty much a sitting duck."

"Yes, there is that," Hawke said, using one hand to vault himself easily off the deck and up onto the narrow varnished teak handrail. He then stood upright, perched atop the slender rail, facing the sea, perfectly balanced, arms at his side, smiling.

"I could launch two men in an inflatable to keep an eye on you, Skipper. Not a bad idea under the current—"

"No need of that," Hawke said. "Cheers."

Dumbstruck, Quick watched Alex Hawke rise up onto the tips of his toes and fly off the rail, executing a pretty good jackknife, extending to his full length to break the surface with little more than a ripple. Quick looked down in time to see Hawke's curly black head pop back up in the dead center of his entry point, a huge grin on his face.

"Repel all boarders!" his employer shouted and then he dove down, disappearing amongst schools of varicolored fish, swimming rapidly beneath the huge black hull.

"Jesus H. Christ!" a voice exploded in Quick's earpiece.

"What is it?" Quick said, adjusting the lip-mike of his Motorola headset.

"Oh, nothing much, sir," one of the underwater video technicians stationed in the fire control center replied. "The owner just swam up, shoved a shark out of the way and stuck his face in my fisheye lens, that's all. Big smile on his face. This is not foul play, roger, Sarge? His idea to jump into the deep dark sea full of sharks?"

"Yeah, his idea, affirmative," Quick replied.

"Sounds about right, sir."

"Yeah. Not that it'll do any good, but you guys keep the underwater telephotos on him as long as you can. Cycle a 360 sweep every five minutes. And gimme a heads-up the second he returns."

"Aye, aye."

"Sonar?"

"Still down, sir."

"How long till the Aegis is back up?"

"Techs are saying two hours, minimum."

"Christ. A sitting duck."

"You could say that again."

Sitting duck! Sitting duck! Sniper said.

Hawke swam as hard as he could, slicing through the slight chop. He stopped suddenly, muscles aflame, somehow always knowing precisely where his halfway mark was. Buoyant in mind and body, he let the current take him, relaxing into a dead man's float, face submerged, limbs hanging down, so heavy they felt more like logs, going with the flow. He let his thoughts float as well, go where they would, and he stayed in this meditative state for some time, lifting his head for air only as often as required.

He remained that way until a deep cold began to seep into his muscles, telling him it was time to head back. Lifting his head for a deep draught of air before starting the long swim home, he was surprised to see a small pleasure yacht silhouetted against the sky, a darkened cabin cruiser, perhaps forty feet in length. She had neither running lights nor navigation lights illuminated, her motors were silent; she was drifting with the current just like Hawke, treading water some five hundred yards off her port beam.

Curious.

He swam towards her, instinctively pulling himself slowly and quietly through the waves. As he drew closer, he saw that she was one of those luxury picnic boats. They were built along the lines of a Maine lobster boat, and if you had a million dollars burning a hole in your pocket, she was yours for the asking. He'd swum to within fifty yards of her when he saw someone switch on a flashlight down below. The curtains were not drawn in the main cabin, and he watched the yellow glow bobbing about, moving forward towards the bow.

The moving flashlight gave him a fairly good mental picture of the layout below. A salon amidships and a small v-berth stateroom all the way forward. He'd guess a complete power failure except most boats of this size were equipped with gensets, diesel or gasoline powered generators. So what was this strange duck doing floating around out here in the dark in one of the east coast's major shipping lanes?

He paddled quietly around to her stern. There was just enough ambient light from the fingernail moon and few visible stars to make out her name and hailing port, emblazoned in gold leaf on her dark blue transom.

RUNNING TIDE
Seal Harbor, Maine

He swam up to the swim platform at the stern, grasping it with both hands, trying to decide whether to hail the owner and see if he could offer assistance or slip aboard quietly. The main cabin was dark once more.

Whoever was down there had either extinguished the flashlight, or taken it forward out of sight. That's when he saw the small electric motor jury-rigged on a swivel mount to the swim platform. Twenty horsepower. A tiller for steering. A man standing on the platform had enough power to maneuver the forty-footer anywhere he wanted without making a sound.

Slip aboard quietly.

He timed the waves slapping under the boarding platform at the stern, waiting for one to lift the boat, waiting for the precise moment when he would swing his weight aboard. With any luck, the rising water would disguise the additional weight suddenly added to the stern. Go! Heaving himself up, he sat on the outer edge of the platform, legs dangling in the water, waiting to slide back into the water instantly if anyone took notice of his arrival. After a minute, he got to his feet, slipped over the transom, and stood on the aft deck looking forward.

The door to the enclosed pilothouse was hanging ajar. He crossed the teak deck and stepped inside, letting his eyes grow accustomed to the darkness.

To his right, seated behind the wheel at the helm seat, the figure of a large man in a dark watch cap facing straight ahead, not moving. Asleep? Drugged? Alex edged cautiously forward, waiting for the man to swing around with a gun leveled at him. Why was he so paranoid? Ah, right, someone was trying to kill him. When the man made no move to turn and see who was approaching, Alex reached out and put his hand on the man's shoulder.

The man, dressed in yellow foul-weather gear, slumped backward, and his head suddenly fell back upon the seat cushion with a soft thunk. His mouth gaped in a rictus of death, his eyes were a faint dull gleam under the lowered lids, and the skin of his collapsed cheeks was bluish-white. There was a neat black hole in the middle of his forehead, powder burns around the entrance wound; the coagulated blood puddled in his sunken eyesockets was black in the moonlight.

There was a gun lying on the seat beside him.

He saw that it was a Browning nine, the sidearm favored by the U.S. Army and also a number of American police forces. He patted him down, felt a bulge in a breast pocket under the slicker, reached inside and pulled out an alligator wallet. The man was Alan Outerbridge, age fifty-five, according to his Maine driver's license. Lived at some place called The Pines on Seal Point, Maine. This was, had been, his Hinckley Talaria 44. And Mr. Outerbridge was now very dead.

Roughly a thousand dollars cash was in the wallet, credit cards, a picture of a young girl. He put the back of his hand against the man's cheek. Guessing, he placed the time of death about two hours earlier.

Hawke turned toward the companionway. The man down below with the flashlight had hijacked this yacht at gunpoint, then murdered the owner and not for his money. Whatever brought the killer to Nantucket, it wasn't robbery. And it wasn't tourism. There was a strong possibility that the blood of Deirdre Slade and her two children was on his hands.

Alex ducked out through the pilothouse door and quickly retraced his steps back to the transom. He ejected the mag in the grip of the Browning, saw that it was full of hollow-points, reinserted it, and jacked a fresh cartridge into the chamber. He was counting on

"Engine trouble, old boy? Boats are a bloody bitch, aren't they? If it's not one damn thing, it's another."

"Shit!"

The startled young man's head came up too quickly and he banged it smartly on the underside of the metal deck. He craned around, eyes wide.

"You!" he said, eyeing Hawke and rolling towards the MAC-10.

Hawke pulled the Browning's trigger and a bullet tore into the expensive cherry woodwork inches above the man's head. The crack of the nine was deafening inside the small cabin. The man flattened once again on the deck.

"Itchy trigger finger, Nikos," Hawke said. "Sorry. Lifelong problem. Slide that machine gun over here. Easy. Now, then, you can sit up and toss me that flashlight like a good little scout."

Deputy Nikos Savalas shoved the automatic weapon in Hawke's direction, then sat up, sullenly rubbing the back of his head. He pitched the flashlight. Hawke caught the torch and set it beside him on the top step, aimed at Savalas.

"I see you've shaved off your moustache, Deputy," he said.

The deputy was out of uniform, wearing torn blue jeans and a loose-fitting black rubber slicker. He glared at Hawke who was sitting quietly at the top of the steps, elbow on one knee, chin propped in the upraised palm of his left hand, smiling. He held the gun in his other hand, loosely, but ready.

"How did you know—" he said.

"It was you? Saw the DHYC burgee up on the bow. Dark Harbor Yacht Club. Wasn't completely sure until I saw the 'DHPD' on the butt of your service Browning. I caught a whiff of you when it took you three times to toss me that line at the Slades' dock. A kid from the Maine coast who doesn't *coil* a line prior to tossing it? And who else had access to my airplane all night? You cut those aileron cables all by yourself, did you?"

"I told my father it wouldn't work. We should have just—"

"Credit where it's due, it was a close thing," Hawke said. "We almost bought it. Lucky for me, I had a splendid copilot aboard. Look here, I don't have time for this rubbish. You hijacked this boat up in Maine, got the owner to bring you down here and then your gun went off in his face. Why?"

The boy suddenly reached inside his slicker and Hawke put another round approximately one inch from his left ear. Maybe less.

"On your feet. Get your bloody hands up," Hawke said. When the youth did as he was told, Hawke added, "Now, both hands at the collar. Easy. Rip open the Velcro. One smooth motion, all the way open, thank you."

Savalas did as he was told and Hawke saw it wasn't a gun he was going for. He was wearing a heavy webbed vest strapped about his middle, pouches stuffed with thin flat bricks of Semtex. *Suicide bombers in every little village and vale,* Hawke thought.

"Your idea is quite good, really," Hawke said. "Your darkened and disabled vessel drifts into *Blackhawke*'s vicinity. An SOS comes over our radio. We respond. Take you aboard, trusting souls that we are. Boom. We all go to Paradise."

"It gets even better," a second man said, standing in the now open doorway of the forward cabin. Tall and dark, wearing greasy coveralls, he was an older, greying version of the deputy. This was the father. The mechanic who worked out at the airfield. The man had a second MAC-10 aimed at Hawke's head. "Please to drop your weapon," he said, with a lightly inflected American accent. "Kick both guns over here."

Hawke complied.

"Kerim, take the guns."

"Kerim is it, Nikos? Well, Kerim, ask Daddy how could it get any better than this?" Hawke said, kicking the Browning away. He was already calculating the angles, whether to roll right or left, go low or high, which one to take out first, which of them might possess the better reaction time, how many seconds it would take to—

"Kerim! Show this impious Englishman the little surprise we have planned for him tonight! We were just putting the final touches on it, yes? Now, he's a member of his own surprise party. Enough talk! Hands on your head!"

Kerim tossed the stubby machine gun to his father, keeping the Browning auto on Hawke. The younger man then stepped back beyond the square hole in the floor, motioning Alex forward with his free hand. Alex got to his feet and advanced three or four steps to the open hatchway. The father was moving around behind him, had the flashlight on him. The kick, when it came, hard and into the small of Hawke's back, was not unexpected. Hawke pitched forward, headfirst into the hatch.

What was not expected was the blur of Hawke's extended right hand, locking around Kerim's wrist, his gun hand, and pulling the would-be suicide bomber down through the hatch with him, the two of them landing arms and legs akimbo, Kerim's body atop his own, shielding Hawke, for the moment, from the machine gun the man standing above him had aimed at his heart.

"Looks like your son's going to beat me to Paradise," Hawke said. "If you decide to shoot me, I mean."

"Say your prayers," the older man shouted into the hold.

"The devil I will!" Hawke replied.

CHAPTER TWENTY-TWO

Miami

Stokely Jones and Ross Sutherland arrived at Miami International on American 170 from Boston at three-thirty on a hot, humid Saturday afternoon, the fifteenth of June. There were enormous purple clouds stacking up to the southwest, first heralds of the big tropical storm coming up from the Caribbean.

Alex Hawke had dropped them off earlier that morning at Logan. The boss was going to refuel and fly his seaplane back to Nantucket for a big powwow with some State Department honchos. He didn't look good, and Stoke had told him to get some sleep. "You don't want to drink whiskey, fine," Stoke called to him as he walked back across the tarmac toward *Kittyhawke*. "Take sleeping pills. You can't stay awake forever."

The two men had been in Miami for maybe ten minutes and both of them, standing on the curb outside in the sun, waiting for the driver, were drenched in sweat.

"See, Ross," Stoke said, "you forget all about this tropical shit." A black Lincoln Town Car pulled up beside them. The driver, in pearl grey livery, white shirt, black tie, and heavy dreadlocks, jumped out, popped the trunk, and opened both rear doors.

"Forget about what?"

"All this damn humidity," Stoke said, as they climbed into the back seat of the limo. "Feel like you walking around underwater. Like you some kind of damn *merman* or something. Merman, that's the opposite of mermaid, case you didn't know."

"I was aware of that, actually."

"Good. 'Cause they lot a people walking around that don't know that," Stoke said. The driver got behind the wheel and nosed out into the heavy airport traffic. "How you doin', brother?" Stoke asked.

"Good, mon," the driver said, his smile matching his lilting Jamaican accent. "Jah has blessed us with another golden day in paradise, yes, mon!"

"Jah must like it hot," Stoke said, gazing out at the sun-blanched palm trees and tropical vegetation. "Miami. Jamaica. Bahamas. You don't hear too much about Jah, you get up in places like Iceland and Alaska, places like that."

"Jah is everywhere, mon, some people too blind to see is all. My name is Trevor, by de way."

"Stokely Jones, pleased to meet you, Trevor."

"Detective Inspector Ross Sutherland, Trevor," Ross said, "New Scotland Yard."

Stoke gave Ross a knowing smile, guessing why he'd added his occupation.

"Yeah, Trevor," Stoke said. "We cops, just so you know. Don't be selling us no ganja weed, 'less we have to bust your ass."

"Don't smoke de herb, don't drink de rum. I'm a preacher," the driver said, smiling in the rearview. "Preach de word of Jah. Ras Tafari. De Lion of Judah. De King of Kings. De Emperor of—"

"Okay, okay, Preacher, I know the cat. Ethiopian. Question is, do you know where the Delano Hotel is?"

"Mon! Everybody know de Delano! Famous! Movie stars, football players! You sure you not a famous football player, Stokely, mon? I recognize you. You Tiki Barber."

"Tiki Barber," Stoke laughed, elbowing Sutherland. "Cat ain't half as tall, half as big, half as good-looking as me."

"You look famous, mon, is all I sayin'."

"I was famous for about nine minutes," Stoke said, laughing. "Shortest career in NFL history. Badass linebacker for the Jets. You blink, though, you missed my ass. Missed my whole career. Got hurt bad first quarter, first game. First game was my last game."

"Intercepted two passes and ran both back for touchdowns before he got hurt, however," Ross said. "I'm quite sure he's got the videotape of the two picks with him if you'd care to see it."

Half an hour later, having taken the Venetian Causeway across Biscayne Bay to 17th Street, the Lincoln hooked a right on Collins and pulled into the circular drive of South Beach's most famous white Art Deco hotel. Sure enough, Tom Cruise and Brad Pitt, both wearing white Bermuda shorts and matching knee socks, opened the rear doors simultaneously and welcomed Ross and Stokely to the Delano. *Hell,* Stoke thought, *even the damn valet parking guys looked like movie stars.*

"Preacher," Stoke said, slipping the Jamaican a twenty, "me and Ross going to be looking into some stuff around this town. You remember hearing about some SWAT guy getting whacked here in South Beach few weeks ago?"

"Yes, Tiki, mon. All over de papers. Ain't found de guy did it, but I know where dey should be looking, mon."

"Yeah? Where's that, Preacher?"

"De Crazy House, mon! Who else but a stone crazy going to break into a SWAT guy's apartment middle of de night, mon!"

Stoke laughed. "You right, Preacher. Anyway, we be sniffing around a few days. You seem like a kid knows his way around town. How 'bout you stick with us? Say, till Friday?"

"Got to check with de boss, mon, but I clear far as I know."

"That's good, my brother," Stoke said. "Here's my card with my cell number. You call me soon as you know."

J. Lo, looked like, or some other damn movie star checked them in at the movie set reception desk in the movie set lobby. Big sheets of white linen hung from somewhere high above, and they moved with the breezes off the Atlantic that blew through the lobby. Beautiful, like flags from nowhere.

"Good afternoon and welcome to the Delano, gentlemen," J. Lo said. "May I have your names, please?"

"We just plain old Mr. Jones and Mr. Sutherland—ain't even in show business—hope you don't hold that against us."

"Yes, I have you right here," she said, handing them two cards to fill in. No smile, no nothing. Too good looking for her own good, that's what.

Stoke scratched her off the list of women he currently considered to have a shot at the title. The title being the next Mrs. Stokely Jones, Jr. The ex–Mrs. Jones had taken his NYPD pension and moved to a split-level in New Jersey with her podiatrist. Stoke had told the female divorce court judge in Newark that his wife, Tawania, she left him for the podiatrist 'cause she was the kind of woman who liked to have men at her feet.

He was telling that one to Ross when J. Lo handed them the plastic key cards to the rooms.

"Come on, Ross, that was good," Stoke said. "Men at her feet. Admit it. You thought it was funny, right? Always laughing on the inside, that's my man Ross."

Now Ross and Stoke were sitting by a long rectangular aquamarine pool that stretched down to the palm-fringed beach and the ocean beyond, looking at all the suntans and bathing suits. Stokely had just embarked on a philosophical contemplation of women's swimwear while Ross talked on his cell to a captain at Miami Dade PD, making arrangements.

"Ain't a whole lot of things you can count on in this world," Stoke observed to no one in particular, "but the female bathing suit is what they call a constant. Constantly getting smaller every year, is what I'm saying. Ever see 'em getting bigger? No. And, I'm talking about ever since I was damn *born*."

Stoke took a pull on the straw in his cherry Diet Coke, surveying the whole Delano pool scene. Women floating in the pool talking secret female stuff to each other, worried about getting their hair wet; shiny, oiled-down white guys lying on the pool chairs talking to their cell phones, everybody wearing trendoid little cat-eyed sunglasses from *The Matrix Reloaded* Part 9. A killer blonde music video star emerged from the pool and Stoke was amazed to see she was topless. Tits way out to here. Topless? Was that legal?

He looked over at Sutherland, trying to figure out what was on the boy's mind. The sun was hot and the Scotsman had finished his call and put his phone away, then put his white linen handkerchief on top of his head kinda like a do-rag.

"Ross, what you thinking? I *know* what you looking at, boy, but tell me what the hell you thinking about?"

"I'm thinking two hours at a stone cold crime scene this afternoon is an utter waste of time."

"See? That's professional teamwork. Scotland Yard meets NYPD. I was thinking the same damn thing, exactly! Ain't likely there's anything there we don't already know about the dead SWAT guy, right?"

"Right."

Stoke's cell phone vibrated and he pulled it out of the inside coat pocket of his new lightweight sports coat, flipped it open and said, "Jones." He fingered the lapel of the sports jacket, looked over at Ross and mouthed the word, "Seersucker."

Preacher was on the phone saying he'd gotten the okay from the limo service to stick with them. Stoke told him, cool, to keep the engine warm and the inside chilly. They'd be out front in five minutes.

"Two choices, way I see it, Ross," Stoke said, snapping the phone shut. "We head over to Little Havana and start asking folks up and down *Calle Oche* questions. Or, we go see that Cuban Resistance guy Conch put us on to, her uncle, Cesar de Santos."

"Aye, the latter," Ross said, putting down his half-finished Bud Light and getting to his feet. "Let's go. We'll call him from the car and tell him we're on our way. One thing, Stokely. We absolutely cannot dis-cuss Hawke's involvement during that Cuban insurrection. With anybody. Ever. Strictly black ops, off the radar."

Stoke looked at him like he was crazy.

"Sorry, mate," Ross said.

"Damn right you are, Flyboy. All this time together, you still see me as some football-playing, ex-SEAL badass. I was a gold shield–carrying NYPD detective when your mama was still rubbing Johnson's baby oil on your skinny white Scottish ass. And take that do-rag off your head. Look ridiculous, you trying to look street."

The architectural firm of de Santos & Mendoza occupied the entire top floor of a jet-black glass tower situated on an island just over a bridge from the heart of downtown Miami. Called Brickell Key, its office towers, hotels, and apartment complexes all boasted panoramic views of Biscayne Bay. The Port of Miami, with giant cruise ships parallel parked along the pier, was to the north; Rickenbacker Causeway and Key Biscayne lay to the south. Ross and Stokely stood in reception, waiting for *Señor* de Santos, staring out the floor-to-ceiling windows at all the activity on the sparkling blue bay.

"Mr. Jones? Mr. Sutherland?" the pretty, Prada-clad receptionist said. "*Señor* de Santos will see you now. I'll buzz you in."

They pushed through heavy double black lacquered doors into a room they were totally unprepared for. The four walls were draped in heavy black velvet, and the only light in the room came from countless tiny windows and miniature streetlamps. Spread out before them was an exquisite scale model of the entire city of Havana, at least thirty feet square, on a raised platform. The architectural detail was astounding. Every statue in every plaza, every fountain, every shrub, tree, and tiny climbing bougainvillea was perfect.

"*Bienvenidos,*" said the elegant white-haired man dressed completely in black who was coming towards them with his hand extended. "Welcome to *la Habana.*"

"Inspector Ross Sutherland," Ross said, shaking his hand. "Thank you for taking the time to meet with us."

"A pleasure," he said, smiling. "You've probably guessed I am Cesar de Santos. You must be Stokely Jones."

"Thank you for seeing us, *Señor* de Santos," Stoke said, looking at the twinkling lights of the miniature city. "I got to tell you, this is the most amazing thing I've ever seen."

"*Muchas gracias, señor.* I chair an organization called the New Foundation For Old Havana," de Santos said. "One day, my precious *Habana* will look just like this. See, the many ancient and beautiful buildings with the blue flags are to be completely restored to former glory. Red flags are the hideous monstrosities built by the Russians. Dynamite. White flags are much-needed new buildings that Cuban-American architects are designing for us even now. But, please, this is not why you're here. My niece, Consuelo de los Reyes, has told me much about you. How may I be of service?"

"*Señor* de Santos," Ross said, "I'm a senior inspector with Scotland Yard. Mr. Jones and I are investigating a murder that took place in England little more than one month ago. We have reason to suspect the murderer may be a Cuban national. Possibly living somewhere here in the Miami area. Or down in the islands. The American secretary of state was kind enough to suggest you might be of help."

"Yes, my niece Consuelo told me about this horrific murder. A bride on the steps of a church! Despicable! Unfortunately, there are many—how shall I say it, low-lifes, living in Miami's Cuban community. *Las cucarachas.* Such a cockroach will be hard to find, I'm afraid."

"I understand precisely," said Ross, "but this particular low-life is likely to be living the high life. Our suspect was high in Castro's government, feeding at the trough of Fidel. I shouldn't be at all surprised if he hadn't siphoned tens of millions offshore."

"Ah, a rich low-life. We have those, too."

"*Señor* de Santos," Stoke said, "those three generals who tried to overthrow Fidel a few years ago?" He got a look from Ross but ignored it.

"I remember this attempted coup, yes," de Santos said. "It was in all the papers. *The New York Times.* Fox TV."

"Well, our boy, this suspect, he was double-dipping back then. The U.S. government discovered hundreds of millions the generals put in offshore banks. Cayman Islands, Bermuda, not to mention Miami. CIA found some of it, but not all of it."

"We believe our suspect has access to these funds, *Señor* de Santos," Ross said. "If he's here, I would imagine he has created a new identity for himself. Changed his name and appearance. Possibly living as a wealthy, highly respectable member of society."

"There are many, many Cubans who fit that description in the exile community, Inspector," de Santos said, lighting a cigar. He offered his opened gold case to Ross and Stokely who declined. "What does he look like, may I ask? Age, et cetera?"

"He's got no eyes," Stoke said.

"No *eyes, señor?*"

"No color in his eyes. Like some zombie in a horror flick."

Ross said, "I'm sure this man kept a low profile when he first arrived. But he may feel sufficient time has passed for him to surface. Enjoy his wealth."

"Ah, I see. Perhaps I have an idea," Cesar said. "There is a party tonight. My foundation's annual benefit dinner. The very top echelons of Cuban society will attend because we will award this year's Medal of Freedom."

"That just might be a very good place to start, *Señor* de Santos," Ross said. "Thank you."

"Cocktails are at seven, dinner at eight. The Grand Ballroom of the Fontainebleau Hotel on Miami Beach. Invitations will be in your names at the registration table. I look forward to seeing you there. It's black tie, I'm afraid."

"That means tuxedos, Ross," Stoke said and got another look from Ross going out the door.

CHAPTER TWENTY-THREE

Paris

Monique Delacroix stood by the tall French windows of the Ambassador's study, dragging on a Gauloise while she watched the media circus. Preparations for today's press conference in the embassy gardens had started at dawn. It had been a hectic morning. The French press as well as the FOX, CNN, SKY, and BBC crews had arrived at eight. Beyond the high walls surrounding the large embassy compound, she could see the forest of telescoping dishes mounted atop their various uplink video trucks. Delacroix, Ambassador Duke Merriman's personal assistant for the last few months, had made all the press arrangements at Merriman's insistence.

The event was scheduled to begin at noon, today, Saturday.

"Happy now?" Agent McIntosh asked her. She let the question hang in the air amidst her clouds of blue smoke. She knew he didn't like her. He didn't trust her. And she certainly didn't like him. She resented taking orders from anyone but the ambassador. Especially this gruff bear of an American who'd suddenly appeared at the embassy. It was an awkward situation. The new chief of security wanted Monique out of this house every bit as badly as the ambassador wanted her in his bed. It was a battle of wills that, so far, Ambassador Merriman was clearly winning. DSS had, after all, only so much power over a bullheaded ambassador in love.

She knew McIntosh was "looking for dirt" on her, as the Americans say. Her friend, Noel, the chief housekeeper at the embassy, had overheard two of his agents in the kitchen talking about her. Let him look, she'd told Noel, she was a good girl of good Swiss stock from the Canton de Vaud. She had always been a good girl. No?

The DSS Special Agent who'd been assigned to protect America's ambassador to France and his family, Agent Rip McIntosh, was, on this warm June morning, not a happy camper. The leathery, sharp-featured man with the brush-cut grey hair was sitting across the room in a leather armchair, glaring at the woman in the sharply tailored red and black Chanel suit.

"I said, are you happy now?" he repeated.

"Unlike you, I am always happy, Agent McIntosh," she said without looking at him. She expelled a thin plume upwards, lifting the bangs of dark hair off her pale forehead, a blithe spirit.

Rip McIntosh was happy now and then, on those rare occasions when all the hatches were battened down, all the guards were posted, the perimeter was secure, and everybody was accounted for, all snug in their wee beds. But Rip McIntosh was not happy now. There were any number of reasons, the foremost being that he definitely did not like the idea of this impending press conference. Even though he didn't know exactly what Ambassador Merriman was going to say, he had a fairly rough idea.

"You could at the very least be a little more supportive, Miss Delacroix," McIntosh said to the statuesque brunette, breaking the silence. "My agents and I are charged with the protection of the ambassador and his children. Not to mention all embassy personnel within these walls, including, God help us, *you*. And, by God, that's what we're going to do."

"This ground, it has been covered, *Monsieur* McIntosh," Delacroix said, her face still turned towards the sunny window. "I work for this man. And he say to me, Monique, arrange a press conference. I am supposed to say, 'No, no, so sorry, *Monsieur l'Ambassadeur*. Special Agent McIntosh, he say it's a bad idea'?"

"No, you say that the secretary of state herself thinks it's a bad idea and that—"

"It is your problem, *monsieur*, not mine."

"I keep forgetting. You're French."

"You keep forgetting. I'm Swiss."

"Oh, yeah. Neutral. Great. Even better."

At that moment two nine-year-old boys, tow-headed identical twins, roared into the room, both wielding tommy-gun shaped water guns. Ambassador Merriman, who had been widowed in September 2001, had his hands full with his two sons. Especially now that he, his children, and the entire embassy staff were all basically under house arrest by the State Department's Diplomatic Security Service.

The spring term at l'Ecole du Roi du Soleil had just ended, the boys were home for the summer, and it looked to be a long one. The children had grown accustomed to having the run of the three-acre embassy grounds and the many beautiful Parisian parks beyond their walls. Now, since the tragic events involving

Ambassador Slade's family in Maine, the boys suddenly found themselves confined to the house itself. It was a lovely old mansion just off the Bois de Boulogne in the heart of Paris; but it was not nearly big enough to contain Duncan and Zachary Merriman.

"You can't run, you're dead!" Duncan screamed as his brother dove for cover behind a large upholstered sofa. *"Tu es mort, tu es mort!"*

Zachary popped up from behind the couch and squeezed off a stream at his brother.

"Au putant! It was only a flesh wound," Zachary laughed at his brother.

"Yeah, right," Duncan grinned, "the flesh right between your eyes!" Duncan then charged, aimed his gun and fired back.

"Christ," McIntosh muttered. He didn't blame the kids. He'd raised two boys himself. Twins. Those long Wisconsin winters were a nightmare for a couple of cooped-up ten-year-old kids. He could escape to his ice-fishing hut out on the frozen Lake Wausau, but the boys—

"Duncan, enough! *Ça suffit!"* Mlle. Delacroix shouted, and McIntosh saw Duncan had nailed her, a big wet spot right on her red Chanel fanny. She turned and grabbed the back of Duncan's T-shirt to prevent him from running away. "Behave! Both of you! What is the matter with you?"

"Cabin fever!" Zachary shouted from his hiding place behind the sofa. "That's what Papa says we've all got! Cabin fever!"

Zachary popped up from behind the sofa and trained his weapon on Delacroix. "You let my brother go or I'll blast you!"

"You can't shoot her, son, she's Swiss," McIntosh said mildly, enjoying himself for the first time all day.

"Zachary Merriman!" a deep voice boomed from the doorway. "You come out from behind that sofa immediately! I told you no water guns inside. And, Duncan, apologize to Miss Delacroix. You, too, Zach. Now!"

Duke Merriman strode into the room. He was lanky, six-five, and elegantly attired in an English bespoke navy three-piece with a dark tie. He had the same white-blond hair and bright blue eyes as his two sons. Born and bred Boston Brahmin from Beacon Hill and no mistaking it. "Zachary, you've got two seconds to come out from behind that sofa!"

"*Oui, Papa,*" the boy said, and edged his way out.

"Now, both of you, apologize," Merriman said.

"Sorry, Mademoiselle Delacroix," the boys said in unison, with a singsong cadence devoid of sincerity.

Duke scowled at his two boys.

"Now, both of you upstairs to your rooms and get dressed. Blazers and ties. White shirts. Hair combed. Nanny will help you. Daddy is giving a press conference in fifteen minutes and you two are going to be standing right beside me looking, hopefully, like proper little gentlemen. And you're not going to say a single word, *comprenez-vous? Sans un mot.*"

"*Oui, Papa,*" the boys said, and ran shouting and laughing from the room. "*Sans un mot! Sans un mot!*"

"Sorry about that, Miss Delacroix," Merriman said, as he and McIntosh watched her twisting around and bending from the waist, trying to dry off her soaking wet derriere with a small linen handkerchief clearly unsuited to the purpose.

McIntosh, trying to hide a smile, got to his feet. "Boys will be boys, Mr. Ambassador, it's only water," he said. "We used to mix it with India ink when I was a kid. Now that would be a problem for Miss Delacroix here."

He cast a quick glance at the pertinent posterior and earned himself a look from Delacroix. He ignored it. "Mr. Ambassador, at the risk of getting my ass kicked the hell out of here, I really wish there was some way I could convince you to reconsider this press conference. It's not too late. We have some remarks prepared by Madame Secretary's own staff that make your point but stop just short of—" He saw the look in Merriman's eyes and gave up. "Anyway, sir, the Secretary herself called me early this morning and said—"

"With all due respect, McIntosh," Merriman interrupted, "I know exactly what she said. God knows, she's said it often enough to me. And I understand your position, and I actually sympathize with it. Your department has an outstanding record, and you are clearly just doing your jobs. However, I have deep convictions about this current situation and I feel it is my duty to our country to express them publicly. Now, if you'll excuse me?"

Ambassador Merriman strode from the room on his long legs, not waiting for any reply. McIntosh sat back down in his chair.

Monique Delacroix grabbed the remote and flipped on the large-screen television mounted within the bookcase. She then collapsed into the armchair, crossing her long legs and facing the security man. They regarded each other in silence for a few moments.

McIntosh let out a long breath of air. "You know something, Miss Delacroix? I took a bullet for Secretary Albright in Uzbekistan back in 2000. I was attached to the SD then, the Secretary's Detail. I've been around the planet fifteen times, foiled an attempt by Moroccan terrorists to dump cyanide in the water supply of our embassy in Rome, pulled smoking bodies out of three embassy bombings, and helped prevent about two hundred more."

"The great American hero."

"Yeah? Well. First time in the line of duty I ever got caught in a firefight by two American kids with friggin' water guns."

"I am the one who got caught, not you."

"Ironic, ain't it? You being so neutral and all."

They stared at each other in silence a moment, and then McIntosh, looking at his watch, said, "It's almost noon. Turn on CNN and let's watch this goddamn press conference."

The camera went from a wide shot of the ambassador and his two well-scrubbed children to a tight shot of Merriman as he took the podium emblazoned with the Great Seal of the United States. The sun was shining and the red rhododendron bushes in the background made the embassy gardens a colorful backdrop.

"*Bonjour et bienvenue,*" Merriman said into the microphone and smiled, acknowledging a smattering of applause. He'd long been popular with the French press corps, primarily because of his unwavering candor and reputation for never ducking the issues.

"Freedom and fear are at war. And fear will not win. I've invited my two sons, Zachary and Duncan, to join me here in the garden this morning," he began, "for a very specific reason. It's the first time they've been allowed out in the sunshine in over two weeks."

He paused here, looked back, smiled at his beaming sons, and then continued.

"The reason? Fear. As you all know, American diplomats and their families around the world are under attack. Five colleagues have died tragically in the last month alone. As a result of this unprecedented attack on America's diplomatic corps, embassy and consulate personnel and their families have been forced to retreat behind closed doors. There is a wholly justifiable sense of fear among many. I have enormous sympathy for them. But I believe such fears are in direct conflict with all America stands for. Freedom. Autonomy. Free will. Independence. The simple everyday pursuit of happiness. The very people who represent those precious notions around the world have been forced to take cover. I find this unacceptable. I lost my wife on September 11th. My boys lost their mother. That is war. But, when American diplomats go into hiding, freedom has lost and fear has won this war. This American ambassador, for one, refuses to live in fear of the terrorists. I believe that it is the *raison d'être* of every ambassador to walk freely among the people of the host country, hear their concerns and understand them firsthand. My family and I will pursue our lives normally, we will not be cowed, and we will let the world see that the heart and spirit of the American diplomatic community remains unbroken. That terrorism shall not prevail. That we will walk in sunshine every day of our lives, and may God have mercy on those who would try to prevent us from doing so. Thank you all very much.

Look up there, boys. Here comes the sun. Let's go for a walk along the river."

"Holy Christ," McIntosh said, hitting the mute button on the remote.

Delacroix said, "Show me the American diplomat who hides behind his walls and his guards after this speech, and I show you cowards. It was brilliant."

"No," the DSS man replied, rubbing his face in his hands. "It was suicidal." The secretary should have recalled the man to Washington. Now how the hell were he and his men scattered around the planet supposed to do their jobs? The task had just grown exponentially more difficult. McIntosh was suddenly tired beyond exhaustion.

"Suicide, Agent McIntosh?" she said, reaching into her purse and fishing around for her cigarettes. "Why do you say something so ridiculous?"

"Look, he's taking questions. The press is going to have a field day."

McIntosh grimaced, hit the mute button again and the sound resumed. The press was clearly excited, smelling blood here.

"Mr. Ambassador," a Fox News reporter at the rear of the crowd shouted, "your remarks are clearly a departure from what we've been hearing out of Washington. Does the secretary of state approve of your position? We are hearing, sir, that she definitely does not."

"I have expressed my personal views to the secretary. I am sure— Excuse me. Something is— Jesus Christ!"

Merriman staggered back from the podium, bending as if to untie his shoes. There was thick white smoke around his feet, seeming to come from the sole of one of his shoes, his right shoe.

"Holy God!" McIntosh screamed at the television, jumping to his feet. "Willie Pete!"

"What?" Delacroix said.

"White phosphorus!" the man yelled over his shoulder as he crashed, shattering wood and glass, through the French doors leading to the garden. Delacroix remained seated, her eyes glued to the television. Like her own eyes, the screen was filled with madness.

Merriman rolled on the ground in agony. The DSS agents were screaming at the press and embassy staff to get back. Every agent knew white phosphorus, colloquially referred to as Willie Pete, when he saw it, knew it had a six-second fuse and a casualty radius of thirty yards or more. They also knew the chemical ignited upon contact with air and instantaneously reached a temperature of three thousand degrees, enough to burn through steel armor.

An aide, who'd been standing just behind the ambassador, had the large pitcher of water from the podium and was approaching Merriman. Zachary and Duncan were frozen in place, watching in horror at the sight of their father writhing on the ground, thick white smoke streaming from his shoe.

"No!" McIntosh shouted, racing towards the aide with the pitcher. "Water is useless! You have to smother it! Christ! Get those kids out of here! Don't let them see this!"

Merriman rolled towards his boys, his face a mask of pain. Aides were desperately trying to cover their eyes and pull them away from him, but the boys were kicking and screaming to be let go, trying to pull their arms free, looking back and crying out to their father.

Daddy! Oh, please, Daddy! Please don't die, Daddy . . .

The only possible way to extinguish white phosphorus was by smothering it. Ripping his suit coat off, knowing it was probably already too late for that, Agent Rip McIntosh dove onto Merriman, rolling with him, trying desperately to smother the goddamn Willie Pete with his jacket and his body. McIntosh was slapping at the ambassador's shoe soles, ignoring the flecks of phosphorus already burning gaping holes in his bare palms.

That's when the white phosphorus packed into the heels of both of Ambassador Merriman's shoes burned completely through. Once exposed to air, it ignited into a flash of searing flame. The two Americans rolling on the ground were instantly incinerated, their bodies unrecognizable three seconds later.

The cameras were still rolling, broadcasting to every corner of the globe the image of the two screaming boys being dragged away from the charred black sticks that had once been an American ambassador and his would-be savior.

The beautiful *hashishiyyun* extinguished her cigarette in the crystal ashtray that bore the engraved seal of the American State Department. She rose from her chair and plucked the sprig of lily of the valley from the buttonhole of her jacket. Tossing the fragrant flower into the ashtray, she took one final look out into the garden and then strode from the room. She made her way through the embassy, past screaming and panicked

CHAPTER TWENTY-FOUR

Nantucket Island

Alexander Hawke seized Kerim in a bear grip, clasping both arms around his violently twisting body, pinning his arms to his sides, and saying to the man standing above with the machine gun, "If you want me, you have to go through him."

The man laughed.

"We're all going the same place tonight, my friend."

"Maybe. Maybe not."

"Paradise by any other name," the man said with a smile in his voice, "would smell as sweet."

"Doesn't matter a damn to me, Shakespeare."

"I am a sheikh, not Shakespeare. I write only death sentences."

"Spare me."

The man grunted as he bent down and lifted the metal hatch cover by one corner, positioning it with his foot, keeping the gun on Hawke and his own struggling son. He fitted one edge of the cover into the hatch and let it fall with a heavy metallic clang.

"No!" Kerim cried in the sudden darkness. "Father!"

"You heard Papa, Kerim," Alex said. We're all in the same boat, as it were."

"I can't breathe!"

"Then drop the bleeding pistol like I told you to do. Ready?"

"Shit!"

"Exactly my feeling."

Hawke tightened his grip sharply and the boy dropped the Browning. Hawke immediately released him, seized the weapon, and brought both his knees up off the floor, catapulting Kerim over his head and slamming him against the bulkhead. There was a whuff of expelled air, a groan, and then silence. Hawke sat up and turned to face the one-time officer of the Dark Harbor PD.

Single portholes on either side of the engine room allowed him just enough moonlight to make out the dark shape crouching by the port-side engine. One hand out, crabbing across the greasy metal floor, the boy was searching for something to throw at him, no doubt. Looking for a loose wrench or a screwdriver. Above, sounds of Kerim's father moving about, making final preparations for his oceangoing jihad. A scraping noise above just then, a large piece of furniture being shoved into place, sealing the hatch cover.

The stink of motor oil and fear sweat down here would make the hold a lousy tomb.

"Don't even think about it!" Hawke said, squeezing the trigger. The vicious crack of the round was enough to send Kerim scuttling back into hiding behind one of the diesels. Hawke felt the sensation of water now moving past the hull. After a second, he heard the thin whirr of the electric prop coming from the stern. Kerim's father was out on the swim platform, steering *Running Tide* into the westerly current where it would soon drift down on *Blackhawke*.

If Hawke had this scenario right, time was rapidly running out.

He fired another round and blew out the porthole just above the boy's head. "Hello?" Hawke said. "Still with me?" He squeezed the trigger once more and heard the sharp click of a dry-fired hammer. Empty.

"Y-yes?" the boy said, as the weapon clattered across the steel deck.

"Has to be a rechargeable flashlight mounted somewhere on the engine room bulkhead, Kerim. Where?"

"I d-don't know."

"Right. I forgot. You're a policeman, not a sailor."

"I like being a policeman."

"You should have thought of that earlier."

"I like Maine, too. I like America. I don't want to die. I have . . . a friend. The most beautiful girl. Her name is Millie and—"

"Let's make sure I understand this. A cop running around the Maine woods in a suicide belt who loves America."

"My father, he made me do this. Wear the belt. He hates America. He and my mother have killed many Americans. When she injected the children at the—"

"The woman who posed as the nurse, murdered all those children. That was your mother?"

"Y-yes."

"And the girl who killed the Slade family. Your sister."

"Yes."

"Chief Ainslie never suspected you? Surely there was a background check."

"We come from Pakistan. But we lived in Athens for many years before coming to this country. My father met a man there. The Emir, he was called. He and my father killed a poor farm family named Savalas and we took their identities. I've been a police officer for five years. Three locations. Decorated for heroism in Seattle. A fire."

"And your mother?"

"She is a registered nurse. Trained at Mt. Sinai. Really. Good cover."

"Christ."

"Yes. We are highly trained. We spend years learning how to weave threads into the fabric. Once we strike, we move on to another town and begin again."

"Schoolchildren, Kerim. Babies, damn you!"

"My people have suffered, too. This is blood vengeance. We seek only justice."

"You call it justice? Your mother poisons children. Your sister slaughters a mother and two children sleeping in their beds. Bloody hell, boy, it's murder!"

"I—saw them in that house. The children. It was horrible. I believe that—I am sorry for what my sister did. Truly sorry."

"Beyond nauseating what now passes for evangelism. Religious fascism. Talk fast, Kerim. Tell me what you and your father are doing on this boat. Now."

"We have—a bomb."

"Bomb. I assumed as much. Where?"

"Up in the bow. He packed TNT up there. Almost half of a ton—"

"Who dies for righteousness this time? The good citizens of Nantucket Island?"

"No. You, Mr. Hawke."

"Me? I'm hardly worth the effort."

"Our plan is to go along beside your boat. Pretending to have engine trouble. Then explode the bomb."

"And you're just along for the ride."

"My father, he knows my true feelings. He made me wear the belt always so I would not warn Chief Ainslie what we were—there is a lock on the belt. I cannot remove it. He has a remote detonator always. He says he will sacrifice me if—if I try to . . ."

The boy was whimpering now, rocking back and forth with his arms around his knees. Pitiful, if not pathetic.

"Christ. The TNT, Kerim, focus on that. Is it on a remote as well?"

"No. A timer."

"Where's the timer?"

"Up there. Wired to the explosives."

"Don't move," Hawke said, "I'll be right back. Try not to blow yourself up while I'm gone."

Blackhawke was completely vulnerable right now, Alex thought, feeling his way forward, moving as quickly as possible in the tight quarters of the dark engine room. Good Christ Almighty.

Security levels were at full alert, well and good, but a million-dollar lobster yacht with a Maine hailing port in gold leaf on her transom just might be sufficiently far-fetched to get through.

He found the half-ton of justice neatly packaged in waterproof oilskins, enough to level a city block. The water flowing outside the hull was moving faster. They would be getting close to *Blackhawke* now. Christ. He'd never find the timer in time. Hawke scrambled back to the love-struck terrorist.

"We're all out of time, Kerim. The explosives are definitely on a timer, not an impact detonator, is that right?"

"Yes, sir."

"When is it set to explode?"

"At exactly four a.m."

Alex looked at his watch. Less than six minutes! They were drifting now, floating with the current towards *Blackhawke*. Suddenly, a powerful searchlight swept across *Running Tide*, lighting up her engine room. He heard the muffled voice of one of his own crewmen, hailing the disabled vessel over a loud-speaker. The voice lacked the authoritarian harshness of a direct challenge. They were clearly buying this act. It would be a close thing. Looking feverishly about, he saw the outline of a small door in the aft bulkhead. It must lead to the crawl space beneath the after deck where he'd boarded. There were two access hatches there, aft of the pilothouse, opening directly up onto the outside deck. He'd seen them when he first boarded.

"One more question, Kerim. Who sent you and your family to America? This Emir?"

"No. Another man. He is called by some the Dog."

"Is this Dog still alive?"

"I believe that he is, yes, sir."

"What is his real name?"

Silence.

"You dare not speak it, or you don't know?"

"Yes."

"All right. I'm going to get us out of here. It will most likely be necessary for me to kill your father. Do you want to come along or not?"

"Yes, sir."

"Do what I tell you, then. You say you can't get rid of that bloody vest?"

"No, sir. It's locked to my body."

"Christ. Let me take a look. Good God, it's . . ."

"Secured with a metal pin through my pelvis. My mother implanted it."

Hawke looked at the boy's punctured hip, unable to speak. What kind of mother could do that to—he heard voices above. Time to move. "All right, Kerim. Let's go."

"Ahoy, *Running Tide!*" came the muffled voice of one of his crew. "Captain! Do you require assistance?"

No reply.

The door, fitted into the bulkhead and leading aft, was, as Alex had prayed, not locked. Hawke went through first, followed closely by Kerim. They crouched in the semidarkness of the crawl space, listening. One of the two hatches above was forward of the spot where the boy's father was now standing.

Hawke drew a breath. The boat's stern had dipped ever so slightly. The terrorist's weight had just shifted aft. He must have climbed up onto the transom. Hawke could almost see him, waving his hands, his face a mask of embarrassment and abject apology. The question was, would Tom Quick recognize the Middle Eastern inflection in his voice or would it be lost in the wind? The man's speech patterns were definitely not Down East Maine.

Hawke pressed one hand up against the underside of the hatch cover and applied pressure. It moved.

"Kerim," he whispered, looking at the glowing numerals of his dive watch and then at the dark figure crouched beside him. "I'm going up through this hatch. Give me thirty seconds, then you use the other hatch. Come up fast and roll to either side. No matter what you see, just get yourself overboard and swim away from this boat as quickly as you can."

Hawke wouldn't wish seeing your own father die on anyone. He'd been there. He saw it still. He would always see it.

Kerim said nothing, just stared at Hawke with an unreadable expression. Alex looked at the sweep second hand of his watch. Coming up on four minutes before the hour. Bloody hell, it might already be too late.

Hawke coiled his body, squatting deeply to get as much leverage out of his legs as possible. He reached up and placed both palms on the underside of the hatch cover, filled his lungs with air, and then exploded upwards in a single fluid movement.

He heaved the heavy cover out of the way as he rolled left across the deck. Kerim's father, now disguised in the dead man's yellow slicker, stood atop the transom shouting to a crewman aboard *Blackhawke.* The gleaming black side of her massive hull loomed above the small yacht's deck. There were perhaps twenty feet of water remaining between the two rapidly closing vessels.

The hatch cover landed with a thud and the Arab jerked his head around, astounded at the sight of Hawke rolling across the deck. He glanced hurriedly at his watch, then looked back up at the crew lining the rail above him, clearly unsure of which way to play this out in the time and distance remaining.

Running Tide now lay directly alongside *Black-*

hawke's towering hull, dwarfed by the yacht. A crew-man above was throwing down a line as the terrorist pulled a pistol from inside the yellow slicker and swung the muzzle of the gun towards Alex, who was now rolling right. He squeezed off two shots, the rounds ripping into the teak deck less than a foot in front of his target. Hawke scrambled to his feet, raised the Browning, and put two rounds through the terrorist's heart. The wallop of the parabellum hollow points slammed the dead man backwards, pinwheeling him into the water.

"Kerim!" Alex shouted, scrambling over the transom and onto the swim platform. "Go! Go!" He twisted the electric motor's throttle and the Hinckley moved off. It was painfully slow.

The shadowy figure of the boy appeared. He climbed up out of the hold, rolled across the deck, and got unsteadily to his feet.

"Jump!" Hawke said. "Get away as fast as you can!"

"I don't—the belt! The weight. I don't know if I can swim."

"Yes you can. Use your arms. You've got to go, now." Hawke turned away to get his bearings. He heard a splash and saw Kerim's head bobbing above the surface a few feet away. He was paddling frantically, coughing and swallowing water. He wasn't going any-where, but he was afloat.

Alex Hawke knew he now had perhaps three min-utes, maybe less. He pushed the electric motor's tiller hard over and twisted the throttle, angling his bow away from *Blackhawke.* Every searchlight was trained on him now and sirens were wailing from stem to stern. Crewmen lined the rails on every deck, all of them with automatic weapons trained on the suddenly suspicious vessel. Battle stations.

Twelve feet above the waterline on the yacht's port side, individual hatch covers slid open simultaneously and a long row of gleaming surface-to-air and short-range missiles protruded, the vessel presenting a very modern version of an English man-o'-war.

But no shots were fired, and no missiles were launched.

Someone had recognized Hawke on *Tide*'s aft swim platform, and told the crew to hold their fire. He could only guess what Tommy Quick must be thinking.

Complete insanity.

He'd opened up almost three hundred yards of choppy water between himself and *Blackhawke* now. Eyes glued to the sweep second hand, he could see there wasn't nearly enough time. He needed at least a thousand yards distance between the two vessels. And an additional thirty seconds swimming to have any hope of not getting killed by the concussion—he looked for Kerim and didn't see him. He'd either gotten safely away, or he'd gone down with the weight of his heavy belt.

The second hand on his watch was relentlessly spinning towards oblivion. In desperation, he twisted the throttle grip harder, trying to get even a fraction more out of the ridiculously underpowered electric motor. He felt a click and realized the throttle was now locked wide open. Nice time to discover this handy feature, he thought; and then he arched backwards, executing a back-flip off the platform and into the cold sea.

Hawke swam desperately towards *Blackhawke*, ticking off the remaining seconds in his head. He looked back. *Running Tide* was maybe a thousand yards away now, maybe just enough, still moving off at about three knots. But, she'd begun a hard turn to starboard! Without his hand on the tiller to counteract the natural torque of the motor, she was automatically veering around. And now, she was once more on a course directly towards *Blackhawke.*

Christ. He was out of options. He could hardly swim into *Tide*'s path, hope to reboard her and correct her heading. No time. Nor could he continue to tread water where he was and allow the boat to get close enough to take him out when she blew.

He strained his eyes, looking for any sight of Kerim on the surface. Nothing. Suddenly, his eyes were fixed on the Hinckley. He'd seen movement at the edge of his vision. Something moving at the stern. At this distance it was hard to make out quite what—there! A black figure rising on the platform, climbing up out of the sea. Kerim. What was he doing! It was only a matter of seconds until—wait.

He saw the bow of *Tide* swing to port, beginning a turn away from him and the big yacht behind him. Kerim had realized what was happening and was manning the electric motor. Yes, that was it. He had her back on a course for open water!

Hawke cupped his hands around his mouth and screamed, "Kerim! Jump! Now!" But the boy either did not hear or did not respond and Alex had no choice but to start clawing the water, swimming furiously away from certain death.

A second later, the massive, blinding explosion of TNT rent the fabric of the air, cratered the ocean, and lit up the night sky. A fountain of fiery debris and burning fuel shot up hundreds of feet into the heavens. Hawke opened his mouth wide in anticipation of the concussion. It was the only way his lungs would survive it.

The outer perimeter of the shock wave hit him hard, blowing him backwards through the water and taking his breath away; burning sections of wood and fiberglass were raining down all around him and a sea of flaming fuel was racing rapidly across the surface. He could feel the intense temperatures of the fireball on his face, feel his eyebrows starting to singe, the surfaces of his eyeballs aching with the heat.

He spun around and took one long look at *Blackhawke*. He was deeply relieved to see she'd already got three launches lowered away, started her massive engines, and was even now under way, steaming rapidly away from the explosion and the spread of flaming fuel.

He gulped air and dove deep, angling down and away from the burning gas and flaming debris. Two minutes later, he broke the surface and saw the figure of Tommy Quick, illuminated a brilliant orange in the light of the flames, standing in the bow of the first launch, heaving a life-saving ring in his direction. Hawke cast a final glance over his shoulder at what had once been the handsome yacht *Running Tide*.

She was gone.

Along with Kerim, the reluctant martyr. Blown to Paradise.

A bloody good cop after all.

CHAPTER TWENTY-FIVE

Miami

The Black Lincoln turned out of the inexorable river of heavy evening traffic along Collins Avenue and into the long sweeping drive of the fifties-era Miami Beach hotel. Colored landscape lights hidden amidst the flowering shrubbery on the Fontainebleau Hotel grounds and at the tops of the royal palms along the tree-lined drive cast a greenish underwater glow on a line of bumper-to-bumper limos snaking towards the entrance.

To Stoke, the neon-lit scene had all the boyhood glitz of a Technicolor Frank Sinatra movie. Those were the days. Frankie and his Rat Pack were lucky enough to live in a time when even the baddest of the bad didn't murder brides in wedding dresses on the steps of no church. That, at least, is what Stoke was thinking as he and Ross climbed out of the back of the Lincoln. Heat hit him like a wall.

He rapped the driver's side window, and Trevor lowered it, expelling a blast of icy air. Outside, the air was thick, heavy, hot. Just the right conditions for an explosive storm. The electric charge in the air made the hair on his forearms stand up.

"Okay, Preacher, listen up. Here's the program. Me and Ross, we going inside the Grand Ballroom for a coupla hours and rub elbows with the rich and semifamous. Eat us some gourmet rubber chicken. Maybe even find us a murder suspect doing the cha-cha-cha out on the dance floor, who knows? Can you wait somewhere 'round here?"

"I be right here, don't you worry," Trevor said. "De head doorman, Cholo, he is from my hometown of Port Antonio. Member to my congregation. He already knows about you, Tiki-mon. I told him we were coming."

"Listen. You got to stop calling me that," Stoke said, bending down to look Trevor in the eye. "Tiki, okay, he's good, I'll grant you that, but he plays for the Giants. Candy-ass. Stoke was a Jet, awright? Badass. Get this shit straight, now, you want to stay on the A-team."

"Yes, mon, no more Tiki."

"Good. Listen, I don't think this is going to happen. But you tell your homeboy, Cholo, he sees me and Ross come out that main entrance behind some guy with his hands in the air? That tells Cholo something. Tells him to call your cell, get you up to the front door in hurry. We collar one of these fat cats, there's likely to be some pissed off people around. Need to cut and run."

The very idea caused Trevor to slam his fist against the steering wheel in excitement.

"Yes, mon! I love it! You ever see *True Lies*? *Bad Boys Two*? *CSI: Miami* on the TV? Same ting as dis, mon! Exact same ting!"

"You ain't seen nothin' yet, Preacher," Stoke said. "Me and Ross here, we badass lawmen of the hop and pop, snatch and grab variety. We find this pencil-dicked shithead killed our lady friend, he only going to be *wishing* his ass was still grass."

There was a deep rumble of thunder above, brilliant lightning blooming in the towering clouds, and the wind gusting up, bending the crowns of the royal palms. No rain yet, but Stoke could smell the sharp ozone in the air as they made their way up the drive to the hotel's entrance. A big doorman smiled at Stoke, holding the door open for them. The homeboy Cholo, who looked like some four-star general in Rasta National Guard.

"Most cordial welcome to de Fontainebleau, Tikimon," Cholo said.

Stoke shook his head, didn't say anything, just followed Ross inside.

"When's the last time you see a hotel lobby like this, Ross?" Stoke asked rhetorically. *"Ocean's Eleven,* 1960, that's when. Damn, that was a good movie. Shit!"

As they made their way through the vast sea of candlelit tables filling the Grand Ballroom, a lot of heads swiveled in Stokely's direction. They were headed towards Table 27, the designated location inscribed neatly on the invitations waiting for them at the entrance where all the little old red-, white-, and blue-haired Latino ladies sat. Patriotic, you had to say that.

"Hell they all looking at, Ross?" Stoke whispered.

"Stoke, if you could see yourself right now, you wouldn't be asking that question," Ross said, smiling.

Unable to find black formal wear large enough to fit him, Stoke had been forced to rent a white tuxedo with wide white satin lapels and white satin stripes down each pants leg. Normally, he would have been embarrassed, but, earlier, when he'd met Ross for a drink down in the lobby bar at the Delano, the Scotland Yard detective had told him he looked resplendent. Resplendent sounded pretty damn good to Stoke, and, he had to admit, it wasn't a half-bad look. Be honest about it, way all these Cuban folks looking at him now, he must look pretty damn resplendent.

You got it, you strut it, Stoke thought, strutting through the endless maze of rich folk. Ring-a-ding-ding, and call me a cab, Calloway.

They took the last two empty gold bamboo chairs at the round table for ten and smiled all around at their dinner companions. The handsome black-tied men all looked like Don Ameche or Fernando Lamas and all the pretty ladies had low-cut dresses and more diamonds than the whole damn Tiffany store on Fifth Avenue. The appearance of this strange duet at the last minute was met with obvious surprise.

"No society like high society, am I right?" Stoke asked his dinner companions, a big smile on his face. "I'm Stokely Jones Jr. One of the Joneses of the West 138th Street Joneses of New York City. How you doing?" He stuck out his huge hand, and shook hands with a beautiful white-haired woman seated next to him. No one seemed to know quite what to do.

"Dolores Velasqueno," the lovely woman said. "How nice to meet you, Mr. Jones."

"Charmed," Stoke said. "I'm sure."

Then Ross said something that sounded like "ahem" that diverted everyone's attention from the giant black man dressed all in glittering white.

"Good evening, everyone. How do you do," Ross said to the startled table, bowing slightly from the waist. "I'm Detective Inspector Ross Sutherland, New Scotland Yard. My colleague and I are last-minute invitees, actually. Sorry we're a bit late. Traffic, you know."

Ross breathed a sigh of relief as Cesar de Santos took the podium. Everyone became silent, eyes on the elegant silver-haired chairman. Ross looked out over the crowd, pleased with the location of their table. They were near the front and on the edge of the ballroom, two or three steps higher than the main floor. He could get a pretty good look at the entire crowd from this vantage point. White-jacketed waiters were already circulating among the tables serving the first course. There had to be a thousand people in the room.

It was going to be fiendishly difficult to pick out a chap just by looking at his eyes, even if they'd gotten outrageously lucky and the man was in this very room. But Ross's investigative instincts were all telling him this was a good place to start, no matter what transpired.

"Good evening, ladies and gentlemen, and *bienvenidos*," de Santos said, his voice filling the huge room over the p.a. system. He launched into his remarks in beautifully accented English, thanking everyone for their generosity over the past year, highlighting individual achievements.

Stokely was far more interested when the lady seated to his right, *Senora* Velasqueno, opened her small white sequined evening bag and withdrew a tiny pair of pearl and gold binoculars. She put them to her eyes and focused on the podium. After a moment, she set them on the tablecloth.

"What power are those things, Dolores?" he asked, pointing at the jeweled binoculars.

"I beg your pardon?"

"How strong are they?"

"Strong as I could get them, *señor*," she said. "I'm blind as a bat."

"Can I take a look?" Stoke asked.

She smiled and handed them to him. "Please, be my guest. I've been to this dinner every year since 1975. It doesn't change much except for the surgery sisters over there at Table 25. They all have brand-new faces every year."

She giggled and put her hand over her mouth and Stoke slapped his knee and laughed.

She was right about the binocs, though. They were small, but powerful. While de Santos continued with his remarks, Stokely used them to scan the faces of the men in the crowd. "Ross," he said suddenly, handing the instrument to Sutherland. "Check out glamour boy over there sitting at the table by the exit sign."

"He's wearing sunglasses."

"Damn right. And these candles ain't all that bright either. So, who's that hiding behind them mirrored Foster Grants?"

". . . and now we come to the moment you've all been waiting for," de Santos was saying. "It is time to bestow our cherished *Ca d'Oro* award to that individual who has most thoroughly distinguished himself in the eyes of not only our judges, but our great Cuban community . . . will you bring the house lights down, please?"

As the lights went down, the music of the orchestra swelled. There was a collective gasp from the audience as a single spotlight picked out an object descending from out of the darkness above. Stokely put his glasses on the thing. It was a model of some kind of futuristic building, all towering glass wings with gold and silver beams inside. Suspended on a huge platform, it stopped just above the heads of a crowd who instantly burst into loud and sustained applause.

"Ladies and gentlemen," de Santos said, "may I present the new Quixote Fox Center for Special Surgery at Sisters of Mercy Hospital! It is my very great honor to announce the man who made this magnificent addition possible. Although new to our cause, already his great humanity and generosity have made him a revered figure in the community. The winner of *Ca d'Oro* is *Señor* Quixote Fox! *Señor* Fox, unfortunately, was called away to an emergency this evening. Please be so kind as to welcome his representative at the podium to receive the award."

All eyes turned towards the table of honor in the center of the room. A single spotlight swept the table. No one stood up. Stokely trained his binoculars on the table. It was where the guy with the mirrored sunglasses had been sitting. Now, his chair was empty. No man made a move to rise, but a woman did. Stokely never took his eyes off her as she made her shimmering way to the podium. She was maybe the best-looking woman Stoke had ever laid eyes on in his life.

"Dolores," Stoke whispered to his new friend, "who is that?"

"Her name is Fancha. She is a famous recording star from the Cape Verde Islands off the west coast of Africa. Very beautiful. She is the . . . friend . . . of Don Quixote Fox."

"This Don Quixote's a pretty lucky fella," Stokely said, watching through the glasses as de Santos tried to get the blue ribbon with the medal around Fancha's lovely neck without rearranging her hairstyle.

"They say he is very handsome, but I wouldn't know. I am not surprised he is not here this evening. He rarely appears in public."

"Really?" Stoke asked. "That's interesting. Why is that?"

"He's going blind. Apparently he suffers some very rare form of eye disease. He cannot bear exposure to any kind of light, natural or artificial."

"Eye disease, huh?" Stoke said, thinking about the mirrored sunglasses guy. "Tell me something, Dolores. This Don Quixote, he been down here in Miami a long time?"

"Oh, no, not at all. Two years perhaps. He's quite young for such a very wealthy man. No one is quite sure where he made his fortune. Or, even where he came from. Very generous. And very mysterious."

"Mysterious. Like, what kind of mysterious?"

"Well, there are a number of things. All very curious."

"Tell me one."

"Ah. Well, someone proposed him for membership at the Dinner Key Yacht Club. He was unanimously rejected by the membership committee. No one will say why. These things are strictly confidential. Then, a month later, the president of the club overturned the board's decision and extended him an invitation to join. Some people said that some kind of pressure was involved in the president's decision to . . . admit him."

"Yeah, well, country club politics can be a can of worms all right, and Lord knows I've seen no end of that stuff myself, but—"

"There was something, hmm, else . . ."

"Talk to me, Dolores. Quixote Fox sounds fascinating."

"This is all beauty parlor gossip, *señor,* but . . . somebody apparently tried to kill him. Unsuccessfully, yes. But, I hear there have been other attempts on his life. He rides in an armored Rolls-Royce motorcar and his home has many guards."

"Is that right?" He looked from Dolores to Ross.

Stokely suddenly got up from the table, motioning to Ross to do the same.

"You got to excuse me a while, Dolores. I got to talk to my man Ross outside for a couple a minutes."

CHAPTER TWENTY-SIX

Nantucket Island

Alex Hawke and Chief Jack Patterson stood in the sunshine on the bow of *Blackhawke*, some thirty feet above the choppy waters of Nantucket Harbor. It was just before seven o'clock on a fine, clear Saturday morning, little more than twenty-four hours after the barely averted attack on the yacht. There were few signs of life aboard the many craft moored along the docks and out at the buoys. Summer sailors traditionally liked to party on Friday nights, and most of them were sleeping in this morning, having closed down the Straight Wharf, the Summer House, or even the notoriously rowdy Chicken Box in the wee small hours.

The air was full of snapping ensigns and diving seagulls and terns. The brisk wind and sharp iodine bite of the sea air made Hawke keenly aware of all his senses. He could feel it. He could feel everything. He was coming back. The recent episode on board *Running Tide* had cleared out a lot of cobwebs; more importantly, it had revealed a number of serious chinks in his well-worn armor.

Numb with grief and anger, his defenses down

both literally and figuratively, Hawke had managed to stumble into one very nasty trap. Despite warnings from the man he'd entrusted with his security, he had underestimated the level of terrorist threat by a stupidly wide margin. As it happened, the incident was providential. He'd prevented a disaster that could have cost the lives of many of his friends and crew. Had the Arab simply locked down all the hatches leading to the deck, trapping Hawke below, the terrorist attack might have succeeded. But cheap luck like that ran out quickly.

After a year of bliss that had ended in tragedy, Alex Hawke was once again in the thick of it. Congreve had announced over after-dinner coffee that it was officially cloak and dagger time again.

DSS Chief Patterson had arrived from Maine via Coast Guard chopper just at twilight. Alex had watched the approach of the big red-and-white helicopter from *Blackhawke*'s launch. The helicopter flared up for a landing on the waters just beyond the breakwater. Alex leaned on the twin stainless steel throttles and the launch sped out to the chopper, bobbing on its pontoons, where the head of the State Department's security forces stood waiting with a small duffel bag. On the short trip back to the yacht, he'd brought Patterson up to speed on the latest events. The near-disastrous flight he and Ambrose had experienced returning to the island from Maine. And the narrowly averted terrorist attack on *Blackhawke* itself.

"Father and son act," Hawke said. "They almost pulled it off."

"Yup. Babysitter's father and her brother the rookie

cop," Patterson said, in his slow Texas drawl. "Makes sense. Father'd been a mechanic over at the airport since he'd moved his charming little sleeper cell family up from New York City. This kid Kerim. You say he tagged the Dog?"

"Yeah. It's the Dog, all right. But some guy called the Emir is apparently pulling everybody's strings. Has been for a long time, too. Ever heard of him?"

"I got emirs and sheiks coming out the wazoo, Hawkeye. You gotta do a lot better than that."

"I plan to. At any rate, no doubt you, too, are on this particular Emir's hit list."

"Hell, Alex, ain't a shit list or hit list I ain't on—for so long I can't hardly remember when I wasn't. Sometimes I feel like the entire radical Islamic world's got a *fatwa* on my head. But you, now that's a different story. Why in hell would they go after you? You poke your stick in any hives lately?"

"Let's just say I don't have a lot of close friends in the worldwide terrorist community," Alex said.

"Show me your boat and we'll talk all about it."

Hawke, listening intently to the latest intel from the DSS team as they walked, had already shown Patterson far more than most visitors ever got to see. He'd seen things inconceivable on anything less than one of the U.S. Navy's own Spruance-class destroyers. *Blackhawke* featured a balanced combat systems suite with towed array and active sonars, medium-range surface-to-air missile systems mounted inside the ship's hull on both the port and starboard sides, and two long-range 7.6mm guns, also concealed, mounted both fore and aft. This integrated combat system centered on the Aegis weapon system, now up and running again, and the SPY-1 multifunction, phased array radar. All located on the very lowest deck in what was known as the War Room.

"Hell, Hawkeye," Patterson said, looking around the massive bridge deck, "this ain't no yacht. It's a goddamn battleship disguised as a yacht."

Alex smiled. "I wouldn't go quite that far, Tex," he said, "light destroyer, perhaps, but not battleship."

Tommy Quick now approached the two men quietly talking at the bow. He stopped a respectful distance away and caught Alex's eye by saluting.

"Morning, Skipper," Quick said. "Sorry to disturb you."

"Not at all, Sarge," Alex replied. "Mr. Patterson and I are just standing up here trying to figure out how to save the goddamn world."

"Yes, sir," Quick said. "Call for you, Skipper. Mr. Congreve down in the War Room. He says it's important. Some kinda press conference being televised in about five minutes."

Hawke said, "Tell him we're on our way."

"Christ, what time is it?" Patterson asked. "Alex, I clean forgot about this."

"Exactly six-fifty-five Eastern, Chief."

"Which makes it almost noon in Paris," Jack Patterson said, as he and Alex entered an elevator. "Unfortunately, I think I know exactly what this is about, Alex. Our ambassador in Paris has gone completely off the doggone rails."

"After what happened up in Dark Harbor, I should be surprised if all of your ambassadors weren't all a little shaky, Tex."

"Yeah, you bet."

They rode down six decks in silence, emerged and turned left into a long corridor lit with red domed lights every four feet or so. Hawke paused at a massive steel door and punched a seven-digit pass code into a small black box mounted on the wall. A cover in the center of the door slid back, and behind it was a fingerprint identification pad. Hawke pressed his thumb to it and the thick door slid silently into the bulkhead, revealing the War Room.

It was surprisingly small, packed with computer screens, radar screens, and TV monitors. Two young crewmen wearing earphones sat before a bewildering array of switches and controls, monitoring the integrated search, track, and weapons systems. The information displayed above them was an electronic visualization of the world out to some one hundred miles or more from the ship. The blue lighting inside the War Room was designed to enhance the video displays. At the far end of a conference table, a seated figure was wreathed in smoke.

"Some setup, Hawkeye," Tex said, whistling softly.

"Thanks. We like it."

"Who the heck is that in the velvet jacket?"

"That? That would be Chief Constable Ambrose Congreve, WMD."

"WMD?"

"Weapon of Mass Deduction."

CHAPTER TWENTY-SEVEN

Miami

Half an hour later, Stoke was shivering in the front seat, busily pulling all the small gold studs out of his shirtfront. The pleated shirt with the gold doodads down the front had to go. A man doesn't feel so damn resplendent when he is all wet and cold and shit, soaked to the bone.

They had made a run for the car the same moment as the furious storm finally unloaded over Miami Beach. Stoke and Ross raced out of the hotel and made a mad dash down the drive, looking for Preacher's Lincoln. Torrential rain and wind lashed them, and the near-hurricane-force winds of the tropical squall were strong enough to rock the cars parked along the drive. Even though Trevor was flashing the high beams, man, you couldn't see a goddamn thing.

"What'd I tell you 'bout the tropics, Ross?" Stoke asked as they jumped inside the Town Car and pulled the doors shut, straining against heavy winds.

"I can't remember," Ross said, jumping in the rear.

"Three little words is all I got to say," Stoke said, fumbling with the AC controls. "Humidity, humidity, humidity."

"Call this humidity?" Ross said.

"Wet, ain't it? What the hell else would you call it?"

Preacher's cell phone started playing the *William Tell* Overture. Have to talk to him 'bout that. So nineties.

"Yes?" Trevor said, flipping it open. "Okay. Good."

"What?" Stokely said.

"She's coming out now, Cholo says."

"Move up, Preacher," Ross said. "What you waiting for?"

The headlights were practically useless it was raining so hard, but Trevor managed to negotiate the curving drive without sideswiping any limos. Preacher edged forward, trying to get his nose under the covered entrance.

"Okay, let's wait here," Ross said.

They could see Fancha standing at the valet desk. She was flanked by two double extra large Cubanos in tuxedos. One look at them, Stokely knew they were all carrying. Suddenly, a midnight blue Bentley Azure convertible raced up out of the rain and screeched to a halt at the curb. The passenger side door swung open and some hombre in a white *guayabera* jumped out and helped the two tuxedos hustle the singer into the backseat.

The tires chirped as the big Bentley swept away from the curb and disappeared into the rain.

"Move it," Stoke said to Trevor.

The Bentley's large and distinctive red taillights made tailing it a good deal easier in the blinding rainstorm. It hooked a left onto Collins Avenue, heading south, the storm-whipped breakers of the Atlantic and Hotel Row on their left. Trevor did as he was told, always at least one or two cars between the Lincoln and the Bentley, keeping the Bentley in sight.

"Where are they headed, Trevor?" Ross asked after they'd passed a number of intersections.

"All you can do is go west 'cross Biscayne Bay to downtown on the MacArthur Causeway."

Which is exactly what the big Bentley did, turn right on 5th and head across the causeway connecting South Beach to the mainland. Five minutes later, at the intersection of Brickell Avenue, in the heart of downtown Miami, the car took another left, heading south on South Miami Avenue.

"He's headed for Coconut Grove," Trevor said, excited, accelerating.

"Easy. Easy. You get any closer, he's going to make us, Preacher," Stoke said. "Man looks like he slowing down, fixing to turn in somewhere."

Trevor hit the brakes seconds before the Bentley's taillights flashed red and the car swerved into a wide drive, coming to a stop at a massive, ornate set of iron gates.

"This not making no sense, mon. No sense a'tall."

"Don't stop, Trevor, don't slow down, keep going," Ross said from the backseat. "It's a residence, is it?"

"Was a residence built by some millionaire back in de twenties," Trevor said. "Now, de house got to be de biggest tourist attraction in South Florida. Called Vizcaya. A beautiful museum, mon! Sitting on a huge piece of land sticking right out into de bay. Tell you one thing for sure. It's not open this time of night."

"Hang a right here, and turn around," Stokely said, craning his head around to keep the Bentley in sight. "Let's go back and see what the hell he's up to."

Trevor backtracked to Vizcaya, slowed, turned right into the drive and pulled to a stop before the gate. The Azure had disappeared inside. On the right was a three-story stucco guardhouse, and a huge man wearing a black poncho came out into the downpour. He sloshed through the puddles at the front of the car and rapped his knuckles on Trevor's window. Hard rain was beating down on the man's clean-shaven head but it didn't seem to bother him much. Trevor cracked his window down about a foot and looked up at the guy.

"What can I do for you, bud?" the guy asked Trevor. Stoke leaned across Trevor's chest and favored the big bald guy with one of his biggest smiles.

"How you doing tonight? We just want to drive in and take a look around, that's all."

"Sorry. It ain't open," the guy said, heavy New York bad-ass accent. One look at the guy and two words popped into Stoke's brain. Mobbed up. Yeah, this was one seriously mobbed-up individual.

"Funny, we just saw somebody go in there," Stoke said. "It's a tourist attraction, right? A museum? Open to the public, is what I'm saying."

"You got a hearing problem, asshole? I said it ain't open."

"You want to watch who you call an asshole, asshole," Stoke said, still smiling.

"Listen close, asshole. This is private property. A private residence."

"You work for the man, right? You got any ID? Rap sheet, maybe? All them prison tats on your wrists? Look to me like some jive-ass con fresh out of the joint. Guy who's done more time than a clock, you know what I'm sayin'?"

"You wanna fuck with me?"

"Maybe later. I swear I know this jailbird, Preacher. I think maybe I even sent him up once. Aggravated stupidity. Hey! This is the Vizcaya Museum, isn't that right, hard case?"

"Right. But it ain't no museum no more. Guy who owns it now shoots trespassers and apologizes later. You're trespassing. Now, you two get your black asses out of here or I'm going to fuck you up."

"Oh. Oh, I see. It's a racial thing. Hey, there's another guy in the back. He white. Can he go in?"

"Fuck are you, wiseguy, or somethin'?"

"Stokely Jones, NYPD," Stoke said, flashing his old shield and forgetting to add the "retired" part as he sometimes did in situations of stress.

"Yeah? Is that right? A plainclothes cop, huh? Tailing the boss's Bentley looks like. Maybe you better come in after all," the guy said, pulling a double-barreled sawed-off shotgun out from under his poncho and pressing the muzzle against Trevor's temple. To his credit, the Preacher didn't even flinch.

The big black gates swung inward.

"Bada-boom, bada-bing!" Stoke said, getting right up in the guy's grille, trying not to smile too much when he said it.

The guy, pissed, pulled the shotgun away from Trevor's head. Stoke saw Preacher's lips moving, guessed he was praying.

Stoke looked past Preacher and smiled at the mob guy. "Now, you listenin' to reason, see? I knew you come around eventually."

"Fuck you," the guy said.

"Your place or mine?" Stoke said.

He was showing him a lot of pearly whites as Trevor accelerated the big Lincoln away and up the curving drive. Stokely swung his massive arm over the back of the seat and looked at Ross, seeing a big smile on his face.

"What you smiling at?"

"You, mate," Ross said. "Just you, Stoke."

"Shit," Stoke said. "A guy like that? Kind of guy can't make it as a real person, so he trying to make it as a character."

CHAPTER TWENTY-EIGHT

Nantucket Island

Ambrose Congreve was sitting with slippered feet upon the table. Still in his pajamas, the man was also wearing, for some reason, a quilted black velvet smoking jacket with a scarlet spotted handkerchief in the breast pocket. He was smoking his pipe and looking up at a large television monitor hung from the ceiling. A graphic on the screen read:

FOX BREAKING NEWS!

"Top of the morning, Ambrose," Hawke said cheerfully. "You're up awfully early. Something good on the telly?"

Congreve turned and smiled at the newcomers through a haze of blue smoke. "I don't normally watch the television at this hour, as you know, Alex. I don't normally watch anything at this bloody hour except the angels of my dreams. But your dear friend Conch called from Washington at the hellish hour of six and got me out of my very warm bed. Apparently, something alarming is afoot with your ambassador in Paris, Mr. Patterson."

"Grab a seat, Tex," Hawke said, "and pay him no mind. He's always grouchy until his midday eye-opener." Congreve shot Hawke a narrow look out of the corner of his eye and then returned his attention to the monitor.

"This could be mighty damn interesting, Alex," Patterson said, as everyone took a chair.

"What does he—"

"Here it is," Patterson said.

Fox TV cut from a tight shot of their reporter to a wide shot of the ambassador and his two children out in the embassy gardens. He was bent over, whispering something to the two blond boys, putting his mouth to each of their ears. Then he stood upright, smiled broadly and approached the podium.

"Bonjour et bienvenue," he began.

The camera zoomed in slowly on the ambassador's face as he spoke, catching the blazing patriotism and the power of his conviction in his clear blue eyes.

"Freedom and fear are at war," he began. Ten minutes later, having finished his speech, the ambassador began fielding questions from the press.

"Christ almighty, Duke, what the hell are you thinking?" Patterson said to the screen, slamming his open hand down on the table when the speech ended.

"I admire his stand, actually," Hawke said, gazing thoughtfully at the ambassador's face. "He's right, you know."

"Hell with right," Patterson said angrily. "This ain't the time for who's right or who's wrong. My team is charged with protecting the lives of these people! Now, you got this guy telling his colleagues around the world that—holy hell—now what?"

Everyone in the War Room stared up in horror at the images now unfolding on the monitor. The American ambassador writhing on the ground, white smoke pouring from his shoes. The shocked, disbelieving faces of his two young boys, desperately trying to rush to their father's aid, but held back by the security agents trying to shield them from the sight of horrendous flames igniting at his feet.

"White phosphorus," Tex Patterson said. "Christ! Somebody got to his shoes and—"

Ambrose saw the anguished look on Alex's face, riveted by the vision of two little boys watching their father die before their eyes. "Turn it off!" Ambrose said, getting to his feet. "Turn the bloody thing off!"

Someone hit the remote and the screen went dark.

The men gathered around the table were silent. Everyone knew Hawke had witnessed the torture-slaying of his father and mother on a cruise to the Bahamas.

"Tex," Alex said, lifting his head and turning his burning gaze towards the DSS man. "You got a real fight on your hands. A carefully orchestrated jihad. And, it's personal. The Dog is killing your guys one at a time. And he likes to fight dirty."

"You know what the worst part is, Hawkeye? We don't know how to fight dirty anymore."

"Oh, there still may be a few of us left around," Alex said.

"Suggestion?" said Congreve. "Unless anyone has more pressing engagements, no one should leave this ship until we reach a very clear understanding of two things. How to run down this wretched Dog. And how to take him out. Mr. Patterson?"

Tex leaned back in his chair, an unlit cigarette dangling from his sun-chapped lips.

"Yeah. Let me start at the beginning of this thing. We had a case. DSS had a case, I mean. A serial killer in London in the mid-nineties. Most of his victims were young, attractive women. Shop girls. Prostitutes. My team only got involved when he murdered a State Department employee. Girl he'd picked up in a pub in Soho."

"What was her name?" Congreve asked.

"Alice Kearns. Low-level staffer. African Affairs section at our embassy in Grosvenor Square."

"She was his last victim?"

"Correct. Late spring, 1998. May."

"American, I assume."

"As a matter of fact, yes. The only American victim. Why would you assume that?"

Congreve stroked his moustache, ignoring the question. "So the man you suspected of orchestrating the murders in Maine, fingered by the young deputy before he died, he was the suspect in these London serial murders as well?"

"Yes."

"I see. And how did this 'Dog,' as you call him, come by his unfortunate moniker?"

"His laugh," Patterson said.

"I don't follow."

"Videotapes were found in his penthouse on Park Lane after he disappeared. In each tape, the murderer is seen wearing a black hooded kaftan. Very careful never to show his face. But, by God, you can hear his laugh. Cackling. Howling. Shrieking. Just like a wild dog."

"The Dog wore a kaftan," Alex said. "Arabic."

"Definitely," Patterson replied. "We were getting very close. He was a well-known business figure in London, but somehow we managed to keep our suspicions out of the press, the whole story. He had no idea we were onto him. No one did."

"Name?" Hawke asked.

"Snay bin Wazir," Patterson said. "Had an Emirate passport, but he'd been around. Africa. Indonesia—"

"The Pasha! The Pasha of Knightsbridge. Brick Kelly and I had a lovely evening with him one night at the Connaught. Very well dressed chap. Polished. He wanted to join Nell's."

"Yes. That was late December, just a few days before we decided to move. On New Year's Eve, 1999, a team of our boys went in with SAS commandos. Roped down from choppers to the terrace of his penthouse on Park Lane. One small problem: the guy was just gone. Appeared to have been forcibly abducted. He and his wife, Yasmin. There were signs of a struggle in the apartment. But, a lot of incriminating evidence left scattered about. Photographs of the victims. Tapes. Relics. Murder souvenirs."

"Did anyone at the time think your serial killer might have been politically motivated, Chief Patterson?" Congreve asked.

"No. Why?"

"Just thinking. Alice Kearns was the last to die before bin Wazir disappeared. She was also the only American to die. She worked for the State Department. African Affairs, I believe you said. It occurs to me that Miss Kearns may well have been the beginning of your current troubles. Was she tortured? Mutilated?"

"Yes. How would you know that?"

"The others the same?"

"Uh, no. She was the only one."

"Hmm."

Congreve got up from the table and began pacing around it, puffing thoughtfully on his pipe. "Please continue, Mr. Patterson. This is most interesting."

"Included in bin Wazir's grisly personal murder video collection was another tape. This one was of the bombings of our embassies in Dar es Salaam and Nairobi. You remember that—" He stopped suddenly and looked at Congreve. "Inspector, I believe I just figured out where the hell you're going with this. I've got it now. Africa."

"Yes," Congreve said. "The Dar es Salaam and Nairobi embassy attacks in Africa. I believe they took place sometime in late summer 1998?"

"August 7. We lost eleven in our Dar es Salaam embassy that day. Two hundred thirteen died in Nairobi the very same day. These were the first two terrorist acts against U.S. interests in Africa. No one knew the attacks were just the beginning of a worldwide war, of course."

"Attacks which occurred just two months after the Kearns girl was murdered in May," Congreve said, studying Patterson's face. "The Kearns girl would have had access to embassy files and information, no? Architectural plans, personnel, schedules, et cetera."

Tex nodded his head, favoring Congreve with a grim smile of appreciation. "Yes, she would have, Inspector. That's how he did it. He extracted what he needed from that poor girl in order to plan the two bombings."

"Tell us, please, about the videotape of the bombings?"

"The African videos were apparently shot from vehicles parked across the street from our embassies at the time of the explosions. Just far enough away to avoid damage and shot with a long lens. The man operating the camera can be heard laughing. Especially when the rescue workers begin removing corpses from the rubble."

Congreve rose from the table, puffing on his briar. He looked at Hawke and Patterson for a moment, thinking. "If I may," he asked mildly.

"Please," Patterson said.

"Snay bin Wazir is not a maniac at all," Congreve said. "A murderous psychopath, yes. Fiendishly clever. But he's no lunatic nor religious zealot, either. One has only to look at his lifestyle in London. He seems to have embraced Western fashion with a passion. Clothing, habits, mannerisms. So the man was, by all appearances, completely apolitical. If anything, a dyed-in-the-wool capitalist. Few al-Qaeda apply for membership at Nell's. Suddenly, he kills a young woman for her secrets and attacks American interests in Africa. Why? And then he just disappears."

"It doesn't make any sense at all," Hawke put in. "An unlikely political terrorist if ever I saw one."

"Unless he became a pawn of someone else. Someone who actually is fundamentalist, who is a zealot, who does have a burning hatred for the West."

"Yes. The Dog is a henchman for a terrorist network. But why would he do that?" Patterson asked. "Become a pawn?"

"Motive? Ah. Money, I suppose," Congreve said. "He lost his shirt in London real estate, don't forget."

"If you're looking for a zealot, I've got a candidate,"

Hawke said. "This Emir the boy Kerim mentioned before he died. The man who controls all the sleepers. Someone with apparently limitless resources. Power and influence."

"Yes," Tex said, excitement creeping into his voice. They were finally getting somewhere. "That's how this bin Wazir does it. He has some massive organization behind him, founded by the Emir. Why, the bastard just pulled off the assassination of one of our most prominent ambassadors in front of the whole world!"

"Meanwhile this Emir hides out in a cave or a bunker somewhere, keeping his own hands clean," Hawke said.

"But, think about *why* this Dog is doing what he is doing, Chief Patterson," Congreve said. "He is calmly and systematically destroying your entire diplomatic corps. Paralyzing you. Why? Why would he do that?"

"Ambassadors and their families make an ideal target. Potent symbols of the country's ideals. And a projection of America's power abroad."

"All true. But, still, why target your ambassadors? Yankee go home?" Congreve asked. "Perhaps. But I think not."

"Ambrose?" Alex said, seeing the man's thoughtful expression.

"Where does it all lead?" Congreve mused. "These attacks are not random; they are systematic, beginning with the first two embassy attacks in Africa. And they will lead, eventually, to total paralysis. So why does one, this Emir for argument's sake, wish to paralyze one's enemy? Obvious, isn't it? A paralyzed enemy cannot fight back. Can't react. Incapable of retaliation when the killer or killers finally move in for the ultimate and perhaps cataclysmic objective."

"Yeah," Patterson agreed. "Looking at our recent digital cell intercepts, I'd say cataclysmic is a pretty good description. It is no secret our embassies are our primary intelligence platforms around the world. You paralyze our diplomatic corps and you cripple a lot of our intelligence-gathering capability. Hell, I see traffic almost every day alluding to some great 'day of reckoning.'"

"Every dog has his day," Congreve said.

"We just have to make damn sure this dog's days are numbered," said Hawke.

"Chief Patterson?" a young technician said.

"Yes?"

"A flash traffic e-mail for you, sir, just coming in from your Paris chief of station. Marked Top Secret."

"Acquire and verify. Then just decode it and print it, son," Patterson said. Because of *Blackhawke*'s almost constant communication with the U.S. State Department and British MI6, all but the most sensitive U.S. and U.K. codes were permanently loaded in her computer servers.

A minute later, the crewman handed him a single sheet of paper inside a black folder bearing the words "TOP SECRET" in red.

"Aw, damn it to hell," Patterson said, quickly scanning the thing.

"Tell me," Alex said.

"Regret to inform you," Patterson read aloud, "that Special Agent Rip McIntosh died in the line of duty at 1220 hours this afternoon, in a valiant attempt to save the life of Ambassador Duke Merriman."

CHAPTER TWENTY-NINE

The Emirate

Blessed and accursed. That is my life, the fate I have made for myself, Snay bin Wazir thought, gazing upon the lovely face of his Rose. The Pasha and the Rose, lounging atop silken pillows scattered across the parquetry flooring, watched the two sweating sumos inside the *dohyo,* the ring, watched them collide, grunting loudly as they did so.

Snay bin Wazir was also watching Rose, keenly aware of her reaction to the private demonstration he'd arranged for the two of them, alone, in the beautiful shrine he'd had built for his sumos. Her lips were parted and she was breathing rapidly. Her bosom swelled rhythmically. There was a light sheen of perspiration on her forehead. Far from being repelled by the sight and sounds of two nearly naked giants grappling with each other, she was, it seemed, decidedly excited.

The sight of her erect nipples, etched in perfect relief against the taut yellow silk of her chemise, was having an increasingly noticeable effect on the Pasha as well.

The Pasha looked down upon this growing evidence of passion beneath his robes and sighed. The

potent admixture of desire and frustration was something he'd always dealt with badly.

All of his latest efforts to bed this most prized of all
the *hashishiyyun* in his seraglio of assassins had failed.
Since Francesca had arrived at his palace from Rome, he
had plied her with jewels, enormous rubies and diamonds. One sapphire as big as a plum. Gifts of sable and
myrrh and gold. Nothing, it seemed, had any effect on
this most sublime of creatures. She was, as he constantly
reminded himself, one of the world's most beautiful and
desirable women.

Francesca. Even her name stirred him, inflamed
him, ignited fireworks of fantasy deep in his brain.
Francesca. Sleeping alone in the desert, a fortnight ago,
he'd written the word in the sand outside his Bedouin
tent. Awakening, he saw the wind had erased her
name. Why did he torture himself? It was foolishness.
This forlorn desire of his did nothing but demean him.
She was a world-famous film star with a considerable
personal fortune. A creature of such transcendent
beauty, she could bat one of her enormous brown eyes
and instantly have any man she might desire groveling
at her feet.

Hopeless!

He could not force himself upon her, she was far
too valuable. Should he lose her, there would be hell to
pay with the Emir, who rightfully considered her a
great asset. Born of a Roman father and a Syrian
mother, Francesca had grown up begging on the backstreets of Damascus. Abused as a child by her cruel
Italian father, she had, since childhood, nursed a
fevered hatred for the impious Westerners who ruled
the world. Her celebrity cover, achieved over the last

decade, was ideal. A rabid holy warrior in the guise of a glamourous Italian film star. It was too delicious for words.

Still, it meant he could not buy her affection with gems or gold. Yet there was something powerful between them. A bond. A thirst, a hunger that bound them together. A kind of lust, yes. Bloodlust?

He had been afraid this rejection was because of his recently acquired girth, his now enormous size. But, no, watching her watching the massive sumos, it was clear this was not the problem. Ah, well. This was not the first time he'd faced this insoluble and most distressing dilemma. Nor would it be the last. He could have as many wives as he wished, of course, as long as they were approved by Yasmin. And Yasmin approved only drudges and dogs. Thus, Francesca was forbidden fruit.

He was as eternally bound to Yasmin as the sea is to its bed, as the earth to its orbit, as the moth is wedded to the flame. Yes, he loved her, he supposed. In his way. And she him. But it was love without passion.

His anger for this gilded steel trap called his life, on the other hand, blazed with passion. Fueled each day as, in a thousand tiny ways, his wife Yasmin threw oil on the fire. A look, a word, a stare.

The Emir's daughter was both his salvation and his doom. With all his money and power, he was still Yasmin's slave. A prisoner here, inside his own palace. As long as he behaved himself, he could keep his head. *Keep your head down and you might keep it,* he reminded himself daily. Meanwhile, the Emir was biding his time, waiting for him to make a single misstep. Even a cross word with Yasmin behind closed doors somehow got back to her father. A word floated into his feverish mind, the word that came to him whenever the impossibility of his marital situation reared up and seared his brain.

Poison.

He wasted endless hours plotting his escape, as if it were remotely possible. Yes, he lay beside his wife, awake those countless nights, conjuring up accidents, mishaps, catastrophes that might befall this woman he no longer desired. Over the years, love had atrophied, which was not unusual. But resentment had grown in its stead. All because of her father's sword, dangling over his head. A situation she never hesitated to exploit in even the smallest disagreement. Even though she claimed to love him deeply!

To the Emir, and to the Pasha's world at large, they were a picture of mature wedded bliss. But, as the old saying has it, one never knows what goes on inside a marriage unless one sleeps under the tent. Unbearable.

So he fantasized endlessly of slips and falls; he conjured Yasmin's tragic demise and his ensuing freedom. Yet, no matter how delicate and elegant the scheme, no matter how sublimely he plotted his dreams, in the end, the Emir always found him out. His would be just one more among the countless heads the Emir had sent dry and scuttling across the desert sands.

Now, if the Emir himself were dead . . .

Suddenly, he couldn't breathe. His ribcage was taking a terrible battering from his heart, an organ that threatened to detonate at any moment. He looked down, startled and astounded to see Rose's beautiful white hand resting lightly upon the folds of crimson silk that draped his thighs. The hand traveled upwards, the fingers parted, searching. He was hard as stone when the hand seized the object of its desire.

"My Pasha," she said, turning those eyes toward him as she caressed him through the silk, wrapped him in it, tightening and then easing her grip.

He opened his mouth to speak, but she pressed a finger to his lips and stopped whatever mad, mindless, unspeakable words he was about to utter.

"No, Pasha," she whispered hoarsely, taking his hand and crushing it against her lush bosom where he felt one nipple already engorged under the silk. "My lips will speak for both of us."

He collapsed back against the pillows as she bent her head to his lap, parting the hem of his robes, yanking them upwards and then taking him in, her thick mane of blond hair cascading over the great expanse of his girth, her darting tongue everywhere at once.

Licks of fire.

Suddenly, her mouth was at his ear, nibbling, her breath hot and loud.

"I want you," she whispered. "Here. Now."

"But the sumos . . . Ichi and Kato . . ."

"In front of the sumos. I want them to see. Now."

That night, the four sumos carried the lovers through the orange groves in the Pasha's sedan chair. Once the sumos had been dismissed, the two alighted and walked deep into the heavily scented gardens. The evening sky was shot with stars, blazing in the clear mountain air. She was his now, and he took her, roughly, and pressed her to him.

"Put a dagger in my heart," he said, "we might as well get it over with."

"The two sumos' lips are sealed," she said. "She will never know."

"Yasmin knows everything."

"No one knows everything."

"In this house there are no secrets. How do you know the sumos—"

"Trust me."

He laughed then, almost giddy that such a woman as this could care for him, let alone exist. He could only imagine how she had managed to guarantee their silence.

"Venice was thrilling, but Paris was exquisite," he said, kissing her forehead. *"Grazie mille."*

"You enjoyed watching it, *caro?"*

"Yes. But, far more importantly, the Emir is ecstatic. He went so far as to say that it was good."

"Grazie."

He smiled at her and said, "She is first-rate, this Parisian one. This Lily. But, then, she learned from the best."

"I thought the white phosphorus would be more cinematic on CNN than a simple shot to the head."

It was such a perfectly outrageous statement he threw his head back and laughed, entwining a lock of her hair in his fingers.

"Genius," he said. "Pure genius."

"The hard part was thinking where to put it. The idea of the shoes, it was Lily's."

"It was perfection itself. Now, you must listen. Business. I have spoken to the Emir. We move to the next phase."

"Yes. It's time. To be honest, I was myself enjoying

this first part. But already we have the Americans running in circles."

"The next few moves will be the more challenging. Far more complex, intricate. It will not surprise you to learn that this assignment is yours."

"I am ready."

"I know."

"Tell me, Pasha."

"There is one more ambassador."

"He's a dead man."

"No, no. You are not to kill him. We will do that when we have what we want from him. We want him alive. He has certain information that is vital to our purposes."

"What, then?"

"A clean abduction. Snatch him. I will arrange for him to be brought here."

"How? *Caro*, it's one thing to kill. The . . . how you call it . . . logistics . . . of a kidnapping of such a public figure . . . *molto difficile.*"

"You'll think of something, my precious Rose."

He kissed her hard on the lips, crushed her against him, wanting to do more than possess her, wanting to both devour her and own her at the same time. Have his cake and eat it . . . he bent his head to her bosom.

Blessed and accursed.

"What was that," Francesca whispered, whirling her head about.

"What, darling girl?"

"I heard a sound. Over there. In the jasmine bushes."

"It is nothing. A peacock, perhaps. Come, now. To bed."

The man lingered in the bed of jasmine for an hour after the two lovers had returned to the palace, savoring both the scent of the flowers and the sweetness of his situation. Finally, he rose and went to the fountain he still visited daily, listening to the songs of the splashing waters, longing to hear the voice that haunted his every waking moment.

He lowered himself to the broad rim of the fountain and spoke quietly to his love. His words were full of hope and joy and promise.

The heartbroken sumo, Ichi, enslaved by the Pasha for so long, now had both the means and the opportunity to escape this prison and return to his homeland, to the source of the sun, his beloved Michiko.

He stole back through the gardens.

Ichi moved as quickly and as quietly as his great bulk would allow. Someone was waiting for him. He would find her sitting on the small marble bench, she said. The far end of the reflecting pool in the secret heart of her private meditation garden, she had told him. What he would say to her would both break her heart and steel her spine. But, no longer would Ichi be alone in his determination to be free of bin Wazir's velvet bonds.

He would have an ally in his struggle.

Yasmin.

CHAPTER THIRTY

The Cotswolds

Ambrose Congreve's feelings regarding the shooting of upland game birds were rivaled only remotely by his feelings in regard to fishing. He would as soon grasp a wriggling, slimy creature and wrench its lips from a fishhook as he would pluck a bloody pheasant from the gorse and stuff the still-warm corpse inside his waxed jacket, which was precisely what he was doing at this very moment.

A fishhook, the symbol used in logic to represent an "if-then" proposition, captured his sentiments at this moment perfectly. If you catch something, or shoot something, you've ultimately got to *do* something with the bloody thing.

He was still amazed he'd managed to hit the damned bird. His gun, a fine prewar Purdey twelve-bore, one of a brace lent him for the occasion by Alex Hawke—Alex being an ardent practitioner of the sport and one-time runner-up for the King's Cup—had not seen a lot of action today. The birds got up quickly, often too close or too far away to get off a shot, and, every time he mounted the gun to his shoulder, all he could see were dogs, beaters, and his fellow guns. He was so terrified of perhaps shooting any of them, that, until just moments ago, he hadn't pulled a trigger all day.

It was late in the day, and he was cold and wet and thoroughly tired of mucking about in the thickets of gorse and bramble in tight-fitting green gumboots. And more than ready to head home, shed these damp tweeds, and settle in for a cozy whiskey by the crackling fireside. His morning had gotten off to a rotten start, with Alex practically lecturing him, *lecturing,* for all love, about sporting behavior in the field. Not that he didn't need such a tutorial; God help him, he hadn't picked up a shotgun in years.

On one of the many bookshelves in his small flat in London was a book he'd read and loved as a child. One of his favorites, actually, an extraordinary book by a man named Dacre Balsdon. Its title still spoke volumes to Congreve.

The Pheasant Shoots Back.

Congreve had been a successful young inspector at Scotland Yard when he first met Alex Hawke, age nine. The trail of a notorious jewel thief had led him to the smallest of the Channel Islands, a fog-shrouded place called Greybeard Island. In the course of his investigation, he visited the home where Alex lived in the care of his elderly grandfather, the chief suspect in the bizarre case.

The very idea that one of England's wealthiest men, an island recluse named Lord Richard Hawke, had pirated his own late wife's jewelry in a daring daytime heist at Sotheby's in London had drawn the young inspector to the matter. Congreve, with the assistance of his suspect, Lord Hawke, solved that case. Ironically enough, it was the butler who had done it. A fellow named Edward Eding, who had faithfully served in his lordship's employ for decades, had masterminded the crime. In the process, priceless emeralds, tiaras, and Fabergé eggs belonging to Alex Hawke's late grandmother were returned to the London auction house. And Ambrose Congreve's burgeoning reputation as a master criminalist was solidified.

The clever young detective and the aging inhabitant of the drafty old pile known as Castle Hawke thereafter became fast friends. Congreve became a frequent guest at the great house on a rocky bluff overlooking the channel; and he was to prove an important figure and mentor in the life of young Alex Hawke.

Brutally orphaned at age seven, Alex was easily the most curious boy Ambrose had ever encountered. As Congreve would remark years later, "He questions the questions more than the answers." So Alex Hawke had relied on young Detective Congreve and his aging grandfather, Lord Hawke, to teach him everything they knew of the nature of the world and its inhabitants.

These early years of his childhood were spent covering even the most arcane of subjects; and for Ambrose to sit here now, silently feigning rapt attention while Alex Hawke, his erstwhile pupil, expounded on the art of killing small animals with high-powered weapons, was tiresome in the extreme.

He had learned, at breakfast that very morning, that to wound birds by very long shots was almost a crime. And that to destroy game meant for the table by shooting birds that were too near was almost as serious an error. A man who can shoot, Alex had informed him later, as they bounced along in the mud-splashed Range Rover, picks off his birds in the head or neck so as to avoid damaging the body for the cooks and the table.

"Look here, Alex, I must say," he'd replied, "I haven't picked up a field gun in thirty years and now you're telling me I'm supposed to shoot the wee beasties only in the *head?*"

So, whilst all around him guns had been blazing all day long, his beautifully engraved and checkered Purdey side-by-side had been notable only for its silence. The poor dead fellow he'd just stuffed into the game pocket of his waxed jacket was the result of a bit of bad luck on the bird's part, brought down without benefit of dog or beater.

Ambrose had just emerged from a remote covert where he'd gone to answer nature's call, and was quite alone. He had paused for a moment, contemplating the notion of pulling out his pipe, watching, with some degree of pleasure, the spaniels working a distant field, when a crowing pheasant suddenly rose up from a nearby bramble patch, perhaps some fifty yards to his left.

"My word," he said aloud, and instinctively mounted the gun to his shoulder, sighting down the twin barrels. The bird's low route of flight would bring him right past Congreve, neither too near nor too far nor too high. He swung his gun, aimed, and shot. Three pounds of flesh and feathers dropped on the spot. "My word," he said again, walking toward the fallen prey. Despite his mixed emotions about the shoot and thoroughly dampened spirits, he'd been delighted to find that it was indeed a head shot, no damage at all to the body.

Ambrose relished the moment of handing the bird

over to Alex to add to the bag at day's end. *Head shot, you see, dear boy. Wouldn't be sporting otherwise.*

There was one added bit of drama as they headed home, down the back roads of Gloucestershire leading to Hawkesmoor. In the rapidly fading sunlight, they were bouncing along the muddy, deeply rutted single country lane, Alex at the wheel, Patterson in the rear. Privet hedges lined both sides of the road, a good fifteen feet high. As they rounded a sharp hairpin bend, another vehicle, going ridiculously fast, came around from the opposite direction and both cars fishtailed, swerving to avoid a collision, skidding to a muddy stop, their front bumpers inches apart.

"Christ," Alex said, angrily eyeing the driver of the other car. "That was bloody close!"

"Sketchy lot," Congreve allowed, eyeing the men inside the vehicle. There were six thoroughly disreputable-looking chaps crammed into the offending car, a battered old Land Rover, all of them covered with mud and blood.

"Poachers, by God," Alex Hawke said, glaring at the driver and his passengers. "Let's bust 'em, Constable. Here's my mobile. Quick call to Officer Twining at the local constabulary and the game warden wouldn't hurt."

When Alex started to open his own door, a gun protruded out of the other Land Rover's driver's side window. The face of a rough-looking chap appeared in the window above the barrel. "Move yer arse, damn yer eyes!" the ruddy-faced and red-eyed driver shouted, slurring his words. "Move yer bleedin' arse out of me way!"

"Moving smartly, old chap!" Alex shouted, opening his door and climbing out. "Very smartly, as it were."

"Wot's up wit you, guv'nor?" the driver snarled as Alex approached the window, seemingly oblivious to the double-barreled twelve-bore aimed at his midsection. Congreve had seen the man load two shells into the chambers as Hawke approached him. He could hear Patterson in the back, spinning the cylinder of his old six-shooter, ready to step in.

"No need for that, Mr. Patterson," Congreve said, flipping the mobile shut and turning to the rear. "Alex will make short work of these sods. Couple of lads from the local gendarmerie on the way, at any rate. Should arrive in about two minutes."

"Wot's up? I'll tell you wot's up," Alex said, smiling at the inebriated poacher. "The jig is up, for one thing. Poaching is illegal, as you know."

"Bugger off, mate, and get yer bleedin' car out of my way then, before I—"

"Before you what?" Alex said, grabbing the shotgun's muzzle in his right hand. He ripped the gun out of the man's grasp and flung it backwards over his shoulder in a single motion.

"Wot the bloody—"

Alex then tore open the driver's door, grabbed the lout by the scruff of his neck, snatched him from behind the wheel, shook him like a rag doll, and then slammed him face down across the mud-spattered bonnet. From a sheath on his belt, Alex produced a stubby hunting knife, the tip of which he now inserted into the man's left ear. He leaned down on the bonnet to whisper directly into his right ear.

"What you're doing is against the law," Hawke said,

quietly. "If I ever see you out here again, you're going to meet with a very serious accident. Got that?"

"Back in the car, lads," Alex said, as the rusted-out rear doors swung open and two of the driver's fellow poachers started to get out, guns in hand. "I'm not a qualified surgeon, and if I have to remove your friend's ear, I might make a bad job of it. You gentlemen are under arrest. Cops should be here in a tick. Hear that siren? That's them now. Sit tight. Shouldn't be long, I don't think."

"A good afternoon's sport, wouldn't you say, Tex?" Alex Hawke said, stamping the mud from his knee-high rubber boots and stroking the feathers of a dead bird he held in his hands. He'd arranged the shoot as a brief and much-needed respite in the middle of Patterson's encampment at Hawkesmoor. Since Hawke and Patterson had arrived back in England ten days earlier, the house had become an absolute beehive of DSS intelligence operations and communications.

Senior intelligence staff from both the United States and Britain were swarming about the place, and occupied most of a warren of rooms of the east wing's upper floor. Hawke and Patterson had a briefing at six every morning with senior staff. Impromptu meetings were held throughout the day and night as necessary. No one was getting much sleep. A forest of the very latest electronic eavesdropping devices had been mounted on the rooftops, and the normally sleepy household was now a twenty-four-hour-a-day hubbub of activity. An intense hunt for the Dog was on but, so far at least, the Hawkesmoor spooks had met with only limited success. Hawke thought a few hours out in the field might rejuvenate them all.

What outraged Hawke most was what he saw on television.

Al-Jazeera, the Arab television network, had long been broadcasting images of gleeful celebrations over the deaths of America's soldiers in Afghanistan and Iraq. A terrorist fires a shoulder-mounted missile and an Apache helicopter full of young American boys explodes in a ball of fire. A truck bomb explodes outside the American command post. People in the streets below erupt into cheers. Now, in the homes and coffee shops, a new reality show: the murder of American diplomats and their families. Each assassination was professionally filmed and edited. No grainy, shaky, hand-held images here. Every gory detail was shot in close-up. And so the grisly deaths of these innocent men, women, and children were now broadcast daily for the rapt enjoyment of an increasingly bloodthirsty segment of the general population.

Hawke, Patterson, and Congreve were stowing their gear and muddy boots in the gun room, having bagged sixty-some birds, not to mention six drunken poachers. The gun room was one of Alex's favorite rooms at Hawkesmoor. In addition to the rows of mounted stags' antlers on all four walls, a row of Georgian servants' bells hung above a large oak armorial. The faded names beneath each bell had fascinated him since childhood. *Blue Room, Water Room, Chintz Room, King's Room, Priest's Room, Dressing Room.* Below the bells hung a warrant to execute Mary Queen of Scots in 1587.

"Drinks are waiting in the library, m'lord," said Pelham, standing in the doorway. "Dinner will be served promptly at eight, which is in one hour. You have an intelligence briefing at nine, sharp, and a video conference with Mr. Sann at Langley at ten."

"Thank you, Pelham," Hawke said. "Ample warning. That gives Mr. Congreve here exactly sixty minutes to consume as much whiskey as he possibly can."

"Really, Alex," Congreve muttered. "You do try my patience on a regular basis." Ever since Hawke had stopped drinking whiskey, he'd been on this bloody holier-than-thou jag.

"Just teasing you, Constable. To shore myself up."

"I stopped drinking once," Congreve said. "Worst twelve hours of my life."

"If I may, Mr. Patterson," Pelham continued. "Another courier arrived earlier, down from London by motorcycle, with a personal message for you. I've left the envelope by the telephone on the desk in your room, sir."

Ten minutes later, a showered, shaved, and much-refreshed Hawke stood with his back to the fire in the eighteenth-century library. The room contained some three thousand volumes. Two globes, celestial and terrestrial, stood on either side of the hearth and peering down from the ceiling cove above Alex's head were the marble busts of classical authors. As a boy, curled up and reading his adventure stories on a winter's afternoon, Alex had always imagined them fiercely critical of his reading habits.

All three men had briefing papers in their hands in preparation for a meeting immediately following supper. There had been some progress during the hours of their absence, but it promised to be a long night.

"Look here. It's been seven days since the last diplomatic assassination," Congreve said. He paused and took a sip of his whiskey. "A hiatus. This bin Wazir is gearing up for something big."

"Unfortunately, that's not accurate, Chief Inspector," Patterson said quietly. After a silence, Patterson drained his bourbon and looked solemnly at his two friends.

"Matter of fact, we've lost another ambassador," he said softly, the corners of his eyes glistening in the firelight. "Just this morning."

"God, I'm sorry, Tex," Alex said. "I knew something was wrong. What's happened now?"

At that moment, Pelham entered the library. "Dinner is served, m'lord."

"I'll tell you at the supper table. It's god-dang awful, is what it is," Patterson said, visibly shaken. "The worst."

CHAPTER THIRTY-ONE

Miami

Stokely Jones regained consciousness in one of the most spectacularly beautiful rooms he'd ever seen. Sitting in a plump upholstered chair that seemed to be made out of gold, he was slightly concerned, as his senses gradually returned, that this might be heaven. Last thing he remembered, he'd been standing at the entrance to Vizcaya, talking to Ross. Then somebody had swung the big door open and plunged a hypo into the side of his neck.

"Look up there, Ross," he said to his fellow traveler. "All them golden angels. Looks like Paradise to me."

The room was all white and gold. Ceilings had to be twenty feet high. Gold and marble statues and big crystal chandeliers and paintings up on the ceiling like out of some fancy picture book. Fireplace so big you could walk inside, invite folks over to supper inside it, and marble columns like in some kind of damn palace over in Europe somewhere.

There was even a pipe organ. Big gold pipes just like Radio City only maybe smaller. Yeah, a modest little place all right. Cozy.

"Well, we ain't in Harlem anymore, Ross," Stoke said. "Yo. Ross?"

Ross didn't answer. His friend was ten feet away. He was sitting in a chair just like Stokely's but his head was down, his chin resting on his chest. Taking a siesta, Stoke decided, definitely traveling in the land of Nod. Then he saw the preacher. The kid was sprawled face down on the marble floor. There was a large pool of liquid, spread out all around his head. Red liquid. Blood? Yeah. It was blood.

Aw, shit, Preacher.

He tried to stand up and couldn't. Couldn't move his arms or his legs. He was connected to the gold chair somehow. That's why he couldn't get up and go help the preacher. Maybe he should wake up Ross and get him to do it. Help Trevor. His throat was dry and he was still feeling dizzy, but his eyes weren't so fuzzy anymore.

"Ross? Hey, Ross, you sleepin'? C'mon, my brother. Wake up, son, somebody got to help Preacher. I can't seem to do it."

No answer.

Any feeling he'd had about being in heaven was gone. He looked down at his arms and saw that they were taped to the damn chair. Legs, too. Ross? Yeah, same situation. And didn't look like anybody could help the poor little preacher boy now, no how, no way. He looked around the room, seeing it clearly now. Oh, yeah. He remembered.

Vizcaya.

Used to be a museum. Now this guy—who was he?—Quixote Fox, owned it. Stoke knew a lot of rich folks, hanging around Alex Hawke all these years.

There was money and there was money. This was one seriously rich cat, buy a museum and just move in. This was offshore money, saved for a rainy day. Hell, a cocaine cowboy who'd been tight with Fidel? Moved out all the cash he could while the getting was good.

Cop brain kicking back in. He could feel it. Little police peanut at the back of his skull. That was good, he was going to need his peanut just in case he had a snowball's chance in hell of getting out of this damn museum without becoming part of the permanent collection.

"Feeling well rested?" somebody asked him.

Tall, thin guy. Snazzy. Wearing mirrored aviator sunglasses. Voilà. Yeah, the guy who disappeared from the Fontainebleau, standing in the front of a group of ten or twelve Chinese guys, all wearing matching black pajamas and all pointing Chicom assault rifles at him and Ross.

Boss himself had on a pretty white linen suit, shiny white shoes, long black hair all slicked back. Had a skinny little black moustache on him, looked like an anchovy stuck on his upper lip. Big white teeth. Had the chick with him, Fancha. He walked across the terrazzo flooring, tapping his white cane in front of him, and stopped two feet short of Stokely.

"Who the fuck are you, kill my friend Preacher?" Stoke said.

"No, *señor*, who the fuck are you?"

"I asked you first, Slick."

"Why did you follow my car?"

"I like Bentleys. That's an Azure, right? Brand-new? What do those go for now? Two-fifty? Three?"

"You find yourself amusing?"

"Somebody got to."

"It's a small group."

"Yeah? Why she smiling?"

"Maybe I just let her play with the big dog."

"See. I knew it. Any man start to talk about his own dick size, you automatically know the underlying problem."

"What problem?"

"The little dick problem."

"Really? How about the no dick problem?"

Guy had pulled out a pair of silver scissors from inside his shirt. Wore them on a black ribbon around his neck. He took a few steps closer, stopped, and turned around, smiling at his squeeze. Stoke thinking, *Yeah, you Scissorhands all right. Found your ass, Rodrigo. Man who goes around killing brides on church steps. Innocent young kids like that speedy English kid who stepped on your landmine in the churchyard. Or little Preacher over there, never hurt nobody. Had a heart of gold, you worthless piece of shit.*

The scissors flashed and Stoke felt his cheek burn.

Yeah. Got you just where I want you now, Scissorhands, your ass is mine.

"Hey. You ain't as blind as you make out, are you? You—"

"Silence! You want to do it, *Chica?*" the guy said to Fancha, snickering his shiny silver scissors, making a kind of whispery noise. "Or, you want to watch?"

Stoke gave him a big smile, catch his attention.

"What t'hell's wrong with you? Seriously. Before you go cutting anybody's private parts off, you got to know something, fool. You mess with my ass, you in a world of hurt."

"Really? Why do I not believe you?"

"You stupid, that's why. You don't bother to ask for information, find out what's going on. You think we just dropped by here for the package tour, me and my friend over there and that poor little Rastafari kid you killed? You think we just showed up 'cause we curious about lifestyles of the rich and famous?"

"I pretend curiosity about you for thirty seconds. Mr. Jones, sí? From New York."

"You spend a lot of time in England?"

"No."

"How 'bout Cuba?"

"No."

"How 'bout South Beach? The Blue Moon Apartments over on Washington Avenue? Specifically apartment 3-A where that SWAT guy got himself whacked in his bed?"

"No."

"Slip your mind, maybe. You stole his Leupold & Stevens sniper scope."

"One more dead cop, what does it matter if I did?"

"See? That's better. Won't do you any good to lie. The truth set you free. Take them mirror glasses off, my man. Look me in the eye."

"You want the truth? I'm going to enjoy killing you. Slowly, with my scissors, because you have insulted me. Then, I'm going to kill your friend over there. The same way. Three more bodies for the alligator fiesta out in the Everglades. End of story, señor."

"Maybe for me. Ain't the end for you, Scissorhands. We got folks expecting us. We don't show up back home, your trouble is just beginning, if it isn't bad enough already."

"Where do you get this name?"

"Scissorhands? What your homeboys all call you, man, you know that. Back in the old country. Before you stuck your scissors in Fidel's back and sided with them cocaine cowboy generals. You talk to Fidel lately? I imagine he's pissed at your ass. Wouldn't surprise me he wasn't the one been trying to whack your ass lately. That's what I'd do, I was him."

"Shit! Guards!"

"See? Now you're raising your voice. Means I got your attention. Take those glasses off, Slick. Let me see your eyes. Maybe you're not even the guy we looking for. If not, we say we sorry, we're out of here, no hard feelings. Come back when you open to the public."

"You fuck now with the wrong man, *señor*."

"My friend over there. One you drugged? Name is Ross. He's Scotland Yard. You look in his pocket, you'll see a warrant for your extradition and arrest."

"Arrest? Ridiculous." That's when the guy flashed the scissors right under Stoke's nose.

"Leaving a murder weapon stuck up in a tree at the crime scene, now that's ridiculous—hey, get them scissors out my nose. You liable to do something you regret later, you—"

"You are under arrest for the murder of Lady Victoria Hawke," Ross said suddenly. Sound of his voice, Stoke could tell he'd been awake for a while, just playing possum. "On the steps of the Church of St. John's, Gloucestershire, at eleven o'clock on the morning of May 15th last. You bloody bastard."

"See? Ross is back. That's good. Now you got Scotland Yard plus a big-city homicide dick on your ass. Now the odds are better, traitor. Two against twelve, you don't count Fancha. Look at her, girl be smiling at the old Stoke again."

"Guards!" the Cuban guy shouted and he heard them all rack the bolts on their assault weapons.

"I'll kill this one," the Cuban guy said to the guards, "just blow the other one away."

Stokely felt a white-hot pain as the man slowly drove the razor sharp scissors upward inside his left nostril, headed no doubt for his brain. He tried to twist his head away, but the thing was too far up his nose. He thought he heard Ross yell something about getting down, and then he was sure he was going to black out from the unbelievable pain, and then all the windows and doors of Vizcaya exploded inward.

Stokely jerked his head back, planted his feet and rocked his chair backwards, getting away from the damn scissors, the flying shards of glass, the flash-bang and smoke grenades somebody was now lobbing in from outside the house, and all the wild bullets the panicked Chinese pajama guys were spraying all over.

That's when the main explosion occurred, blowing all four walls apart to make room for the roof and chimneys and all kinds of damn shit to come down on top of them. Just before all his lights went out, Stokely had one last thought.

Hey, Stoke, guess what?
You one dead cat.

CHAPTER
THIRTY-TWO

The Cotswolds

A fire was blazing in the massive hearth at the far end of the dining hall. The three men sat at one end of the long mahogany table. Down the length of the table stood a row of gleaming silver candelabra and Pelham had lit every candle.

It was a fine, richly paneled room, with a vaulted Adam ceiling picked out in blue and white. A massive Victorian chandelier hung from the center, modeled after a nineteenth-century hot air balloon. Alex himself had purchased it, upon learning that the huge glass balloon had been originally designed to contain live goldfish. He'd intended to try it himself, but had never quite gotten around to it.

After the wine had been poured, Pelham withdrew from the room and returned to the kitchen to ensure the first course was ready.

"Tell us about it, Tex," Alex said, as gently as he could manage. It was obvious that the aging Texas Ranger was suffering deeply.

"That message," Patterson said, "the one came down here by courier from London. It was from my station chief in Madrid. I knew what it was before I even opened the thing. Heck, I knew this was comin', sooner or later."

"What happened, Tex?" Alex asked.

"The father of those two wonderful little kids up in Dark Harbor," Patterson said, choking the words out. "The husband of the beautiful Deirdre. Evan Slade was his name. As fine a gentleman, father, and husband as ever I met. A great American."

"The bastards got him too, Tex?" Hawke said, leaning forward, lacing his fingers under his chin.

"Naw, it wasn't like that, Alex. Evan was sitting at his desk at the embassy over there this morning. Had the al-Jazeera network on the TV. All of a sudden they showed the—the pictures—the goddamn *movies* of Dierdre and the children, Alex! The whole thing. He put a .45-caliber gun in his mouth and pulled the trigger. He just wasn't—strong enough—to see that, Alex. To see his kids—in their beds—"

Hawke stood up and went around to where Patterson sat, slumped forward. He put his hand on the man's shoulder. "Tex," Alex said, looking down at Patterson's shattered expression. "None of us would be strong enough to see that. None of us. You know that."

"Dreadful business," Congreve said. "Horrific."

And then everyone was silent while Pelham served the first course. It was some kind of creamed soup, served hot. Leeks or celery or something like that. Hawke could care less. He'd lost his appetite.

Each man picked up his spoon. Hawke, a bit unsure about what to do with the sprig of rosemary that lay atop the soup, put down his spoon, plucked the sprig of rosemary from the soup bowl and held it to his nose.

"Don't touch that soup!" he barked at his two companions who were in the midst of lifting their spoons to their open mouths. "Drop the spoons!"

Patterson and Congreve looked up at him in shock, lowering their soupspoons.

"What on earth, Alex?" Congreve said.

"I intend to find out," Hawke said, pressing the button mounted under the table that would summon Pelham from the butler's pantry. A moment later, he was at Hawke's side.

"Something wrong with the soup, m'lord?"

"Pelham, do we have any new staff in the kitchen? Any recent hires, I mean?"

"Well, there is the one, sir, joined us the month before you arrived home from America. Excellent qualifications. She was sous-chef at *l'Hôtel de Paris* and—"

"Would you kindly ask her to join us?" Hawke said, and Pelham, a look of distress on his face, rushed from the dining room.

"You thinkin' what I'm thinkin', Alex?" Tex said gravely.

"We'll know in a moment," Hawke said, and sniffed the soup once more.

Pelham ushered in a pretty, dark-eyed young woman, mid-twenties, wearing a white apron with a *toque blanche* atop her black curls. She wore an expression of calm despite the unusual summons. Pelham looked stricken. Something clearly was amiss.

"Good evening, I'm Alex Hawke. You're new here, I understand."

"*Oui, Monsieur Hawke.* One month since I arrive from Paris."

"*Bienvenue, mademoiselle.* I wonder. Why would a

pretty young woman want to leave Paris and move to the dreary English countryside? Seems a bit odd."

"To learn some English. And, because of my boyfriend, he have a job at the Lygon Arms in town."

"Did you prepare this soup?"

"*Mais oui, monsieur.* I hope you are enjoying it. *C'est bon? Encore un peu?*"

"Quite delicious. Has an odd, nutty aroma I can't quite identify."

"*C'est un pâté de noix moulues, monsieur,* a paste of ground walnuts. *Peut-être cela*—perhaps that is—"

"*Eh bien.* No. That's not it," Hawke said, dipping his spoon into the soup. "Here, you taste it and tell me what you think it is." He handed her the spoon but she simply stared at it.

"Is there a problem?" said Hawke.

"*Non, monsieur.*"

"Then taste it."

"I cannot, *monsieur.* It is not proper."

"Did you put something in this soup that should not be there, *mademoiselle?*"

"What are you saying, *monsieur?*"

"I am saying that if you don't taste that bloody soup in the next two seconds I'm going to have my friend Chief Inspector Congreve over there arrest you."

"On what charge, *monsieur?*"

"Attempted murder should do it."

The girl's eyes flared angrily and she flung the spoon to the floor. Before Alex could react, she bent forward and grabbed his soup bowl from the table and raised it to her lips.

"I would sooner eat all of it!" she shouted defiantly and tilted the bowl toward her open mouth, wolfing down the contents in one long, single swallow. She stood then, looking down at them, eyes blazing, yellow soup smeared on her chin and down the front of her apron.

She wiped her mouth with the back of her hand, eyeing all of them insolently.

"Porcs infidels! Je vais au paradis sachant que mon valeureux successeur réussira là où j'ai échoué!" she said, smiling at them.

A second later, she made a small noise and collapsed to the floor.

Congreve shoved back his chair and went to her, kneeling at her side. He placed two fingers at the carotid artery just beneath her ear, paused a moment, then shook his head.

"Unconscious?" Alex Hawke asked.

"Dead," Ambrose said. "What was it, Alex, in the soup?"

"Aflatoxin, most probably. Derivative of the extremely toxic mold produced by peanuts when they go bad. Brilliantly disguised, I almost missed it. She was very good at her trade, this one. She'd most likely have gotten away with it."

"Alex is right," Tex said, holding the soup bowl under his nose. "Aflatoxin's a tough one to catch. Our postmortems would show only damage to the liver. Shucks, after all the port wine we've had today, nobody would—" He put the bowl down.

"What was her name?" Alex asked Pelham.

"She called herself Rose-Marie, sir," a very shaken Pelham said, gazing down at the lifeless figure. "I must say I'm thoroughly mortified, your lordship. Someone should have—"

"Rose-Marie . . . Rosemary . . ." Congreve said, more

to himself than anyone in the room. He placed the sprig of herb on his linen serviette and doubled it over.

"Now, you listen here, old thing," Alex said, putting an arm around Pelham's frail and trembling shoulders. "There's no way anyone in this household is to blame. You're shaking. I want you to go into the library, pour yourself a largish whiskey, and put the whole matter behind you. We'll join you in a moment. It's quite over as far as I'm concerned."

"I'll just go ring the constabulary, your lordship," Pelham said, and disappeared as if in a daze.

Alex eyed the fragrant twig in his fingers. "Rosemary. It appears you're quite right, Ambrose. First Iris in Maine, then Lily in Paris, and now I find this little sprig of rosemary right here under my own nose."

"You're forgetting one, Alex," Patterson said. "Rose."

"Rose?"

"When we pulled Simon Stanfield out of the Grand Canal, he was wearing a single rosebud in his lapel. According to his wife, he hated flowers, especially roses."

"This Dog calls all of his sharp teeth by the names of flowers, or, in this case, he takes a wee license with an aromatic shrub," Hawke said. "Quite the romantic, our homicidal assassin. Please tell me, Ambrose, the late unlamented, what were her final words?"

"She addressed us as 'infidel swine,'" Ambrose said, staring down at the dead assassin, and shaking his head. "And then informed us that 'I go to Paradise knowing my worthy successor will succeed where I have failed.'"

"Let's keep a weather eye out for her successor, shall we, Ambrose?" Hawke said.

"The supply would seem endless," Congreve said, and sipped his wine.

CHAPTER THIRTY-THREE

London

Body of Lies was the hottest ticket in London. If you could even get your hands on one, that is. The tabloids joked that the sizzling waiting list for tomorrow night's gala premiere was so long some members of the Royal Family were embarrassingly midlist. Adverts for the latest epic spy flick were everywhere. Marketing declared war on every square inch of London. Space not plastered with Nick Hitchcock's picture was space wasted. Airtime, radio or television, without a mention of the "Sexiest Spy Alive" was precious time lost forever.

Marketing had spoken. Cry havoc, and let slip the hounds of publicity, they said. Legions went forth, and it seemed every corner of the capital was plastered with Ian Flynn's cruelly handsome visage.

Looming above a rain-soaked Piccadilly Circus, a giant billboard cutout of a smirking Nick Hitchcock dominated the skyline. There was the prerequisite luscious babe on his left arm and a lethal-looking black automatic in his right hand. Every ten seconds, his gun emitted a loud pop, and a perfect round smoke ring wafted from the gun's muzzle to be borne aloft high above the hurry of swirling umbrellas, the glistening red buses and gleaming black taxis. The sound effect of Nick's gun, the *Lies* marketing gurus soon learned to their chagrin, unfortunately could be heard only in the quiet of the wee small hours, when the hooting armies of the night had tented down.

Francesca, emerging from a Soho theatre into a surging sea of paparazzi shouting her name, glanced up at her giant cardboard costar just as Nick's gun went off. "Firing blanks," she said to Lily and her director, Vittorio de Pinta.

Vittorio, who clearly had a lot more riding on this picture than she did, mainly his future, draped an arm around his star's bare shoulders.

"Mi amore," the handsome Italian said, smiling broadly for the flashing cameras, "please do not behave this way. Be a good girl. Smile for the cameras."

"What's my motivation?" Francesca said.

"Money, darling."

"She's got a lot on her mind," Lily said, casting a sideways glance at Francesca.

Lily, for a time known as Monique Delacroix and formerly personal assistant to the late American ambassador Duke Merriman, had arrived from Paris earlier that week. With a variety of makeup, wigs, and sunglasses, she managed to make herself unrecognizable. Francesca had spent two days bringing her beautiful young protégée up to speed on the plot to kidnap an American ambassador. Francesca, along with Mustapha Ahmed al-Fazad, the mastermind behind many of the Emir's most deadly attacks in Europe, the Philippines, and the Far East, had spent the last weeks in intense planning sessions in Francesca's suite overlooking Hyde Park. The plans were now complete.

But it was Francesca and Lily who would ultimately be responsible for the success or failure of this most audacious action.

The next day, the day of the world premiere dawned bright and clear over London. But the luscious babe depicted on Hitchcock's arm, the current rage of London, was clearly in a state of rage herself. She stormed about her rose-filled three-bedroom corner suite at the Dorchester, screaming at all of her handlers in general and one in particular. The new Hitchcock Girl had practically reduced Luigi Sant'Angelo, her wardrobe assistant on *Lies*, to tears.

"Non abbastanza petto! Desidero più petto!" she cried, yanking down the neckline of her yellow de la Renta and thrusting her breasts upward.

"Scusi, scusi, signorina, ma . . ." Luigi sputtered, cringing on the sofa with his legs tucked beneath him. "But you cannot show any more bosom, *signorina*. Not with this gown—"

"Sciocco! Fool! What did I tell you a thousand times, eh? Bosom, bosom, bosom!"

She plucked a few dozen long-stems from the nearest vase and flung them at the cowering creature. The man ran screaming from the room, hands flailing about his head like diving birds, tears pouring down his cheeks.

Francesca looked over at the dark-haired man sitting serenely in an armchair by the sunny window. He was scribbling furiously in a small notebook, intense, making sure he was getting all this. She went over to him and collapsed at his feet.

"Roberto, caro, do you think I was too mean to him?"

Bob Fiori was senior correspondent for *Vanity Fair,*

the American magazine, which had exclusive rights to
the London premiere of *Body of Lies*. He was working
hard. The film and its star-studded premiere would be
next month's cover story. He looked up from his small
spiral notebook, pushing his heavy black glasses higher
on the bridge of his nose. He was one of the few men
on earth capable of ignoring a direct question put to
him by Francesca d'Agnelli.

"Roberto! Answer me!"

"Sorry, did you say something, Francesca?"
Jonathan Decker said from behind his camera. He was
the photographer covering the story. He was very
happy about the stuff he'd just gotten, Luigi being
attacked with roses.

"My God! Does no one around here listen to me?"

"Calm down, Francesca," Fiori said. "Sorry, I didn't
hear what you said just now. I was concentrating on
what you said before that."

"I feel bad about Luigi."

"Maybe you were a little mean. But you're under a
lot of stress. Tonight is a big night for you, dear
Francesca. Here, have a glass of champagne."

"I wouldn't let my dog drink this piss the studio
sends up. Will you be a darling and order me the Pol
Roger or the Krug? *Scusi, Roberto,* you're right, I'm just
a wreck about tonight."

"Darling, Jonathan and I went to the screening,
remember? You've got nothing to worry about, I
promise."

"Nothing at all, baby," Decker added, with the wry
smile that was his trademark.

Of course, it wasn't the movie she was worried about.
The London audience's reaction to *Body of Lies*

that evening at the Odeon in Mayfair was astonish-
ing by any measure. The sexual *frisson* between Ian
Flynn, the fifth actor to play Nick Hitchcock, and his
latest Hitchcock Girl, as played by Italian bombshell
Francesca d'Agnelli, was palpable. Riveting. You
could, as one L.A. film critic said next morning,
tongue firmly in cheek, "cut it with a knife."

No Oscar nominations, certainly, but big box office,
definitely.

Raed, the black-liveried chauffeur, who was in reality a heavily armed Syrian assassin Lily had organized
for the evening, nosed the big silver Rolls up to the red
carpet extending from the Park Lane entrance of the
fabled Grosvenor House Hotel. This was the site of the
international *Body of Lies* premiere gala now at full tilt
in the Great Room, the largest ballroom in all Europe.
There was a gaggle of jostling paparazzi and crush of
screaming, cheering fans as Francesca exited the Rolls.
In the life of most stars, it was a moment to be cherished. For Francesca it was merely necessary, a moment
to be endured, a prelude to the evening's true climax.

The international press was out in force. Mobile
video units lined both the north and south sides of Park
Lane and the airspace above the hotel was host to four
or five helicopters, their pilots and cameramen all vying
for the best angle to cover the arrival of the celebrities.
Casting her eyes upwards, Francesca wondered how
they managed to avoid one another. An air collision
tonight would be a disaster in more ways than one.

Security, as she'd expected, was pervasive. Metal
detectors at every conceivable entrance, names and
pictures on every invitation, British and American security men with skinny ties talking to their lapels every-

where you looked. Francesca, Lily, and the slightly drunk director Vittorio, fully accredited, blew through without a problem, according to plan.

Entering the tightly packed and raucous ballroom, Francesca, with Lily in tow, moved with the confidence of a woman who knew she possessed more sheer wattage than any other woman in the room.

"Darling!" a famous American gossip columnist said, taking her arm, "I've just been with Steven. He thought you were brilliant! He wants to breakfast with you tomorrow morning in his suite at Claridge's! Isn't that fabulous?"

"Fabulous," Francesca said. "Darling, have you met Lily? Wasn't she enchanting as Nick's secret paramour?"

Without waiting for a reply, Francesca left Lily with Liz and made her way through the press of bodies, dodging the flashing capped smiles and breezing past the wafting air kisses proffered by the botox brigade. She was looking for a man wearing a star sapphire ring on his left index finger. She didn't know what he looked like, but she didn't need to. He would recognize her. After tonight, the whole world would recognize her.

"Lovely ring," she said. A bulky mustachioed man in a white silk Nehru jacket had smiled at her from his post at one of the many, many bars. This one was just to the right of a pair of French doors opening onto a small balconied terrace. Beyond the traffic of Park Lane, the heavy leafy green of Hyde Park lay under the dark summer sky.

"Thank you," the dark man said, "I bought it in Cairo."

"So he's here," Francesca replied, and motioned to him to follow her out to the terrace.

Lily found the photographer Jonathan Decker five minutes later, chatting up the Duke and Duchess of Somewhere.

"Oh, Johnnie," she breathed, "may I steal you for a small tiny minute, *s'il vous plaît?*"

Decker turned away from the duchess and regarded the budding starlet with the towering, diamond-studded red hairdo and the neckline plunging due south. "Hey, baby," he said.

"Johnnie?"

"Yes?"

"Was I good?"

"Phenomenal."

"It was only the one line. *Merde.* Everything else, they cut me."

"It was the delivery of that one line, baby, believe me. Sultry. You could feel the testosterone levels spiking all over the goddamn theatre. Say it for me."

She smiled through pouted lips and repeated the line.

"I've been a naughty girl, Nicky."

"Yeah, baby. Just like that."

"I don't know anybody here."

"Count yourself lucky. I know everybody here."

"Really? Who's that?"

"Who's who?"

"That tall one over there. The incredibly good-looking one with the curly black hair. He looks bored. I like that in a man."

"Good eye, my dear girl. That is Alexander Hawke. One of the richest men in Britain, or so everybody says. He's got a title, too, a good one. Not a 'Your Grace' or anything, but still. Christ, I hope I get old enough and rich enough to look down on new money some day."

"My God. Beautiful. Is he married? Say no. Who is he talking to and why isn't it me?"

"Want to meet him?"

Ten minutes later, Lily found herself alone with the most attractive man she'd ever seen. He asked her if she'd like to join him for a drink at the bar.

"I drink too much at these damn things," he said, "everything I say bores me to tears. I'm having a spot of rum, Goslings Black Seal. Bermudian. Quite good, if you've never tried it."

"Just a glass of white wine would be fine."

"*Pisse-de-chat,*" Hawke said. "Try the rum."

"*Oui, c'est bon. Merci.*"

Hawke nodded at the barman who came right over and took the order. A minute later, the drinks arrived. He raised his glass to her and smiled.

"You look familiar. Are you?"

"Pardon?"

"You know my name, but I don't know yours. Sorry, I didn't stick around for all the closing credits."

"Lily Delacroix, *Monsieur Hawke, une plaisir.*"

"Pleasure," Hawke replied, and realized he had nothing to add. He looked around the massive room, having no idea where to take this. He was slightly amused with his situation. This little red-headed star-let wasn't much over twenty, he was sure. What on earth was he thinking when he—

"I don't know anyone here, I'm so sorry," she finally said.

"Don't be sorry. I'll fill you in. That group over there, for instance. Finance men from the City. The fat one doing all the talking is Lord Mowbray. The others are Barings, Rothschild, Hambro. The one who's laughing at whatever Mowbray just said is Oppenheimer. Diamond chap from South Africa. Throw in a couple of wealthy dukes and you've got the whole lot."

"*Merci.*"

"*Je vous en prie, mademoiselle.*"

"You speak French."

"Not if I can help it. There are one or two French idiomatic expressions I find amusing. A way of describing a woman with a figure like this latest Hitchcock Girl, for instance. Francesca something or other."

"D'Agnelli. What is the expression, *Monsieur* Hawke?"

"*Il y a du monde au balcon.*"

"Everyone is seated in the balcony," she said, laughing. "Big bosoms."

"Precisely. Now, my dear girl, if you'll excuse me, here comes young Tom Jefferson, an old American friend of mine. I must—"

"Hello, Hawke, old buddy. Helluva movie, wasn't it? The boys loved it. And this pretty young lady was in it if I'm not mistaken. How do you do, I'm Patrick Kelly. What's your name?"

"Back off, Brick. I saw her first. Don't pay any attention to him, Lily, he's married."

"*Bonsoir, monsieur l'Ambassadeur.* I am Lily."

"Now, how in God's name do you all know what I do for a living?"

"Because my closest friend, she told me you might come tonight. I will tell you a secret. She hopes to get a chance to speak with you, *monsieur*, if you still remember her."

"All right, now you've piqued my curiosity, *mademoiselle*. Who is this mystery woman?"

"Francesca d'Agnelli."

"Francesca?" Brick said. "Good lord!"

"Leave me out of this," Hawke said, and sipped his rum.

"Where is she? I'd love to say hello," Brick said.

"She'll be so happy. I just saw her walk out onto one of the balconies over there. For a cigarette, I'm sure."

"Which one?"

"By that bar. Come along, I'll take you to her."

"Alex, you hold down the fort," Kelly said. "Order me a Ketel One on the rocks with a twist. I'll be right back."

CHAPTER THIRTY-FOUR

Miami

Stokely woke up when a raindrop bounced off his forehead. He opened his eyes. Chalky dust made them sting. He blinked out tears to clear them, and did a quick survey. What hurt and what did not. His nose still hurt like hell, inside the left nostril where the guy had stuck his trademark silver scissors. Legs hurt too, like a weight on them. It was, shit, a big chunk of plaster on top of him. Heavy mother, too. Pinned his arms and legs both. Oh, right, the ceiling fell down when the bombs went off. And now it was dark clouds up above, crackling with lightning, spitting out rain, and there were guys with flashlights climbing all over the rubble. Rescue team. *Hey, over here,* he almost said.

No. This wasn't Dade County EMS on the scene. These guys were all shouting in Spanish. That wasn't the thing, though; the thing was they were all in black and had camo paint and all had automatic weapons. He heard one go off. A Chinese guy, had to be one of Don Quixote's guards, screamed in pain, another burst, quiet once more. They were shooting the survivors.

He closed his eyes. Dead again. Listening.

You spend enough time, like he had, standing on

street corners in Spanish Harlem selling product, you're bound to pick up a lot of español. And Stoke had. *Donde está del Rio?* he heard one say. Where's the river?

They were shining flashlights all around him, now. They were looking for a river? Calling out the name, over and over. Del Rio! Del Rio! The river, right? No.

Don Quixote. The star formerly known in Cuba as Rodrigo del Rio. This blown-up museum used to be his house. These guys, Cuban forces most likely, were the ones who'd knocked it down. The guy they were looking for had a pair of scissors up Stoke's nose when the lights went out. Where was he now? Stoke'd like a piece of this action. Only he couldn't move.

He was wondering about Ross, too. Ross, just before lights out, saying get down, Stoke. Was Ross dead or just playing possum again? He heard another guy scream, not Spanish, Chinese again, and then a burst of automatic fire. Shut the guy up. He could see it now, even with his eyes closed. A blind man could see it. They were going through the rubble, looking for del Rio, and shooting anybody who didn't fit the description.

He had to get to Ross, help him before they found him and shot him. Trying not to make any noise, he got his hands and knees pushing up against the plaster. Didn't move more than half an inch but something slid off, glass most probably, least it sounded like glass when it broke.

Instantly, a guy was shining a light in his face. Another guy kicked him in the head with the toe of his boot. Stoke's eyes popped open and he looked into the flashlight, smiling even though he couldn't see anything but a ball of fire that made him squint. Jesus. Hurt like hell.

"*Buenas noches,*" Stoke said, "*Americano. Amigo.*"

Having pretty much established his ties to the Hispanic community, he was surprised when the boot caught him just behind the ear. A couple of guys were lifting the roof off him and four other guys had him by the arms, yanking him out. He wondered if four would be enough. Alex always described him as being about the size of your average armoire. Actually, he was bigger, from what little he'd seen of armoires.

Anyway, they finally got him on his feet and shoved him back against something that was still upright. A beam or a column felt like. Then they got his arms behind him. He was still groggy and there was a guy with a pistol in his ear. Otherwise no way they would have tied his wrists together with the plastic military handcuffs.

"Stoke? You alive, then?" It was Ross, his voice cracked and broken sounding.

"*Silencio!*" another Cuban guy said, and he heard the thud of metal on bone, somebody taking a pistol to Ross's face. This Miami vacation was not going in the right direction. He'd rather be checking the action poolside at the Delano anytime.

"Hey, listen up," Stoke said to the guy in his face, "*habla inglés, aquí?* Somebody speak English? Who's the *jefe* around here?"

"*Sí, señor,* I speak English," the little guy with the gun in his ear said. "So I am able to understand your last fucking words." He cocked the hammer. "Say them."

"Oh, man, hold up."

"Where is he, *señor?*" the Cuban said. He was short and had terrible acne scars which probably accounted for his bad attitude toward life. "Tell me where your *jefe* is and maybe we can talk." He slammed his fist into Stoke's ribcage for emphasis, most probably broke a few of his fingers in the process.

"Hey. We got a problem here? You talking about Don Quixote, right, a.k.a. Rodrigo del Rio, right? He ain't my *jefe,* man. I'm Stokely Jones, NYPD retired. Me and that guy you beating up on over there, we both cops. We're looking to bust this Rodrigo's ass just like you. You guys're all Cuban right, 'less I'm wrong."

"How would you know this?"

"I know a lot of shit, you let me talk. You in command of this outfit? You the *jefe?*"

"*Sí.* Talk fast."

"This cat del Rio betrayed your government a while back, I know that. Switch-hitter. He was Fidel's chief of security. But he ratted out Fidel to them three rebel generals who took over. But me and another guy, who shall remain nameless, we went down there and spoiled their little military coup. Killed two, sent one away for life. That's how Fidel got his banana republic back. And that's how come Rodrigo, with a price tag on his head, he cut and run. Now, Fidel got you boys out trying to whack him, right? You're Cuban Special Forces, right? RDF? Shit, amigo, I know your boss. The *comandante* himself."

"Shoot these two fucking gringos," the bad-skinned guy said, taking his gun away and stepping out of range. Stoke heard three or four automatics racking their bolts. "No witnesses."

"Wait! You're not thinking straight. Two things.

One, my friend over there ain't no gringo! He's
English. Royalty. Put it together, pal. *English. Royalty.*
You shoot him, you got a major international crisis on
your ass. Two. You talking to a personal friend of
Fidel's. As in Castro. We tight, motherfucker. You
whack me, you in the land of pain soon as you get back
to sunny Havana. You shoot me, Fidel shoots you,
okay? Boom. Boom."

"Shoot him."

Stoke closed his eyes. Didn't want to see it.

"Shoot me first, boyo!" Ross shouted, sounding
stronger. "I don't want to see my friend die. But before
you shoot either of us, take a look at the medal he's
wearing around his neck."

"What stinking medal?" the little *jefe* asked.

The medal? Oh, yeah. That medal. Stoke smiled
over at Sutherland and then shouted at his interroga-
tor, getting right up in his business.

"Hey! You! Focus! What are you, ADD?"

"ADD?"

"Attention Deficit Syndrome, man! Try and concentrate, all right, till I can drum you up some Ritalin?
You don't believe what I'm sayin'? Look inside my shirt!
Rip it open! You looking at one bona fide Cuban Medal
of Honor winner, boy. Just check it out. You don't recognize what you see, I'm shit out of luck, you boys go
right ahead and shoot us."

Stoke held his breath. Ross may have just saved his
life. These low-level special ops guys were usually
what, in the SEALs, they used to call risk averse. Don't
like to take chances. Works in your favor sometimes,
you get lucky enough.

Like now, the guy ripping open his fancy dress shirt

seeing that bright gold medal hanging on a twenty-four karat chain around his twenty-four-inch neck. A nice shiny Cuban flag on the front. Man lifting it off his chest, looking at it up close. "Where you get this?"

"Cuba, where else? When I saved your *comandante*'s ass from those rebel generals couple of years ago, like I told you. You probably don't remember all that. Probably still in grade school."

"Shut up! Enough of this bullshit."

"Tell him to read what's on the other side," Ross said.

"Yeah! Turn it over," Stoke said. "Shine your damn light on it. Read what's on the back. Out loud, *por favor,* so all your trigger-happy commandos with their guns on me know who they dealing with here."

"Presented to Stokely Jones Jr.," the guy read in English, shaking his head, not believing what he was reading. "In recognition of his heroic service to the Republic of Cuba. Fidel Castro, January 2002."

"See what I'm saying? Fidel and me, we are two coats of paint. We are tight."

"It's—real? This is real?"

"*Sí. Es real.* Damn right it's real. Think I went out and bought it in case I ran into some Cuban commandos didn't believe my story?"

"Okay. *Bueno,*" the guy said, finally. Risk averse, all right. "Okay. I believe you."

"Good. I'm Stoke, he's Ross. What's your name?"

The guy actually reached up and patted Stoke on the cheek. "*Me llamo Pepe,*" he said, "Lieutenant Pepe Alvarez." Big smile, like they friends now. Not taking any chances whatsoever just like Stoke knew he would. Or would not. Whichever way you want to say it.

"Let these two gringos go," he said to the guy behind him. "Cut them loose."

"Good, Lieutenant. Now you focused. Lucky, too. You got two world-class cops here, help you go find this skanky piece of human garbage Rodrigo."

"Right," Ross said, rubbing his wrists. "This man you're after murdered a friend of ours. A bride on her wedding day. And a Miami police officer in his bed, and now this poor lad here." Ross knelt beside Preacher, covering him up best he could with his torn and bloody black tuxedo jacket.

"Scissorhands is going down, Ross," Stoke said, looking at the dead boy on the floor. "When we catch hold of him. All the way down. Look at me. I promise you that." He'd loved the kid. Planned to take him under his wing.

Somewhere out beyond the house, down the great sweep of lawn that ended at the edge of the bay, there was a heavy rumble. Two powerful and deep-throated engines erupted into life. Sounded like one of those hundred-mile-an-hour Cigarette powerboats. Also, there was the sound of about fifty Miami PD squad car sirens coming up the long drive that led to the former residence of Rodrigo del Rio; what used to be the Vizcaya Museum. Time to rock and roll.

"You guys come here on spec-ops boats, right?" Stoke asked the little guy, kneading his wrists, trying to make his hands wake up. "Inflatables off some foreign freighter also stops in Havana, way I would do it."

"Sí."

"That's good, 'cause we gonna need 'em if we going to catch Rodrigo. Hear that? Fixing to haul his ass away from the dock."

"*Vámonos!*" Alvarez shouted, and everybody bolted from the rubble and ran down through the gardens to the Vizcaya docks where the Cubans had moored four high-speed inflatables. Stoke was bringing up the rear with his arm around Ross, who'd busted up his leg. Everybody jumped in, cranking the big outboards, throwing off lines. Stoke and Ross jumped down into Pepe's boat as it roared away from the dock.

Stoke peered over the bow, the salt spray and rain stinging his eyes. All they could see of Rodrigo now was the huge white plume of his speedboat's rooster tail as he raced away from the elaborate Venetian-style harbor, slashing southeast across storm-tossed Biscayne Bay. Boy had worked out his escape plan a long time ago, Stoke imagined. Saw this day coming. Contingency planning was what they called it.

Stoke was happy. He'd always liked being some-body's contingency.

CHAPTER THIRTY-FIVE

Suva Island

Snay bin Wazir relaxed back into the deep leather cushions of the armchair in his sitting room and fired up another Baghdaddy. The ornately carved door hushed shut; he was alone. Smoking with the cigarette held between thumb and forefinger, he inhaled deeply, the long yellow cigarette going to ash like a firecracker fuse. He gazed out the large oval window beside his chair. The Mountain of Fire lay smoldering some three thousand feet below him. The peak of the active volcano, rising up from the dense green carpet of rain forest, was wreathed with swirling scuds of rain clouds and tendrils of fog.

He heaved a sigh of contentment and pressed his face closer to the glass. Everything was going according to schedule in London. An attendant had just handed him a downloaded e-mail sent via the high-speed air-ground data link from Lily's BlackBerry PDA. Lily and the Rose had just arrived at Grosvenor House and cleared security. The target was present. They were proceeding.

All good, he thought, gazing at the idyllic scene below.

But it wasn't really. There'd been a second down-loaded message from the Emir. Crumpled into a ball, it now lay on the Persian carpet at Snay's feet. The message could not have been clearer. One of his flowers had grown too tall for the garden. She would have to be cut down to size. Bin Wazir sighed. His beautiful Rose. Ah, well.

Fanning out from the base of the mountain, he could see the farmers and their oxen spread across the vast rice paddies. The volcano had erupted just last year, the fiery lava flow killing hundreds. But the farmers had rebuilt their homes near the volcano because it was the ash that made this region of the island's soil so fertile.

If you look at a chart of the South China Sea and, more specifically, Indonesia, in the area just south of the Equator and just north of latitude 15 degrees south, you'll see that 120 degrees of longitude perfectly bisects the small island of Suva, due west of Timor. Like all of Indonesia, it is Muslim; the largest Muslim nation on earth. In the seventies and early eighties, Suva Island was a vacation mecca for wealthy Arabs and their families. A long landing strip was slashed into the jungle to accommodate private planes. And then came the jumbo jets packed with rich young Arab tourists. The men in search of, not sun and sand, which they had more than their share of, but whiskey, wine, and casual sex.

The one hotel on the island is a sprawling resort set amidst many lush acres on the southern coast, with beautiful curving white beaches gently washed by the blue Suva Sea. It is called the Bambah. The Pink Palace. For most of the eighties and early nineties, it was a very chic destination. When it later fell out of fashion, it lay vacant for years, crumbling into a state of decay. Islamic guerillas discovered it, and, for years, it was a terrorist training camp before the guerillas were finally routed by government forces. Once more, the jungle asserted itself. The once beautiful buildings and grounds of the Bambah were overrun with riotous vegetation; the old hotel was left to molder and rot.

Snay bin Wazir was a sharp-eyed man who knew a bargain when he saw one. He bought it, and poured his wife's millions into it. But, after a brief renaissance in the late nineties, the hotel fell once more onto hard times. The rambling pale pink Bambah hotel below was the last remaining link in bin Wazir's once-golden chain. Gazing down upon its steep, fish-scale blue tile rooftops, he had to admit that the beautiful old hotel, once the jewel of his global real estate empire, had been a flawed stone.

As his 747 banked sharply, lining up for its final approach to the 10,000-foot jungle airstrip, Snay's mind was crowded with dreams of future glory. His efforts to destabilize and terrify the American diplomatic service had succeeded beyond anyone's hopes. Here at Suva, he was to set in motion the final phase of the Emir's Grand Jihad. His *hashishiyyun* had rocked the Great Satan back on his heels. Now he would lay him low. As the big jet touched down, reversed its thrusters and lumbered down the runway, he was filled with hope. After many humiliations, glory would finally be his.

Bin Wazir stood in the opened cabin door and thanked his trusted and very British pilot Khalid al-Abdullah, and his copilot, an Irishman named Johnny Adare, for a smooth flight. Their work had just begun.

They would supervise a waiting army of technicians and mechanics. They would create the Angel of Death.

Snay took a long, loving look back at his airplane as he descended the aluminum stairway to the ancient black hotel limousine. He knew the next time he saw his splendid green and gold Boeing 747, one of only three such privately owned aircraft in the world, he would scarcely recognize it.

The long black Daimler wound its way through the tenebrous jungle. The old pink palace sat on a rocky point of land jutting out into the Suva Sea. The hotel boasted a vast jumble of blue-tiled rooflines and minarets and other Middle Eastern architectural conceits. As the big car lurched to a stop at the covered entrance, he could see that a fresh coat of pink paint had been hurriedly applied to the rambling main structure.

The doormen and bellboys, in their faded pink jackets, were bowing and scraping before he and his bodyguard, Tippu Tip, had even climbed out of the rear of the car.

He'd given Ali al-Fazir, who ran the hotel, a few weeks' notice. The owner was coming. Snay bin Wazir was going to host a convention of some four hundred "travel agents" gathering for a two-day training seminar. The theme of the seminar, created by Snay himself, was "Travel in a Changed World." The attendees were scheduled to begin arriving first thing next morning. Al-Fazir had arranged a lavish welcome dinner for them, a traditional Indonesian *selametan* dedicating various foods to spirits and combining Muslim prayers with this spirit worship.

As Tippu and the elderly hotel driver removed three

antique Louis Vuitton steamer trunks from the cavernous boot of the old Daimler, Snay bin Wazir climbed the wide semicircular steps leading up to the verandah. He was surprised not to see the normally obsequious al-Fazir standing in the doorway to welcome him with open arms. Some feverish last-minute preparations for his arrival, no doubt.

"Hello, Saddam," he said to the dragon.

The Komodo dragon, traditionally kept chained to a stout metal post in one corner of the Bambah verandah, strained at the heavy links of its leash and bared its sharp, saw-like teeth. The animal, at just over ten feet in length, weighed nearly three hundred pounds. Komodos were the world's largest living reptiles. Very quick and very strong, with razor-sharp claws, the lizard could easily overcome wild pigs, deer, and even water buffalo.

Before he'd finally been captured and adopted as official mascot of the Bambah, Saddam had eaten at least fifteen human beings alive. Farmers' children, mostly, and one very old woman. He'd been weaned from such exotic fare twenty years ago. But Snay believed the dragon had never really lost his taste for human flesh. When you approached him, you could see his coal black pupils dilate, sense his fetid breath quickening.

Komodos are extremely fearsome creatures. Contrary to popular belief, the dragons don't kill you with their sawlike teeth. When they bite you, bacteria in their saliva goes right into your bloodstream. It can take you three or four days to die. A horrible death, knowing the dragon is tracking you, waiting for the chance to enjoy you at its leisure.

Saddam dreams of us at night, Snay had once told Ali al-Fazir, who was terrified of the dragon. Yes.

Colorful, exciting dreams. Stalking us, playing with us, seeing how long he can wait, waiting until he can stand it no longer. Then pouncing, gripping us with his claws as he opens his jaws, the taste of our warm meat and hot blood not nearly so exciting to his reptile brain as the sound of our cracking bones. Look, Ali, look at those eyes! He's dreaming of you!

For weeks, Ali would use another entrance to the hotel, avoiding Saddam at all costs.

Since human flesh was no longer a regular item on Saddam's menu, however, he'd acquired a great fondness for monkey heads, and there was always a pail full of them at the top of the hotel steps. Bin Wazir reached into the pail, plucked out a nice fresh one, and tossed it at the hissing beast. The lightning speed with which Saddam managed to snap the monkey's head up and pulverize it with his powerful jaws never failed to amaze him.

Despite the thick iron collar bolted round his neck and the heavy stainless steel chain that held the creature in check, the very sight of him was enough to cause heart palpitations in man, woman, or child. Saddam had long been a bone of contention between Snay and his manager al-Fazir. Bin Wazir, who had personally captured Saddam and installed him at the entrance, contended he was a great attraction. The terrified manager, who had to submit his monthly booking figures to the owner's wife, Yasmin, argued quite the opposite. "You could live with a man-eating dragon snarling at your door, but why would you?" he would ask Yasmin.

"Excellency!" al-Fazir shouted, rushing out of the entrance and embracing bin Wazir. "Allah has granted you safe journey! It has been a long time, my good friend. Much too long!" The man tried to hide his surprise at bin Wazir's enormous girth, which had tripled to sumo size since last they'd met.

Snay bin Wazir made a show of returning the awkward embrace and then held the other man at arm's length, looking at him carefully. He'd never completely trusted this al-Fazir. He always suspected his manager went behind his back, dealing with Yasmin on important hotel issues. Also, even the most cursory look at the books revealed a long history of inconsistencies. At any rate, year after year the hotel managed to eke out a small profit, Yasmin seemed to like the fellow, and so Snay tended to let it go.

"My great friend," he said, looking down at the bleary-eyed man, for Ali was a good head shorter, "are you all right? Have you been ill? Look, you are trembling."

"No, not at all," al-Fazir said with a thin smile. "A touch of monkey fever, perhaps, that's all. I'm much better now, Excellency. Quinine, you know. Nothing better."

Especially with vast quantities of Tanqueray gin, Snay bin Wazir thought. Actually he looked not good at all. His hands were damp and clammy, his skin sallow, his cheeks hollow, and his bloodshot eyes glassy and furtive. He had a long-standing bottle problem, Snay bin Wazir knew. Perhaps it had worsened. He smiled at the man and took his arm.

"Good, good," bin Wazir said. "If you need care, I'll arrange a charter. My pilots can fly you out to the hospital in Jakarta. The doctors are shit on this island as we learned during the last outbreak of the dengue." Ali had lost his wife to dengue fever. He had not been the same man since.

"Come, we will speak of it later," the bleary manager replied. "Let me take you up to the Owner's Suite. It was a long flight. A drink, perhaps, first? In the bar? While your luggage is being unpacked?" The man looked desperate for a drink himself.

They sat drinking Bali Hai beer in a booth in the cool dark of the main bar, just off the lobby. The room smelled of spice and mildew and leather. Overhead in the gloom, the paddle fans spun silently. The room was richly paneled with various Indonesian hardwoods, with a soaring beamed raffia ceiling. Snay bin Wazir himself had designed the room, modeling it after the Long Bar at Raffles in Singapore. His ideas on hotel interior decoration were much changed, less extravagant and more traditional since the Beauchamps debacle.

There was a white man sitting at the far end of the bar, talking quietly with the bartender. He wore a soiled linen jacket over khaki shorts and had leather sandals on his bare feet. His longish hair and beard were bleached by the sun, and he was deeply tanned. Clearly, he was someone who spent most of his time in the bush.

"A guest?" Snay bin Wazir asked, the question laced lightly with venom. He took a long, slow draught of his lager as he eyed the man at the bar. He'd specifically told his manager this seminar was to be strictly a closed, private affair; absolutely no outside guests when the attendees began arriving.

"Yes, yes, but do not worry, Excellency," Ali replied. "Name's Nash. He's checking out first thing. Tomorrow morning."

"No. He is checking out first thing this afternoon, Ali.

What did I tell you?" Snay strained to contain himself. An outsider in the hotel was the last thing he needed.

"He has a charter, Excellency, flying in from Java. Picking him up at first light and heading back there. You have my humblest apologies that he—"

"Who is he, anyway? Looks like a fucking Brit to me."

"Doesn't he? He's Australian. Perth, I believe. But he speaks perfect *Bahasa*. Like a native. He's some kind of scientist, I believe, studying the fauna and—"

"Idiot."

Snay bin Wazir rose from the table and strode deliberately across the room to the bar. Ali al-Fazir watched with his heart in his throat as bin Wazir stopped and whispered a few words to the bartender polishing glasses at the near end of the bar, then proceeded to the other end, taking the two stools next to Nash. As the two men spoke, Ali al-Fazir's head sunk lower and lower until his chin was resting upon his sternum. Was the Pasha a day early? He couldn't remember anymore. He was lost, drowning in the bottle.

"Hello," Snay said to the foreigner. "I am Mr. bin Wazir, the owner of this establishment."

"G'day, mate, Owen Nash is my name," the man said, extending a strong brown hand, which bin Wazir shook.

"I'm afraid I've some bad news for you, Mr. Nash. The hotel is fully booked."

"Right, I understand there is a large group arriving tomorrow."

"Ah. Who might have told you that?"

"Your manager over there, Mr. al-Fazir. Great bloke, awright. We had a few beers together just last night."

"Yes, he's a fountain of information, isn't he? What else did he tell you?"

"Oh, nothing really. Hotel gossip and such. Soul of discretion, I assure you. No worries, mate."

"No worries. But, how unfortunate that Mr. al-Fazir has his dates mixed up. The group is arriving this very afternoon."

"Today? But my charter flight out arrives at dawn. Surely you can find a spot for me for just the one night, Mr. bin Wazir. A linen closet would suit me just fine."

"What do you do, Mr. Nash?"

"I'm a photographer, in actuality. On assignment here for the *National Geo* magazine. Big feature on the Komodo dragons coming up. Might make the cover if I get lucky. Quite a few of them on this island, actually. Besides that bloody big bloke at the front door, I mean."

"Yes, I know. I've captured quite a few dragons on Suva myself. My mascot Saddam, as you see, is getting a little long in the tooth. I've got a pair of healthy young fellows just waiting to take his place. Not quite as large as Saddam, but a lot quicker and stronger."

"In captivity?"

"Yes. A large cage the hotel maintains on the property. You can take a look at it on your way to the airstrip, Mr. Nash. Take pictures."

"Thank you, Mr. bin Wazir. Light should be great that time of morning, actually."

"Actually, you're going out there now, Mr. Nash. I've instructed the bellman to collect your things and put them in the boot of the hotel Daimler. As it happens, I have a plane at the airstrip. My pilots will be only too happy to give you a ride on the short hop over to Java."

"But—"

"Ah, here's my driver now. He'll take you to the airstrip. Say hello to Tippu Tip, Mr. Nash."

The towering African chieftain in the red dashiki stuck out his hand and Nash had little choice but to stick his own out as well. The African crushed his hand and smiled broadly, revealing his red-stained teeth.

Nash picked up the antiquated bakelite speaking tube hanging from a hook beneath the rear window of the Daimler.

"Why are we stopping here, driver?" he said into the tube. "The airstrip's up just ahead. Let's press on, mate."

"Boss say you lak take picture of baby dragons."

"Oh, never mind that. Let's just get to the airstrip if it's all the same to you, mate."

"Boss say you take picture, you take picture."

"Yeah, well your boss isn't my boss, is he? Now, you—Christ!"

Tippu suddenly swung the big car off the side of the road and skidded violently to a dusty stop in the short grass. Even with the air-conditioning on and all the windows up, you could hear the thrashing and roaring of the two young Komodo lizards from their cage somewhere just inside the solid green wall of jungle. His passenger grabbed frantically for the rear door handle but Tippu had locked all the doors. He turned his massive bulk around in the front seat and looked at the plainly terrified white man.

"Ar take you see dragons," he said. "You lucky, Mr. Nash. Dragons' feeding time."

CHAPTER THIRTY-SIX

London

Brick Kelly trailed in Lily's scented, alluring wake. He watched the lavish redhead in pearlescent *peau de soie* sashay silkily through the French doors onto a balcony terrace. There were a number of these semi-circular terraces off the ballroom, all overlooking small gardens on the hotel's north side. But for the deep thump-thump of the news chopper hovering overhead, it would have been a peaceful spot to escape the tumult of the sharp-elbowed crowd inside. Across Park Lane, the trees of Hyde Park loomed black against the evening sky.

Ambassador Patrick Brickhouse Kelly felt a twinge of guilt.

Tish and the boys were somewhere at the far side of the ballroom, getting autographs from the star, Ian Flynn. It was the reason he'd brought his family out tonight, despite all Jack Patterson's words of caution. C'mon, Tex, he'd said. A chance for his cooped-up boys to see the world premiere of the new Nick Hitchcock thriller? And, perhaps meet the star himself? In the end, Patterson and his DSS detail had finally relented. Half the royal family and all of their security would be there after all. The ambassador's family might be a little more secure at a spring garden party inside the walls of Buck House perhaps, but not much.

He cast a guilty glance over his shoulder, looking for Tish and the boys. They were sure to be taking pictures, now, and where was Daddy? Why isn't Daddy in any of the Nick Hitchcock pictures, Mummy? Because Daddy had slipped away to have a clandestine word with an old friend, darling.

Lily paused just outside the doors, allowing Brick to advance alone. Francesca had her back to him, her elbows resting on the wide stone balustrade, gazing into the deep summer night. Her lush blonde hair was pulled back into a chignon, held in place by glittering diamond clips. She seemed to be whistling softly or whispering to chipmunks playing below among the chestnut trees.

Long-buried memories stirred. A week with her, lost in the sanctuary of a small bedroom overlooking the Spanish Steps. Brick, having survived the sandstorms and tank battles in the deserts south of Baghdad with his skin mostly intact, had elected to stop in Rome for a week before heading home to Richmond. A refueling stop, he'd told his mother on the phone, and she'd suggested a hotel he'd find at *Trinità dei Monti 6,* the Hassler. The intimate old-world atmosphere of the hotel proved perfect for nursing war wounds.

It was on his second night in Rome, dining alone at *La Carbonara,* a lively *trattoria* he'd discovered in the *Piazza Campo del Fiore,* that the young American army captain had first glimpsed the beauty. She happened to be working in the kitchen, slicing salami at a heavy wooden table, and every time the kitchen door swung inwards or outwards, he tried to catch her eye.

In the warm, steamy light of the kitchen, surrounded by frenetic cooks, busboys, and black-jacketed waiters, she seemed serene, and, save the gleaming knife in her hand, even angelic.

The kitchen door swung like a camera's clicking shutter. She'd catch his eye as one waiter pushed into the kitchen with a tray of empty dishes; and he would return the favor as another emerged bearing plates of steaming pasta. Finally, there was that one smile. Neither would remember nor care who'd smiled into the camera first. He fell in love. He thought, at the beginning, she might just be a little bit in love with him, too.

Still blood runs deep, she'd said to him after their first fight. It was one evening after two or three bottles of rough Chianti in a *taverna* in Testevere, and he spent the rest of the night trying to explain why what he'd meant was not an insult. She was easily hurt, and prone to quick anger. One lesson Brick learned that week was that threading an Abrams M1-A battle tank through Iraqi minefields made tiptoes across the eggshells of the female psyche look suicidal.

When the young Francesca, having asked about his bright decorations, had learned the extent of her handsome new lover's recent activities in the Persian Gulf, her eyes had flashed with righteous anger.

It ended badly in a quarrel that last night, just before his flight to Andrews AFB and then on to Richmond. A horribly public outburst over the recent Iraqi defeat in the "mother of all battles." He'd innocently proposed a toast, raising a glass to his fallen comrades in the 100th Armored Division.

"Here's to us, our noble selves," Brick said. "None finer, and many a damn sight worse!"

She'd lowered her goblet and, with a thin smile, emptied her full glass onto the white linen tablecloth. The table looked bloodsoaked.

"Still blood runs deep," she said, gazing at the spreading crimson stain. "This war is not over. It is just beginning."

Brick looked into her eyes and realized he was seeing her for the very first time. "Tell me about it," he said, and she did.

Her father, now the proprietor of La Carbonara, was a sixth-generation Roman. Her mother was Syrian. Francesca had grown up in the backstreets of Damascus. She lived in an abusive, tortured household rife with political and religious fervor. She'd listened to both sides all her life, and ended up passionately siding with her blessed mother in her hatred for the impious capitalist imperialists bent on ruling the world. Now her poor mother was dead. Of a broken heart, Francesca always screamed at her abusive father when her anger flared. Her father's abuse of his daughter was knotted irrevocably with his religion. And her hatred.

What Brick decided he did not need, after a tour of duty in the Gulf in which many of his friends had died horribly in the defense of freedom, was a raging Islamic fundamentalist in his bed. They parted. He never saw Francesca again. Until this moment.

Crossing the terrace now, his mind was filled only with memories of her body in different poses and shifting shades of light in the beautiful old bed. He felt his heartbeat accelerate. "Francesca," he said quietly, the accent on the first syllable, and she turned around. The soft light of the garden on her exquisite face, bare shoulders, and deep bosom was unbearably unfair to a long and very happily married man.

"Caro?" she said, the big brown doe eyes gleaming. *"Sí.* It is you. Tank. My great American war hero. *Ecco, mi amore,* come here, eh, Tank Commander? Give your old friend a kiss, eh?"

She held out her arms and Brick went to her. He sincerely meant to give her a chaste peck on the cheek, but she wasn't having any of that. Both hands went around his neck and she pulled him to her, red lips parted, and the kiss on the voluptuous mouth was unavoidable. He was trying to pull away when he felt a sharp bite just under his left ear.

"What the—"

He caught a glimpse of her right hand, saw her big sapphire ring with the silver needle protruding from the center of the stone and then, nothing more.

"He's slipping. Help me hold him up," the Rose whispered.

Lily grabbed Brick's arm just as the nylon harness dropped from the sky to the terrace below. A hovering helicopter, indistinguishable from any of the press choppers still circling above the hotel, now dangled a hundred-foot-long nylon sling from its opened bay. Together, the two women quickly looped the harness down over Kelly's head and shoulders and then cinched it upwards under his arms. Rose looked up at the man leaning out of the open chopper bay just above and gave the visual signal. The unconscious American ambassador shot straight up into the night sky, instantly winched up and hauled inside the helicopter. The chopper, white with large blue ITV NEWS logos on its flanks, roared away over the treetops of Hyde Park.

Rose looked at her watch. "Under ten seconds," she said to Lily. *"Va bene, eh?"*

"Molto bene," Lily said, and something in her voice made Rose look up. Lily was reaching up inside the wig of red hair arranged atop her head and festooned with emeralds.

"Che cosa . . . what are you—" Francesca said, but Lily was one step ahead of her.

"Un cadeau," Lily said, pulling a small black object out of the nest of her hair. "A farewell gift. From our Pasha. In memory of your brilliant performance in the sumo shrine. You remember, darling? You costarred with him."

"No," Rose said, moving backwards, "don't. Don't."

"Surely you knew what would happen if you got too close to him. The Pasha kills what he loves in order to survive. If one flower grows too tall, he cuts it off. Chop, chop."

Lily advanced toward her with the snub-nosed object extended at the end of her arm, pressed the muzzle into Rose's bosom, and fired the weapon into her heart. With the choppers still throbbing overhead, and the noise inside the ballroom, the muffled sound of the single round was barely audible. Rose fell toward her, knocking the gun from Lily's hand, her body landing with a dull thud on top of the weapon. Lily saw that she was dead and vaulted over the balustrade. She fell a good ten feet into the waiting arms of Raed, the driver she had arranged for the evening.

Raed put her down on the ground and looked up, waiting for the next woman to tumble into his arms. Lily grabbed his hand, taking him in tow, and started racing along the narrow dirt path between the curved wall and the thick privet hedge.

"I thought there were two of you," Raed said, moving swiftly and easily along just behind her.

"No," she said over her shoulder. "Just me. Hurry. We're late. The Pasha's plane is wheels up at Gatwick in less than an hour."

Alex Hawke was watching the ice melt in Brick's vodka when he heard something from beyond the open doors he didn't like at all. A muffled thump followed by a noise that sounded like a hundred-pound sack of flour hitting the bricks. He slammed down his rum and walked quickly towards the French doors, cursing himself and knowing instinctively it was probably already over. All of his alarm systems, usually so reliable, had gone off thirty seconds late.

Still, he was unprepared for what he found. The Italian movie star, alone, face down in a rapidly spreading pool of blood. No sign of the little starlet. And, bleeding hell, no sign of his friend Brick. How the hell? He ran to the balustrade and peered down over the side. The garden below was empty. Nothing.

He dropped to his knees beside the woman, getting an arm under and turning her over, cradling her head as gouts of aortic blood pumped directly from the small entrance wound over her heart. She was moaning and her breathing was keening and shallow. She was conscious, but he knew instantly she wasn't going to make it. No one could save her now.

He had less than a minute with her. Maybe seconds.

"Who shot you?"

"Oh . . . so cold."

"You're going to be all right. But, you must tell me, my poor woman. Who shot you? Where is the ambassador? Tell me."

"That . . . bitch. Lily . . . she shot . . . they have all betrayed me . . ."

"Who? Who betrayed you?"

"All of them . . . the Pasha and . . . *un fottuto disastro*."

"The American ambassador. Where have they taken him?"

"B-Brick? Beautiful Brick . . . ?"

"Yes. Brick."

"The Blue Palace . . . Fatin . . . you know . . . in the mountains . . ."

Her eyes closed. He was losing her.

"Stay with me! The Americans, Francesca, who has been killing all the Americans?"

"Snay bin Wazir," she whispered, "the Pasha. He . . . has killed me, too . . . millions more . . . Americans . . . soon . . . justice."

And then she was gone.

Lowering her gently to the blood-soaked bricks, he saw the gun. He picked it up carefully with his handkerchief. It was sticky with blood. Plastic, he saw, to avoid the detectors. One shot. One to the heart was usually enough.

"Good God, man, shall I get a doctor?"

Hawke looked up to see Lord Mowbray in the act of lighting his cigar.

"Too late for that I'm afraid. If you'd be so kind as to ask Jack Patterson to step outside. Tall American chap at the bar just to the left of the door. Cowboy boots. Also, get an MI6 agent out here. Anyone will do, but the more senior the better. Tell them to hurry, please, Lord Mowbray. But, don't cause a stir. I need to have a quiet word alone with Ambassador Kelly's wife."

As Mowbray turned to go, Patterson appeared in the doorway. Hawke handed him the murder weapon wrapped in his handkerchief.

"Who is it?" Patterson said, kneeling beside him.

"Francesca d'Agnelli."

"Dead?"

"Very."

"The movie star. Damn it. The woman we grilled in Venice. Three times, and came up empty. She was with Stanfield the night he exploded in the Grand Canal. This is 'the Rose.'"

"Yes," Hawke said. "Murdered two minutes ago by the Lily. They snatched Brick, Jack. They've got my best bloody friend."

"Did she talk?"

"Yeah. Apparently, a hell of a lot of Americans are scheduled to die at the hand of Snay bin Wazir."

"Jesus Christ," Patterson said, his face a mask of failure and despair. He took out his satellite mobile phone, flipped it open, and punched in the emergency code for Secretary of State Consuelo de los Reyes. Seconds later, the high-low sound of wailing sirens filled the streets of Mayfair and Hyde Park.

CHAPTER THIRTY-SEVEN

South Biscayne Bay

Couple of minutes into watching the young Cuban spec ops guy handle the inflatable boat, Stoke flashed his old Navy SEAL ID at Pepe. It was enough to convince the Cuban commander to let him drive the damn boat, since his own guy seemed scared shitless about going flat out in the rough seas and had the thing running at half throttle. Kid even had trouble keeping the thing going in a straight line.

"Your wake look more like a snake than a stick, son," Stoke said to the guy, relieving him of duty. "Best let a professional do this heavy weather shit. Find a place to sit and hold on!"

Stoke grabbed the helm, shoved the throttles all the way forward, and the nearly flat-bottomed boat leapt forward, up and out of the water the way it had been designed to run. Boat was fast for a reason. It was basically a cafeteria tray with five hundred horsepower stuck on the back.

Stoke got the twin Yamaha 250's powering the thing over the wave tops. Waves too big, curling overhead, he just smashed right through them. Other three boats were having trouble keeping up with them, but Stoke wasn't much for waiting around. As it was, he and Pepe were having a tough time keeping Rodrigo's rooster tail in sight. Cigarette boats were built for serious speed, those deep "V" hulls sliced right through anything.

It had occurred to him to just call in the cavalry, in this case the U.S. Coast Guard. They'd have a chopper shining a spotlight on this guy's head in ten minutes. But Stoke wanted this bad boy for himself. He wanted him for Hawke, too. Hadn't he promised Alex he and Ross would go find him? Run him to ground? Goddamn it, that's what they were going to do. Stoke was a mission-oriented individual.

Dead or alive, he told Alex when they'd said good-bye two days ago at Logan Airport. Stoke liked dead better. Alive, Alex would probably kick Rodrigo's butt and turn whatever was left of him over to Scotland Yard. Best part about dead, ain't nobody got to worry about extraditing your ass, you dead. Or, worry about you disappearing down some loophole.

The four troops sitting in the stern were so excited about his SEAL card, next thing they'd be askin' for was his damn autograph. Stoke was thinking he wished he had his old crew, Thunder and Lightning, on this thing. Some world-class badass hop-and-pop counterterrorists with him, instead of Rambo Jr. and his teenage commandos sitting back there behind him, all amped up about a real-live SEAL driving the boat instead of worrying about kicking ass and taking care of business.

Least he had Ross. Even wounded, you want Ross on your side. Tough as it was, bouncing around like this, Cubans had a medical corpsman trying to get some kind of splint on Ross's busted lower left leg.

"Hey, Ross," Stoke said, shouting at the man over the roar of wind and engines. "How you doin' back there, my brother? Okay?"

Ross smiled and gave him the thumbs up. Man was stone badass. He was lying down on a thwart seat in the stern, holding on to the guy who was working on his leg by the scruff of his neck, trying to keep the medic from bouncing out of the boat. Every time they pounded through a wave, a wall of seawater washed over the boat. "Hoo-hah," Stoke shouted into the salty spray. Just then, the outboards sputtered and he looked down at his fuel gauge.

"Shit, Pepe, what were you thinking about? We're about to run out of gas, man! How you plan to catch this asshole without fuel? You ain't even got extra jerry cans aboard?"

"In the other boats! We only plan for enough to get back to Port of Miami, *señor!*" Pepe shouted, holding on to the windscreen with his left hand, and the night-vision binocs with his right. "Not this!"

"Plans don't always work out, do they, Pepe?"

Stoke thought about the situation for a second.

"Listen up, Pepe, I got a thought."

"*Sí, Señor* Stokely."

"We don't need the other boats, they're only slowing us down. We can deal with this all by our lonesomes, we got enough gas. I'm going to slow down, let 'em catch up, off-load those extra jerry cans. You keep your binocs on Rodrigo."

Stoke hauled back on the throttles, back to idle, let the boat settle, ride up the front of the big waves, crest, and slide down the back. In a couple of minutes, the other three boats had reached them. Stoke waved them in close, ready to throw lines and raft up. Start the fuel transfer. He knew the three boatloads of commandos wouldn't be too happy about this but—

"*Señor!*" Pepe said. "We will not need the gas! Look!"

He handed Stoke the night-vision binocs. The boat had slid down to the bottom of a trough so he had to wait till they crested to get a look. He couldn't believe what he was seeing through the luminous green lenses. Seven or eight ramshackle old wooden houses rising up on stilts, 'bout twenty feet over the water. Old, looked like, and deserted. Stiltsville! Yeah, he'd read about the place on the plane down. Old gambling and rum-running settlement, built in the '30s. Been a ghost town since the last big hurricane. But, the really weird thing? Rodrigo's sixty-foot speedboat was moored to a ladder going up to one of the bigger houses. Boat looked empty, just bobbing up and down. Now, why would he want to do that?

"*Fantástico! Lo tenemos! La rata!* We got the rat!" Pepe shouted, looking at the troops in the other boats and pointing to the Cigarette. "*Vámonos!*"

"Hey! Hold up, Pepe!" Stoke said, quickly grabbing a lifeline on the nearest boat before the guy driving it could take off. He pulled the boat alongside and pointed at two large jerry cans of gas in the stern. "*Dos más, por favor,*" he said to the young commando. Kid was built like a small gorilla. He picked up the two heavy gas cans like a couple of super-sized Pepsis and handed them over to Stoke. By the time Stoke had them, the three inflatables had already gunned their motors and raced away.

"What you wait for, *señor?* Let's go get him!"

"This is a major goatfuck, man, I'm tellin' you. Get on the damn radio and call 'em back. Pronto if not sooner!" Stoke turned his back on the guy and started filling his tanks.

"This is my operation, *señor*, not yours! I take my orders from *el comandante,* not *norteamericanos.* Now, go!"

"You always this stupid, or you just making a special effort today?" Stoke said, shaking his head in wonder.

The other three flat-bottoms were still racing toward Stiltsville and closing fast. Total and complete fuck-up, you could see it coming a mile away.

Stokely had the Cuban commander's Glock nine sidearm out of its holster and jammed up against Pepe's head before the guy even knew how or even if it might happen.

"How you say 'mutiny' in Spanish, *jefe?* 'Cause that's what's happening. First thing you do? You tell your guys here to hand their guns nice and slow to Ross, *comprende?* 'Less you want your brains in the water."

Lieutenant Alvarez gave the order, and Stoke knew enough Spanish to know the man wanted to keep his brains intact, though, from what Stoke could see, there wasn't a whole lot to go around. Ross, sitting up now, accepted the weapons and stowed all but one, an AK-47 Chinese assault rifle, under the thwart seat. The AK he cradled loosely, but his finger was on the trigger.

"Assault knives?" Stoke asked the guy.

"*Sí.*"

"Feed 'em to the fishies."

Four knives splashed into the bay.

"Yours too, *Comandante.* I'll keep it safe for you."

After the guy had handed him the knife, Stoke took the gun away from his head and pushed him down into the seat. The three assault boats were now closing to within maybe a couple hundred yards of the nearest stilt house, the big one where Rodrigo's black Cigarette boat was moored.

"One last chance, amigo," Stoke said, handing Pepe the radio. "Call 'em back."

The guy shook his head no.

"Ask you a relevant question, Pepe," Stoke said. "You seen much combat? Or you just a special ops guy? Dragging folks kicking and screaming out of their houses in the middle of the night and shit. Kidnapping their children? Or, maybe you just got a sinus problem? Your nose so stuffed up you can't smell a trap stinks to high heaven right in front of you?"

"My men will take him, you will see."

"Well, look at it this way, *Comandante,* however it goes down? We sittin' tight. We got us a front-row seat. Ain't that right, Ross?"

"Trap, Stoke," Ross said quietly, eyes following the three boats, going slowly now, ghosting up to the ram-shackle house where the black boat was tied. Troops on their feet, weapons all trained on the Cigarette.

"Bet your ass, trap. Nothing else makes sense, Ross. Rodrigo, he knows we after him. Why he stop? Tie up? Take a nap? Catch him some *bonita*? He got Fancha with him. Maybe catch a little trim?"

"The boat doesn't make any sense."

"That's what I'm working on, too. He can't be in it. He knows he's outnumbered. Twelve guys with automatic weapons, RPGs. Shoot his boat up, sink it. So, then, what, he's up in one of the houses? Lure them in?

House-to-house? Twelve against one? Make any sense to you?"

"Better off running, Stoke. Head south for the Keys. Bags of hidey holes down in the mangrove swamps."

"What I try to tell the military genius here."

"Right."

"Rebel without a clue. Boy like to snatch his troops from the jaws of victory."

"His call."

"Keep your eyes open, Ross. Looks like *Señor* McHale's Navy is going in without him."

"Here's a thought," Ross said, rubbing his stubbly chin. "Maybe that Cigarette's not Rodrigo's only boat."

CHAPTER THIRTY-EIGHT

Suva Island

He took a small sip of the ice-cold gin, and savored the juniper bite of it on his tongue. In no aspect of his appearance or attitude was there any hint that here was a man about to ignite the fuse of what could conceivably be World War Three.

The dense din of insect music provided a natural background for the man and his two companions. The three of them were sitting on the broad Bambah verandah, bathed in the pale equatorial light of late afternoon. The owner himself was seated in a tall white wicker rocking chair, regal as a fat old maharajah, sipping his gin fizz and lime. The cane and wicker rocker was creaking under the burden of his weight.

Bin Wazir wore his favorite evening attire, an aged white dinner jacket made up long ago at Huntsman's of Savile Row. He'd had his tailor enlarge it any number of times, still he had to be very careful not to strain the seams. Age and the brutal Indonesian heat had turned the vast silk jacket almost yellow, which made it even more elegant. He was wearing black striped silk trousers, black tie, and a pair of black velvet evening pumps without socks. He had rubbed oil of macassar into his thick dark hair and combed it straight back off his domed forehead.

In the distance, out beyond the sweeping ring of the bay, the peak of the towering volcano was sending plumes of grey ash into the whitish-yellow sky. Occasionally, brilliant red and orange jets of molten fire would streak upwards, pause, and then fall back into the mouth of the volcano. There were reports of increased activity. Reports? Anyone who'd lived around volcanoes long enough knew it was early days. The old mountain was just building up a head of steam. Even Saddam, his tail whispering across the floorboards, knew it was only a matter of time.

From time to time, barefoot servants in gold and red sarongs would appear, padding out onto the verandah with bowed heads and hands clasped as if in prayer, silently topping off bin Wazir's gin, adding tinkling ice from a silver bucket. Or, another might insert a fresh yellow Baghdaddie into his long ebony holder, while yet another held his flaming gold Dunhill to the tip.

Tonight was clearly a very special occasion in the long and storied history of the Hotel Bambah. A sense of nervous excitement was obvious among the staff and guests throughout the hotel, even out here on the verandah. Especially out here on the verandah.

"Most kind," the owner would say to the servants, and then the verandah, save the constant insect hum, fell quiet once more.

His two companions sat in silence. Three, really, if you counted the dragon, Saddam. Earlier, Tippu Tip had been playing with the Komodo, rolling monkey heads across the floor. He aimed them carefully, keeping them all a foot, and no more, outside the range of Saddam's jaws, the dragon snapping and straining at his steel leash. The African had tired of this game well before the dragon, and was now lying stretched to his full length atop the cushions of a bamboo divan, snoring quietly.

Saddam was coiled in his corner, his great scaly tail swishing slowly, snaking across the old wooden floorboards, head down, eyeing the various occupants of the porch carefully with his yellow eyes. He had varying degrees of interest in these three humans. He regarded the sleeping African for a while, his eyes flashing, then he turned his attention to Snay bin Wazir rocking in his chair at the top of the steps.

The sight of his owner seemed to calm him. The man never teased or threatened him. And never failed to toss a monkey head or two his way when he came up the steps from walks in the gardens. Pacified, he would even allow the human to stroke his great snout. Satisfied that all was well with Snay bin Wazir, Saddam directed his gaze to the third man on the verandah, Ali al-Fazir. The bright eyes flashed again and the long forked tongue shot out, licked the air, and retracted.

The hotel manager was Saddam's chief tormenter when the owner or guests weren't around. He was sitting on the steps below Snay bin Wazir with his arms wrapped morosely around his knees. He was gazing out into the darkening gardens. The old dragon smelled fear and flight; at any moment the much-hated old sack of bones might stand up and sprint off into the encroaching gloom.

Snay spoke, breaking the long silence.

"All of the guests have arrived and are checked in?"

"Yes, Excellency," Ali al-Fazir said, "all four hundred. All very beautiful, may I say, sire. Exquisite."

"Yes. But, chosen for their brains and training, my dear Ali. The *crème* of the camps the world over. The preparations for this evening's reception? And the welcome dinner?"

"Complete."

"The menu?"

"Beef Rendang, Ikan Pedis, and Babi Panggang for the main course. Sate Ajam, Gado Gado, and Kroepoek udang to begin. As you ordered, sir."

"Ah, well," Snay said with a sigh, "I suppose there's really nothing left for you to do then, is there, Ali old friend?" He took another sip of gin.

The silence continued thus until Ali could stand it no longer. "I was wondering, Excellency, about . . ." He realized he had no idea what he was wondering about, that he was just desperate to say something, anything, to prolong the inevitable. "About . . ."

"About?"

"Trees," Ali said, a lost look filling his bloodshot, red-rimmed eyes.

"Trees."

"Yes, sire, all the trees you planted so long ago out there in the garden. I've always wondered what they are."

"Ah, curious, after all these years."

"Well, I am curious, sire, about the various—"

"No, no. I meant it *is* curious that after all this time on the property, you suddenly develop an interest in its horticulture."

"I only meant—"

"Quiet, Ali. Silence. At any rate, these plantings here at the foot of the steps are East Indian snakewood from Java and Timor. The seeds yield strychnine. And, just over there, those evergreens beyond the path, are my favorite. From Borneo. They call it the ordeal-tree, or poison tanghin as the fruit contains tanghinine, a toxic asthenic. These spectacular Hawaiian climbing lilies, *Gloriosa superba,* are a wonderful source of colchicine, three grains of which are fatal. The castor bean plants at your feet contain the seed which produces ricin, a quite fashionable poison once again."

"All poisonous. Everything."

"With few exceptions, yes. A lovely thought isn't it? The Poison Garden. Thinking of going for a walk, are you not?"

"I was, yes."

Ali got slowly to his feet, pushing down with his hands on his knees for leverage.

"How far will I get, sire?"

"Depends on your herb of choice, I suppose."

"Yes."

Snay turned and looked at the African and saw the big rheumy red eyes staring at him in the growing darkness. "I believe we're ready," he said to Tippu Tip and the big head nodded once in acknowledgment.

He looked back at al-Fazir and saw that the man was rooted to the spot, his chin down on his sternum. He was shaking like a leafless stalk in a strong breeze.

"I-I've been a good soldier," he blurted out, more to himself than Snay.

"Good-bye, Ali," Snay said pleasantly. "One last thing. That tree by the gate. If you get that far, it's a chinaberry tree. The fruit contains a narcotic that instantly shuts down the entire central nervous system. It might be of some help."

Ali bowed deeply from the waist.

"Sire."

The man leapt from the steps and hit the ground running. Bin Wazir let him get twenty feet away and then looked over his shoulder and nodded. Tippu already had the key in the security lock. The glass cover of the device slid back and he pulled the red ring. The steel pole the dragon was chained to descended silently into the verandah's floor.

"Saddam!" Snay whispered to his roaring dragon. "Kill!"

Ali did make it to the chinaberry tree, such was his desperation and fleetness of foot. He leapt up and caught the lowest hanging branch and managed to swing himself up into the tree. The ten-foot lizard was racing through the gardens at over forty miles an hour with its jaws open. Ali screamed and started climbing desperately for the top branches, his leather shoes making it difficult to find purchase.

The fruit? Where was the fruit?

Saddam was at the base of the tree now, his fore-claws making huge gashing swipes at the bark. He looked up at his hated prey, for that's what Ali could see in the watery yellow eyes, hate, let out a bellowing roar, and started upwards, climbing swiftly and easily.

Ali was snatching handfuls of leaves and berries, shoving everything down his throat, choking it all down, chewing desperately on the fruit, swallowing the bitter juice, waiting for darkness. He felt Saddam's hot breath on his bare ankles and screamed when the dragon bit off his left foot in one quick bite. Then Saddam started on his other leg.

It wasn't just the sound of screaming coming from

the top of one of the poison garden trees that brought the few guests not already massing down at the beach pavilion to their windows. It was the horrible sound of cracking bones. Snay sat back in his rocker, a satisfied smile on his face.

"Why you kill him?" Tippu rumbled from the shadows.

"He was due. And he couldn't keep his fucking mouth shut."

"Heh-heh. Lak Saddam."

"Tippu," Snay said after a long moment, "would you get a couple of fellows and fetch Saddam? I think he's quite finished with Ali for the time being." Snay knew Saddam's eating habits. He would take an appetizer from a soft portion of the victim, wait for the blood poison to take effect, then return to the main course when he was hungry again. Meanwhile, what was left of Ali would remain in the treetops, ropy strings of flesh draped in the higher branches.

Tippu clapped his hands smartly and two young native boys appeared out of the bush. One had a high-powered rifle loaded with tranquilizing rounds, the other a thickly meshed steel net. The African descended the steps heavily, took the rifle from the boy, and the trio disappeared into the garden.

"Sire?" the receptionist said as Snay passed the front desk on his way up to the main ballroom to check on the arrangements. "So sorry to disturb you. There is an urgent telephone call for His Excellency. I'll put it through to the telephone room, sir."

"Pasha," the voice said. It was Lily, calling on a secure line. Bin Wazir sat on the small chair and pulled the folding door closed after him. A small table lamp with a red shade was illuminated. He lit a cigarette. His nerves were thrumming.

"Yes, dear girl. I've been waiting for word. All is well?"

"The mission was—a complete success, sire."

"We have him? We have Ambassador Kelly?"

"Yes, sire. We have him. He is at this very moment en route to the Blue Palace. The plane left Gatwick ten minutes ago."

"And, the world-famous movie star?"

"Another flower grows in Paradise."

Snay entered the hotel's grand ballroom. The sea of red tables was just as he had ordered. The centerpieces consisted of many small flags, all emblazoned with the official emblem of the Emir's jihad, a raised sword dripping blood. Row upon row of larger versions of the red flag were mounted high on all four walls of the room. The effect was all he hoped it would be. A room bedecked with the colors and symbols of blood and vengeance.

"Ah, sire," the small dark man with steel spectacles said, rushing forward from the projection room. "You are here for the tech check. All is in readiness, sir."

"Good, good, Seti," he replied, his eyes sweeping the room, relishing the moment to come. "Could you put up the first three slides?"

"It shall be done!" Seti said, and rushed back into the projection booth. The large wall behind the podium from which Snay bin Wazir would address the audience contained a concealed theater-sized screen. Snay bin Wazir merely had to press a button on the podium's remote to reveal the screen. He climbed the few steps up to the stage and strode across to the podium and lit up another of his yellow Baghdaddies.

"First slide," he said, puffing into the microphone.

"Coming up," Seti's voice replied over the speaker system.

Snay turned and faced the screen, pressing a button on the remote in his hand. The wall disappeared. A slide came up.

"TRAVEL IN A NEW WORLD"

A trace of a smile played about bin Wazir's lips. He took a secret delight in his own wit and irony. New world, indeed, he thought. "Next," brought up a new slide: an old picture of the Emir on horseback, with sword raised in righteous anger. He could hear the swelling applause that would soon fill the room. "Next."

A detailed map of the United States of America, some fifty feet across. All the major airports, railroads, and highways were clearly designated. National parks and monuments were starred, as were famous tourist attractions. The Alamo in Texas. Mount Vernon. Williamsburg, Virginia. A vast shopping mecca called the Mall of America. There were also two sets of black mouse ears. One near the coast of southern California and one in the dead center of the state of Florida. Another nice touch, he thought.

Black flags marked America's one hundred most populous cities. Number one, New York City, with well over eight million in the 2000 census. At number fifty, Wichita City, Kansas, with roughly 350,000. Last on the list, Irving City, Texas, with 191,615 souls. The combined population of the top hundred was well over one hundred million. On the black flag pinpointing each designated city was a symbol. It was the familiar circular yellow and black spoked wheel of the trefoil; the international warning for radiation.

Snay bin Wazir clasped his hands together as an indescribable shiver of pleasure rushed over him. Such a state of bliss must surely have a name. Yes.

Paradise.

He called for the next slide.

It was a carefully illustrated diagram. A step-by-step guide to the final assembly of a nuclear device that one hundred of the lucky attendees would find waiting for them at safe houses located at their designated destinations within America's most populous cities. Each plutonium device, designed by Dr. I.V. Soong, the Emir's chief weapons expert, contained the explosive power of the weapons used to destroy Nagasaki and Hiroshima. The two-kiloton bomb was almost exactly the size and shape of an American football.

The Indian scientist Soong was a brilliant graduate of Cal Tech who had given his bomb an American nickname no one understood. Still, the infamous name had stuck among the female attendees, all veterans of terrorist training camps throughout the world, all highly trained in the development and deployment of the most sophisticated small radioactive explosive device on the face of the earth.

The Pigskin.

Snay smiled and a single red spotlight picked out his gleaming canines, the pointed teeth between the incisors and the first bicuspids.

Every dog has his day, the man said to himself, crossing the stage.

CHAPTER THIRTY-NINE

London

Alexander Hawke and Ambrose Congreve arrived at the world-famous black door at precisely eleven o'clock in the morning. Hawke had been to a number of state dinners and meetings at No. 10 Downing, but it was a first visit for Ambrose Congreve. The worldly detective had feigned nonchalance all morning, but his best navy chalk-striped suit, Windsor-knotted regimental tie, and highly polished Peale wing-tipped shoes belied his efforts. He was even wearing, Hawke noticed with some amusement, his favorite brown trilby.

For a man who prided himself on his sartorial indifference, Congreve was surprisingly *à la mode* on this sunny morning in July. His socks even matched. Bright yellow.

"You look festive this morning," Hawke said, nodding in his direction.

"Festive?"

"Hmm," Hawke murmured.

"May I quote Thomas Jefferson?"

"Always."

"On matters of style, swim with the current. On matters of principle, stand like a rock."

Ambrose drew himself up, adjusted the round, tortoiseshell spectacles perched at the tip of his nose, bent, and carefully inspected the lion's head brass knocker, brass numbers, and the letterbox inscribed "First Lord of the Treasury."

"You know why that particular title is there?" Ambrose said, pointing to the letterbox.

"No," Hawke replied. "No idea."

"Ah. Dates from 1760, when the Duke of Newcastle was prime minister. He was also first lord of the treasury. All subsequent prime ministers have resided here at No. 10 by their right as first lord of the treasury."

"Imagine that."

The discreet black door, once wooden, now Kevlar, swung open.

Hawke and Congreve were escorted across the black and white checkered entrance hall to a small alcove containing some modern British sculpture. Their escort, a rather severe gentleman in a cutaway over a starched white bibfront, bowed slightly and departed to attend to far more pressing and important business, as an attractive young female staff member approached with her hand extended. "Good morning," Hawke said, shaking her cool hand.

"Lord Hawke, how do you do? And Inspector Congreve," the pretty brunette said, "what an honor. We're delighted to have you gentlemen here at the prime minister's residence. I'm Guinevere Guinness."

"Thank you, Miss Guinness," Congreve said, bowing slightly and favoring her with his most sparkling smile. "An honor."

"Yes, honored," Hawke said, inwardly wincing at the young woman's use of his title. Hawke had long discouraged anyone at all from using it. However, here at No. 10, everyone stood on ceremony.

"Gentlemen, if you'll be so kind as to follow me upstairs? You'll be in the Terracotta Room for just a few minutes. Meeting is starting a bit late, I'm afraid. The prime minister has a surprise visitor from Washington this morning. Let's just take the stairs, shall we?"

The two men followed Miss Guinness's decorous ascent up the grand staircase. The stairway was quite impressive, cantilevered as it was out of the curving wall with no visible means of support. On the pale yellow wallpaper to their left were hung black and white portraits of every prime minister, ascending in chronological order.

At the foot of the stairway, a giant globe, a gift from French president Mitterrand, Congreve had noted, and, on the wall, a small portrait of the first prime minister, Sir Robert Walpole. Gaining the top, Congreve paused to point out that, by tradition, the prime minister in residence was never displayed.

"Really?" Hawke said. "I had no idea."

Hawke smiled inwardly. Having known Ambrose since his own early childhood, he knew precisely what was going on here. This little history lesson was nothing but tit for tat. Ambrose was exacting his revenge for the upland game shooting lectures he'd endured from Alex the week prior. It wasn't knowledge the man was doling out; it was retaliation.

"Here we are, then," Miss Guinness said. "There's tea, I believe . . . and cress sandwiches."

"Lovely," Congreve twinkled, touching the tip of his forefinger to his perfectly upturned moustache.

They were soon comfortably seated in the Terracotta Room on two facing Chippendale sofas, admiring the historic portraits hung on walls the color of warm brick. Tea had indeed been laid, and Alex let his eyes roam about the room while Ambrose poured. Every item in the room was polished or brushed or plumped to perfection. It was a room where foreign visitors to Downing Street might get some sense of Britain's cultural heritage. Above a door, a gilt-framed portrait of Lord Nelson, who had defeated the French fleet at Trafalgar.

"Do you happen to know, Ambrose, the precise number of French soldiers required to defend the city of Paris?" Hawke asked.

"Why, no, I don't."

"No one does."

"Why not?"

"It's never been attempted," Hawke deadpanned.

"Jolly good," Congreve said, trying desperately not to laugh out loud. "I daresay, yes. Never been attempted, hah." He looked up, and leapt to his feet.

At that moment, the American president strode into the room, a smile on his weathered, craggy face. He had the look of a man who'd spent most of his life at sea, which indeed he had, and yet somehow the ravages of wind and salt and sun had never managed to get to his sharp grey eyes. His salt-and-pepper hair was cut short and brushed back.

"Well! Look who we've got here! It's young Alex Hawke! Good God, it's great to see you, Hawkeye! I heard nagging rumors from Tex Patterson you were going to be here."

Alex stood up and the two old friends shook hands

warmly, then, after a moment's hesitation, embraced each other, each clapping the other man soundly on the back.

"Mr. President, it's good to see you again," Hawke said. "Too damn long since we didn't catch any bonefish in the Keys. Are you the surprise visitor? I understood that you were huddled at Camp David this weekend."

"I am, at least as far as CNN is concerned," President Jack McAtee said. "Came over last night. This thing has rapidly gone from bad to worse, as you know, Alex, so I'm glad you're on board. Consuelo tells me you're making significant progress."

"I hope so, sir. You'll see what we've got in the meeting."

"Good, good. Now. Tell me. Who is your friend here? This isn't the redoubtable Chief Inspector Ambrose Congreve by any chance?"

Congreve shook the man's hand. "How do you do, Mr. President. A very great honor to meet you, sir. A privilege, indeed."

"A great pleasure to meet you at last, Chief Inspector. The legendary Congreve of Scotland Yard. There are endless tales about you from young Alex here. His secret weapon, he calls you, behind your back. His own personal demon of deduction and derring-do, isn't that right, Alex?"

"Ambrose takes a mystery and bends it to his will, Mr. President," Alex said with a tilt of his head.

Congreve sputtered, "Well, I hardly—"

"Wonderful meeting you, Inspector. You must come for a chili supper with Betsy and me at the White House sometime. I'll get Hawkeye here to arrange it. Anyway, I've got five minutes alone with your PM before the meeting, Inspector. This thing is a certified bitch, as you gentlemen well know."

The president turned away and, trailing secret service agents, headed for the door. Alex looked at Congreve and saw that, for the moment anyway, the man had been rendered speechless.

"Forty-fourth president of the United States," Alex said to Ambrose, with a nod towards his departing friend's back. "Lives in the White House, as you may know, one thousand six hundred Pennsylvania Avenue to be precise."

Hawke looked away just in time to miss Congreve's withering stare.

"Gentlemen, if you'll come this way?" It was the comely staffer Guinevere and they gratefully followed in her silky wake down the elegant hallway to the Cabinet Room.

The room, with its long, boat-shaped table, was full of buzzing H.M. government and American diplomats, plus high-ranking military and spook types from both sides of the pond. The only people Alex recognized instantly among the lumpy, bestriped crowd round the table were Conch and, right next to her, Texas Patterson. There were charts and maps projected on three monitors placed around the room. Hawke nodded at Tex and pulled an envelope containing two CD-ROM discs from his inside pocket, handing it to a junior man at the near end of the table. The discs represented everything Alex, Congreve, Tex, and the worldwide DSS team assembled at Hawkesmoor had learned in the last ten days.

The young man inserted the first disc into a slot on the laptop and began scrolling through aerial images of a mountain stronghold, adjusting color and contrast.

Conch came around from her seat opposite the door and shook hands warmly with Congreve, then, very professionally, with Hawke. She held his eyes a moment too long and Alex squeezed her hand gently before releasing it.

"Hello, heartbreaker," she whispered.

"Hey, good-looking," Hawke said under his breath.

"You have everything you need? Tough audience."

"Yes, one hopes, thank you."

After the secretary had made the more formal introductions, Alex and Ambrose took two empty chairs to her left. The seat opposite the fireplace was always, Alex knew, reserved for the PM. The chair beside that was being held for the American president.

"Let's get started," Conch said, remaining on her feet. "My boss will be here in a few minutes, but he told me to go ahead. He already knows what I'm going to say. Slide, please."

On all three screens was a picture of an object very closely resembling an American-style football.

There were a few stifled chuckles and some not so sotto voce murmuring up and down the length of the table. Hawke heard his name mentioned. Something about his having handed over the wrong slides.

"Looks like a goddamn football to me," said a four-star general with a heavy Texas drawl, and there was some snickering from the American contingent.

"Doesn't it, though?" Conch said. "It's not. It's a linear implosion nuclear device containing a single critical mass of plutonium, or U-233, at maximum density under normal conditions. It weighs only 10.5 kilograms and is 10.1 centimeters across. Fusion boosted, it is capable of destroying a city roughly the size of, oh, let's just say for argument's sake, General, Fort Worth, Texas."

"Still looks like a football," the general muttered.

"Dr. Bissinger?" Conch said, nodding at a rumpled old gentleman seated across the table who had his nose buried in a book.

"Sorry?"

"Linear implosion?" Conch said, smiling at him and nodding at the football on the screens. "Could you enlighten us?"

"Ah, yes-s-s-s," the rumpled man said, getting slowly to his feet. With a quick underhand toss, he flipped a silver mock-up of the Pigskin to the startled general. "Good catch! This is the design approach known as 'linear implosion.'"

Dr. H. Gerard Bissinger, the American Undersecretary for Nuclear Affairs, was a gangly bespectacled former Harvard professor. Known in Washington circles as the "Bomb Babysitter," he was charged with knowing the precise whereabouts of every nuke on the planet.

"Slide?" Bissinger said. "In laymen's terms, the weapon the general is holding, shown here in cross-section, is capable of being fielded with a 'neutron bomb' or enhanced radiation option. Simply put, the 'linear implosion' concept is that an elongated, or 'football-shaped,' lower density subcritical mass of material can be compressed and deformed into a higher density spherical configuration by embedding it in a cylinder of explosives which are initiated at each end, thus squeezing the fissle mass to the center into a supercritical shape."

"Say what?" the American general said.

"Beg pardon?" Bissinger said.

"Excuse me all to hell, Doc," the American general said, "but if that's layman talk, I guess I ain't a layman. Does anybody in this room know what the hell this man said?"

Alex couldn't help himself. With a slight cough, he took the floor and all eyes were on him.

"In a vernacular you might well understand, General," Hawke said evenly, "Dr. Bissinger has just informed you that it's very late in the fourth quarter and the opposing team has the ability to throw the long bomb."

"The long bomb?" the general asked, turning the silver football in his hands.

"Precisely," Alex Hawke said. "The ultimate 'Hail Mary,' as it were, General."

CHAPTER FORTY

Stiltsville

Stokely Jones looked down at the glowering *jefe* and shrugged his shoulders. What the hell were you going to do? Man is on a mission. Tell the man, fucking loud and fucking clear, his mission is a suicide mission. Little shit doesn't want to hear about it. He's in for the kill, baby, means to bring home the bacon. Problem with acting all badass, like Lieutenant Alvarez was acting, was that you got to actually be badass if you were going to live long enough to pull it off.

"Ross, I dunno, what do you think?" Stoke said finally, sick of all the punk Cuban's gangbanger attitude, the little guy sitting there staring eye-daggers at him. Ross was feeling better. Sitting up now, running a big hand through his strawberry blond crewcut, the drugs having kicked in. His leg probably still hurt like hell, but he was back on the case. That was good because it doubled the number of people on this boat with half a brain to two.

"I think you let the little bugger go," Ross said, wincing as he stretched his bad leg.

"Into a trap."

"Aye, maybe so. Not from his point of view, however. Christ, Stoke. Rodrigo's got to be the most

wanted man in Cuba. Somebody delivers his head to
Fidel on a platter? The lieutenant here sees this whole
thing as a once-in-a-lifetime career opportunity."

"Got that part right."

"Let him go, Stoke."

Stoke nodded, yeah, that's what he was thinking,
too.

"Okay. One last time, *jefe*, listen up. This is as close
as we going to get to that damn sea-going ghost town,"
he told him. "Now, you and your compadres, you want
to swim over there, I can't stop you. I *can*, but I won't.
So, what I'm saying, go do what you got to do and *vaya
con dios, muchachos*. Okay?"

Guy didn't even say, hey, thanks a million.

"You get in trouble, *jefe*, you know who not to call."

"*Vaya en agua!*" Pepe shouted to the four young
commandos seated on the stern. Kids didn't need a lot
of encouragement. Each one executed a frogman back-
flip into the black water. Pepe stood up, not sure how
he was supposed to go over the side and still be looking
cool about it.

"You want your knife back, Lieutenant? Bad idea,
you swim into the man's trap empty-handed."

"The knife, *sí*. And the gun," Pepe demanded, hand
out like he was some kind of authority figure. Stoke
shook his head.

"The gun? Shit. You are crazy. You the one with the
death wish, not me. I give you your Glock back, first
one you shoot is me."

The man took the knife, hawked a looey into the
water. "Fucking gringo coward," he spit out, and then
did a kind of half-dive, half-jump over the side and
started swimming fast towards Stiltsville before Stoke

had a chance to jump in on top of him and rip his pea-brained head off.

"Yeah!" Stoke called after him. "That's right! I'm the chickenshit. Not you! Go get 'em, *el tigre!* Balls to the walls! Hoo-ah!"

The black silhouettes of the seven ramshackle houses stood maybe a thousand yards away. The hard rain had stopped. Rain-heavy clouds still covered most of the stars, but there was a sliver of orange on the eastern horizon. Dawn was maybe an hour away. The Cubano contingent would or would not be around for it, depending.

"Now you know why they call 'em 'banana republics,'" Stoke said. "Damn commie guerillas down there all went bananas in the sixties and they ain't got their shit back together yet."

"Castro's outlasted ten American presidents," Ross pointed out.

"True. But old Fidel, he's more movie star than Communist. He only shoots people to keep them from walking out of the theatre before his movie's over."

Ross was standing at his side now, both of them watching the Cubans. Stoke had dosed Ross up pretty good with morphine from the Cuban's medical kit. Ross said the leg wasn't broken anyway, just a torn tendon he got when the museum roof fell down on top of him. 'Course, Ross would say just a scratch even if there was a big white jagged thighbone poking out his skin.

The first of the three Cuban commando boats to arrive in Stiltsville ghosted up to the black-hulled Cigarette. When nobody killed them instantly, two men scrambled aboard the speedboat's bow and sprayed the cockpit with automatic fire, blowing out the windshield and ripping up a whole lot of very expensive fiberglass. One guy jumped down into the cockpit and tossed a flash-bang grenade through the open companionway, on the off chance the guy Rodrigo was chillin' down there, whipping up a pitcher of rum *Cuba Libres* or something.

No reaction from the shot-up speedboat with *Diablo* in blood red letters flaming down the sides, none from the stilt house where she was tied up, not a peep from any of the other six houses in the ghost town.

Nada.

Surprise, surprise. Nobody home, just like I told you, Pepe. So, where is the legendary Scissorhands? Split already for the Keys on another boat, the way Ross had it? Maybe. Man had put a lot of thinking into his exit strategy. Boy liked drama. Liked to stick around see how it all played out. Plus, he's got to stay close enough to Stiltsville to pull the trigger when the time was right, at least the way Stoke saw the thing unfolding.

The squad split into three teams, each team going up the rickety wooden ladders to clear a different deserted house. Looked like Pepe and his boys would make it over there for the fireworks. Stoke saw the swimmers reach the ladder of the nearest stilt house. Pepe, the fearless leader himself, in the lead. With the night-vision binocs, Stoke could see he was swimming with his head above water, the assault knife clenched in his teeth, Rambo-style.

Like all the houses in the deserted community, Pepe's objective was a handyman special. The house was sitting on top of four stilts at a weird angle, like an old dog with one leg shorter than the others. No windows left, just lopsided holes with rotted pieces of fabric fluttering in the wind. No doors, just more black holes. This forgotten town had seen too many hard times, too many hurricanes. Tough to believe this many houses still standing.

Probably not a bad life out here at one time. Row over to your buddy's house, drink beer and fish off his porch all day. Sun go down, you drink rum and play gin rummy by gas lantern light all night. No horns blowing, no TV going, no phone ringing. Little woman rags your ass, you come home late, just tell her to take a long walk on a short pier. Yeah. He could see the original Stiltsville attraction. A blind man could do that.

The littlest Rambo went up the rickety ladder first, and fearlessly signaled his squad to follow. What the hell Pepe planned to do next, if that guy del Rio actually happened to be up in the house, was unclear to Stoke. Attention! Operation Total Goatfuck is now about to commence! Shit. Warning! I have an assault knife! He saw Pepe dive through the open door, going in low, four more guys right behind him, rolling left and right. Least they got that part right.

Anyway, all five of them got safely inside and that's exactly when the little tinderbox house blew sky high, nothing left but blackened and burning stilt poles poking up in the sky like four big Tiki torches.

Then the fancy black Cigarette blew, all that expensive gasoline and pricey plastic going up with an explosive whoosh so hot Stoke could feel the heat on his face and forearms at a thousand yards. He'd seen a Cuban commando in a window just before the explosion, one from the first wave of armed Cubans who'd sped away. Guy had fired an RPG grenade into the Cigarette's stern, where the big gas tanks were, just for the pure hell of it. Last stupid thing he did, too, because a second later the house he and his comrades were standing in wasn't there anymore, just a huge fireball climbing into the dark purple night like a little A-bomb mushroom.

Stoke hit the throttles, and opened up another two thousand yards between him and what was left of Stiltsville. Seconds later, the remaining five houses exploded almost simultaneously. Night was day.

"Pepe, goddamn your dumb ass," Stoke said aloud. Even if Alvarez was a dickhead moron, he hated seeing all those young kids die for no good reason. The stupidity and arrogance of the Cuban commander made him sick. He looked at Ross and shook his head.

"Scissorhands wired up all the houses, Ross. Long time ago. Dynamite, probably packed up watertight under the floorboards of each house. Disguised so all the tourista tour boats who still bother to come out to look at these empty shacks couldn't see nothing. You think he's waitin' around to see this? I guess yes. I guess he wouldn't miss these fireworks for anything."

Pretty good contingency plan, Stoke thought. Blow the hell out of whoever is chasing you. Blow your own boat up while you're at it, too, although the Cubans had beat him to that part. Coast Guard or Customs guys, cops show up, think you're dead and gone, and you're gone all right, already running for your back-up mansion somewhere down in the islands. So, how'd he do it? Fuses? Blasting cap timers? No. Couldn't be timers or fuses. Too time-critical. Had to be radio detonators. Cell phone. Had to make sure everybody was at the party before he pushed the pound key and lit the candles. Make sure he was clean, leaving the scene.

Which meant he had to be an eyewitness. Which meant Scissorhands was still close by.

Ross was looking aft, scanning the horizon with the glasses. Had his back turned to the action, concentrating, didn't even bother to look around when the really big explosions started. Three more houses went up, boom, boom, boom, huge, about five seconds apart. Might as well have been high noon out on the bay the way the sky lit up. Ross didn't even flinch. Man knew how to focus.

"Good Christ, there he is, Stoke!" Ross said, handing over the glasses. He'd picked out the silhouette of another Cigarette, identical length to the one that had just burned and gone to the bottom. Different paint job, Stoke figured. Different name on the registration. New passport, ID papers and a couple million bucks in Ziplocs stuffed somewhere behind a fake bulkhead.

"Where?"

"Two o'clock! The cut between those two islands. See his rooster tail? He's moving south—"

"*Diablo II!* Let's go get him," Stoke said, cranking the two big 250 Yamaha outboards to life. Good thing he'd gotten this thing gassed up. He leaned on the throttles and the RIB leapt forward, arcing a wide flat turn to the southeast. The wind was down and so was the chop out on the bay. No extra weight on the stern now, slowing him down. Hell, two guys in a three-hundred-horsepower Frisbee, man, you are one screaming cat skimming over flat water.

"What about survivors?" Ross screamed over the roar of the twin engines.

"No such thing as a survivor back there."

Ross craned his head around, looking over his shoulder at the flaming remains of Stiltsville. Nothing left but twenty or so of the wooden supports, all burning like torches, sparks and licks of fire against the night sky. Stoke was right. Instant incineration. No one could have survived it.

"Boy got one big advantage on us, Ross," Stoke said, flipping the wheel hard over and missing a clanging steel channel marker by maybe two inches.

"Namely?"

"Horsepower. Got at least twice as much."

"That's a big one."

"Yeah, but he's got a big disadvantage, too."

"I'm waiting."

"Brainpower. See how bad he's outrunning us now?"

"I was going to comment on that."

"He's gone outside the intracoastal channel markers, see, headed for open water where he can totally lose our ass."

"Smart move."

"Maybe. Boy's headed for the sawgrass flats out there just north of Sands Key. Usually ain't but about a foot of water where he's headed now. That big boat's got props, not jets. She draws at least three, maybe four feet of water. We draw two, max, another advantage on our side." The boat flew off a wave top and landed, hard.

Ross, squinting his eyes with pain, said, "So he's in the box, is he?"

"Maybe. Maybe not. He's smart, he's probably got his depth-sounder alarm set to go off at maybe five, five and a half feet. He ain't smart, we got him. You watch him. Boy hits a solid sandbank at sixty miles an hour, that'll be something to see. Pitchpole city. Go cartwheelin' 'cross the water, yeah, ass over teakettle."

But the Cigarette screamed ahead, trailing a deep roar in her wake, kept heading due east, racing across the flats for the open waters of the Atlantic.

Stoke couldn't believe it. They must have, what, dredged out a new channel down here? Why do that? Nobody living round here but turtles and gators, lotsa skeets, sand fleas, and no-see-ums. He leaned harder on the throttles, even though there was nothing left. Seeing Vicky lying on the church steps, the memory of it like somebody kicking him in the back of his eyeballs. He could not lose this guy now, not this damn close.

He sucked it up, all his anxiety, and said to Ross, "Alarm on that big boat's bound to go off any second now, beep, beep, beep. Then you see him turn, one way or the other, fast, else he runs hard aground, sticks his dick in the dirt, pitchpoles, and we snatch his ass right out of mid-air."

Ross had the chart in his hand, studying lower Biscayne Bay. "Right. Well, at the moment it doesn't look like he—"

The big Cigarette suddenly banked hard over to starboard, going on its side, throwing up a wall of white water as it carved a tight turn away from the mangrove swamp projecting from the northern end of the island.

Ross said, "Looks like we better pretend he's smart."

"Okay. Okay. We can deal with this. Next, he's got to run southeast or southwest, inside or outside of what they call the Ragged Keys."

"Which way is better for us?"

"The way he's going right now, see? Boy turning inside. Yeah, going to try to shake us in all them mangroves. SEALs used to call that the 'Deep Severe' back in there."

"Sounds like an ideal spot to lose us. Or, more likely, tuck in somewhere and wait. That's the smart option," Ross said.

"Maybe smart, maybe not. Mangrove swamp's a lot like a marriage, Ross. Whole lot easier to stay out than get out."

"We're the last witnesses. He's not going to let it go. All kinds of firepower undoubtedly prestashed aboard that thing, Stokely—he could be trying to set us up."

"Of course he is, my brother! You right, as usual. One reason Alex Hawke holds you in such high esteem. Now. Look at him. See? What'd I tell you? He got to slow down in those shallows. Hold on to something, Ross, we 'bout to make up a little time and distance on this nouveau cracker."

CHAPTER FORTY-ONE

London

"This device was developed on a crash basis by the Iraqis in the waning Saddam years," Consuelo de los Reyes continued. All eyes in the room at No. 10 Downing were on her. She asked for another slide. A group of low buildings in the rocky desert.

"Designed and built right here, at the former Tikrit al-Fahd laboratories northwest of Baghdad. Slide. A brilliant former Cal Tech scientist born in Bombay named Dr. I.V. Soong is the prerequisite evil genius behind this and many other little nightmares. The poison gas formulas used against the Kurds in northern Iraq, for example—"

"Poison Ivy, himself," the home secretary said, "in cahoots with Chemical Ali."

Conch smiled grimly. "Yes. Poison Ivy. Soong is also the scientific mastermind behind the miniature smart bomb which killed Ambassador Stanfield in Venice. He's behind the recent revival of the ancient Indian sect known as Thuggee, by the way. Practitioners of ritual murder who view the wholesale taking of human life as a pious act. CIA and NSA sources have linked this group to al-Qaeda. So far, Soong has successfully eluded extreme prejudice."

"This bloody Thug renaissance," a mustachioed officer said. "I thought we'd seen the last of them at the end of the Raj, and now they are in league with these bloody terrorists—"

"Afraid you're correct, General," Conch interrupted, "Dr. Soong's Pigskin is one of the primary weapons of mass destruction our troops went looking for but never found. The perfect little Doomsday machine. Hard evidence at State indicates unknown numbers of these small bombs were smuggled into Syria. The labs were long gone, but I saw troops playing touch football with mock-ups just like the general's holding."

"Sorry, Madame Secretary," Sir Anthony Hayden, the home secretary, said. "This football design. Just to put us all in the picture. Is it meant to be some kind of inside joke? Like the president's 'nuclear football'? Is this Dr. Soong some kind of homicidal practical joker? Or, does the design have some actual basis in science?"

"Let's ask Dr. Bissinger."

"The latter," he said. "In plain English, the weapon's football form is purely coincidental. A function of physics. Pinch the ends of a tube and you exponentially increase the destructive power of what were formerly known as suitcase nukes. Soong's football nukes were flown out of Iraq by Saddam's son Uday six days before the fall of Baghdad."

"Christ in a goddamn wheelbarrow," a shiny-domed American Air Force general said. "How many of those bastards got out?"

"Over a hundred of them, General. Flown out of Saddam International on a Russian Antonov cargo plane. Landed here. Emirate of Sharjah. That's the bad news. The good news is they were all purchased by one particular individual. In the last month, that individual got careless. All it took was one time. NSA zeroed in on digital cellphone intercepts, matched voiceprints, and we got close. Now, the work of a lone MI6 agent has confirmed who that individual is. Jack?"

Patterson looked over at Hawke, then got to his feet and took the laser pointer. "Thanks, Madame Secretary. Slide?"

On all three monitors, a photograph of a rugged-looking middle-aged man in khakis, shielding his eyes from the glaring sun.

"This is Owen Nash," Texas Patterson said, moving the laser point across the screen. "Or was. British MI6 operative working western Indonesia. Covered as a nature photographer for *National Geographic* out of Sydney. Australian national. Missing, presumed dead. His last transmission was forty-eight hours ago. He was on the remote Indonesian island of Suva, slide please, located just here, due west of Timor. These recons were shot by U-2 and dedicated birds in the last twenty-four hours. Questions?"

There weren't any.

"Nash's recent signals had him checked into a Hotel Bambah, the sole structure on the island. Slide. Sorry, there is another structure here on the island, as the next slide will show. Thank you. Airstrip here. Ten thousand feet, believe it or not. Used by jumbos ferrying Arab tourists in the eighties. And, here, a very large airplane hangar, newly built, with an older adjoining corrugated tin structure. An equipment shed; barracks possibly. According to Nash's last transmission, travel agents from throughout Indonesia, Malaysia, and the

Philippines, numbering approximately 400, were due to start arriving at the Bambah the next day."

"Christ," the home secretary said. "Travel agents. Clean passports. Visas. Immunization. Ideal cover stories."

Patterson said, "Exactly. Agent Nash was wondering why four hundred Arab travel agents were suddenly getting together for a hullabaloo in the middle of nowhere. Suva's not exactly Honolulu."

"Let me guess," the sardonic British prime minister's principal secretary said, rubbing his chin. "Encourage more Arab air travel to America?"

"You got it, sir. Exactly our thinking. Anyway, your man Nash promised to confirm or refute prior intelligence at 0800 GMT yesterday. He never made that call. All efforts to contact him have failed. Questions?"

"Yes," General Sir Oswald Pray said. "When were those photos taken? The Suva Island surveillance?"

"1800 hours yesterday, General. I think most everyone here knows Commander Hawke. I'd like to turn it over to him. Alex?"

"Good morning," Hawke said, taking the laser pointer. "Slide, please. A surveillance photo of the mountainous Fatin region of the southern Emirate. Slide, please. Massive fortified structure. Built over the last three decades in a virtually inaccessible mountain pass. Elevation, 18,000 feet. Something regionally known as the Blue Palace."

"Extraordinary!" Hayden said. "Looks like the evil version of Shangri-la!"

"Yes," Hawke replied. "Now, the most interesting part of this morning's slide show, gentlemen. Both the Bambah Hotel on Suva Island and the Blue Palace atop this mountain belong to the same man. Slide. Snay bin Wazir. The name on the lips of the dying woman involved in the abduction of Ambassador Kelly at Grosvenor House last week."

A great deal of murmuring around the table ensued and Conch asked for quiet.

"Question regarding this chap bin Wazir, Lord Hawke," Sir Howard Cox, a very senior Whitehall ministerial type with longish hair and gold-rimmed spectacles, said, tipping back his chair and lacing his fingers over his expansive waistcoat. "His name was given to whom? First I've bloody well heard of it. I'm supposed to be in the loop, you know."

"Indeed you are, sir."

"Hell, Alex, I *am* the loop," Cox said. There were chuckles around the table.

"Name was given to me, sir," Hawke said. "The woman actually died in my arms a few moments after the abduction at the film gala."

"Good Lord, Hawke," Sir Howard said. "My reports said she died instantly. You chaps certainly managed to keep the lid on this bit, I daresay. What else did she give you?"

Alex nodded, accepting the equally implicit compliment, or criticism, in stride. Over the years, he'd been forced to become an adept at avoiding the byzantine politics of Buckingham Palace, Whitehall, No. 10 Downing, and New Scotland Yard. Politics, if carefully avoided, could be relegated to a necessary nuisance.

"Yes, Sir Howard, the dead woman implicated this bin Wazir in her murder," Hawke said. "Her dying words, in fact. We've yet to determine any motive. She also indicated that bin Wazir was the man responsible for the worldwide spate of attacks on American State Department officers and their families. She suggested it was only the beginning of action on a much greater scale."

A portly, turnip-faced British Army officer wearing a spiffy Sam Browne belt spoke up. "This bin Wazir. Same fellow who owned Beauchamps here in London back in the nineties, if I'm not mistaken, m'lord."

"Yes, General," Hawke said, "the same man. Bin Wazir was under DSS surveillance at that time, suspected of slaying a junior State Department employee. Jack Patterson can speak to that. Jack?"

Patterson said, "Snay bin Wazir was responsible for the grisly murders of at least five young women here in London in 1997 and 1998. As well as terrorist attacks on the Lebanese Marine barracks that killed 166 of our boys, the two embassy bombings in Africa in 1998. On New Year's Day, 1999, Mr. bin Wazir and his wife, Yasmin, disappeared without a trace."

"You kept looking, I daresay?" Sir Howard asked.

"He's been at the top of the DSS Most Wanted List for five long years. We've come close, that's all I can say," said Patterson.

"Until now," Conch interrupted. "We've hit the jackpot. Langley has current cell traffic intercepts indicating that Mr. bin Wazir is at this very moment on the small Indonesian island of Suva. He got sloppy. Just once, but that was enough. Instead of his old analog phone, he used a hot phone, one Langley had coded in. Transcript I saw this morning indicates he's preparing to leave Indonesia and return to his base of operations in the Emirate—excuse me—Mr. President, Prime Minister, welcome, please join us. Chief Patterson and

Commander Hawke have just completed their presentations."

The two new arrivals took their seats, and it was clear from their expressions that they'd been engaged in very serious discussions. Gone from President Jack McAtee's face, Hawke noticed, was the genial bonhomie he'd seen earlier in the Terracotta Room. The prime minister cleared his throat and let his gaze range round the table.

"First of all, I want to go on record straightaway," Prime Minister Anthony Tempest began, "and say the president and I have just had a most candid conversation regarding this horrific threat to the U.S. mainland. Tens of thousands of American lives are evidently at risk, maybe far more. I've just sent a signal to the First Sea Lord, Admiral Sir Alan Seabrooke, regarding the disposition of Royal Navy forces on station in the South China Sea and the *HMS Ark Royal* group in the Persian Gulf. I told Sir Alan that while I do not underestimate the challenges and difficulties we face in this new crisis, I have every confidence in our resolution and determination to see this through. I have given my great good friend, the president here, every assurance we in Britain will fully support whatever actions he intends to take."

McAtee nodded and said, gravely, "Thank you, Mr. Prime Minister. The abduction of our ambassador to the Court of St. James is just the latest in a recent series of unprovoked and unspeakable attacks on our State Department. We believe these attacks are intended to destabilize American diplomatic officers around the world. To induce a state of paralysis and fear which would cripple America's ability to prevent, or respond to, a devastating assault on our homeland."

There was a discreet cough at the far end of the table and all eyes turned towards a ramrod-straight officer with a perfectly manicured moustache.

"Mr. President, if I may, Major General Giles Lycett here, Base Commander, RAF Leuchars in Scotland. My Tornado F-3 fighter aircraft patrolling the no-fly zone have just been grounded. Why? And, might I ask just what America's immediate intentions are?"

"Yes, General, you may ask. Within the next seventy-two hours, American bomber wings based here in England as well as Tomahawk cruise missiles launched from both British and American fleets patrolling in the South China Sea and Persian Gulf are going to level both the command and control center in the Fatin Mountains and the terrorist base on Suva Island."

"A preemptive strike?"

"A preemptive strike. Anything else?"

"Any truth to the rumor that some kind of 9/11–type attack is planned against numerous major American cities, Mr. President? Using civilian or private aircraft as weapons?"

"No comment."

"Mr. President," a senior staffer said, "rumors floating about Whitehall suggest that a rogue stealth bomber is now prowling the North Atlantic and that the *HMS Turbulent* has been deployed to find this sub."

"No comment."

"Have you raised the threat level in New York and Washington?"

"No comment."

"A hundred of these bloody Pigskin bombs have

gone missing. And no one has even the foggiest notion where they are?"

"No comment."

"Mr. President," Hawke said, coming to his rescue, "if it's all right with you, I'd like to move on. British and American intelligence sources are convinced Ambassador Kelly is being held hostage at bin Wazir's Fatin Mountain location. Would you agree?"

"Yes. The seventh floor at Langley is almost one hundred percent on that, Alex. That's hard intelligence. We have thermal imaging and other, boots-on-the-ground, HUMINT confirmation."

"Ah, Mr. President," Hayden said, "any idea why they'd want to kidnap Ambassador Kelly rather than assassinate him?"

"No comment."

"May I ask then, sir, what immediate plans are being made to effect the ambassador's rescue?" Hayden persisted.

"Mr. bin Wazir has demanded three things in return for the safe return of Ambassador Kelly. The immediate departure of all coalition forces from Arab soil. The cessation of U.S. and British control of all Gulf State pipelines. And the release of all terrorist POWs now held prisoner in U.S. detention centers at Guantánamo and elsewhere. We flatly reject all three. Naturally."

"And, in answer to my earlier question, the plans for the ambassador's rescue?"

"No comment."

"But, with all due respect, Mr. President," Hawke said, "I assume there are plans well under way for a hostage rescue prior to the bombing?"

"No. There are no such plans. I cannot risk the wel-

fare of the entire nation for a single life. Were
Ambassador Kelly in my position, you can rest assured
he would make the same decision. Is that all, gentlemen?"

Alex Hawke leaned forward across the table, his
hard blue eyes locked on those of the president.

"Sir. I understand the extreme gravity of the situation. And the sense of urgency. But whatever we do,
we've got a moral obligation to get Brick safely out of
there, Mr. President."

"I'm under enormous cabinet pressure to take this
madman out now, Alex. And they're absolutely right.
The B-52s are warming up their engines."

"Brickhouse Kelly is a great statesman, sir. He
almost single-handedly brokered the current Mideast
ceasefire. A war hero. The father of five fine young
boys. We've got seventy-two hours, sir. I strenuously
urge you—"

"I am well aware of all that," the president said
sharply, shoving his chair back from the table. "I certainly don't need to be reminded by you that—"

"I'll get him out if I have to do it myself, sir."

The president and Alex stared at each other for
several long moments, the president considering his
reply. The president could count on one hand the
number of men in the world who could publicly challenge his authority and get away with it. But, finally,
he had to smile. Alex Hawke was certainly one of
them.

"Then I'm goddamn glad somebody invited you to
this tea party, Mr. Hawke. You're probably the only
man in this room who might actually be able to pull
something like that off."

"So, you would have no objection, Mr. President," Hawke interjected, pressing his advantage, "to an independently mounted hostage rescue operation?"

His question was met with a wry smile.

"Let me put it this way, Alex. If someone can get up to the top of that goddamn mountain and get Brick Kelly out of there in seventy-two hours without compromising the American mission or the security of the republic, I assure you neither Secretary de los Reyes nor I would have any objection."

"Thank you, sir."

"Then, with your permission, Mr. President," Conch jumped in, "I'd like to put the Hostage Rescue Team at DSS under the joint control of Chief Patterson and Commander Hawke. Effective immediately."

The president looked at her sharply; then at Hawke. It was no secret in Washington that Conch and Alex went way back and they shared a lot, including their love for Brick Kelly. Hell, he loved the man himself. But he had no doubt that, sometime earlier this morning, there had been a little *a priori* collusion between his two friends.

If Hawke could save Brick Kelly, God bless him. If not, he knew Alex Hawke would probably die trying.

"Done," the president finally said, getting to his feet. "Good morning then, gentlemen. Appreciate your coming on such short notice."

"Thank you very much, Mr. President," Jack Patterson said, also rising. Then, looking at Hawke, he added, "C'mon, Alex, let's saddle up. We got a long way to ride and a short time to get there."

But Alex Hawke was looking at the beautiful Secretary de los Reyes still seated across the table. She gazed at him with her soft brown eyes as Hawke said, quietly, "We'll get Brick out, Conch."

"I don't doubt that for one minute, Alex."

"You wanted to see me, Mr. President?"

"Yes."

Hawke had joined the president in the small sitting room used by the prime minister's family on the top floor of Number Ten. McAtee was standing by a window, looking down into the garden. He turned around and faced Alex. He seemed to have aged since the earlier encounter in the Terracotta Room.

"Good show down there."

"You wrote the script, sir. My role was fairly believable. Stereotypical, one might say."

"Alex, listen. The spooks on both sides are in total agreement for once. There are at least a hundred of these goddamn suitcase nukes unaccounted for out there. Hell, they may already be on the way. They may already be inside U.S. borders. Homeland Security doesn't know. Much as I love Brick, if it were up to me I'd blow the shit out of this bin Wazir right this goddamn minute. But to placate the other side of the aisle, I've got to try to cobble together this goddamn European coalition. Thank God for Anthony Tempest and the Brits. True grit, that man."

"Indeed, sir."

"Look me in the eye and listen to this, Alex. The Nimitz Carrier Battle Group is on station in the Indian Ocean. The fire control systems aboard those cruisers and destroyers are keyed to launch Tomahawk land attack missiles in exactly seventy-one hours and forty-eight minutes. Coalition or no coalition. It would take an act of Congress to alter that launch schedule. Okay?"

"Yes, sir."

"And I pray even *that* timing is soon enough to catch this little bastard holding all his high cards."

"Yes, sir."

"But I don't have that option. I need to *know*, Alex. Just exactly, precisely, where those bombs are and what the living hell this maniac is up to."

"Yes, sir."

"And I need to know now. You get yourself inside this palace of his, you find Brick still alive, fine. I pray to God that will be the case. He's a great American. But you've got one job and one job only. Get this bin Wazir up against a wall and make him tell you exactly where all those goddamn Pigskins are and what the hell he plans to do with them. Got it?"

"Got it."

The president suddenly looked very, very tired. But Alex Hawke had one more question.

"Why the hell kidnap Brick, sir? Instead of taking him out like the others?"

"I've got a leak, Alex. A bad one. Inside Langley."

"Tell me."

"I had two candidates slotted to succeed Ted Sann on the seventh floor. Ambassadors Evan Slade and Brick Kelly. Six weeks ago, there was a top-secret meeting at the 'Farm' down in Virginia. Sann briefed both candidates on our imminent Middle East operations. This is need-to-know, so I can't reveal the players. But we've got hard intel that Country A is ramping up for a nuke strike against Country B. We are going to preempt A without B's knowledge in hopes of averting an all-out regional war. Somebody who shouldn't have been there was in that room with Sann at that meeting. So far, we haven't got him. Anyway, these bastards have penetrated the highest levels at Langley."

"So they murdered Slade's family up in Maine? To what end?"

"They obviously expected Slade to be there at the house. It was a long-planned family vacation. At an isolated location where they could prime Evan to talk by murdering his family one at a time in front of him. A standard tactic. Evan changed his plans at the last minute and sent his family ahead without him. But the sleepers pretty much kept their plans intact. Then Evan shot himself before they could get to him and get anything out of him. So now they'll go to work on Brick by threatening his family with the same courtesy they showed the Slades."

"Jesus."

"Yep. The Queen invited the whole Kelly family to stay in a royal apartment at Kensington Palace for a week. Safe enough there. Brick, of course, has no way of knowing that. Still, Brick won't talk, Alex. No matter what they threaten or do to him. They'll figure that out pretty fast. So—"

The president looked up to see Hawke halfway out the door, pulling it closed after him.

CHAPTER FORTY-TWO

Suva Island

The smell of women. Snay bin Wazir inhaled deeply, a shiver of pleasure tripping lightly down his spine at the fragrant memory. His linen shirt was still soaked with sweat, sticking to his skin. An hour earlier, at the climax of his oration, the temperature outside, in the lush gardens of the Bambah Hotel, was nearly ninety. For the hour he spoke inside the great room, it was well over one hundred.

Snay giggled. Earlier that evening, he'd ordered the staff to light the furnace and turn up the heat. Filled to capacity with over four hundred nearly delirious young women, the great room had been redolent with the moist heat of pungent femininity. It was as if some great mound of exotic fruit had been placed there in the hall and had begun to ferment.

The women were screaming. They were on fire.

Having ignited them with his facile tongue, Snay now stood back from his podium, head bowed, and let them burn. They chanted. They raved. Had they been able to sweat blood, they would have done so.

"Death! Death! Death!"

He whipped out his silk handkerchief and mopped

his brow. Finished, drained, utterly spent, bin Wazir allowed the delicious scents and sounds to wash over him. He lifted his gaze to the rafters. To row upon row of crimson banners, faded over these many years to the color of old blood. Ten minutes became twenty. Half an hour passed. Still, pitched cries and moans issued from the mass of writhing bodies.

Ah. It had been glorious. It had been vindication. A bulwark erected against the slights and humiliations he had endured at the hands of his enemies for so very long. A kind of purification. A kind of redemption. He smiled.

Vengeance is mine, sayeth the Prophet.

The wails of his disciples still reverberated within his brain as he stood now, in the shadows of the moonlit palms at the water's edge, looking up at his beautiful Bambah on the hill.

The pink hotel was quiet now, her public rooms and long dank hallways devoid of ringing echoes, darkened. But not desolate, oh no. The old hotel was humming with restive energy, waiting to be unleashed. A small yellow chin of moon hung in a black sky peppered with silver stars. The gardens were still, save the gentle rustle of the palms. The only other sound Snay could hear was the singsong wish-wash of the surf at his feet.

He fired up a Baghdaddie and listened to the night.

Even Saddam up on the verandah was silent, although Snay knew the wily old dragon was not sleeping. The women had excited him as well. Caressing his snout, looking into those gleaming yellow eyes, Snay had seen something most familiar. There on the verandah, saying good-bye to his aged beast, it came to him just how much alike they were, he and the Komodo.

Ravenous, primitive creatures. Feral. Equipped with sharp claws. Yes, all that and one more trait they shared: they were both poisonous. A light burning on an upper floor winked out.

Sleep, little flowers.

Almost all the hotel's lights had been extinguished. His *fleurs du mal* were deep in slumber now. In a few hours they would rise up and begin their epic and final journey. Praise Allah, what joyous havoc this old dog was about to wreak upon this world! He threw his head back and laughed at the sheer outrageousness of it all. For some moments, he cackled and capered about in the soft white sand, a fat white devil in the moonlight.

What was the name they had all called him, friend and foe alike? Tippu Tip had told him one night, many years before. Confessed it in a drunken stupor, the two of them buckled against a piss-stained wall in some dank alley in Africa, roaring over some horrible blood-soaked deed just done.

The Dog. Yes, that was it, the name they all said behind his back. The Dog.

Soon the whole world would learn that this Dog had a very jagged set of canines. He looked at the phosphorescent glow of his watch in the darkness. Almost one. What was keeping Tippu and his all-important passenger? It was late, and there was much to be accomplished before the sun rose over Suva.

At that moment, from up at the top of the drive, the engine of the ancient Daimler reluctantly turned over. He took a deep breath and allowed himself a brief moment of relaxation, perhaps the first in weeks. Months of intense planning were nearly finished. No detail of this stage had escaped him, from the sublimely technical and logistical, to the most ridiculously mundane. He'd had the most fun with the inexpensive Western-style female wardrobe (he'd ordered it all online from a Lands' End catalog!) and even choosing the supple leather shoulder bags each woman would carry tomorrow.

Bags to hold the American city maps he'd ordered over the Internet from something called Triple A. Very good maps, indeed! Maps, and, of course, the precious Pigskins.

He'd even designed the New World Travel logo for the bags himself: a blue and green globe enwreathed in olive branches, suspended from the beaks of two doves. Then, he'd written the perfect slogan:

We come in peace.

He watched the Lucas headlamps of the Daimler snake down the drive, the twin yellow beams intermittently streaking through the black trunks of the palms. A moment later, the mammoth black car rolled to a stop beside him, hissing and pinging. He waited for the usual death rattle but Tippu somehow managed to keep the ancient motor at idle. He heard a heavy click and a man seated in the shadows of the rear seat pushed the door open for him.

"Good evening, Snay," the man said in his peculiar accent. The wiry old Indian had a high-pitched girlish voice and was prone to fits of giggling. "Get in, get in! You are good, I am hoping? Yes?"

"Very good, thank you," Snay replied settling into the deep leather cushions. The car listed to one side under his weight. He eyed the other man carefully. *Snay?* The manner was far too casual and he didn't like it. The doctor was an ugly little bugger. A lank ponytail of greasy grey hair was stuck to the back of his balding head. A pair of thick black spectacles perched on his beaky nose, magnifying two already enormous buglike eyes.

He always kept his fingers laced protectively over his little potbelly, as if it were a pot of gold, a repository of precious coins. No, bin Wazir thought, irritated, there was little to admire here but the brain.

Tippu noisily engaged first gear and they rumbled down into the thick jungle.

The Indian, Dr. Soong, was always in a hurry to get his words out, as if his mind had a constant backlog of bottle-necked sentences.

"I am having no idea you are such a fiery orator, my dear Snay! Such stimulation! All those beauties! Oh my word! Not a dry eye in the house. Or a dry anything else, for that matter, I am suspecting. Hee-hee."

"You were there? You were not invited, Doctor."

"I slipped in a side door, you see, and sat at the rear. Look at my jacket! Soaked to the skin. You are having boiler problems, yes? The old place is finally falling down around your ears! You must—"

"And no one stopped you? You just came in and sat down."

The little man seemed delighted at bin Wazir's evident irritation.

"Yes, no one. Very aphrodisiacal qualities, your speech produced, Snay," he said. "Oh, yes. Labial engorgement! I checked a few of them, you see, when I gave them their vaccinations. Don't worry, said I. It's all right. I am a doctor! Tee-hee. Most amusing, what?"

"So. All is in readiness?" Snay interrupted.

"In a manner of speaking. Most excellent, your lecture about my little Pigskin bombs. Pity I am having so much trouble with them, you see."

"Trouble?" Snay sat forward, his pulse rate zooming. If this little shit was— "What kind of trouble?"

"They are not working, you see," the man giggled. "Not working."

"Not working."

"No. Not."

"Tippu Tip," Snay said, speaking evenly into the speaking tube, "pull over when we get to the cage. I want to show the doctor the baby lizards." Blood pounded at his temples. He stood on the threshold of triumph. Nothing must interfere—

"The dragons? No-no, it's not necessary, Pasha. I am only trying to tickle you. Tee-hee. No problem, Snay, no problem. Please be—"

"Some minor adjustments, then? The Pigskins?"

"No. Not really minor, no."

"No? No!" Snay lunged for the man and instantly had his hands around the fellow's scrawny neck, yanking him sideways, his thumbs already applying sufficient pressure to crush the doctor's rattling windpipe.

"Stop!" the little man managed to get out.

"You think you can fuck with me?" the enraged Pasha screamed into his left ear. "Who will protect you now? The Americans and British have killed all your Iraqi friends, your playmates Ouday and Qusay! Pulled your glorious benefactor Saddam out of one rathole and tossed him into another! And sent the rest crawling under rocks! The Saudis, the Iranians, even your own countrymen have disowned you. Even the bloody Pakis hate your guts! Now, you tell me that everything is in readiness or I'll kill you right here!"

"Let me go! I can't breathe! I will talk!"

Snay hurled him back into his corner like a sack of chicken bones. The little masochist. The problem was, he liked it. It was one of the great secrets of his success and long life. Since you couldn't hurt the man, you were at his mercy. The threat of the dragons was another matter.

"You've got thirty seconds before we arrive at the Komodos, you ugly little wog. Start talking."

The doctor had his hands at his throat, massaging his cruelly bruised flesh.

"Patience? Allow me to finish? My God, you are a madman. You are now a personage of great responsibility. You must learn to control these murderous impulses. Why, the Emir himself was saying to me just the other day that—"

Bin Wazir felt hot beads of perspiration popping out at the corners of his eyes at the mere mention of the Emir. Failure now was unthinkable. Unacceptable. "Tell me what I want to hear. Or I'm feeding you to the dragons."

"It's the bombs are the problem. Well. Who would believe it? Not the bombs, but the fissile matter inside. The design is flawless. Feel free to call me a genius, everyone does. But! But, but, but—and here is the problem. There was unfortunately this last-minute problem with the fissile material. It was not the specific grade I paid for and—"

"Fuck! You're dead. Tippu! Pull over!"

"Wait! Wait! Let me finish! I am not stupid, you know. I had a much better idea, you see! Ready-made. No delays. No problems. Simpler. Keep driving, I beg you, let me explain."

Tippu braked the big car on the verge opposite the dragon cage, got out and stamped around the side. He opened the doctor's door, reached in and grabbed his ponytail, lifting him a foot off the seat. The African looked at his master, waiting for instruction. "Ar kill him?"

"Please!" the man screeched. "Let me show you, Pasha! In the big suitcase! Open it!"

"What is in the suitcase, you miserable worm?" Snay had assumed the two polished black metal cases contained the doctor's personal effects for the flight across the Pacific.

"The perfect weapon, dear boy! Genetically altered smallpox," the doctor cried. "Designed it myself, I did. Impervious to the American vaccine! Nothing can stop it! Let me go and I'll show you."

"Bugs. Fucking bugs, I knew it," Snay said. "Where are the bombs? I want to know now! One hundred million dollars worth of suitcase nuclear bombs, bought and paid for. Now where fucking are they?"

"You have them! They are yours! They are all stored down in your catacombs, Pasha. Inside the Blue Palace! When I return, I will make certain adjustments to make them more stable and—"

Snay could not listen to one more word, such was his fury. He nodded at Tippu and the African whipped the man out of the open door and started through the underbrush toward the cage.

"I paid a hundred million for some fucking bugs?" bin Wazir said, trotting alongside Tippu Tip, leaning down and shouting in Soong's ear as he was being bounced along like a desperate puppet. His feet were dragging through the grass, clawing for purchase.

"A plague! A pox!" Soong cried out. "An infinite

plague. Much, much deadlier than the Pigskin! The bombs, they would only kill a million perhaps. But this— NO!"

They came to the cage. The dragons were hurling themselves against the bars, thrusting glistening tongues through the bars; long and black, darting. Tippu pulled a heavy ring of keys from his robes and handed them to bin Wazir.

"I'm going to open the cage, now, Pundit," he said, his words barely audible over the voracious roars of the Komodo dragons. They were snapping in anticipation at the steel cage rods with their viciously curved incisors. A few bones were scattered in the dirt, the remains of the British MI6 agent.

"Pasha," the doctor said in a strangled voice, "if you kill me, you are finished. You must know this! It is over. Everything. The Emir has told me many times that if we fail in this, we both will wish we were dead long before our heads roll. Please. I beg you."

Snay bin Wazir looked at the wizened little elf in disgust. Finally, realizing the incontrovertible truth of what the man was saying, he told Tippu to release him. As fervently as he wished to rip off this disgusting weasel's head and toss it into the cage, the fact was, he had no choice at all. In order to make tomorrow's absolutely critical deadline 35,000 feet above the Pacific, Snay's newly refurbished 747 had to be wheels up before sunrise. Three hours from now.

Tippu dropped the man into the weeds like a soiled tissue. "Ar don lak this one," he said. "He stink."

"Good, good," the doctor said, gasping for breath, crawling on all fours away from the cage and the enraged Komodos. "Very good."

"Talk," bin Wazir said, lowering his great bulk to the ground beside the shaking creature. The man was hugging his knees to his chest and rocking, thrilled to be alive. Snay lit up a Baghdaddie while Tippu hovered, throwing a fistful of betel nuts into his mouth and pulverizing them, the red juice leaking out the corners of his mouth. They waited until the doctor regained his ability to speak.

"So. You know Mr. Kim, naturally? Friend and ally of our most revered Emir?"

"In Pyongang. Yes, yes. Go on."

"Yes. So, I have been doing some, how do you call it, freelance work for his North Korean government. Division 39, they call it. Top-secret fund. I am helping him to process spent fuel rods from his Yongbyon nuclear complex. We are making plutonium units the size of baseballs! Plus a ballistic missile which will reach the heart of Tokyo! But, sadly, North Korea is under the American microscope, you know. But, ha, good for me because Mr. Kim always has me looking for alternatives to plutonium. Lucky me, I recently found him a very, very good one."

"Biological."

"Correct. I have created a genetically altered v-virus," the doctor said. "Like smallpox, a derivative, only better. There is no prevention. Oh, the Americans have stockpiled something called vaccinia immune globulin, VIG, but it is useless against my hybrid smallpox virus."

"Smallpox."

"Yes. The very best bio-terror weapon on earth. It, it is transmitted by expulsion of minute droplets from the nose and mouth from person to person. Through the air. Thoroughly human-tested on political prisoners by Mr. Kim's Division 39 scientists. One hundred percent success rate. *Cha-ching!*"

"Go on."

"So you see? We're ready to go! No delays. Unlike the Pigskin bombs, my I-Virus, the Koreans are nicely calling it the I-Virus in my honor, it has no radioactive half-life. Once the carriers are infected—"

"Carriers? What fucking carriers?"

"Ah. The Barbie Doll terrorists, who else? Tee-hee. Four hundred perfect walking time bombs." The doctor had recovered rapidly. He saw he once again had bin Wazir where he liked to keep him, wholly dependent. Harmless.

"You mean—"

"Yes, yes! Your lovelies will all be infected with the I-Virus during the flight over the Pacific! The first dosage they got when I 'vaccinated' them at the hotel. Ease your mind! They're not being infectious until the second massive exposure they will receive once airborne. I will explain it all at the hangar, Pasha. May we remove ourselves from these beasts? I cannot possibly hear myself think."

Thwarted, the two ravenous lizards were now visiting their frustration upon each other. And what little was left of Owen Nash.

Soong smiled quietly to himself. He'd already been paid handsomely by the North Korean dictator. The second, smaller, suitcase on the floor was full to bursting with dollars. Now, it appeared, he'd live long enough to also dine extravagantly at the Emir's bottomless trough.

The Daimler exploded fitfully into life. Resuming

the short trip to the airstrip, Dr. Soong carefully explained why the I-Virus concealed in titanium canisters inside his black case was vastly more lethal than even one hundred small nuclear devices.

"Think exponentially, my dear Snay," he said, rapping the case with his bony knuckles. "Do you understand what I am saying?" Bin Wazir nodded sagely, still having only a vague idea what he was talking about, keeping the man alive only out of sheer desperation.

"Exponential," he repeated in a hollow voice. He was at this juncture, he knew, leaning on a slender reed.

"Yes! The transcendental number e, you see. The base of all natural logarithms, raised to an exponent. Confused? I mean simply that the I-Virus will expand extremely rapidly through the population, becoming ever greater in size, Pasha. Spin out of control right under the American noses! Under their noses! You get it? You understand now why this is perfect? It cannot possibly be stopped! Ha!"

"I kill with knives, not bugs. Explain."

"Pleasure. Why is smallpox the perfect weapon? Good question. Why, because the symptoms of smallpox are never apparent until twelve to fourteen days after infection. During that time, the carriers are all extremely infectious to anyone with whom they come in contact. But, during this period, to all appearances, they appear perfectly healthy."

"They have no visible symptoms?"

"None! For at least two whole weeks! So the virus is spreading exponentially and yet completely undetected. Tee-hee. It's the difference between a true global plague and a little isolated head cold like SARS or monkey pox. You see?"

Snay leaned his head back and allowed himself a glimmer of hope that it was not all lost after all. He stared at the doctor, a kind of desperate hope in his eyes. He said, "The Americans can't catch it in time to stop it." Bin Wazir grinned slyly.

"By the time they catch it, they've already caught it!"

"The entire country."

"Yes!"

"I'm beginning to like this."

"The Emir underestimates you. But I do not."

"Projections, Doctor. How many will die?"

"Perhaps ten million. A few more, a few less. At any rate, catastrophic results. The American infrastructure will overload. National, state, and local governments will come apart at the seams. Loss of electrical power, communications, septic systems, water filtration. Widespread panic, total chaos, rampant disease, virulent sepsis. Mob rule followed by anarchy. Vigilantism. Fundamental meltdown."

"Meltdown."

"Basically, the end of the America we all know and hate, Pasha."

"Keep talking, Doctor."

"The basic plan remains the same. No deviation from your schedule. After the airplane arrives at its destination, the highly infectious army will disgorge and fan out across America. They will travel to your designated hundred most populous cities. All that you have prearranged remains precisely as planned. But, once in place, instead of detonating my beloved Pigskins, your lovely agents are mingling with the infidel masses within those hundred cities. Going to movies, train stations, amusement parks, zoos. Making boyfriends and girlfriends, you see? Then newly infected masses of American carriers, undetected, mingle and travel and create exponentially new armies of infected carriers."

Snay bin Wazir eyed the little man narrowly, all of his vivid dreams of cities and mushroom clouds going up in smoke. Replaced by legions of scabrous American zombies, rioting in the streets. For the first time since leaving the hotel, he allowed himself a smile. Two whole weeks before the first case was diagnosed. It could work.

"You say ten million of the Americans will die?"

"Yes, indeed. At least."

"It is not without a certain appeal," he said.

CHAPTER
FORTY-THREE

The Ragged Keys

Stoke gunned the inflatable across the shallow saw-grass flats, grabbing a hard southwesterly angle towards the northernmost tip of the Florida Keys, taking a route the big Cigarette couldn't possibly navigate. The new angle narrowed the distance between the two boats rapidly. Stoke got just close enough, eased back on the throttles, and let the black rubber boat settle. He scratched the stubble of beard on his chin, thinking it over.

"Ross, you can manage it, I think maybe you ought to be up on the bow with Pepe's AK. We get much closer, Scissor is going to put up a big fight. We ain't ready yet."

"You may not be, Stokely, but I am. This is the bastard who murdered Vicky."

"Yeah, that's what I'm saying, man. I want to talk to his ass before he's dead. Tell him face-to-face my emotional reaction to what he did back in England. Get up close and personal with him about the sacredness of the house of the Lord. Know what I'm saying? Talk to him about my religious convictions. You think he's got that Fancha aboard still?"

"I do. Wouldn't you?"

"One fine chick. Notice how she was smiling at me back at Vizcaya? I got the feeling she was only with Scissor because she was under—something. You know what I mean."

"Duress?"

"That's it. Duress. Thinking about her under all that duress. Be kinda nice to save her sweet ass. You know, for the benefit of all mankind."

"Ever the humanitarian."

"Natural born do-gooder."

Stoke smiled, and eased the throttles back as the speedboat slipped through the razor-sharp sawgrass into the outskirts of the mangrove swamps. Scissor was poking his nose here and there, scoping it all out. Casual. Like he didn't have a care in the world.

"See? Look at him. He thinks he's smart, that's his problem. Simply does not understand I'm hip to his stupid self."

"Stupid? Rather considerate, Stoke. For a murderous psychopath."

"What? C'mon, flyboy. That man is a born loser."

"He didn't kill us. That was nice of him."

"Losers got time to be nice."

Ross had no comment for that observation.

"Besides, he killed the Preacher," Stoke said, seeing the kid when he said it.

"Right," Ross said, after a beat. He, too, saw the smiling Jamaican boy, so delighted with the game of cops and robbers. "You're the SEAL, Stoke. How do we play this quagmire game?"

Stoke knew exactly how to play it. Fact was, he'd played enough war games down here in the Keys to have a very good idea. Namely, keep pushing him. Force him deeper and deeper into the mangroves. Limit his options. Close. Eliminate.

In the mid-sixties, a secret Navy operation down at the old Key West Station had trained his squad back in here for a coupla months. Heat 'n Skeet, his knuckle-busters had called this bug-infested swamp, where paradise is hell. Twisty-turny channels snaking this way and that, no rhyme or reason. Nothing on the charts. Some of them lead to open water, but most don't. So, if Scissor just happened onto one that goes straight out to sea, Stoke knew he was shit out of luck.

Stoke said, "I'm betting I know a lot more about this swamp than he does. Maybe his horsepower advantage 'bout to run out."

Ross limped forward to the bow with the heavy automatic weapon and Stoke eased the throttles forward once Ross was comfortably situated up there, one hand on the grab rail, gun in the other. The inflatable's hull wouldn't provide Ross much in the way of protection, but it was a definite plus to post a stone warrior up front with an AK-47, you running up on somebody's ass in a little rubber boat.

Diablo II was moving slowly now, because of the shallow water and all. The man was trying to feel his way along the Ragged Keys using his depth sounder and his GPS, trying to find an escape route without running aground. Stoke kept his distance, knowing the guy most likely had an RPG tube aboard, not wanting to get anywhere near inside the grenade launcher's thousand-yard range.

The two boats moved south like that for a good ten minutes, Stoke stalking him, taking Sands Key on his port side, still way east of the Intercoastal Waterway. *Diablo II* accelerated now, sensing deeper water, and Stoke sped up too. Cat and mouse all right, but who was who?

Sand Cut was coming up fast now, just off the port bow. This was the cut which separated Sands Key from Ragged Key to the south. Stoke swore under his breath. Rodrigo gets through there, he's out in the open Atlantic and gone *adios, muchachos*. Problem he had, though, unless the Corps of Engineers had widened it since he was down here, no way the big *Diablo* could squeeze through that channel. Which the cat had obviously just figured out, because he suddenly hung a hard left and blasted into a wide opening in the mangroves. *Okay*, Stoke thought, grinning like a barracuda, *here we go*.

Now, we in it, boy.

Stoke slowed the engines to a crawl entering the swamps. It was a twisting maze, sea grapes and mangroves you could reach out and touch on either side of the boat. Plenty of deep water back in here, though, and *Diablo* disappeared around a sharp bend. Stoke heard him throttle back. The Cigarette's big motors made a deep rumble no matter how low the RPMs. This was good. He could just track the sound, stay out of sight but stay with him, turn for turn, wait for his chance. On the bow, Ross suddenly held up his hand. Halt. Then, a slashing motion across his throat.

"Kill the engines," Ross turned to him and whispered. "He's stopped."

Ain't that interesting, Stoke thought, hitting the two red kill switches on the console that instantly shut down the outboards. He listened carefully to the swamp sounds. Crickets, tree frogs, skeets, that was it.

Must've, what, run aground? Fouled his props in mangrove roots maybe? Or, he's up to something. Playing games. Either way, old Stoke was not about to be going around any corners blind.

Stoke left the console and stepped aft, stooping to grab another one of the confiscated Glock nines stowed in the stern lazarette. He popped the clip, saw it was full, rammed it back into the grip. He jacked a round into the chamber and shoved this second pistol inside the black cummerbund still wrapped around the waist of his nonresplendent dirt- and grease- and blood-stained white satin trousers. The Fontainebleau Hotel seemed long ago and far away.

"You know—" Stoke started to say something but Ross held up the flat of his hand, signaling for silence. Stoke edged his way forward and crouched beside Ross in the bow. The current had moved the inflatable to the right side of the narrow channel and they'd drifted up under some overhanging sea grape and mangrove branches.

"Listen," Ross whispered.

"Yeah. I hear it."

A woman crying, sounded like. Yeah, that's what it was. Fancha. Begging, maybe. He could see the guy doing that. Bait. Using the woman, hurting her, trying to draw him in.

Damn.

"He's playing games, all right," Stoke whispered, ripping off his torn and ruined pleated formal shirt. "Motherfucka think he playing Cat and Mouse."

"He is."

"No. He ain't."

The ex-SEAL swung his legs silently over the side

and lowered himself feet first down into the warm black water. He gripped an overhanging mangrove root with one hand and used the other to slice off a thick cattail reed with an assault knife. Then he looked up at Ross.

"Ever try this? Works great. I stayed submerged, breathed through one just like this for over an hour one time, Mr. Victor Charlie stalking my squad up some Mekong backwater."

"You were riverine, Stoke. I was the Navy flyboy. Remember?"

"Yeah. I forgot. Rocket man. You okay? You too doped up to do this? I don't want alligators sneaking up on you." He'd felt kinda bad earlier, not leaving Ross at Vizcaya where the Dade County EMS guys would have fixed his leg up. Not that Ross would have ever in a million years let himself get left behind, they going after the man who killed Vicky, hot on his trail now.

"Come on, Stoke. Who do you think you're talking to? I eat morphine for breakfast."

"You're right. Sorry. Tell you one thing, though, Ross," Stoke said, easing himself soundlessly deeper into the brackish water until only his head was visible.

"Yeah?"

"Like I say, this boy, he thinks he playing Cat and Mouse, but he ain't," Stoke said.

"No? What's he playing?"

"Cat and Cat," Stoke said, and, flashing a huge white grin, he disappeared beneath the surface.

"Boo!"

Stoke popped up right next to the Cigarette. He'd been underwater, breathing through the reed, treading water and watching for movement of the hull above. See where everybody was up there. The hull hadn't moved in sixty seconds. Before that, he'd swum for eight minutes without taking a breath. Hell, it wasn't even a record. In his old SEAL Team Six days, they'd called him the Human Draeger. Draeger was the German underwater breathing apparatus used by SEAL insertion teams to swim great distances without a telltale trail of bubbles.

He surfaced, took a gulp of air, and swung the Glock back and forth above his head, expecting to see Scissor peering down at him over the gunwale. The sun was up now, and the temperature back in the deep severe was climbing fast. He banged the muzzle of the pistol on the hull a couple of times. A loud, hollow thud. Then rapped it a couple more times, harder. Still nothing.

"Hey! Ahoy, there, Captain! Big black dude down here in the water about to blow a big fat hole in your yacht!" He aimed the pistol just where he expected Scissor's head to appear.

Nothing.

He kicked his legs, lunged up and grabbed a shiny cleat, rocking the boat side-to-side, singing one of his old favorites to himself.

"Rock the boat, don't rock the boat, baby . . . rock the boat, don't rock the boat, baby!"

That's when the drop of blood plopped down, splat, right in the middle of his forehead.

Scissoring his legs hard, he shot up out of the water, grabbed the stainless rail with one hand, and hauled himself up and over into the cockpit in a single move. The deck was sticky under his feet. Whole mess of confused bloody footprints. Fancha was sitting with her back to the transom, head down. Blood matted in her hair. Stoke stared hard at the blood spatters and foot-prints until he could begin to make it all jell.

He'd been right. Scissor had used her for bait. Lure them in on his own terms. But she put up a fight. Guy fights girl. Guy wins. Guy ties girl up, hands and feet with anchor chain, hurts her with scissors, and then goes over the stern.

He pressed two fingers on the side of the naked woman's neck. Strong pulse. Out cold, though. Big contusion on her forehead, like she'd hit her head on the gunwale going down. Going to the stern, he stared at the footprints, then saw more blood smears on the big overhanging mangrove, the one Rodrigo must have grabbed in order to haul himself over the side and climb ashore.

Stoke was ticking off the possibilities as to what Rodrigo might be up to when he heard a low moan from Fancha. Girl was going to wake up in a world of hurt from what he could see. He knelt down beside her, scooped her up in his arms and quickly carried her below. The whole interior was done in creamy white leather and he lay her down on a long sofa, getting a lot of blood on the man's custom upholstery.

He got the ropes and chains off, talking softly to her and trying to get her to come around.

She was whimpering now, saying something he couldn't understand but could guess at, rolling her head back and forth. He ducked into the head and stuck a couple of hand towels in the sink, turned on the cold water. Wringing them out, he returned and sat down on the floor beside the sofa where she lay. He wiped off a lot of the blood, saw where the guy had slashed her with the scissors.

Mostly superficial. Upper torso. A long thin wound that started below her belly-button and disappeared into her pubic hair. He found a blanket and covered her, then stepped back into the head and ripped open the medicine chest looking for the first aid kit. There was a good one and a couple of minutes later, he'd mostly cleaned her up and swabbed her with the bacitracin cream and applied gauze bandages. Her eyelids were fluttering but she was still way out of it.

Suddenly, an explosion cracked the air. A thousand birds lit out from the surrounding swamp and the noise and concussion of the blast rocked the *Diablo*. Stoke knew instantly what had happened.

"Aw, goddamn it," he said, and bolted up the steps to the cockpit. He could see and smell the flames licking up through the mangroves. Burning gas. Rubber. Smoke was rising out of the swamp into the pink dawn sky. It was coming from back downstream, right where he and Ross had tied the inflatable.

He looked back at the girl. Still out. He removed one of the two automatics jammed in his cummerbund and jacked a hollow-point into the chamber; then he wrapped the girl's right hand around the grip and stuck her finger through the trigger guard. Left her like that. Said, "Stay cool, Fancha, I'll be right back," and bolted up the steps to the cockpit. If she'd been awake, he would have told her to definitely not wait until she saw the whites of his eyes—all this guy had was white. White with little black pinpoints.

There was a secondary explosion. *Whoompf.* Whatever munitions Pepe and his boys had been carrying in the inflatable's stern storage just went sky-high.

"Ross!" he screamed, and leapt onto the bank, ripping mangroves out by the roots as he clawed his way through the dense undergrowth. Leaping over roots and saltwater pools, he couldn't stop seeing that hinky little smile on Ross's face when he'd left him. Pupils dilated with morphine, lopsided grin. How'd you get to be so stupid, Stokely, man your age? All this time, all the crazy shit you saw Charlie pull down in the Delta; and all the gangsta stuff up in the Bronx? Man, you are supposed to *know* by now how this shit goes down!

He'd been a damn fool.

Cat one. Mouse zero.

CHAPTER FORTY-FOUR

The Emirate

Fudo Myo-o was wielding the sword of instructive wisdom and holding a coiled rope to bind any evildoers who failed to heed his message.

"He looks very powerful, Ichi-san," Yasmin said to the sumo. He was lost in concentration and didn't look up. She was draped in peacock blue silk. She plucked another bright green grape from the bunch she had brought into the garden, and asked, "Who is it, in the painting?"

They were sitting in Yasmin's private meditation garden. Ichi had been working there every morning for some days now. He was putting the finishing touches on a painting. Yasmin had promised to smuggle it out to his beloved Michiko. The beautiful Yasmin had made a surprise appearance this morning, settling herself upon the marble bench and watching quietly while he painted.

"It is a rendering of Fudo Myo-o," Ichi said, smiling. "I am pleased that you like it. I have great respect for the feminine eye."

"Is Fudo your God?"

"One of them."

Yasmin and Ichi spoke quietly. Discretion was always their habit, ever since the night he had first come to her here in the garden; the night he revealed her husband's sexual betrayal with the treacherous Rose. They had to whisper because, even here in Yasmin's most private garden, there was no privacy. Eyes and ears were everywhere.

Behind the thick stone walls of her opulent prison, Yasmin sometimes wondered if there was any privacy left at all, even within the walls of her own mind.

"You have many gods, Ichi-san?"

"Fudo is an old one," Ichi said. "Since I was a boy. He is the patron saint of Budo. Budo in my country is the way of brave and enlightened activity. For the warrior, Fudo represents steadfastness and resolve. He who is immovable."

"And, Myo-o?"

"Myo-o means 'King of Light.'"

"So, Budo is—your religion?"

"Perhaps. Budo has three essential elements. The timing of heaven, the utility of the earth, and the harmonization of human beings. I suppose for some that is a kind of religion."

He returned to his painting and the silence between them stretched out, languorous and comfortable. Morning sunlight dappled the garden with shadows. The scent of the climbing yellow jasmine was heavy, soporific. Yasmin would have loved to lay her head upon Ichi's lap and drift away beyond her walls. But she could not. She had bad news.

"I have just heard from my husband, Ichi-san. His plane will shortly leave Suva Island. He will be here late in the evening."

Ichi did not reply. He just absorbed. And harmonized.

"I am so sorry," Yasmin said. "I thought we had more time."

There were large elephant and camel caravans departing at first light the next day. Yasmin had arranged for Ichi to be smuggled outside the walls in one of many large baskets even now being stacked just inside the walls. Tonight, with the palace security forces once more under the ever-watchful eye of bin Wazir and his inner circle, the guards would be sure to check every container leaving the Blue Palace.

Ichi closed his eyes and lifted his head so that the sun struck him fully on his upturned face.

"Do not mistake my heart. It is steadfast. Another day of hope will come," Ichi said. He opened his eyes. "Look. The light. It is still visible in the valley beyond the wall, is it not?"

"I will help you to escape. You will be one with your Michiko again, my dearest Ichi-san. I promise you."

Ichi added brushstrokes, his touch like tiny wings batting here and there against the painting.

"How do you know when it is finished?" Yasmin asked, after a time. "The painting."

Ichi looked up at her and smiled. He liked the question.

"You never finish," he said. "You abandon it."

The silence resumed. Finally, Yasmin rose to her feet and made as if to leave the garden. She stopped and looked at the gentle sumo, lost in his art and sorrow.

"Have the *rikishi* killed the American?" she asked him.

"We have been told to wait. Until your husband

returns. The torture has not yet broken him. His body yields only pieces of secrets."

"But you still take him the food I send?"

"Without it, he would starve."

"I am sick to death of it. Prisons. Torture. All the killing."

"It is just beginning. A great storm of death gathers here."

"Shh—servants."

Ichi returned to his painting, pretending to add a stroke just here and just there to the image of the fierce god Fudo Myo-o. Two young females appeared, dropping to their knees before Yasmin, their foreheads to the ground.

"Yes? Why have you disturbed me?" she demanded.

"A letter, Most Revered One. From the American. He begged us to bring it. He said that—that you would understand and not treat us harshly."

"Give it."

Yasmin took the envelope from the shaking hand of the servant and turned her back. The two young women rose silently and melted away into the shadows of a graceful archway. She opened the message with a fingernail and pulled out two handwritten pages. After reading them, she put a hand on Ichi's enormous shoulder.

"Yes?" he said, turning from his painting.

"A farewell letter, Ichi-san, written to his wife—and children—oh—"

Ichi looked up and saw her tears.

He said, "I am sorry for your pain."

"This is how you know your life is finished, Ichi-san," she said, holding up the American's scrawled letter to his loved ones. "It is—like your painting. You abandon it."

"Yes," the sumo said, gathering himself up. "This American, he is a good man. He has suffered long enough."

"Oh, God," Yasmin said, hiding the letter in the folds of her robes, "hasn't everyone suffered enough?"

CHAPTER FORTY-FIVE

The Ragged Keys

The mosquito that had been biting Stokely's neck was now just a red smear in the palm of his left hand. In his right, the dead Cuban's nine millimeter. In the Glock, thirteen hollow-point bullets, one spare mag in his cummerbund. In his eyes, nose, and throat, the acrid bite of burning rubber and gasoline. He edged up behind a still-smoldering scrub palmetto and pushed a charred frond aside with his pistol. The blackened and flattened mangroves and sea grapes extended back a hundred yards or so on both sides of the narrow waterway.

Nothing on the surface of the water other than some burning fuel and a couple of smoking life vests.

"Ross!" Stoke hissed, keeping it low. "Hey, Ross! You okay? Where are you, buddy?"

He waited, not expecting any damn answer, seeing the thing, how it happened. Yeah, Ross would have been right where he left him, up in the bow with the AK, watching the bend in the water. Perking up his ears all of a sudden when he hears his buddy Stoke up ahead, shouting and banging on the *Cigarette* hull with his pistol, then splashing around, climbing aboard. Ross mentally focused on that. Meanwhile, Scissor sneaking past him on the bank, moving quietly, taking his time, getting behind the inflatable, settling down in the mangroves with a clear shot.

Scissor enjoying this part, was probably eating it up. Resting his RPG tube carefully on a sturdy branch. Sighting the thing, maybe on the jerry cans full of gasoline in the stern. Yeah. Or, maybe, right between Ross's shoulder blades. Squeezing the trigger slowly— Ross maybe shaking his head in that last second, trying to concentrate, clear the morphine cobwebs out— hears a *THUNK-WHOOSH* behind him.

Shit, Ross.

You were riverine. I was the flyboy.

"Okay, muthafucka, that's it!" Stoke screamed, not giving a shit anymore, getting to his feet. "I'm coming to get you! You got a shot? Take it! Take your shot 'cause it's going to be your last!"

He stood up on the bank, eyes peeled, breathing hard.

There was still a little blood, dried blood, on the leaves and branches of the mangrove down by the water, the spot where Scissor must have been when he fired the grenade launcher at Ross. Something shiny caught his eye, a spot on a root sticking out of the muddy bank above his head. He reached up and felt it, pulling his hand away and looking at the bright red smear. Fresh blood. So Fancha had cut his ass, too, somehow. When he was hurting her. During the struggle. Got his scissors away from him for a second or maybe just raked his face with her nails. Didn't matter. It was something.

He worked along the bank, dead calm now, knowing what he had to do. Follow the blood.

He stayed close to the water a couple of minutes.

Saw more shiny blood on a scrub palm frond to his left and headed inland. Seeing the whole thing in his mind, staying low, pausing every twenty seconds to listen. Skeets and birds were back. Tree frogs. Fiddler crabs scurrying over the sand everywhere. Sun was up and hot. The deep severe. Heat 'n skeet. Fresh blood on the dried grass where he crouched in the scrubs. Where the hell are you, Scissor? You doubling back to the *Cigarette*?

Yeah, that's it. Gone back to his boat. That's exactly what he'd be doing. Boy must have had himself a very startling realization.

There he is, smiling, lining up his mouth-watering shot, but something nagging at his ass, just before he squeezed the trigger. What's wrong with this picture? Oh, yeah. No big black guy on the rubber boat with the white guy, that's what's wrong. Didn't pass any big colored fellas slipping and sliding back along the bank, so, where the fuck is he? He's got to be in the water. Or, he left his boat and swam up the channel. Right, Scissor thinks, black man swam upriver to the *Diablo*.

Stoke was glad he'd given Fancha the other gun.

He got to his feet and was running through the thick low scrub of the small clearing towards the *Cigarette*, when a single round whistled past his ear. He hit the dirt hard, scrambling and rolling right into a thicket of palmettos. Not good cover. Two more bullets kicked up dirt three feet to his left. Steep angle. Shooting from elevation. Stoke lifted his head and saw the big Gumbo Limbo tree at the far edge of the clearing. Bunch of cypress trees, too, but you couldn't hide in a cypress.

Scissor liked to shoot people from out of trees. His M.O.

Stoke stood up and pumped four bullets into the

gumbo. Then he ran at a crouch towards a stubby little Calusa tree over on his left that would provide a little cover. The Calusa exploded before he got there. A white trail of smoke led back to the top of the Gumbo, right where Stoke had him.

Gotcha.

Stoke ran forward, right at him, squeezing off three careful shots in a tight pattern at the top of the tree, right where the RPG trail came from. Waiting to see the guy come tumbling down, and that's when he heard a pop from up there in the treetops and somebody took a Louisville Slugger to his left thigh, bam. Spun him around good, maybe twice, but he stayed on his feet, only a hundred yards more now, pumping his legs, and then his feet stopped moving so good. Mud or something.

He made it almost to the base of the Gumbo, firing the Glock, screaming at the guy, "C'mon, Scissor! C'mon down! Les' see what you got! Show me something! Shit! You ain't got nothin', shoot a bride down front of a church!"

He splashed through a mudhole full of water, twisted something, pitched forward, the Glock dry-firing now, empty. He kept his balance, moving forward and digging the fresh mag of ammo out of his waistband. Hell, he'd climb the tree and pull the little shit down by his ankles. Stick the Glock in the guy's mouth and see if he could beg God's forgiveness that way. He would do that, and then some, but his feet wouldn't move anymore. Couldn't even lift his heels, like in that nightmare when you try and run but nothing will move.

He heard a sucking noise when he tried to lift his right leg and looked down at his feet. Couldn't see 'em anymore. They had disappeared into some mucky stuff near the base of the tree. Past his ankles now, damn, almost halfway up to his knees. He heard some leaves rustling above him and then the guy just drops out of the Gumbo tree, lands on his feet in a patch of swamp grass next to the muck. Got a nickel-plated .357 mag aimed at Stoke's forehead.

"*Hola,*" the man with no eyes said. No more mirrored shades. He had three ragged claw marks down his left cheek, still bleeding. Fancha had caught him good, bless her sweet little soul. Stoke smiled at the guy.

"Hey. How you doing? Where's your grenade launcher?" he said, grinning. "Get stuck up in that tree?"

Scissor smiling at him with those horror movie eyes. Clear as marbles. Man had aged some since Vizcaya, life on the run and all. Wearing a Kevlar sportcoat, which explained why he hadn't got shot out of the tree. Stoke's left leg hurt like a bitch now, like a nest of hornets had put down stakes in his thigh muscle. He couldn't pull his damn feet out of the muck. He started looking around for something to grab on to, a bush or something. Wasn't anything near close enough. Maybe if he stretched out flat, he could get his fingers in the thick grass round the edge and haul himself out.

Stoke raised the Glock, but they'd both heard it dry-firing and they both knew it was empty. He couldn't decide whether to throw it at the guy's face or ask him to give him a hand here, get out of this crap. The mud was almost up to his knees now. You could feel it rising.

"Hey. Look. Do me a favor. Give me a hand here. I'm stuck in the mud."

"Is not mud, *señor.* It's quicksand."

So he'd known about the quicksand. Pretty good

trap. Shit, you had to give him credit for that at least. The guy sat down on the mound of grass, his legs crossed under him, smiling at Stoke, cradling the big silver magnum in his lap. Chilled. Happy. Like he was waiting on the perfect sunset down at Pier House on Key West. Wouldn't leave till it had gone all the way down. Then he'd ooh and aah and go have a margarita at Sloppy Joe's.

Stoke's mind was racing as he tried to stifle all the bad stuff he remembered about quicksand. More you struggle, worse it gets, he knew that. Saw a scary movie when he was a kid and he could see it now. Guy in Africa in a situation just like this. Guy kept his nose sticking up till the end—his mouth filling up with muck so he couldn't scream anymore. Then, nothing but a couple bubbles on the surface.

"Hey. I got an idea. See that old cypress branch? That'll reach. Then we can have us a fair fight."

"I don't give a fuck about fair."

"I forgot. The brave bride killer."

"How is your amigo? Hawke? Still in mourning?"

"You help me get out, we'll talk all day long."

Stoke had managed to eject the Glock's empty mag without the guy seeing it. Sank instantly, sucked down. You could feel the pull. Strong. Had to be fed by an underground spring. Even if he managed to reload and shoot this evil bastard, it was all over anyway. He was going down. He knew that. Seen this movie, pal. The hero dies in the end.

I can live with that, Stokely suddenly thought. What the hell, you know? It even made him smile. Business he was in, your number's bound to be up one day, why not this one? Good as any. *Just don't go out all by yourself, Stoke. No matter what. You do that, you just break Alex*

Hawke's heart one more time. One way or another, you got to take this dirtbag along for the ride. Headed my way? Step right in.

"What's so funny, *señor?*"

"You, that's all. Instead of running Cuba, you running from me, bigshot. You know who saved Fidel? Who got him out of your hostage hacienda? You're looking at him. I'm one half the reason all those Navy *Super Hornets* bombed all you little banana republican dictator assholes into oblivion. That's right. Alexander Hawke and Stokely Jones, Jr., we the ones teach you not to fuck with the US of A, dickhead."

Rodrigo del Rio laughed out loud.

"You want me to end it, huh? Is that it? Shoot you, no?"

"Not really. I plan to live a short and happy life."

While he was lecturing Scissorhands on politics of the Caribbean he'd slipped the fresh mag into the Glock's grip with just a soft click. Didn't see any eye movement from the guy, not a flicker. Good. Muck was now climbing up near his waist. Bad. Not a whole lot of time here. Extremely unfortunate situation you find yourself in, Stokely.

"Ask you a couple questions," Stoke said, finger lightly on the trigger, waiting for his moment. "You Catholic? *Iglesia Católica?*"

"*Sí.*"

"I'd spit, but why waste good saliva? Your mamma back in Cuba, she know you killed a bride? At a church? How do you possibly go any lower than that? Tell me something. Back in England. You aiming for Hawke? Or Vicky? Which?"

The guy laughed. "I am not Cuban. Colombian,

Señor. From Cali. We Colombians kill the circle around the center. The bride was first because I knew she would cause the most pain. What better place to kill her than on the steps of the church? She was first. Hawke will be last."

"Really? So who's supposed to be next?"

"You, of course. Why do you think you're here?"

"You ain't that smart."

"No? I knew one of you would come. Avenge the bride. I knew it was you who saved that fucking Castro's life, no? Twenty years ago, Fidel disappeared my family and put me in a hole. I lived in the hole for twelve years. No sunlight, no artificial light. Ever. He did this to my eyes. Twelve years in blackness, this is what happens. But I got out and I was going to bury Fidel in that very hole. I was close. And then you and this man Hawke, you ruin everything."

"Yeah, we got a bad habit of doing that," Stoke said. He raised the Glock and fired as he said it. "Messing with people's long-range plans."

Shit.

"You missed," Scissor said, unhurt, and pulled the trigger of the .357.

Stoke's shoulder exploded in pain, and his gun smacked in the muck close enough to reach. He tried to grab it but he couldn't move his arm and, besides, the damn gun sank instantly. What the hell? He'd missed? He never missed. Glock sounded funny when it fired. Mud in the muzzle maybe. Wasn't his day, but, hell, it was still early.

Stoke looked at the guy, sitting there with the smoking .357, pulling the hammer back again. Cocky. He could see the guy trying to decide what would be more fun, shooting him in a lot of nonlethal places or just watching him sink.

"That must hurt, eh?" Rodrigo said.

"Hey, look!" Stoke said suddenly. "Here comes the dead guy. Why don't you ask him yourself?" Stoke grabbed his right shoulder with his left hand. Bones felt okay. It was just a flesh wound but it was bleeding like hell and the muck was creeping up over his ribcage and the new bullet hole in his shoulder made him forget all about the one in his leg. That, and the fact that—

"Oldest trick in the book—" the guy was saying when Ross hit him high, square between the shoulder blades and drove Rodrigo forward, not stopping, pumping his legs, shoving him into the quicksand not six feet from Stokely.

The guy started screaming, flopping around. Digging his own grave, which would save Stoke a lot of trouble.

" 'Bout damn time," Stoke said to Ross.

"Sorry. Just woke up," Ross said. He picked up the cypress branch and it was long enough.

"You just about burned beyond recognition."

"I got blown up."

"Looks like it."

"*Señor*, I beg you!" Scissor screamed. He was up to his waist already. "Save me—"

"Save you?" Stoke said, whipping around furiously and looking at him dead in the eyes, one last time. "*Save* you?"

"Please!"

"Ain't nobody can save you, Rodrigo. Take a good look at yourself. You going straight to hell. And you halfway there already."

*   *   *

It took the man with no eyes a long time to die. He
flapped his arms back and forth, making snow angels in
the muck, but it didn't help much. He was going down
all right, just as Stoke had told Ross he would, back at
Vizcaya. Stokely and Ross sat on the clump of dry grass
and watched. He pleaded and begged for a while. In the
end, all that was still showing was the tip of his nose,
just like in that movie about Africa that Stoke saw
when he was a little kid.

He was there, and then a half-second later he
wasn't. Right after that, the exact same two little bubbles from the jungle movie.

Pop. Pop.

"You hurt?" Stoke finally asked Ross.

"A little. Heard him coming. Slipped over the side.
Tried your reed-breathing technique. It worked okay
until the ammo went up and blew me out of the water.
You?"

"Couple of boo-boos, that's all."

"I don't think you need your cummerbund anymore. You could tie that around your leg."

"Good idea. Thanks."

"Don't mention it."

"You know what I like about this, Ross?"

"Can't imagine."

"At the end, I mean the very end, I do believe
Rodrigo truly knew which direction he was headed in."

"Yeah."

"You see that, too?"

"Yeah."

"Vicky, she was standing on the church steps. The
girl was already halfway to heaven when she died."

"Yeah."

"Well. I guess that's all you can ask for."

Stoke got up and stuck his hand out to help Ross get back on his feet.

"I guess it is," Ross said.

CHAPTER FORTY-SIX

Suva Island

The big Daimler rolled up just outside the massive corrugated hangar and hissed to a creaky stop. The sleek little Gulfstream jet that would very shortly whisk bin Wazir home to the Blue Mountains was parked just outside on the tarmac, engines warming.

As Tippu hauled his ancient Vuitton steamer trunk up the steps of the G-3, Snay and the doctor stood for a moment outside the cavernous hangar filled with blazing arc lights. Snay bin Wazir's heart was beating wildly. He knew what to expect inside, and still he was ill-prepared for the sight of the freshly painted behemoth standing in the glare of endless banks of lights.

It was beyond perfection. An exact copy. Down to the last nut and bolt.

His chief pilot, Khalid, strode forward out of the mass of technicians huddled under the nose of Snay's now-unrecognizable 747-400. Thick cables, connected to two ancient Cray supercomputers on rolling platforms, snaked out of the nose wheel bay. Snay, grinning like a ten-year-old, opened his arms and embraced Khalid, clapping him on the back.

"It's magnificent! Absolutely flawless!"

"Thank you, indeed, sir," Khalid said, in his crisp

English accent. He took a step back. "It does rather look like the real thing, doesn't it?" The handsome, middle-aged pilot, whom, along with his copilot, bin Wazir had lured away from British Airways years earlier by doubling their salaries, was dressed in a perfectly pressed black pilot's uniform, another exact copy of the original, right down to the last gold button. The pilot removed his cap and saluted. At that moment, his first officer, Johnny Adare, approached and snapped to attention. Like his senior officer, he was wearing a crisp black uniform.

"Sir!" Adare said smartly to bin Wazir. "The aircraft is nearly fueled. We have almost completed the downloading of the pirated transponder codes and GPS coordinates. My lads on the ground at Singapore Changi International Airport were able to 'borrow' the original flight plan for an hour and replace it onboard the BA plane without notice. As you assured us, security at the hangar there was conveniently absent. All we will need now is our friend's squawk number, which we can easily obtain from the radio. As soon as we have finished downloading and fueling, we can begin boarding. Sir."

"How long?" bin Wazir asked Adare, looking at his watch. The incident at the dragon cage had cost him nearly an hour. In order to avoid any high-altitude surveillance cameras, and make its rendezvous over the Pacific, his plane had to be airborne an hour before dawn.

"Two hours, sir."

"Make it one."

"Done," Adare said. "I'll whip these wog bastards a little harder." Bin Wazir smiled. Adare still had a bit of the rowdy IRA kneecapper about him. Adare paused. "One thing, sir, a bit curious to me if you don't mind. Passengers are due to start loading in half an hour. We have not yet received the . . . cargo."

"Last-minute change of plans," bin Wazir said. "The good doctor here will explain it in some detail. A colleague of mine. His name is Dr. I.V. Soong. He'll be joining you in the cockpit. Stick him in the jumpseat."

"Very good, sir," Khalid said, looking closely first at Soong and then at his employer. "No changes to the flight plan? The destination is unchanged?"

"Nothing to be concerned about, Khalid. The blessings of Allah be upon your epic journey. I wish you a good flight."

"Very good, sir. We'll get moving, then. Doctor Soong? If you'll follow us?" The pilot and second officer turned on their heels and headed for the rolling stairway leading up to the opened cabin door just aft of the nose. Adare looked back over his shoulder at this strange little figure struggling with the two big black Halliburton cases. He was making a series of unintelligible noises.

"Is there something else?" Adare asked the man.

"Yes," Dr. Soong said. "There is. You must get someone to help me, please. A mechanic. I need to make some last-minute changes in the aircraft's emergency oxygen system. Minor alterations. Good, good! Let's go!"

The man lugging the big black suitcases followed the two pilots up the steps to the open door of the gleaming, freshly painted Boeing 747.

"I don't like it," Adare whispered to Khalid, stepping inside the plane. "Not a bit of it. No payload.

Now, this little bleeder wants to screw around with our air. If that's not Poison Ivy himself, I'm Lady Margaret Thatcher."

"I don't much like it either," Khalid replied. "But it's payday, isn't it, Johnny boy? We just drive the bus. So who the bloody hell cares."

When this was over, Khalid was going to use his million dollars to buy that little semidetached cottage in Burton-on-Water. Send his kids to a good public school, give his wife some pretty dresses and a little garden, finally read all of T. E. Lawrence, starting with *Seven Pillars of Wisdom*. Johnny was going to buy that corner pub in his old Belfast neighborhood, the one he'd had his eye on for so long. He already had the clever name. *The Quilted Camel.*

With 63,000 pounds of thrust per engine, the roaring jumbo jet sent volleys of thunder through the dark jungle, scattering such wildlife as perched, scurried, or slithered there, the deep rumble rolling right up the western slope of the smoldering volcano, waking up every bone-weary farmer's wife an hour early.

Carrying vast quantities of extra fuel in her wings and tail section, and with four hundred passengers aboard, the heavily overloaded airplane still managed to reach her takeoff speed of 180 miles per hour before she ran out of runway. She rotated, and lifted off into the predawn sky. The few early risers, farmers who stood beside their oxen at the edges of their fields to watch, shuddered at the sight. They could not have said why, but there is something unnatural and malevolent about a large airplane flying into a dark sky with no lights illuminated.

Something secret and threatening.

Lumbering down the runway in the pale light of the dying moon, a long row of darkened windows glinting from her fuselage, she looked like a ghost plane. No red flashes at the wingtips, not a single light from within, not a bulb, interior or exterior, was lit. Now, airborne, the stark black flying machine was a moving silhouette against the stars. Accelerating low out over the rooftops of the old Bambah Hotel, the pilot could now see what all the fuss was about on his radar screen. A rapidly approaching black wall; a storm front moving in from the South China Sea.

Normally, the pilot would just vector around it, or climb quickly above it. Not today. Not now. He was staying right here, right down on the deck.

Crests of the wind-whipped waves below, some as high as a three-story building, lapped at the airplane's broad belly and spattered the undersides of her fuel-laden wings. A typhoon had been building in the South China Sea and this was the leading edge. The four Pratt & Whitney engines howled ahead into the teeth of the headwind.

"Pull up! Pull up!" Dr. Soong said, after a long minute in which the aircraft did not appear to him to be climbing. "What is the matter? Are we going down?"

There was a faint reddish glow inside the cockpit, coming from the instrument panels, and the copilot, Adare, could see the terrified expression on the man's face. The doctor wore thick black glasses, and the greasy lenses seemed to be made of waxed paper, but Johnny Adare could still see that this was not a happy flyer.

Adare, amused, looked at this little man seated in the jumpseat just aft of the captain and gave him an ironic and assuring thumbs-up. It was a gesture the doctor found most unconvincing. Something was very wrong. Look! They were about to fly through a big wave! He covered his eyes with both hands and waited for the impact.

The 747 was carefully following a well-thought-out flight plan. Unfiled with any aviation authority, but still, her flight plan. She would fly north-northwest for one hundred miles at an altitude of fifty feet above sea level. It was dangerous and made more so by the storm, but it was necessary. For now. A hundred miles out over the Pacific, safely out of Indonesian airspace, and any radar anywhere, she would begin an ascent to an altitude above normal commercial operating routes. 45,000 feet was the plan. Barring any unforeseen difficulties, the 747 would be touching down at LAX International Airport in Los Angeles, California, in just less than twelve hours.

Two minutes after takeoff, Doctor I.V. Soong, still very agitated, said from the jumpseat, "I am wondering, Captain, how long we must stay so low to the sea? Dangerous. Very dangerous. Ground effect, you know."

The captain turned in his seat and glared. The prospect of this hyperactive little gnome sitting behind him for twelve long hours was not appealing. He now understood why the Suva technicians referred to him as Poison Ivy. The man was indeed poisonous. It seeped from his pores. Even his breath was tainted and foul. He silently cursed bin Wazir for saddling him with this toxic little toad.

Ten long minutes into the flight they were still

skimming the wave tops of the South China Sea. It was a bumpy ride, flashes of lightning lit up the cockpit, and they could hear the shouts of the passengers through the locked cockpit door. Khalid could only imagine what it must be like back there, flying through this mess in pitch-black darkness. When he'd agreed to the Pasha's instructions, he hadn't known about the storm.

"Cabin and cockpit lights," he said to the copilot, and Adare flipped the two switches that turned them both on.

"Cabin and cockpit on," Johnny said, as the cockpit was fully illuminated. "Nav lights? Wings? Beacon and strobe?"

Khalid looked at his watch. If bin Wazir ever found out about any of this, he'd most certainly be dead. He'd certainly been fired for less. Many times. But by the time bin Wazir did find out, he'd be long gone. The reins had begun to chafe long ago. In twelve short hours, he'd be out of the harness forever.

"Light her up," Khalid finally said, easing back on the wheel. He'd turn all the goddamn lights on and take the airplane up to five hundred feet. Flying this low to the water in these conditions was suicidal.

"Oh!" Soong cried. "Oh, my God!"

It was even rougher at five hundred feet. Khalid's metal flight binder went flying across the cockpit. Soong knew they might have to fly lower than normal to avoid radar, but he'd had no idea they'd be flying at this altitude through a typhoon. He slipped out of his shoulder straps and staggered to his feet. He grabbed the back of the copilot's seat and held on. He couldn't stand it any longer.

"May I be having a small word with you?" Soong said, leaning over the copilot's shoulder and speaking into his ear.

"What?" Adare said, lifting his headphones. He, too, was annoyed and shared Khalid's distaste for the last-minute passenger in the cockpit.

"A word, if you please. Important. We could go down to bin Wazir's kitchen," Soong said, his smile no more than a minute crack, "have a cup of tea. A spot of whiskey."

"Took the bloody galley out," Adare said, speaking above the engines and the storm. "Even the two bedrooms. Everything that used to be back there on the lower deck is now a fuel tank."

"His sitting room, then?"

"Jesus. What is your bloody problem?"

"The Pasha told you. In the hangar. Last-minute change of plans. I need to explain. What needs to be done. We must speak." The captain craned his head around and stared at Soong.

Khalid said, "If you and the Pasha cooked up some plan to do something with my airplane other than fly it across the Pacific, you'd best spit it out. Now."

"My plans will in no way affect you nor your airplane, Captain," Soong said. "In any way. You have my most sincere assurances."

The captain returned his gaze to the black and rain-splashed windshield. This flight, his last official mission, was not getting off to a good start.

"Do it, Johnny," Khalid finally said without looking back at either of them. "Find out what the little bugger's up to. As long as you're back there, you might as well do what you can to calm the ladies down."

"Aye, Skipper, will do," Johnny Adare said, playfully punching Khalid's shoulder. "Ladies aren't happy, nobody's happy." He laughed silently at the thought. Four hundred suicide killers back there, handpicked from the most brutal terrorist training camps on the planet. Wasn't much left that could scare them, he didn't imagine. He unbuckled his shoulder straps and eased out of the right-hand seat. "Come along, Doc, let's see what kind of trouble we can get our ruddy selves into back there."

"Johnny?" Khalid said to his copilot, grabbing his arm.

"Aye?"

"You hear any squawking out of this little bird that sounds even remotely sketchy, you get back up here and tell me all about it."

CHAPTER FORTY-SEVEN

The Emirate

Four skeletal black birds soared high above the white floor of the valley. Jagged snow-blown mountains marched shoulder-to-shoulder up both sides of the wide basin, craggy promontories that scraped the crystalline blue skies. Three of the four gaunt black birds flew up this valley in a fair semblance of formation.

The fourth, mission code *Hawkeye,* putative leader of the flight, did not. This mischievous bird would lag behind the flock; first scribing tight corkscrew arcs downward, she would then ride a rising column of warm air, only to nose over the top and dive once more, the earth rushing crazily up, the airspeed indicator redlined. At the last possible moment, the wayward blackbird would level its wings and climb out, soaring once more on the warm thermals and rejoining the flight.

The pilot of this fourth bird, grinning with exhilaration, heard a squawk in his headphones.

"Hey. Offer you a deal, Hawkeye," Patterson drawled on the intercom. "Limited time only."

"Shoot, Tex."

"You keep this bird on an even keel till we reach the

LZ, set us down gently in one unbusted piece of high-tech plastic, you get use of this aircraft right here for one entire month of playtime."

"You're not serious?"

"I reckon I am."

"Deal," Hawke said, thrilled. With a wingspan of sixty feet, *Hawkeye* was in every sense the world's most sophisticated high-altitude stealth glider. He'd never flown anything remotely like her. Few had.

The lanky Texan, seated two seats aft of the Englishman in the cockpit, heard the huge smile Hawke had put behind that word, *Deal*. Never in his life had he known a boy who just loved flying airplanes so much. And, never once, at least not since this whole nightmare had begun in Venice and on the steps of a little church in England, had he heard Alex Hawke sound so happy.

"Would you like to drive, Tex?"

"Naw, son, you doin' jes fine now."

"I aim to please."

"G'night," the big man said, flipping down the most darkly tinted of the three visors attached to his helmet. Tex stuck a fresh mint toothpick in his teeth, leaned his head back against his headrest and closed his eyes; trying to relax a little in the short time remaining before all hell broke loose.

For some time, *Hawkeye* soared gracefully up valley, riding the thermals, flock in tow, and nothing and no one disturbed the blissful silence of the air.

Now, the ice-encrusted twin peaks of the Blue Mountain loomed ahead. It was monstrous. A dark blue–tinged mass of sharp granite angles, frozen snow and blue-black ice, the rocky pinnacle rose through the few stringy cloud layers to scrape the sky at 18,000 feet. The tallest of the two peaks was just 9,000 feet shy of Everest, the other peak a thousand feet lower.

The narrow snow-filled crevasse that split that pinnacle was the little flock's destination.

"Hey, Tex. You awake?"

"Am now."

"I've got the LZ in sight. I still feel guilty. Flying your plane—these are your men, Tex. Your planes. Your men."

"We been through all this, ain't we? Law of the plains. Injuns got you surrounded, the best shot gets the long rifle. That'd be you, Hawkeye."

"I suppose—"

"Hawke, listen. It ain't like you're hurtin' my feelings. The president gave you this assignment, remember. Not DSS, and not me. Me and the boys will gladly knock down anybody gets within spittin' distance of you. But you got the ball, son."

"I have the ball, sir," Alex said, laughing. It was the expression fighter jocks used in carrier landings to tell Flight Ops they were properly lined up on final approach.

"I got your joke, son. Mixing up metaphors, do it all the time, my wife says. Football and flying."

"Right."

"Glad we got that all straightened out," Tex said, leaning back and closing his eyes. He had that rare ability, when all about him were losing their heads, to nap. Alex Hawke used the flying time remaining trying to envision what kinds of hazards he might soon encounter trying to land four Black Widows on a mountaintop at 18,000 feet. He stopped counting at three.

The DSS pilots had nicknamed the new glider design Black Widow in memory of the legendary P-61. The reedlike glider's twin-barreled fuselage certainly recalled the World War II nightfighter, the P-61 Black Widow. The new high-altitude aircraft even had the red hourglass shape, identifying nature's deadliest spider, painted on its matte black belly. But, while vintage Black Widows were powerful, bulbous, muscular warplanes, bristling with weaponry, *Hawkeye* and her like had no weapons. No engines. Built of carbon fiber composite and thin everywhere the P-61 had been thick, she looked, Patterson said, "like a flying box built out of toothpicks."

Hawke's headphones crackled again.

"*Hawkeye, Hawkeye,* you got *Gabriel* upstairs," a voice said. "I have your LZ in visual contact. You're getting close. Glad as hell it's you landing that thing up there, not me. Over."

"Roger that, *Gabriel.* Appreciate your support as always," Hawke replied.

The ungainly E2-C Navy surveillance plane, mission code *Gabriel,* was monitoring the entire mission and sending a real-time video feed direct to Washington. Earlier, a small group gathered around a monitor at the White House had cheered when the four glider pilots had pulled their release knobs, cast off the towlines from the Navy STOLs and soared away over the range of misty blue mountains. Then they'd lapsed into subdued silence.

A very small number of those watching the White House monitors knew the fate of their country was very likely riding with the men inside those four Black Widows.

The silence in the Oval Office was broken when the quietly excited voice of one of the four pilots crackled over a set of speakers. "This is your captain speaking," the small group heard the pilot say. "Kindly put your seatbacks and tray tables in an upright position."

"Copy that, Skipper," came the laconic reply. "And in the unlikely event of a water landing, I reckon the cheeks of my ass will act as a flotation device?"

"Roger that," the pilot laughed.

"That would be Alex Hawke and Tex Patterson aboard *Hawkeye,* the lead plane," the president said, smiling grimly at the small gathering of people watching with him in the Oval Office. "*Hawkeye* will be first in."

Jack McAtee's eyes were glued to the screen. The tension in the room was more than palpable, it was excruciating.

"This is it, boys," the grim president told the vice president and his chief of staff. "This is the whole damn shooting match, right here."

So far, so good, Hawke thought, easing his stick forward an inch and getting his nose back below the horizon where it belonged. Of course, the method of getting *out* of a high-mountain hot zone would not be nearly so straightforward as getting in—but Hawke had enough on his mind at the moment to stuff those kinds of thoughts back into the semidistant recesses of his brain. He concentrated instead on the good news; uneven, mountainous terrain might shield their approach from visual and electronic monitoring.

"*FlyBaby . . . Widowmaker . . . Phantom,*" Hawke said. "This is *Hawkeye,* copy?"

"Roger, *Hawkeye*, *FlyBaby*'s right behind you, high, wide, and handsome," her skipper, a tough south Florida kid named Mario Mendoza, said. "Can't shake me with all those circus acrobatics."

"Copy that, *Hawkeye*, *Widowmaker* at your five." Jim Ferguson, Ferg, was a good old boy from West Texas, former crop duster and current knucklebuster. Tom Quick, the only non-DSS agent besides Hawke, was two seats behind him.

"That leaves you, *Phantom*," Hawke said. "Copy."

"Uh, roger, *Hawkeye*, *Phantom* copies," Ron Gidwitz, the skinny kid from the south side of Chicago who was flying *Phantom*, said. "We got, uh, got us a minor problem here, sir. Got a warning light lit up and . . . we, uh—"

"Talk to me, *Phantom*," Hawke said. A minute stretched out.

"Disregard, *Hawkeye*," Gidwitz finally said. "Warning light just went out. Some kind of electrical glitch. Over."

"Roger that, *Phantom*. *Hawkeye* over."

The flock of blackbirds flew onward, etching themselves against the bowl of the sky.

CHAPTER FORTY-EIGHT

Flight 77

Cherry Lansing could tell that the extreme hottie seated next to her in the window seat was never in this lifetime going to talk to her. Like, she straight up knew it. He had to be like one of the few remotely hot species she'd seen on this entire vacation. Oh, well. How cool could he be? He was reading the Bible, some foreign bible anyway. He did have an MP3 player, which was a good sign. But he'd tuned out, stuck his headphones on right after takeoff—which was, in her experience with boys, a bad sign. A-hole.

She squished the disgusting ham sandwich into a little ball, put it back in its nice little silver, as if, Styrofoam dish and stuffed it in the seat back in front of her, wondering what her parents were having for lunch up in first class. No wonder she was buggin'. It was so undemocratic, sticking her back here in the ghetto.

Then, when she dared, how dare you, to complain to her mother about how unfair it was, her mother goes getting all up in her business about how spoiled she was—like that was remotely true—so she'd gone into the ladies' room right next to the gate and fired up some chronic she'd bought off this cute street boy back in Sing-Song or Hong Kong, whatever. Really good leaf. She'd gotten baked.

"Hey," she said.

"Hello," he said back. Hello? Is that what he said? Hello? Not, yo, whasup? Like any normal person?

"Like my necklace? Bangin' rocks, huh? My name in lights. Got it in Singapore."

"What?"

Maybe he didn't speak good English. He looked like Middle Eastern or Asian or one of those. Short, dark, and handsome. Cherry flashed her namesake necklace at him again. She was totally iced out for this trip home. Asian bling from Sing-Sing. Couldn't wait to show the new crown jewels to all her hootchie friends back in Darien. Them and her baby daddy who she'd missed so much. Oh, well. It was only twelve hours to L.A. and then another five to New York and then an hour or so up the Merritt by limo to Darien—she pulled the airport book her mother'd bought her out of her bag and opened it. It was named after that famous artist Da Vinci but her mother told her it was about secret codes or something.

"You are interested in numerology?" the boy said, pulling his headphones off and looking at the book. College. Definitely college.

"What?" she said. Like she was annoyed at having her reading interrupted. Like she read books. As if.

"Numbers. Their hidden meanings."

"Oh. Yeah. Fascinating."

"Me, as well." He smiled. Nice grille. Straight and pearly. Big brown eyes. Long, long lashes.

"That's what this is about? Numbers? Jesus Christ. This is a *math* book?"

"It's what everything is about. Flight 77. You see? A mystical number. Powerful. Or, this row number we are this moment sitting in. It's 76. A very important number for you Americans, is it not?"

"76? You mean, like, the gas station? Or, what?"

He just looked at her and then went back to what her dad called the thousand-yard stare.

"My boyfriend gave me this book," she said quickly. "You should see him. What a babe. He looks exactly just like JFK. Identical."

"Which one?"

"Which one?"

"Yes. The president? Or, the airport?"

"*What?*"

The seat belt sign pinged off and the bitchy British Airways stewardess said in her bitchy British accent that they could get up if they wanted to but stay out of the aisle so they could get their crappy carts up and down and keep the belt fastened loosely when they were in their seats because there was some storm or other down in South China.

Get up but stay out of the aisles? Unfasten your seat belt but keep it fastened? Hello? Is this woman two toys short of a Happy Meal, or what?

"Excuse me, please," the hottie-tottie brown-eyed boy said, taking his cheesy plastic shaving kit out of his made-in-Taiwan special backpack. He turned his back and unzipped it like he didn't want her peeking and put his MP3 player inside it. As if she cared about what was in his stupid shaving kit. "I must use the restroom, please. Urgent."

Oh. Like she cared. He was going to shave? Brush his teeth? It was way more information than she needed. Why didn't he just say he was getting up? She'd use the restroom herself and fire up some more leaf but you couldn't even smoke weed in there anymore. She knew, believe me. She'd tried.

Urgent? What could be urgent? Yuk.

Flight 00

The minute Johnny Adare stepped out of the cockpit and into the upper galley with the little doctor in tow, everybody started calming down. It was the uniform, he guessed, and the famous Adare smile he'd inherited from his dad. He'd gotten laid with both so many times he couldn't remember. It had taken every ounce of self-control he had to stay away from the Bambah for the last three days. He'd watched the lassies land, climb on the buses, and head for the hotel. Not one of them much over twenty-five, none of them exactly drop-dead gorgeous, but what the hell. At any rate, they had not been chosen for their looks.

"Don't even think about it," Khalid had told him, the two of them standing by the hangar watching the stream of young women climb up the steps of the buses to the hotel. Yeah, yeah. So, he hadn't ever gone over to the hotel but that didn't mean he ever stopped thinking about it. Ever.

"Sorry 'bout the bumpy ride, ladies," Johnny said on the intercom phone in his pilot voice. One of the prerequisites for the Pasha's death squads was that they all had to speak perfect English, so that made it easier. He had a vague idea of what this was all about but he'd learned long ago that it was a lot easier not to ask a lot of questions. Just shut up and fly the bus, Johnny. He'd learned that lesson long ago from Khalid.

"Just a few potholes in the sky," he continued. "That's all. We'll be flying a little lower than usual for a while, until we get through this stuff, but it shouldn't be much longer. Then, we'll climb to our normal altitude. We're expecting a smooth ride to L.A. today. Everybody sit back and relax. As soon as we can, we'll be serving you a light breakfast. Thanks."

He sounded funny, he thought, hanging up. Ten years with the Pasha. Christ, he'd almost forgotten what a real airplane pilot sounded like.

He nodded thanks to the cabin crew, the Pasha's three beautiful private hostesses seated on fold-downs in the upper galley, two of whom he knew very well. He smiled at them, hung up the phone, and motioned Soong to follow him down the spiral stair. The abbreviated main cabin, six seats abreast, was full of some very nervous female passengers. But, just as it had topside, his appearance on the main deck had a calming effect. That, plus the fact that Khalid had disobeyed orders and turned all the interior lights on and climbed high enough so that the wave tops were no longer threatening to reach up and pull them from the sky.

He flashed his smile, pausing here and there with a brief word of reassurance. He and the doctor were headed all the way aft to what little of the Pasha's private quarters hadn't been turned into auxiliary fuel tanks. About halfway back, he noticed an overhead panel hanging down. The engineer who, at the last minute, had replaced all the oxygen canisters with the ones Soong had brought aboard in his black suitcase had neglected to fasten it properly. Johnny smiled at the three women as he reached over them to snap the panel back into place. They all smiled back. Hell, they were all smiling now.

He started aft. Where was that little bugger?

"Heads up! Doc! I thought you said it was important," he called to him. The guy was still leaning over to talk to one of the travel agents in a tight white Gap T-shirt. She did have a pair that would pop the pennies off a dead Irishman's eyelids, he'd noticed. The doc was practically drooling on her. Scratch the practically.

"Sorry, sorry," he said, and came toddling after Johnny, holding on to seat backs as if he really wanted to keep from falling into somebody's lap.

Adare closed the beautifully carved door behind them, leaned his back against it and shook out a cigarette. He snicked a match with his thumbnail and, for once, it worked. The warmly lit cabin was certainly stunning, but familiar. He'd spent a lot of time back here entertaining the hostesses when the boss wasn't aboard. He went to the liquor cabinet and poured himself two fingers of Jameson's Irish whiskey. His last official voyage. One for the road.

"So?" he said, rolling the delicious whiskey around in his mouth before swallowing. "What's up, Doc?"

The doctor was lighting up, too. He'd taken one of the Pasha's Baghdaddies from the inlaid box next to the leather sofa. His hand was shaking so badly he could barely hold the match.

"We must do an in-flight test," Doctor Soong puffed nervously. "Very important. Sooner the better."

"In-flight test?" Adare said. That didn't sound good. "You've got to be joking, man. A test of what?"

"No-no," Soong said, putting a bony little hand on his arm to reassure him. "Not to worry. Only the emergency oxygen system, Johnny."

Johnny?

Adare's right arm shot out and he slammed the man up against the bulkhead. His ribs felt like chicken bones. And Johnny felt like snapping them. This little shit had definitely gotten Johnny's Irish up.

"I want somebody to call me Johnny, I let them know. And you, you miserable little bugger, are at the very back of a very long fuckin' queue. You better tell me what the bloody hell you've done. Last-minute changes to my airplane, Doc, I don't like 'em."

"Please! The cockpit has its own oxygen supply, no?"

"What of it?"

"And, the cockpit itself has an airtight seal?"

"Jesus Christ, man! Are ye flat crazy? What have ye done to us?"

CHAPTER FORTY-NINE

The Emirate

Hawke looked at his watch, willing the red sweep second hand to slow down. Two days earlier, on a warm morning at No. 10 Downing Street, seventy-two hours had seemed reasonably sufficient. But now that he was down to five hours and counting, he wasn't at all sure. In exactly three hundred and forty minutes, the big B-52s arriving upstairs would open their bomb bays. If that wasn't exciting enough for you, you'd be seeing a goodly number of little blips on your radar screen. Incoming Tomahawk land attack missiles, fired from guided missile cruisers with the Nimitz Carrier Battle Group deployed in the Indian Ocean.

"We're five miles out," Hawke said into the lip-mike. "Squadron climb and maintain two-one-zero—over."

He eased back on the stick and watched his altimeter needle spin. At twenty-one thousand feet, he leveled off. The twin peaks of the mountain were now a whole lot closer. The extensive high-resolution recon photos hadn't lied. The mountain itself was a deep gentian blue against the pale sky. There, like a wound, was the designated LZ; a narrow strip of blinding white at the bottom of a ragged crevasse that cut between the mountain's peaks.

"Squadron . . . turn right to a heading of one-four-niner," Hawke said.

It was roughly one hundred feet across and a bit shy of two thousand feet long. Hawke lifted his visor and knuckled the stinging sweat out of his eyes. Christ. It was going to be a bit like setting down on Pimlico Road during a Saturday afternoon tornado without your wingtips clipping any double-decker buses.

He craned his head around and looked over his shoulder at Patterson. Tex was strapping a Velcro bandolier of four thirty-round mags over his white Kevlar vest. Checking all his gear. Hawke smiled. Tex would be carrying an HK MP-5 submachine gun as an added measure of security in addition to his trusty Colt .45 Peacemaker. The team had given a great deal of thought to weapons. Since they carried no personal effects and wore no insignia, no national or unit markings, it was decided it didn't matter what kind of firepower they brought along. Hell, you could buy anything at all on the open market these days.

Each man on this mission had signed on as a NOC. Spook-speak for "Not On Consular." It meant your name did not appear on any list, Consular or otherwise. If you got caught, you didn't exist. Hardly mattered. You were soon dead anyway.

"I just thought of something, Tex," Hawke said.

"I'm a little busy right now, Alex. What?"

"We're five minutes out and we're still alive."

"Good point. I've just spotted three radar domes. No Sammies. I guess these new-fangled jammer things work okay. Shoot, Hawkeye, in the early days we used to lose about a Widow or two a month, or pretty near."

"Most encouraging," Hawke said. He craned his head around, looking aft, making sure all his little ducks were in a row.

"Squadron turn right to zero-six-zero," Hawke said. "Form up. Stick to your predetermined order going in: *Hawkeye, Widowmaker, FlyBaby, Phantom.* Copy?"

"Dead last," *Phantom*'s ex-Marine pilot Ron Gidwitz said, laughing.

"Bad choice of words, Ronnie," Patterson said over the radio.

"Don't worry, *Phantom,* you're about to kick some serious ass! Semper Fi, man!" came the response from another aircraft.

Hawke recognized Tommy Quick's adrenaline-pumped voice. He was riding along with Ferguson in *Widowmaker*'s aftermost seat. A last-minute member of the team, Hawke had insisted the Army's former number-one sharpshooter would be a vital addition no matter how this all played out.

"Ron, you okay back there? Copy?" Patterson asked *Phantom*'s pilot, the concern in his voice obvious.

"Okay? I'm fuckin' fantastic!" Gidwitz replied. Hawke smiled at the reply. Patterson's Blue Mountain Boys did not need any more motivation. They were psyched. Gung ho.

"Cut the mike chat," Hawke said. "*Hawkeye* is going in." He flipped down his visor and focused every scintilla of his concentration on the narrow slash in the top of the mountain dead ahead.

Alex lined his nose up on the rocky leading edge of the crevasse. From here, the opening in the bloody thing looked to be about six inches wide and a foot long. To make it all the more interesting, the closer he flew to the sheer face of the mountain, the more unpredictable the winds got. The buffeting had increased dramatically in the last thirty seconds.

"Ride 'em, cowboy," Hawke said dryly. They were porpoising severely. Just keeping his spindly wings level was a full-time job.

"Man-oh-man," Patterson drawled, craning around Hawke's helmet for a first-hand look at the snow-scoured jaws of the approach. He'd seen pictures of where they were headed but they didn't do it justice. For one thing, it didn't look anywhere near close to wide enough to accommodate their wingspan. "You honestly believe you can thread this needle, Hawkeye?"

"Tell you something I've always wondered, Tex," Hawke said, struggling to control pitch, yaw, and roll, while maintaining his glide path. The delicate aircraft was being bounced all over the sky by strong cross-winds and hammered by wind shear.

"What's that, son?"

"I wonder how the bloody hell it's possible for a man to break a sweat when the temperature outside his window is –50 Fahrenheit."

"You, too, huh?" Tex said. "You plan to hit the brakes anytime soon?"

"Right about . . . now!"

Hawke hauled back on the dive brake handle with his left hand. He'd waited until the very last possible moment, then got the brakes wide open. The glider would now descend at the steepest possible glide slope. He needed a steep angle because of the short two-thousand-foot rollout, and he was coming in very hot because of the extreme altitude. Thin air. *Hawkeye* was dropping at 400 feet per minute. He eased the brakes and shot a glance at his yaw string. The two-inch-long string of red yarn attached to the leading edge of the canopy was a fail-safe aeronautic instrument invented by Wilbur Wright himself. It was now absolutely straight. The only way to fly.

"Final leg," Hawke announced matter-of-factly.

"Call the ball, son," Tex said.

"I have the ball, sir," Alex replied.

A second later, "Shit. Full dive brakes."

When Hawke realized he was too low instead of too high it was almost too late. The sudden downdraft had him going nose first into something big and hard that didn't move. He had instinctively closed the dive brakes, flared out, prayed, and waited for the crunch of impact. Later, he estimated his skids had cleared the rocky serrated outcropping by less than a foot. It was enough. He popped his twin drogue chutes and his nose came up and he scraped in over the rocks, hitting the snowfield dead center, neatly bisecting the hundred-foot-wide opening.

Once he was inside the shelter of the crevasse, the crosswind died abruptly and he got his tail skid down first, then the nose, and he steered with his rudder. He kept his wings level, skidded and bounced straight up the snowfield as planned, giving the three aircraft coming in behind him some operating room. Using backward stick motion, he managed to keep his tail down. Finally, he lowered the Widow's snow brakes and brought the plane to a stop.

Hawkeye was safely down. By a nose.

"That sure was exciting," Tex said as Alex popped the canopy release. The frigid air, gleaming with ice particles, was startling. Alex cleared the ice from his oxygen mask and looked back at Patterson. Each mask contained a lipmike so communication would be uninterrupted while on the mountain.

"Pretty good landing, son, considering," Tex added.

"Any landing you walk away from is a good landing," Hawke replied, aware of the cliché, finding it unavoidable under the extreme circumstances. Up here, the hackneyed old World War II sentiment was definitely true. He saw the mission time remaining on the digital readout of his instrument panel. He had one plane on the ground and three in the air. Five hours left on the clock. Even if everything from now on went like clockwork, the clock was fast becoming his mortal enemy.

And when had any mission anywhere ever gone like clockwork?

He unsnapped his quick-release harness, hoisted himself up, and swung his legs out over the side of the cockpit. It was only a four-foot drop, but he sank up to his knees in soft snow. The cold took his breath away. So did the view from one notch below the top of the world; his eyes took in the vast sweep of valley far below, stretching away beneath a cobalt blue sky. He reached up to give Tex a hand, his eyes riveted on *Widowmaker*'s approach.

Ferguson was emulating Hawke's successful glide path perfectly, but wisely kept his nose a bit higher and compensated for the last-second wind shear at the mouth of the crevasse. His landing was a thing of beauty; the second Black Widow got her skids down, rushed towards Hawke, twin white drogue chutes billowing out behind her, spraying snow to either side of her nose skid. She slewed to a stop two hundred feet shy of *Hawkeye.* Hawke gave Ferg and Quick a big thumbs-up, then he and Patterson rapidly walked to the rear of the port fuselage and opened the cargo doors. Inside the twin holds on each Widow was everything one might need for an armed assault on an impregnable fortress.

"I don't like the way Ron sounded up there," Patterson said, hurriedly fastening a web belt around his waist. "Too giddy, you ask me." From each man's belt hung assorted frag and flash-bang grenades to both kill and disorient the enemy. Each two-man team would carry the same weapons. Heckler & Koch MP-5 submachine guns, which could be fitted with grenade launchers, and on their hips, the new HK USP .45 pistol with sound suppressor.

"Sounded okay to me. I thought that was just Ron's game voice," Hawke said, wincing as the bitterly cold air seared his lungs. He'd removed the onboard oxygen mask and tossed it back into his seat. His assault and rescue team had spent the last thirty hours at a 12,000-foot base camp. Even though he was somewhat acclimated, it was painful to breathe at 18,000.

"No," Tex said, "definitely not Iceman's game voice." Gidwitz's street nickname back home on the south side of Chicago was "Iceman."

"Hypoxia?" Alex asked, concerned now. At 18,000 feet, oxygen deprivation could be a killer. You got euphoric, cocky, belligerent. A mean drunk. The high-altitude glider Black Widow had internal oxygen for just that reason. *Phantom* had reported a problem earlier, a warning light, then told Hawke to disregard the report. Hawke turned and took a long hard look at *Phantom*'s approach. She was definitely rocking and rolling but there was so much turbulence and shear out there, it was damn near impossible to spot trouble.

His overall pitch and glide level looked pretty good to Hawke's eye. He said, "I don't know, Tex. Anybody crazy enough to land an airplane up here is out of his mind to begin with. What would you look for?"

"Yeah, I reckon," Tex said, eyeing Gidwitz's approach, clearly not reassured. "Let's move it."

First things first. They grabbed two of the portable oxygen and communications units stowed inside the starboard-side hold and strapped them on, fitting the face masks over mouth and nose and jamming the new cylinders onto their regulators. At this altitude, there was sufficient oxygen but insufficient pressure to force that oxygen into your bloodstream. Unless you were fully acclimated, a few minutes without oxygen up here, you started to think you could fly.

FlyBaby was next, and again, the landing was flawless. Mendoza popped his drogue chutes and slid up right behind *Widowmaker*. Three ducks in a nice neat row, and one more on the way. *Phantom* was a quarter of a mile out and looking reasonably good. Hawke zipped up his white-camo thermal outerwear and shouldered into the MP-5 submachine gun, the strap over his shoulder. The gun could be fitted with HK's 40mm grenade launcher and had the pre-ban high-capacity fifteen-round magazines. Time to roll. He'd cleared the chamber of the HK and was checking the mag when he heard something he didn't like at all. He looked up just in time to see Ron Gidwitz and Ian

CHAPTER FIFTY

Inside the catacombs, you could see your breath. You could feel the damp stone beneath your feet begin to climb your bones. She shivered, wrapping her fur-lined silks more tightly about her as she ran. She raced past dark tombs and rooms that could still knife cold fear into her heart. She'd been seven years old when she'd first set foot in this very passageway. She still awoke some nights in a terror of what she'd seen at the very end of it.

In the early seventies, her father, the Emir, commenced construction of a new mountain fortress atop the ruins of a fourteenth-century Moorish fortification. Workers had uncovered a vast network of tunnels and tombs and burial vaults deep inside the mountain. Yasmin had accompanied her father the first time he explored the honeycomb, a small girl following his flickering torch through the endless confusion of dripping and dank passageways.

They'd come at last upon a vast vault, the torchlight suddenly picking out an entire wall of the ancient dead, their eyeless sockets, lipless grins and twisted claws seeming to beckon her forward. *Join us!* She screamed and ran, finally rushing into the arms of her mother who, sensibly, was waiting at the entrance to the tombs. Father says it's the Kingdom of Lost Souls, she'd cried to her mother. Long afterwards, her father would laugh at her childish fears, recounting the story with relish throughout her childhood. As if it was amusing to be afraid of death.

Many of the underground vaults she now hurried past made ideal hiding for the caches of gold and weapons the Emir and her husband were amassing for the coming wars with the infidels. Legions of political enemies were locked away in these catacombs. Many went insane under torture here, and many died or were simply forgotten.

Her father had made her a wedding gift of the present fortress. She'd named it the Blue Palace for the color of its stone. The young bride had immediately demanded the tombs be sealed, but her handsome young husband, Snay bin Wazir, had rescinded that decree. He would find many uses for the underground world, he had assured her. New horrors now occurred beneath her home. She looked but did not see.

Countless innocents had died where she now tred, Yasmin thought, as she hurried through the slimy passages, the grey stone glistening in the light of her torch. But no more. It was time for it all to stop. She herself would end it, or die trying. She'd had another dream the night before. A dream in which she herself wielded the sword of Fudo Myo-o, the god whom Ichi-san called King of Light; she had the power to stop this nightmare. Awaking, she knew she could not act alone. Some in the palace, given the opportunity, would rise up in her defense. But, there was one man whom she could trust completely. She knew where she would find him and she hurried there now.

An occasional oil lamp or guttering candle mounted on the jagged walls of the Kingdom lit the way. Passing guards dropped to the stone, prostrating themselves before her. Rats scurried before her and disappeared like the countless lost souls who had suffered and died in this dismal hell.

No more.

Word had just reached Yasmin that strange black aircraft had been spotted attempting to land atop the Blue Mountain. One plane had crashed, but there were thought to be survivors. It was, the captain of the house guards assured her, most probably a rescue party sent in search of the imprisoned American. It was insane, he laughed. But, nevertheless, quite interesting. In all these many years, no one had ever attempted anything quite so daring or quite so stupid.

Her husband, who had just returned from Suva Island, was also vastly amused by the news of the intrusion. He had just ordered a patrol outside the walls to find and capture the interlopers. Anyone foolish enough to try and land an airplane atop the Blue Mountain was sure to provide him a delightful afternoon's entertainment.

He was ignoring her, busily making his plans for the day's sumo celebration when his wife slipped away.

She arrived at the isolated cellblock vault where the American had been held since his abduction ten days earlier. The duty guard, who had passed food to the American for her and smuggled out his letter, hit the switch that opened the electric security door. Inside one of the dim cells, she could hear Ichi-san speaking softly to the American. Entering the cell, a silent scream caught in her throat.

"The honor in death—the death of honored ancestors—the true and solitary path of all warriors—" Ichi-san was whispering to the pale American kneeling before him on the stone floor. He was gently stroking the man's head, offering him encouragement. The man's frail body wore the scars of recent beatings. His head was bowed and he held the hilt of Ichi-san's Samurai sword with both hands, the trembling tip of the blade already piercing the skin of his emaciated belly. She knew what this was called. In his desperation, Ichi-san had spoken its name often enough.

Hara-kiri.

"Stop!" Yasmin cried. "You cannot do this!"

The American slowly raised his head and looked up at her. His eyes looked like holes in a mask.

"Why?" he croaked, his parched lips barely moving. His hollow eyes were shining with tears. No food, no water, no sleep. He was broken, but he had not given up whatever it was they'd wanted. Had he, he'd be dead.

"Yes," the sumo agreed softly. "Why? Bin Wazir's method will be far less merciful than the blade of the Samurai."

"If you do this now, others will die in vain."

"Yasmin," Ichi-san said. "I do not understand."

"Someone has dared to come here to save him," she said. "Unlike all the others who have died here—this man has not been forgotten."

She fell to her knees beside the shaking prisoner and spoke, the words tumbling out in a rush. "Strange black aircraft have landed atop the mountain. It is believed that men have come for you. Put their lives at risk for your sake. My husband knows. He will surely find them and put them to death. He already intends to make sport of it. In the *dohyo* of the sumos."

"You risk your life coming here," Ichi-san said to her.

"I've had enough of this."

"What can we do, Yasmin?" the sumo asked.

"Can he walk?" she asked. "His feet look—"

"Yes," Ichi-san replied. "Barely."

She pulled the black pajamas of a houseboy from the folds of her silks.

"Here. Dress him in this. And wrap his head in this. And bring that sword. If we are lucky, we will all live long enough to put it to good use."

The sumo looked at Yasmin and smiled. He reached out his hand and stroked her cheek, flushed pink with the running and the damp cold here inside the mountain.

"No doubt. No confusion. No fear," he said to her, his eyes alight for the first time since she'd met him. "We are ready now."

"Yes, Ichi-san, I believe we are."

"We must not be seen together. He is at the *dohyo*, preparing for the ceremony. I must go there now."

Yasmin caught his hand at her cheek and squeezed it.

"The harmonization of human beings," Ichi-san said, smiling at her, "and, the timing of heaven."

CHAPTER FIFTY-ONE

Ron Gidwitz and Ian Wagstaff, the squad's radioman, had escaped from the remains of *Phantom* by sheer luck and good design. She'd sheared off both wings in the crash landing; the weight of the snow had simply ripped them away from the fuselage. But then the monocoque egg-shaped cockpit had detached, as it had been engineered to do, hit a buried slope and gone airborne. It hit the snow once more and skidded directly towards Hawke and Patterson, snow parting in front of the nose skid like a bow wake thrown to either side.

"Jump!" Hawke screamed and he and Patterson dove out of its path. The oblong black egg bounced once again and soared directly over the head of Alexander Hawke, who stared up in amazement as the carbon fiber module containing two good men disappeared over a sheer rock face.

"Good God," Hawke said.

"Designed that way," Patterson shouted over his shoulder, making his way up to the edge of the cliff face. "Modular. Lose the plane, keep the pilots. That's the idea, anyway. We'll soon see."

Hawke, slogging as fast as he could through knee-deep snow, rushed up to join Patterson on the rocky ledge. He was expecting the worst, splintered black shards and broken bodies on the rocks far below. Arriving at the top, he found himself perched, not on the edge of nowhere, but on a simple ledge. Thirty feet below him, down an angled black ice incline, another, larger, snow-covered ledge projected out into thin air. There, he and Patterson first saw the upturned canopy dish lying in the snow about ten feet from the cockpit. The black plastic pod looked as if it had been split open with a hammer. Hawke's face flooded with relief.

Gidwitz and Wagstaff were rolling in the snow, wrestling, and laughing like a pair of punch-drunk palookas. They weren't dead, just drunk, victims of altitude sickness.

"Hypoxia," Hawke said. "You were right."

Phantom's internal systems had malfunctioned. Oxygen deprivation in the cockpit had sent the two DSS rangers into disoriented euphoria that no doubt caused the crash. But, thanks to the Widow's reinforced cockpit module, they were still alive.

Hawke leapt off the edge, landed hard on his butt, and slid easily feet-first down the black-ice face to the bottom. Patterson followed seconds later. Tex removed two gold foil survival suits from his backpack and managed to convince the two giddy men to climb inside. Wagstaff, the communications specialist known traditionally as Sparky, kept trying to tell him a joke about a Texan who owned a pickle factory. Tex finally shut him up and managed to strap emergency oxygen masks over both their faces. He turned to Hawke.

"It'll take at least half an hour before they're in any condition to move around. At least."

"We don't have that long, Pards," Hawke said, flick-

ing his HK machine gun to full auto. Both men turned
to see what was making all the noise.

Emerging from a wide crack in the mountain was a
Hagglund BV 206 all-terrain tracked vehicle. As it rumbled into the open, Hawke saw that it was towing a
tracked troop carrier. The military ATV was built in
the UK for NATO's Rapid Reaction Force, but that
wasn't any NATO insignia painted on the door of the
all-white vehicle. It was a symbol Hawke had seen
before. An upraised sword in a bloody hand. On the
roof, a man behind a swivel-mounted .50-cal. machine
gun. Without warning, the man atop the vehicle
opened up, stitching the snow, kicking up powder,
stopping just short of Alex Hawke.

He and Patterson lowered their weapons.

The double doors at the rear of the troop carrier
flew open and ten armed guards poured out, leaping to
the ground. Two guards immediately opened fire,
squeezing off long, high bursts over their heads; the
rounds splintered rock and ice on the cliff face above,
showering it down on Hawke, Patterson and the two
sick men on the ground. In seconds, the guards had
formed a semicircle around them.

"Got the drop on us, Pards," said Tex out of the
corner of his mouth.

"Yeah, but here's the good news," Hawke said.

"I'm waiting, Hawkeye."

"They take us prisoner in that thing, we don't have
to worry about how to blast our way inside an impregnable fortress anymore. Classic Trojan Horse. Works
every time."

"Yup. Good point, Sunshine. I was kinda hoping
we'd catch a break just like this."

A grinning guard suddenly stepped forward and jabbed the muzzle of his Kalashnikov into Hawke's belly. Hawke staggered backwards against the ice face, collapsing to the snow, feigning pain. Patterson lunged for the man who'd done it, but nine AKs swung in his direction. Hawke had seen the blow coming in the man's eyes and so was ready for it. He'd also caught a glint of light from the cliff above out of the corner of his eye. Now it was gone. With any luck at all, the rest of the team above had not been spotted.

The same guard with the loopy grin came over and kicked Hawke brutally in the ribs with his steel-toed boot. Then stood over him, smiling. Hawke twisted away in the snow, rolling to avoid the next blow to his ribs, gaining precious seconds, talking softly into his lipmike as he moved. He no longer had to feign any pain. His left side was on fire.

"Hey, Tommy," Hawke whispered, "you up there?"

"Got you covered, Skipper," the sniper Tom Quick replied. "In the rocks above and behind, on your left, sir."

The guard advanced and kicked Hawke again, even more viciously. The pain was searing and it took his breath away. This guy was starting to seriously piss him off.

"Got a shot, Tommy?" Hawke managed.

"Oh, yeah."

"Take it."

A neat red hole instantly appeared between the eyes of the grinning man standing over Hawke.

"Old pals of Mr. bin Wazir," Hawke said, smiling up at the guard who was dead on his feet but didn't realize it yet. "We understand he lives nearby. Thought we'd drop in."

Before anyone else could react, Tom Quick took out the tango with the .50-cal on the roof of the Hagglund, and then dropped two more on the ground with clean head shots. Hawke got to his feet, bringing up the HK as he did, moving to give Patterson a clear field of fire as well.

Hawke heard a burst from a weapon on his left, swung instantly that way and fired. His rounds caught the man in the throat. He dropped his weapon and raised both hands to the wound, unable to stop the geyser of bright arterial blood which erupted. The man collapsed in a heap in the blood-soaked snow.

Five of the six remaining guards, unaccustomed to armed resistance, turned to run for their vehicle. All five died on their feet in less than ten seconds, victims of Hawke, Patterson, and the silent but deadly sniper above. Quick had acquired the new lightweight HK 7.62 sniper rifle for the mission. So far, he had no complaints. The sixth guard, spotting Quick on the edge of the overhang, raised his automatic to return fire. Before he could squeeze off a burst, Hawke hit him low, across the knees, and sent him sprawling in the snow. In an instant Hawke was all over him, ignoring his own pain, the snout of his weapon jammed up under the guard's chin.

He looked into the terrified boy's eyes and asked, "Do you want to live? Nod yes if you speak English."

"Yes—"

"Name!"

"Rashid—"

"Get on your feet, Rashid. I'm requisitioning your vehicle. Sorry. Force majeure. You're driving."

"Good work, Pards," Patterson said. "Your friend

Mr. Quick up there makes a fine addition to the squad."

"Still, we do appear to have lost the element of surprise—*Widowmaker, FlyBaby,* you guys get down here on the double. We're taking this ATV inside the Pasha's palazzo. Copy?"

"On our way, skipper."

They loaded Gidwitz and Wagstaff into the troop transport. The two men were still groggy, but coming around courtesy of the oxygen. Mendoza and the rest of the team climbed inside the carrier as well, except for Hawke and Patterson, who would ride up front with the kid driving the snow-cab. Quick would be riding up on the roof, manning the .50-cal.

Hawke looked at his watch. Christ. It would be a very close thing. He had less than eighty minutes to find Kelly, extract vital information from bin Wazir, and get the hell out of there before the B-52s showed up and the big bunker-buster bombs started falling. And the Tomahawks came cruising.

CHAPTER FIFTY-TWO

Flight 00

Johnny Adare stared at the man called Poison Ivy in amazement. They were toe-to-toe in the sitting room aboard the Pasha's 747-400, special edition. The little cretin I.V. Soong was standing before him waving a wad of U.S. dollars in his face. One hundred thousand of them, to be exact. First the guy says he wants to test the aircraft's emergency oxygen system, and then asks, by the way, is the cockpit sealed? Adare immediately grabbed the intercom phone to call Khalid up in the cockpit.

Johnny had started to punch in the cockpit code, but the wiry little fellow grabbed his wrist.

"No!" Soong shouted. "Put it down. You will ruin everything. Just listen for one moment. If you don't like what you hear, then call the cockpit. Okay? Please!"

That's when he opened up the smaller of the two shiny black suitcases he'd stowed under the Pasha's fancy leather sofa. The big one, now empty, had held all the replacement oxygen canisters. This smaller one was full of cash. Johnny eyeballed it carefully. If each wad was U.S. fifty grand, there had to be a million quid in there. A little less than one and a half million dollars.

Just the bloody sight of so much cash in one place was enough to make Johnny quietly replace the receiver.

The sun came out on Dr. Soong's face once more.

"Let's have a drink, shall we?" Soong said. "Another whiskey? I may join you. My nerves, you see. Rough flight. Shaky."

Johnny collapsed into the big leather armchair the Pasha used when he was on the phone. Soong went to the bar and poured them each a tumbler of Jameson's. He handed one to Johnny, took a healthy swig of his own, and sat carefully on the edge of the sofa.

"Good, good," he exclaimed in his high-pitched voice. "A toast! To your new life as a rich man, Captain Adare."

"Tell me what's in the canisters, Doc."

"It is an—experiment—I am conducting, sir. A test."

"I ain't a fucking test pilot, Doc. And I don't do fucking experiments. Eight miles up, anyway."

"Ah! Is a good one! No, you don't have to do anything. You know about what you were originally supposed to be carrying aboard this plane? Something called a Pigskin?"

"Got a rough idea. I don't want to know."

"There was a problem with them. Very unstable. Be glad I did not allow them to be loaded on your airplane, believe me, Johnny. Very lucky. My god."

"I'm a lucky man," Adare said, deciding to let the "Johnny" pass for now. "What's in the bloody canisters?"

"I am coming to this. Please. How much is the Pasha paying you for this trip?"

"Two hundred fifty grand. Free and clear."

"Tsk-tsk. So unfair."

"What?"

"Khalid is getting one million."

"What? You're bloody lying!"

"Shh! Calm yourself, Johnny. It's not a problem."

"The bastard's getting a million?" Johnny said, swallowing his whiskey. "But he tells me he's getting a quarter of that. Son of a bitch! Ten years we're flying together and our last job for that fat bastard bin Wazir, he thinks he can screw me over?"

"Grossly unjust! This is why I picked you, Johnny. To have this little chat back here. I pretended fear back in the cockpit so Khalid would not suspect. See?"

"Yeah? Keep talking. So this—experiment—why not just tell Khalid about it? Why pick me?"

"Because I know Khalid's reputation. By the book. Always by the book. Veddy, veddy British. So that's why I asked for a private word with you. You are a most reasonable and intelligent man with whom I can do business."

"And if I said no?"

"I did my research, Johnny. A wife. A sick daughter. No pension. So. A million dollars cash? You saying no never occurred to me. You ask what is in my canisters, I will tell you. It is like I said, an experiment. I am trying out a new drug."

"A drug."

"Yes," Soong said, lying smoothly, and unceasingly amazed at the easy dexterity of his mind. "A mind-control substance. A hypnotic. It will enable me to have the power of autosuggestion over the subjects of my experiment. I am just trying it out. Bin Wazir has generously allowed me to conduct this test on your airplane to America."

"Mind control, eh? Autosuggestion? Christ. I could see the possibilities in that."

"Yes, yes! Very exciting. I know what you mean! Of course, what the Pasha has in mind for these young women is something much more—serious."

Adare went to the bar and returned with the half-full liter of whiskey. He refilled both their glasses—visions of an army of beautiful zombies wandering around America blowing up nuclear power stations—splashing some on the table. He was staring at the contents of the opened suitcase.

"A million dollars. You're serious?"

"All yours. Count it out for yourself. I trust you."

"Don't have to ask me twice," Adare said, kneeling beside the opened suitcase. "What do I have to do, Doc?"

"Very simple, Johnny. We return now to the cockpit. All you say about our conversation is that there is no problem. Much ado about nothing. The stupid little air-sick wog, whatever. At some point, certainly in the next hour or so, Khalid will need to leave the cockpit to relieve himself. When he does, you and I put our cockpit masks on. Then you seal the cockpit and activate the emergency oxygen in the main cabin. The masks all drop down. Go on the intercom and say there has been a sudden loss of cabin pressure. Inform everyone to stay calm, fit the masks over their faces, and breathe normally."

"That's it?"

"That's it."

"What about Khalid? Comes out of the head and sees all those goddamn masks hanging down? He'll fucking kill me."

"Khalid? He is no problem, Johnny, trust me. I have planned this operation in great detail. Yes, I had a little last-minute problem with the end product to be delivered but it's nothing you cannot handle. You are my man. So simple. We have our scheduled rendezvous over the Pacific and—boom—and Johnny lands in L.A. and Johnny walks away with one million dollars."

Johnny let out a long, low whistle. A bloody millionaire. He could see it, the whole thing. He'd never take any more crap from bin Wazir, his ex-buddy Khalid, anybody. He could even see himself walking away with a lot more than a million. There was almost two million in Soong's black case. What was he going to do if Johnny just picked it up and walked off the plane? Call the cops? He'd be checking into the Beverly Hills Hotel tonight, not that cheesy dump on La Cienega!

He looked at his new best friend Soong and grinned, already tasting his first martinis in the Polo Lounge.

"Locked up with four hundred women on autopilot?" he said. "I'm not sure I wouldn't want to trade places with Khalid."

Poison Ivy laughed so hard Johnny thought he was going to pee in his britches. He stood up and polished off the Jameson's remaining in his glass. There was an old overnight bag of the Pasha's in the head. Vintage Louis Vuitton, cost more than his current salary. He retrieved it and stuffed it with the money, throwing in a couple of extra wads, what the hell. It was all his now anyway.

Flight 77

Cherry scootched her knees over so the hottie-tottie could climb over her and slide his cute little bootie into his seat by the window.

Whatever was so "urgent" had taken old Brown Eyes over half an hour. She'd started to wonder if he'd gotten sucked down the toilet. Laugh. She'd heard it happened to pets and babies all the time. Oops! Sorry, Junior! Bombs away! Anyway, her philosophy on the whole airplane bathroom issue could be explained in three little letters. NPR. No. Public. Restrooms. Except in extreme situations, thank you very much.

They had finally started the movie, which was good. *Clueless,* one of her all-time faves. Leave it to British Airways to show a zillion-year-old movie that everyone on the entire planet had seen a thousand times. Everybody had lowered their shades and the lights were down. She'd been kinda half-watching, half-listening to her headphones (like she didn't know this whole movie by heart) and half-hoping the brown-eyed wonder would be just a teensie bit—friendlier—now that he was back from doing his, you'll pardon the expression, business.

Dream on, Cherry.

"Hi. Everything come out okay?" Omigod, had she really said that? Didn't matter. He hadn't even heard her. You could talk to a tree or a dog and have a far more interesting conversation.

"Hello? Anybody home?"

Nada.

"I said, hi. Whassup?"

Didn't even look at her. Hey, don't wanna talk, that's cool. He had his cheeseball Taiwanese shaving kit perched on his knees. She thought the MP3 player was coming out again and the earphones, but, uh-uh, he just sat there staring straight ahead holding his stupid dopp kit with both hands.

"Hey. You. Foreign person. What ya got in there? A bomb?"

Nothing. What a nutball.

Staring into space. Like she didn't even exist. Asshole. After a while she just spaced. He was talking now; not to her but to himself. Whispering like, repeating something she couldn't hear over and over. She put her seat all the way back and scrunched the crappy cardboard pillow into a little ball under her head.

She must have zonked out because when she opened her eyes, *Clueless* was over, and they were now showing an old episode of *Friends*. Gameboy, right in front of her, was now standing up in his seat, facing her, smiling, with his thumb in his mouth. Cute kid, actually. Curly blond bangs on his forehead, big blue eyes. Sparkly. She was sorry she'd kicked his seat back earlier. Larry of Arabia by the window was still at it, whispering to himself. Only now he'd put his shade up and was staring out at something. Like there was really something to see up here. Like, how do you say "lame" in your language?

What the hell was he looking for? That hole in the ozone maybe.

"You are so *whack*," she said to his back and then she floated back to la-la land and dreamed of her sweet boo baby back in deepest darkest Connecticut.

Hey, she thought just before she fell asleep, what if she *was* pregnant? Would that be so bad? Maybe she'd have a kid cute as Gameboy.

CHAPTER FIFTY-THREE

The Emirate

It was cramped up front. The terrified kid Rashid driving, Hawke in the middle, Patterson on the door. Both men were wearing Type 3 Kevlar body armor, but Alex was strongly considering removing his because of the painful injuries to his ribs. The entire team wore the same armor, plus white balaclavas to protect their heads. Hawke had the muzzle of his USP .45 pistol wedged between two of the driver's ribs. They'd gotten the Hagglund ATV turned around and were retracing its fresh tracks in the snow along the shoulder of a ridge, assuming they would lead them back to the mountain fortress built into the south side of the lower peak.

The .50-cal mounted above him on the roof started chattering before Hawke could see what Quick was shooting at. They came over a rise and he saw the target just below. A tracked Soviet Spetsnaz-style BTR-60 armored personnel carrier and twenty mountain troops all clad in white. The armored vehicle had just finished clanking across a small arched steel bridge which spanned a crevasse maybe sixty feet across. Beyond the bridge, their destination. A whirling red light marked the opening of a tunnel leading inside the mountain. Somebody inside that mountain had heard the shooting and sent this second war party out to see what was going on.

Quick's .50 rattled again, expended brass cartridge cases pinging off the roof. Now this mountain division knew they had unwelcome guests.

"Don't stop!" Hawke yelled at Rashid. "No matter what! Do, and you're dead."

Quick's fire was rapid and lethal. The troops, or what was left of them, had been caught completely unaware. They scattered, diving behind snow banks or the rocks on either side of the steel bridge. The return fire was sporadic and for the most part inaccurate, but a few rounds were surely sizzling around Quick, who was exposed up on the roof. And it was only a matter of seconds before that armored carrier opened up on them. Luckily, Patterson had fitted the .40mm grenade launcher to the muzzle of his HK machine gun. The rooftop .50 was useless against the heavily clad Russian-made vehicle.

Without saying a word, Tex opened his door, swung it outward, and climbed out onto the step-up bar mounted beneath the doorsill. He hung on to the windscreen with one hand and tried to get a bead on the carrier through the open window.

"You got this bastard?" Hawke yelled at him. The troop carrier was getting dangerously close.

"Yeah, Pards, I got this sumbitch!"

Tex fired. There was a whoosh and a white vapor trail and suddenly the carrier's ugly snout exploded and was engulfed in flames. It veered left and stopped, clearing the way to the snow-covered bridge. Then the carrier's gas tank went up with a roar, putting a fiery end to everybody inside. There wasn't much time for a victory celebration.

The Hagglund's windscreen suddenly exploded into a thousand pieces. They were taking heavy fire from the left.

"Go! Go!" Hawke screamed at Rashid. He was leaning across the boy, firing his .45 pistol out the driver's window. He saw two drop and kept firing. Maybe not hitting many hostiles, but keeping up appearances. Unlike their dead comrades on the ground behind him, Hawke thought, these troops meant business. The palace guards, no doubt. Fiercely loyal, fight-to-the-death types. The only way to do this was just blow right by any resistance and get inside that tunnel. Thank God he had Quick on the rooftop fifty and Tex riding shotgun.

Seconds before they reached the bridge, Rashid screamed something in Arabic and yanked the wheel hard right, locking it. Hawke thought he'd taken a bullet but no, the kid was just trying to kill them all. The ATV veered sharply right of the bridge and plowed through a snowbank, accelerating toward the yawning black emptiness of the bottomless crevasse. They were going over an edge where the black ice of the mountain plateau disappeared into nothingness.

"Jump! Now!" Hawke screamed at Patterson, who was still hanging out the open door. "You, too, Tommy!" It was their only chance. He himself was locked in a desperate struggle with the boy for control of the wheel. He smashed his pistol against Rashid's hand on the wheel, but the kid would not let go. Hawke was desperately stabbing at the brake pedal with his left foot. The Hagglund fishtailed, slowing, for he'd finally found the brakes, but it was still headed, skidding wildly now, out of control, straight for the precipice. The vehicle's tracks finally stopped, but not the forward momentum.

It was too late.

The bottom fell out of Alex's stomach as the cab lurched over the edge and dropped into space. Hawke and the boy were thrown forward against the empty windscreen frame. The crazily spinning view below was sickening. A ten-thousand-foot drop into nowhere. There was a screeching metal sound and the cab bounced against the face of the crevasse and jerked to a stop, suspended in nothingness. Hawke remained completely still, his heart pounding, and did nothing for a second, willing himself not to breathe or move a muscle.

He felt the vehicle's weight shift. Tom Quick was somehow still on the roof, most likely clinging to the base of the .50-caliber machine gun though he couldn't see him. Where the hell was Patterson? Had he jumped in time? The door was still attached, at least the small part of it he could see, but it was hanging down at a weird angle.

He knew instinctively what had happened. They were hanging by a thread. The cab itself had gone over the edge but not the troop carrier they were towing. The brakes had slowed them just enough to prevent the entire rig from going over the side. Only the weight of the carrier up on the ledge, and the men inside it, stood between him and the abyss. Without even breathing, he craned his head around and looked up through the cab's rear window. The carrier was up there, all right, tracks perched out over the lip of icy rock. He could hear no automatic fire. It was dead still except for the wind whistling through the cab.

That's when he saw Patterson's bloody hand appear. He hadn't jumped, he was still clinging to the dangling doorframe. Somehow, Tex had reached up and grabbed a visible section of the door. The fingers were clawing at the metal, the joints showing white with strain.

"Hey, Pards," he heard the cracked voice below say, "gimme a hand, here, willya?"

"Hold on!" Hawke shouted. Hawke knew he had only one chance and he had to take it now. He hooked his left foot up under the dashboard and dove for the hand. The cab lurched sickeningly over to the right with his weight shift, the metal door Tex hung from banging against the rock face. Christ. He had one shot here. Hawke shot his right arm out and lunged for Texas Patterson's hand. A fraction of a second more and he might have grabbed it. He watched in horror as five bloody fingers peeled away from the frame one at a time and disappeared before he could reach them.

Tex didn't scream going down.

"Jesus Christ," Hawke whispered, his breath ragged. He used his foot to haul himself back to the center of the seat and the cab swung back, grinding against the ice. Hawke slowly craned his head around and stared at the ashen-faced Rashid. "You bloody bastard," he said to the kid. "Goddamn you to hell for what you did."

Rashid had lost it. He was wide-eyed, staring down through the windscreen at the bottomless gorge below, taking rapid, shallow breaths. Watching Tex plunge ten thousand feet had taken a good deal of the religious fervor out of the holy warrior. Hawke briefly considered two options and opted for his second idea.

"Get out," he said.

The kid stared at him, his eyes unseeing, too scared to understand what Hawke had said, perhaps. Vocal cords paralyzed with fear.

Hawke, barely keeping his emotions under control now, spoke.

"You wanted to go to Paradise? You're looking at it."

"Please—"

"Now! Get the hell out."

Without waiting for a reply, Hawke reached gingerly across Rashid's chest and unlatched the driver's door. The cab had ended up tilted just enough to the driver's side that gravity did the job for him. Rashid screamed and reached out for something, anything to hold on to, but all he got was a fistful of air. He slid straight out and down into oblivion. He fell so far, Hawke lost sight of him. He took a deep breath, said a silent farewell prayer for Tex, and weighed his options.

He noticed the cab had shifted slightly back toward an even keel with the sudden loss of weight on the driver's side. Good. But now he could see one of Quick's bloody boots dangling below the windscreen. Bad.

"Tommy?" Hawke said into his mike, praying they could still communicate.

"Jesus Christ," Quick said, his voice quaking.

"Yeah. I know. Just hold on."

"Oh, God, Skipper. I—I think my hand is broke. I'm having a hard time holding—"

"Just don't move, Tommy. You just hang on, I'm going to get us out of this. *Widowmaker? FlyBaby?* Copy?"

"Copy," was the terse, one-word reply from one of his guys still inside the troop carrier precariously balanced up on the ledge.

"Everybody all right up there?" Hawke asked.

"We're all afraid to move, sir," Gidwitz said. "Weight shift."

"Yeah. Probably wise. This situation is a bit iffy. Can you see anything up there?"

"We've got the rear doors cracked. Tangos are approaching. Cautious, but here they come."

"Listen carefully," Hawke said. "You've got mountaineering equipment in that thing, I saw it. Nylon lines, grapnels, carabiners. Secure one end of a line somewhere solid inside. Anything seriously bolted down. Do it now. Then, two guys go out the door, one high, one low. Start shooting as you go out. No full auto. Three-round bursts and make them count, save your mags. Everybody still in the truck covers the third guy who goes out two seconds later with the bitter end of the line, heads straight for the steel bridge and takes two wraps around the rail. Got that?"

Hawke heard a sharp grinding, screeching sound above him. The cab dropped, a stomach-turning foot or so, maybe more, and jerked to a stop. A hard rain of rock and ice from above clattered on the body of the cab. Then it stopped. Nobody said anything.

"Uh, roger that last, Skipper," Gidwitz said, finally breaking the tense silence. "Line is already secure here inside the carrier. Ring bolt in the floor. Taking it out myself. What about the loss of ballast weight when we bolt out of—"

"I can't blame you if I'm dead, now, can I? It's all we've got, Ronnie. Ready?"

"Aye, aye, sir," Gidwitz said.

"Go."

It was probably not much longer than two minutes, but in the swaying frozen cab it felt more like two hours before the distinctive tune of automatic-weapons fire ceased and he heard Gidwitz's voice through his headphones again. "Double lines rigged to the bridge here, Skipper. Solid. We got six tangos down, nobody else moving up here. We've secured the area."

"Good. Get a slip-harness down here to Sergeant Quick. Now. He's still out on the roof, holding on to the .50 with a broken hand. So make it extremely quick."

"We're on it. Rigging a second one for you, Skipper. Uh, and Chief Patterson's status? We heard—"

"Yeah. You heard. Two rigs will do it. He, uh—"

"For God and country, sir," Gidwitz said, his voice choked with emotion.

CHAPTER FIFTY-FOUR

Flight 00

Khalid slipped off his headphones, raised his arms over his head and stretched, yawning deeply. He looked across at Johnny Adare in the first officer's seat and smiled. They were flying at high altitude, maxed out at the 747's limit, 45,000 feet, on a northwesterly heading, a thick band of clouds beneath them. He was flying at Mach .84, normal cruising speed, 567 miles per hour, helped by a slight tailwind. They were due to descend through the cloud layer to their rendezvous at 0900 hours, local time. Half an hour. Good time to take a leak, grab a cup of coffee and stretch his legs.

He reached down into his black leather flight case and pulled out the red-and-white-striped envelope the boss had given to him back at the hangar. Instructions. Bin Wazir had told him not to open it until 0830 hours, just prior to the time when he was due to initiate his descent to 35,000. At that altitude, he would look for his target. He had a good ten minutes to take a break before initiating his descent for the rendezvous.

"She's all yours," Khalid said, sitting back and relinquishing control of the aircraft to Johnny. "You want any coffee?" He didn't ask the doctor. The man had been sound asleep in the jumpseat for the last two hours and Khalid had learned long ago what they say about sleeping dogs, especially a mangy little cur like this one.

"Sure, Cap'n," Johnny said with his usual cocky grin. "Long as you're up."

Khalid handed him the envelope. "We're supposed to open this just before we begin our descent to 35,000. Try not to open it till I get back."

"Is this a test?"

"Actually, it is."

"One day, maybe you'll trust me."

"Yeah. One day. Ditch the autopilot and keep an eye on this," he said, tapping the dial of a newly installed instrument. It was military, called a TAR, Target Acquisition Radar. As Khalid had told bin Wazir, finding another airplane out here in the middle of the Pacific would be next to impossible without it. The antiquated 747's forward-looking radar was good for only one thing, weather. Locating another airplane in the vastness of open sky and sea that was the North Pacific was going to be difficult, under the best of circumstances. Even if you possessed the plotted waypoints from the target's own main GPS nav systems, which he did. They'd been downloaded in Singapore along with his transponder code.

"His waypoint intercept's not coming up for another twenty-five minutes," Adare pointed out. He had the chart on his knee, with the target's waypoints carefully penned in red ink.

"Yeah, well. Keep an eye on it anyway. This is an uncertain world we live in."

Khalid squeezed past Soong in the jumpseat and

opened the cockpit door. He took one last look at his copilot, smiled and left the cabin, pulling the door shut behind him.

Soong's eyes popped open.

"Yes-s!" he said, pumping his fist like some ridiculous American football hero on television.

Johnny looked over at his new business partner. Couple of million quid, what the hell. He said, "Lock that door, Dr. Soong. It is now officially time to rock and roll."

Soong leapt up and fumbled for the bolt that would secure the cockpit. For a scientist, his knowledge of basic aircraft design was pathetic.

"The red handle," Adare said. "Shove it left until you hear it lock into place. Jesus."

Satisfied the cockpit door was locked, Adare now gave Khalid a few minutes. He knew his routine. He'd stroll aft, go back in the upper cabin galley to chat up the girls for a couple of minutes while he sipped his coffee, then make his way to the head on the lower deck. Satisfied this was now done, Adare reached over and twisted the dial that opened the outflow valves, dumping the cabin pressure. The effect on the passengers in the main cabin would be sudden and unpleasant. Dizziness, lightheadedness. He could already hear them complaining out there. It would only be momentary, however.

"Climb up here where I can keep an eye on you," he said to Soong, indicating the now-vacant pilot's seat. The doctor did as he was told, grinning like a giddy twelve-year-old. If he'd had a little pair of plastic wings, he couldn't have been happier. "Good," Johnny said. "I'm going to seal the cockpit and turn on the emergency oxygen up here. Reach over your left shoulder. Pilot's emergency oxygen mask is located just there." The cockpit had its own system, completely separate from the rest of the aircraft. Drug-free zone, Johnny thought, smiling.

He and Soong both fitted the masks over their faces. Then Johnny thumbed the switch that would cause the masks to drop from the passenger cabin overheads and start the flow of oxygen from the doctor's newly installed canisters. Next, he switched on the intercom and spoke in his most reassuring pilot voice.

"Well, we've just had a loss of cabin pressure as I'm sure you've all noticed. Nothing serious. Some kind of temporary malfunction. Just place the emergency oxygen masks over your faces and breathe normally. I'll begin a descent to a lower altitude. Just relax, ladies, it's all under control."

Only then did First Officer Adare kick off the autopilot and take full command of the 747.

It took Khalid all of ten seconds to appear outside the cockpit and start trying to beat the door down. His muffled screams could be heard clearly but Johnny decided to ignore them. He'd get tired of it after a while, realizing there was absolutely nothing he could do at this point. The new Kevlar door was reinforced. At any rate, pretty soon Dr. Soong's drugs would kick in, and Khalid would be a walking zombie just like the rest of them back there.

Whatever concoction Soong had added to the oxygen flowing throughout the airplane, it was now dispersed. Adare's experience taught him that everyone was mildly panic-stricken when the masks dropped in front of their faces. They tended to gulp the oxygen and suck it deep.

0900. Johnny Adare ripped open the Pasha's envelope and handed it to Soong. "Read it," he said, easing the wheel forward. Time to take her down below the cloud layer and have a look around. They'd stayed at 45,000 to avoid being spotted and for better fuel efficiency in the thinner air. The only thing he was now actually concerned about was fuel consumption. The plane normally carried 64,000 U.S. gallons. Reconfigured, the plane he was flying had an additional 6,000 gallons. His calculations had them getting to LAX, no problem, but how much could he afford to burn down at low levels looking around for the target? It was a question he would have liked to put to Khalid, but Khalid was no longer a factor in his life.

"What's it say?" he asked Soong who was scanning the contents. Soong knew everything that was contained in the document. He'd written it. But there was no need to give Johnny more information than he required. Both Adare and Khalid had been informed that they were to intercept a British passenger plane en route from Singapore to Los Angeles. Precisely what would happen to that airplane, the two pilots had been informed at Suva Island, was contained in the sealed document. They'd both been promised a huge amount of money not to ask any questions.

"It is complete information on the rendezvous target. British Airways flight from Singapore. Flight #77. Waypoint intercepts marked on the charts. Biographical information on the pilot and copilot that we will need if we are challenged. Good stuff! Very thorough!"

Challenged? What the hell did that mean, Adare wondered but knew enough not to ask. Adare descended through the broken cloud layer and leveled off at the target's designated altitude, 35,000 feet above the Pacific Ocean. Empty sky, empty sea. He was now five minutes from the target's next known waypoint. He should acquire the target on his radar screen any minute. He studied the TAR, looking for a tiny blip. Nothing.

He reduced his airspeed and flew on, imagining everything that could have possibly gone wrong. The list was disturbingly long. Ten minutes later, he was starting to sweat. Twenty minutes later, at 0930 hours, he was beginning to think something was seriously wrong. He flew what hurricane hunters called an Alpha pattern, a flight path that looks like a giant X when drawn on a chart. The fact that he was possibly late and not early began to creep into his mind. Then, the TAR began to beep.

"Well, hello there!" Johnny said, easing his throttle back to fifty percent and descending a thousand feet to make room for the new arrival fast approaching from the rear.

"Yes!" Soong echoed, pointing to the glowing blip on the screen. "Our twin brother! Identical twin! Good, good!"

The doctor had removed a small digital video camera from his case. It was wired to a bizarre contraption with a small dish antenna. He now put the camera viewfinder to his eye and began filming the empty sky outside the cockpit window.

"What in God's name are you doing?" Adare asked him.

"Bin Wazir likes to watch," Soong said.

Was there no bleeding end to this little sod's madness?

Flight 77

Captain Simon Breckenridge, a ruddy-faced man with thirty years experience, stared out his cockpit window in utter amazement. He was sitting in the left-hand pilot's seat of British Airways Flight 77 heavy, en route to Los Angeles from Singapore. He couldn't believe his eyes. Another company plane? Flying his precise course heading and altitude? What the bloody hell was going on here?

He looked at his copilot, John Swann, and both of them shook their heads. Mystified. This surrealist apparition did not make the least bit of sense to either man.

"Dee-dee-*dee*-dee . . . dee-dee-*dee*-dee . . ." Swann said, mimicking the old *Twilight Zone* theme.

"Company plane?" Breckenridge barked into his radio transmitter. "Identify yourself, over."

No response.

"Speedbird on track Delta crossing one-four-zero degrees west longitude, say your call sign."

Nothing.

"What the hell is this, Swannie?" Breckenridge eased his throttles forward. The big plane lumbered ahead, gaining on the other company plane now reducing speed and descending. When he was directly aft of the bizarrely positioned aircraft, he thumbed his mike.

"Company plane, this is British Speedbird 77 heavy, Whiskey Zulu Bravo Echo . . . identify yourself immediately."

"Christ, Simon, I cannot believe what I'm seeing here," Swann said. He was leaning forward, peering out his windscreen at the mysterious BA airplane. "He's got—holy Jesus—he's got our bloody tail number!" Tail numbers were deliberately small on commercial craft, to make life tougher on terrorists. But Swann was close enough now to read it.

The two giant aircraft were now flying parallel at roughly the same airspeeds. Breckenridge and Swann watched in amazement as a plane absolutely identical to their own in even the smallest detail now climbed a thousand feet and matched his altitude. The two planes were flying wing-to-wing about a thousand yards apart.

"You lost out here, Captain?" Breckenridge said into his mike and waited for a reply.

"Come back?" he finally said, when none was forthcoming.

Flight 00

"What the hell is that?" Adare asked the doctor. Soong had now pulled another small electronic device, brick-shaped with a flexible antenna, from inside his jacket and was punching in a sequence of numbers on a keypad.

"Radio transmitter," the doctor said, his eyes alight. "In case our young friend over there loses his nerve."

"Young friend?"

"Hmm. Yes. Seat 76-F."

Soong was scanning the long row of windows on the British plane's flank, wondering just which one the good-looking youth was sitting beside. Months earlier, he'd met the boy in a Damascus safe house and spent a week teaching him how to combine two apparently innocent and inert liquids into a powerful explosive apparatus, one triggered by a cheap, simple musical recording device called an MP3 player. If he failed to trigger it himself, Soong would use his radio transmitter and do it for him.

"Nerve? What are you talking about?"

"His name is Rafi," Soong said, putting the camera to his eye once more and filming the British jetliner. "He is the young nephew of our beloved bin Wazir. Incredibly rich, handsome. Girls, girls, girls! Yet, he wishes to martyr himself and— Look! You are getting too close, Johnny! Get away, get away! Now, I tell you!"

Adare banked the plane sharply and rolled away. Oblivious to the cries and shouts of the four-hundred-some-odd terrified souls in his care, he climbed three thousand feet in a matter of seconds. It was barely enough to avoid the jagged chunks of metal flying in all directions.

Flight 77

The sudden and unspeakably violent explosion in row 76 on the starboard side of BA 77 broke the back of the airplane. People seated very close to the blast simply came apart, shards of the bomb and nearby objects fragmenting them. A fire raced through the airplane in the few seconds before it began to break up. The four Pratt & Whitney engines were still providing thrust, but the aircraft was no longer stable. It was experiencing horrific gyrations. Within five or six more seconds, the plane was in chunks. Seat backs were collapsing and severely traumatized human beings were slipping out of their seat belts, thrown into the sky from what little remained of Flight 77.

Their fall from the sky lasted four minutes.

The passengers, and a few of them were still technically alive, fell seven miles, having attained the terminal velocity of any falling body, 120 miles per hour, during the first five hundred feet. Brutal impact against the ocean's surface is what killed anyone aboard Flight 77 who had miraculously survived the explosion, the frigid air, and the horrific velocity. On impact with the water, the ribs break and become sharp jagged knives, eviscerating the heart, lungs, and aorta. The aorta also ruptures because part of it is fixed to the body cavity, and the internal organs keep moving for a fraction of a second even though the body that contains them has stopped dead.

The water stopped the falling bodies short, but not

the aircraft's two black boxes. They tumbled slowly through the lightless depths into a deep gorge that split the ocean floor many thousands of feet beneath the surface. What had happened to Flight 77 would remain a mystery.

Rafi the martyr had not lost his nerve. He'd pushed the Paradise button right on schedule.

Flight 77 simply disappeared from the sky in a massive fireball. In time, the charred and broken bodies, the detritus of clothing, baggage, personal effects, and the scattered jumble of fuselage and wing fragments of the British airliner would slip beneath the waves. No trace of the massive carnage would remain.

But another airplane, Flight 77's identical twin, under the control of First Officer Johnny Adare, instantly assumed the British aircraft's original flight plan. And this airplane flew onward toward the City of Angels.

CHAPTER FIFTY-FIVE

The Emirate

Hawke stacked up his assault team just outside the tunnel's entrance, their jump-off position into the mountain fortress. They were in single file, MP-5s at the ready, set at full auto. They were now thirty-one minutes into an eighty-minute mission parameter. Tight to begin with and then going off the side of the mountain—Christ. Hawke raised his hand, silently communicating a sixty-second countdown until the team would enter the tunnel. Then he and Quick each tossed two flash-bang and smoke grenades deep into the tunnel.

All his mind's eye could see as he watched the whitish smoke fill the tunnel was the image of Patterson dwindling to a tiny white speck in the black nothing below. At least Tex had gone knowing he had done his duty, died in the service of his country. It helped, a little, to think that Tex would at least have known that kind of peace in that last tenuous minute of life. He hoped so, anyway. Maybe you couldn't even think when—he tried in vain to shake off these feelings, force himself into the present moment. It would be a certified bastard soon enough, when and if he had time to think.

Damn it!

Despair and dread were pricking at the edges of

his consciousness. Despair at losing Tex. And dread that he might not find bin Wazir in time or not at all. He could be leading these men into a death trap. How arrogant could he have been to imagine that such a small force could penetrate—no. It *was* certain death to allow this kind of thinking. He deliberately dug his fist deep into his fractured ribcage, causing tears to spring to his eyes and driving every thought but the howling pain in his side out of his mind.

"Go," he said, seconds later, and the team moved forward into the tunnel. After one hundred yards, Hawke signaled a halt. They had encountered zero resistance thus far, which was both good news and bad. He certainly had no desire to see any more live ammo headed his way. Yet, clearly, their presence was known. The lack of any defense, especially here at the back door of the enemy's house, was troublesome in the extreme. A man didn't need Stokely's nose to smell a trap.

He needn't have worried. As they edged forward in the dense smoke, he heard the muffled exhaust of another Hagglund and saw two wavering yellow lights floating toward him in the bluish-white smoke, like flying saucers in a cloud.

"Backs against the wall," Hawke ordered his men, trusting the approaching engine noise to cover his voice. "Tommy, take out the fifty on the roof. Use your suppressor. Two up in the cab are mine. Everybody else at the rear doors. When they open up, waste them."

The ATV rumbled blindly toward them. When it was directly opposite, Quick squeezed off a silent head shot and the man up behind the .50-cal tumbled off the cab. Hawke leaped onto the running bar, his .45 in hand. He shot the startled driver in his left ear, then, as his sidekick was raising his AK-47, he put one between his eyes. From the rear of the carrier, he heard his team's automatic weapons open up and the screams of the dying men inside. The driver's foot was still jammed on the accelerator and Hawke reached inside and grabbed the wheel, steering with one hand. When he'd guided the thing through the smoke into clear air, he reached inside, switched off the ignition and, as the ATV came to a stop, pocketed the keys.

"Might come in handy," he said to Quick, finding him in the dissipating smoke. Wagstaff and Gidwitz were pulling eight newly dead guards out of the rear of the troop carrier.

Forty-four minutes. And counting.

The seven-man squad proceeded cautiously onward into the bowels of the mountain. The tunnel, which now smelled strongly of fuel and oil and machinery, led eventually to a spacious natural vault. It was being used as a motor pool. Here were three more armored personnel carriers, two more Hagglund ATVs, and a fleet of snowmobiles. No secondary cadre of guards, no security cameras mounted above that he could see. The tunnel continued beyond the vault, angling upward. Christ. He didn't have time for all this bloody spelunking.

He didn't notice the stainless steel door inset into the rock to his left until he heard a hiss and saw it begin to open. He and his squad dropped to a crouch, weapons trained on the opening door.

There was someone inside. And, though he was huge, it was only one man. The massive black man Hawke and Kelly had met five years earlier, one night on Mount Street, just outside the Connaught Hotel. Hawke's finger tightened on the trigger of his HK.

Shoot him? Or get him to take them to bin Wazir and save them the precious time and trouble of looking for him?

"Hawke," the big man rumbled. He held up his hands, bright pink palms outward, to show he was unarmed.

"Indeed, I am," Hawke said, making a decision and lowering his weapon. He'd decided against killing the man on the spot; better to simply let this fellow take him to the target. He'd reached a point where every minute counted. On his signal, the squad lowered their guns.

"Ar am Tippu Tip," he said. "The Pasha sent me. You come." He stepped back to make room for them in the large elevator.

"Good. We were hoping to catch him at home."

Hawke stepped back and nodded to the team to enter. What the hell, he thought, an elevator was a lot easier than using the bricks of Semtex they carried to blast a breach in a five-foot-thick wall. Once they were all inside the elevator cab, Tippu touched a panel and the door slid shut.

"I believe we've met," Hawke said, turning to smile at the African. "London, wasn't it?"

Tippu glared at him with his red eyes.

The lift jerked once, then rose swiftly. Roughly calculating the probable speed of ascent, he determined they had already risen a thousand feet. The mountain complex was clearly enormous. When the lift stopped, and the door hissed open, he could see that he'd not been mistaken. The cab was flooded with sunlight. They stepped outside, blinking in the brilliant light and clear air. They'd arrived at the very top of the Blue Mountain.

The first thing Hawke noticed was that there was

no snow underfoot. Subterranean heating system, he thought, as they moved out onto some kind of parade ground. On the far side, he could see a small village of minarets and vast glass domes. From the greenish hue inside, he guessed they housed trees and exotic vegetation. Not a soul in sight, armed or otherwise. Bloody Shangri-La.

A high wall of thick bluish stone surrounded the entire compound. This exterior wall was studded every hundred yards with lookout posts. Winking glints of steel caught the sun in each window. They were expected. He followed the curve of the wall with his eyes. He knew from the recon photos that the main entrance was to his left, beyond the huge Oriental shrine which dominated his view. The structure was a replica of the Japanese sumo shrine in Kyoto.

"Over there," Tippu said, pointing at the shrine. "Sumo temple. He is waiting. Leave guns here."

"Dream on," Hawke said.

On either side of the steel door from which they'd just emerged stood two stone guardhouses, both empty. The wooden door of one hung ajar. Hawke looked at Quick's bloody left arm and mangled hand.

"Tommy, you remain in there. Keep your eyes open. Cover our retreat. When and if."

"No," Tippu said. "He comes. Guns stay."

"No," Hawke said. "He stays. He is wounded."

Tippu looked at the muzzle of Hawke's HK, now an inch from his nose, then he shrugged his great shoulders. He turned and stomped off towards the temple, his broad back presenting a choice target. It was the gesture of a man who knows he has you vastly outnumbered. A moment later, after a brief whispered conversation with Tom Quick, Hawke and the squad followed, leaving Quick behind. To Hawke's enormous relief, the hand Quick had broken was not the one that featured his highly reliable trigger finger.

Speaking quietly into his mike, he ordered Gidwitz to advance with him. The rest of the team was to linger for exactly three minutes, then fan out and get across the open ground to the shrine. Hawke then headed across the empty parade ground at a run in the direction Tippu Tip had gone, a sharp spike of pain in his left side with every loping stride.

A match was already in progress. Two sumos, glistening with sweat, were in the *dohyo,* stomping about the ring, chasing away evil demons, Hawke believed. At the edge of the ring, sitting in solitary splendor, was the man he had met in London in the late nineties. Or, rather, twice the man, for he had doubled in size in the interim. Like the other *rishiki,* he was wearing a ceremonial *mawashi,* a loincloth of crimson silk.

"You come," Tippu said to Hawke. "He stays here."

"Human sacrifice," Hawke shrugged, smiling at Gidwitz.

Hawke quickly surveyed the enormous circular room. It was spectacular. Massive wooden beams, which appeared to be plated with hammered gold, soared above him. Mounted on the beams above the ring, four Sony Jumbotrons, broadcasting the match. There were eight arched doorways, two of bin Wazir's men posted on either side of each. No visible weapons anywhere. An ornate balcony projecting above his head encircled the entire space. No one up there he could see. What small audience there was, a smattering of veiled women on one side, and a group of men on the other, paid no notice to the new arrivals.

This bin Wazir was either very stupid or supremely confident. Hawke imagined the latter. Somewhere in this fortress, he hoped, Brick Kelly was still alive. And somewhere inside the brain of bin Wazir was information the president of the United States needed desperately. The trick, how to extract both while keeping his own skin, and that of his men, intact. No mean feat, it would appear.

"Many guns trained on you," Tippu grunted. "Put down your weapons now. Him, too."

"Certainly," Hawke said, unfastening his web belt and letting his HK slide to the ground. Gidwitz did the same.

Hawke quickly turned away from Tippu, bent, as if to tie his bootlace, and quickly extracted Patterson's old Colt pistol he'd shoved inside his boot. He placed it in Gidwitz's hand as he stood up. He looked into the man's eyes, then deliberately up at the balcony, before he turned to follow the African through the crowd of onlookers. Gidwitz had nodded imperceptibly. He'd understood the unspoken orders, Hawke reassured himself, find a way up to the balcony with the Colt. Cover him.

"Ah," Snay bin Wazir said, smiling broadly, "Lord Alexander Hawke."

Hawke offered a slight bow from the waist. "Mr. bin Wazir. It's been a long time."

"Indeed. I saw your aircraft. Interesting approach. You are here for your friend Mr. Kelly, I imagine."

"Yes, as a matter of fact I am. Is he still alive?"

"For the time being."

"Where is he? I'd like to say hello."

"He is, unfortunately, detained at the moment. However, should you survive the little entertainment I've arranged, I shall see you to his quarters."

"A sumo match?"

"You haven't lost your keen powers of observation, Lord Hawke."

"Never. Who's winning?"

"Right now, Hiro. The bald chap. But Kato is formidable. He could still prevail. You will fight the winner of this match. If you live, you shall have the honor of fighting me."

"A dubious honor. Still, if you insist—"

Snay bin Wazir clapped his hands and the two additional sumo giants who'd been observing the bout in progress approached him, bowing deeply.

"This man will be competing," he said to the two huge Japanese. "One of you, take him away and see that he is suitably prepared."

"I will do it, sire," one said, stepping forward.

"Good. Go with him," bin Wazir said to Hawke, and returned his gaze to the action in the *dohyo*.

"This way," the sumo said.

Hawke followed the man through a set of heavily embroidered draperies to the far right of the ring. They entered a spartan room, smelling richly of the sandalwood that paneled the walls. The sumo sat on a bench and motioned Hawke to join him.

"You know sumo techniques, Hawkeye-san?" he asked Hawke.

"Not exactly," Hawke replied.

CHAPTER FIFTY-SIX

Christ, Hawke said to himself. Thirty-two minutes until the B-52s opened their bomb bay doors. Bombs away.

"Kelly is alive?" Hawke said to the sumo. "That's where you got the name Hawkeye?"

The sumo nodded. "Yes. He is a brave man."

"You know my name. I don't know yours."

"I am Ichi-san."

"Make this quick, Ichi-san," Hawke said, stripping off his balaclava. "I'm a fast learner on a very tight schedule."

"Good. You will fight Hiro. Kato no longer cares enough to win. To win, you must force Hiro from the circle. Or, cause some part of his body other than the soles of his feet to touch the clay. The second is the more likely. Okay?"

"Okay. Why are you doing this?"

"I am going to kill the Pasha and escape from his prison. You have come to help. Such is the timing of heaven. Now you will pay most close attention, please."

The sumo stood in order to demonstrate his lesson.

"Hiro will underestimate you. That is key. Show him no hint of emotion. You will only have one chance. Never take your eyes off Hiro. Assume this stance, the *shikiri*, putting your fists on the line in the clay."

Hawke rose and copied Ichi's squatting stance.

"Like this?"

"Fists farther apart. Feet as well. Good. Now, take a deep breath. Make sure it is deep, because you will only get one. If you take another, you will lose strength. Are you ready?"

"I don't know."

"You will know. When you are ready, explode. It is called the *tachi-ai*. If you hit him here, and just precisely here, you will knock him off his feet. It is over."

"And if not?"

"It is still over."

"I see what you mean."

"Now, explode."

Hawke did, hitting the man's sternum with enormous force. He might as well have hit a granite monument.

"Well, that doesn't work," Hawke said, picking himself up.

"Not against me, Hawkeye-san. I am immovable."

"Then I'm glad we're on the same team," Hawke said, checking his watch. "Shall we go see Hiro? I've got a plane to catch."

Hawke entered the *dohyo*, never once taking his eyes off Hiro. He simply couldn't believe the size of his opponent. He outweighed even Ichi, probably tipping the scales in excess of five hundred pounds. Hiro flexed his muscles and stamped his feet. Hawke followed his example, too focused on what he must do to feel ridiculous. He tried to imagine his opponent to be a small object, to simply be pushed aside, and found this a difficult feat of imagination.

He approached his line in the *dohyo*, staring at the other man implacably. The man squatted, assuming the *shikiri*, supporting his weight upon his fists. Hawke felt an odd calm, stemming no doubt from Ichi's serene confidence in the outcome. He, too, bent and placed his fists on the line, inhaling deeply as he did so.

He gave no warning. A half second after his fists touched the clay, Hawke exploded up and into the man. He launched his body with every ounce of the coiled energy in his legs and caught Hiro precisely where he'd been shown. The man took the unexpectedly vicious blow to his sternum and staggered back. For one horrible moment, Hawke thought he might recover, but the blow had caught him completely off guard. Backpedaling heavily, he briefly lost his balance, and one knee hit the clay.

Hawke didn't hear the cheers that erupted, or the surprising applause coming from the women on the other side of the ring. He walked over to Hiro, who was still kneeling, and offered the man his hand. The great sumo warrior smiled at him and grasped it, rising to his feet.

Hawke showed no emotion.

The first match was over, but his second was already about to begin. Bin Wazir was getting to his feet. Hawk felt light-headed from the pain in his side and black spots were floating before his eyes. He shook his head and willed them away. Just then he noticed an odd thing. The four suspended television monitors were no longer broadcasting a live image of the *dohyo* and the matches. Instead, there was an image of a British airliner in flight. Had he lost it completely? The shaky picture appeared to be taken from another aircraft flying alongside.

He recognized this for what it was, a distraction, and turned his eyes away.

Standing at the edge of the ring, Hawke accepted a sip of water from a ladle handed to him by Ichi, who then handed him a paper towel to wipe his lips. "To cleanse the spirit," Ichi-san said.

Bin Wazir entered the *dohyo*, raising each leg high and bringing it down hard. Hawke followed suit.

Both men cast their salt into the center of the ring. Hawke made his cast high and hard, emulating Hiro's heroic gesture, an early show of strength and confidence. His opponent favored him with a long, hard stare that was, Hawke imagined, the sumo equivalent of trash talk on a football field. The Dog showed no emotion, nor did Hawke, as they squared off opposite each other and bent to place their fists on the clay.

It was a simple game, as Ichi had said. Mass versus speed.

Hawke pulled as much air down into his lungs as he could without blacking out from the sharp knives in his side and waited. He knew instinctively the instantaneous explosion of the *tachi-ai* would not work twice in succession. Eyeing the Dog, and readying himself, he looked for some sign from his opponent. Again, he felt a kind of serenity, imparted perhaps when Ichi had given him the water and the towel for his lips.

To cleanse the spirit.

In the same instant Hawke saw his flicker of intent, Bin Wazir lunged.

He came in low, and Hawke was ready.

He sprang upwards and, placing both hands on the man's massive shoulders, leapfrogged cleanly over his back. The Dog's momentum carried him forward.

Hawke, who had landed on his feet and whirled about, thought for a second the man might need to put a hand down to keep himself from falling, thus ending the match. He was not so lucky. Bin Wazir kept his footing. He then stopped, and turned around to face Hawke, stamping his feet.

They circled each other now, using all of the *dohyo*, still showing each other nothing.

"You're hurt," Bin Wazir said, smiling. "Your whole left side is crushed. Must be painful."

"Just a scratch," Hawke said, advancing.

Hawke's mind was racing, searching every corner for some advantage. Ichi-san had not covered this section of the sumo arts in his lessons. Suddenly, a bright image flickered above him. It caught his eye and he looked up for the briefest instant. What he saw on the television monitors horrified him, and in that moment the Dog had him.

What he saw, before bin Wazir wrapped him in both of his powerful arms and lifted him bodily from the clay, was the British airliner exploding into a huge fireball. The plane was disintegrating before his eyes, flaming jet fuel and pieces of metal and human beings falling earthward in a rain of liquid fire.

The man's grip tightened about his ribcage. The pain was horrific. A jagged splinter of bone must be piercing something inside. Nothing to do but try to ignore it and try to keep the blackness at bay. He realized that biz Wazir had pinioned him in such a way as to make escape all but impossible. He had to find a way to buy a moment to think before he completely blacked out.

"You blew up that airliner yourself," he said,

pushing the single button he knew might work—
Snay bin Wazir's ego.

"Yes, I did," the Dog said. "One of yours. It appears
I will kill a lot of Englishmen today. I could kill you
now—but why spoil the fun? We should complete the
match, no? You appear to have many supporters in the
audience."

"Sporting of you," Hawke grimaced, his voice
scratchy and harsh as the man released him.

Back on his feet, he moved to the edge of the ring,
breathing deeply, trying to regain his strength. A sheen
of perspiration coated his face, grey with pain. Bin
Wazir would be counting on delaying tactics, so Hawke
charged. Speed versus mass, now. Bin Wazir tried to
sidestep him, but Hawke was too quick. He dove for
him, and heard a satisfying crack as his right shoulder
slammed the Dog's left knee. The knee went backward,
the patella shattered. The man grunted in pain, but did
not go down. Hawke rolled away and sprang to his feet.
On the four screens, the rain of fire continued.

"Why pick on England? I thought it was the
Americans you and the Emir were after," Hawke
taunted, circling the enraged man again and again.

"Americans, yes," the Dog said. "My holy warriors
will kill them too. Today. Perhaps ten million or more."

Hawke edged closer, feinting left and right.
Suddenly, the pain was forgotten and he felt a surge of
strength. His mind had finally taken over. "That many?
The Pigskin, Mr. bin Wazir? Tell me, are your little
bombs already inside America?"

Bin Wazir laughed and lashed out, an unexpected
blow. Hawke barely dodged it with a head feint.
Spinning away, he chopped down hard on the man's

shoulder with the flat of his hand. It registered, but the man was unfazed.

"You see that airliner disappear, Mr. Hawke? Look, you can still see the pieces falling from the sky, burning up on the screen. Look!"

"That trick only works once, bin Wazir. The Dog. That's what they call you isn't it? A dog? Some kind of mutt, one would only imagine?"

"One English planeload of fat, happy infidel tourists, see it, Mr. Hawke? Happily bound for Los Angeles, but now a flaming tribute to mark my martyred nephew Rafi's grave. Allah be praised! Another plane, identical, now takes its place. A ship full of warriors who carry death to America."

"Really?" Hawke said, moving in now. "As we speak?"

"In one hour, America as you know it ceases to exist. A scourge far more lethal than the atom is about to be unleashed. An angel of death will descend."

"I think this match is over," Hawke said.

His left leg lashed out and up, catching the man full in the groin. When he bent over in agony, Hawke was on him. He lifted his right knee twice into the Dog's face and drove the small bones of the man's nose and eyesockets inward with tremendous force. Another blow to the side of his head stunned him further; a second slashing flat-handed strike tore the tendons of his neck and caused his head to loll upon his shoulders. A final smash to the back of his skull drove him face down into the clay. He was still alive, but he wasn't getting up anytime soon. Hawke stood above him, his nostrils flaring at the stink of the man, panting, finally allowing himself to believe he had survived.

CHAPTER FIFTY-SEVEN

The cheering was astounding, but what was most surprising was the sudden appearance of all four sumo *rikishi* at his side in the ring. The four giants surrounded him, turned to face outward, and planted themselves, arms folded across their chests, forming a defensive perimeter around him. Apparently, Ichi-san was not the only sumo warrior who had no love for the man who remained face down in the center of the *dohyo*.

Tippu Tip had appeared when bin Wazir went down and now crouched beside his fallen and unmoving master. Making angry, mournful sounds, Tippu looked up, his red eyes flashing at Hawke. Alex had no interest in another round with this brute. That match had been decided one night long ago with Tippu Tip checking into St. Thomas's Hospital on the Thames for an extended visit.

"Ar kill you," Tippu bellowed, getting to his feet. Hawke had heard that line from him before.

"Ichi-san," Hawke said, ducking away from a swipe of Tippu's huge paw. "Could one of you gentlemen please escort this fellow from the ring? We must find Kelly, quickly."

Ichi looked at Hiro, who immediately obliged, seizing the giant African from behind, arms around his thick waist, lifting him off his feet, and simply waltzing him out of the *dohyo*.

"Kelly is here!" a woman's voice cried out. Hawke looked up in amazement. A veiled woman robed in emerald silk stood up amidst the group of women seated on the far side of the ring. Standing next to her was a tall, gaunt figure of a man dressed all in black. He pulled back the burnoose covering his head and that was when Hawke saw the shaggy red hair.

"Brick!" he shouted. "Let's get the bloody hell out of here!"

"Good plan!" Brick replied, but his cry was hoarse and raw.

Brick Kelly was alive. Hawke grabbed Ichi's arm and squeezed it. Smiling, he said, "The timing of heaven, Ichi-san?"

"Yes, Hawkeye-san. The time for freedom."

Phut-phut-phut! A burst of automatic fire kicked up clay a few feet from Hawke's feet.

"Get down! Get down!" Hawke shouted, pulling Ichi to the clay beside him. The three *riskishi* also dove to the clay. The guards at each doorway had their weapons up, and were squeezing off short bursts, but they seemed uncertain. Their lord and master was down, but was it over? Hawke heard a round zip above his head and then saw the man who'd fired at him go down, his head exploding in a fine red haze.

Hawke's eyes lifted instantly to the heavily carved wooden balcony. Tom Quick was up at the rail with his new sniper rifle, not the least uncertain about what to do with it. Every time a new guard appeared in a doorway, Quick waxed him with a clean head shot. Gidwitz was up there, too, behaving like a gunfighter in an old western. He'd pop up and fire, duck down, scramble around to a new location on the balcony and fire again, creating the illusion of four or five gunmen up on the balcony. The illusion was enhanced by the nostalgic roar of Tex Patterson's old Peacemaker.

Everyone was occupied for the moment, his guys seemed to have the situation in hand; but Hawke had information which needed to get to Washington immediately.

"Tommy," Hawke said, having retrieved his Motorola headset from Ichi, "I need Sparky Wagstaff down here in the ring with that sat phone. Now."

"Bad news, Skipper. Sparky was headed here from the guardhouse with the com set. Got halfway across, one of the towers took him out. Fire is murderous out there."

"Get someone out there. I need that phone, Tom."

"Negative, Skipper, we tried that. Phone was smashed. Nothing left of it."

"Anybody else down?"

"Gidwitz took one in the shoulder, sir, but, as you see, he's not down. Just keeps firing that old Colt."

Twenty minutes remained on the mission clock. The guards were all firing up at the elusive Gidwitz up on the balcony now, and it gave Hawke's remaining men, who had somehow made it to the shrine, the chance to clear the hall one doorway at a time. Hawke didn't have the luxury of waiting for the bullets to stop. By now, the big American bombers would have arrived and be circling above. He needed to get on a radio to the president. Now. But the closest radio available was aboard *Hawkeye*.

He and Ichi started in a low crouch towards Kelly, and Hawke saw his friend limping towards him. The man could hardly walk. Torture had broken his body.

Brick Kelly was smiling, but tears were streaming down his face.

Hawke ran the final few steps and Kelly fell into his arms. It was only then that Hawke saw in his eyes how very near to death his friend was.

"Alex," he whispered through parched and cracked lips.

"It's okay, Brick. We're going home now, old buddy."

The woman who'd been with Brick stood, and raised a gleaming Samurai sword high above her head. The enemy fire ceased instantly. "You are Hawke," the beautiful woman in silk said, approaching him. "I am Yasmin. Kelly spoke of you. You did not forget your friend." She lowered her sword.

"He is my friend," Hawke said, embracing the frail body, shocked at how little flesh remained on his bones. He had not eaten much since his abduction. "I don't know how to thank you."

"Take him safely home to his wife and children," she said. "That is more than enough." Smiling sadly, she turned away.

Hawke supported Brick with one arm and headed toward the nearest doorway. It looked clear. He spoke again into his mike. "Okay, Tommy, I have the hostage alive. Give me a fast sitrep, we've got to move out, now! What's it look like from up there?"

"Door opposite you is clear, sir. Working on the rest—"

"You get our guys out of here. I'm out this door with the hostage. Regroup at that elevator. Sixty seconds. How's the parade ground look? Can you take out those bloody towers from up there? Can I get some fire suppression?"

"Negative. Don't have a shot, Skipper. Can't—"

Hawke had been carefully ticking down the remaining mission time in his head. He was at eighteen minutes. He needed to get to his radio, and they would barely have time to rig a snatch for the Black Widows. Even that assumed somehow crossing the parade ground under withering fire from the watchtowers. He cast his eyes about the hall, desperately searching for some way out.

"Ichi-san, is there some other way out of—"

"No harm will come to you now, Hawkeye-san," Ichi said, nodding in the direction of the regal Yasmin. She was deep in conversation with a uniformed man, clearly the captain of the guards, who was nodding his head vigorously, and shouting orders at subordinates and into his walkie-talkie. All automatic weapons were lowered, even as he spoke. Apparently, a new ruler now held dominion over the Blue Palace. And her word was law.

"Come along, Ichi-san," Hawke said, pulling the balaclava down over his head. "You want out of here as badly as I do."

Supporting Kelly with one arm, Hawke ran through the arched doorway of the sumo shrine and into the brilliant sunshine of the parade ground.

"Belay that last, Tommy, cease fire," Hawke said into his lip-mike as he ran across the open ground. "Regime change. We're going out unopposed. Move it."

"Copy. Look up. You got B-52s assembling upstairs."

Hawke shouted over his shoulder at the sumo who was struggling to keep up, "I can make space for you if you want to come along, Ichi-san. In fifteen minutes, this place will not exist. If you wish, go back and tell Yasmin that she must get herself to safety. Deep inside the mountain. Now. Understand?"

"Thank you, Hawkeye-san."

"Don't thank me yet. That elevator—"

"I know it."

"Sixty seconds. No more."

Twelve minutes on the clock. The dead radioman, Ian Wagstaff, sealed inside one of the gold survival bags, had been carefully placed inside the troop carrier. The now delirious ambassador lay upon a makeshift bed between the two facing benches, breathing emergency oxygen. Gidwitz gave him first aid as Hawke raced the vehicle over the bridge at full throttle, out along the narrow shoulder of the mountain and through a narrow gorge. Finally he was heading up a steep icy incline he knew would lead to the crevasse and the long snow-field where they'd left the Black Widows.

Ichi, who sat up front in the cab, was looking at Hawke closely. "The palace is to be destroyed?" he asked.

"Yes. I hope Yasmin and the *rikishi* are taking shelter somewhere inside the mountain."

"There are many bombs buried within that mountain, Hawkeye-san."

"Bombs?" Hawke looked at him, changing down to a lower gear to make the grade.

"Bin Wazir is a death merchant. The mountain is one of his primary factories."

"The British plane that exploded. And the new one to take its place. You know about these?" Ichi nodded, yes.

"Yasmin knows everything. She tells me everything. The new plane is disguised to look like the real one that was destroyed. The passengers aboard the new one are all from terrorist camps."

"Is the new plane carrying bombs? How many?"

Hawke's hands were relaxed upon the wheel, his eyes were calm and focused. But his heart was thudding in his chest.

"Some of the bombs in the mountain were going to America. But, now—"

"What, Ichi-san? You must tell me. There's no time! Millions will die."

"There was a problem with the fissile material. An accident. Many technicians died. Dr. Soong, who made the bombs, is aboard the plane for America now. He has infected those aboard with—"

"The bombs, Ichi, does he have bombs on the plane?"

"I believe that he does. But he is taking no chances now. Because of the problem, he has also infected everyone aboard with a virus. Something he created. Like God."

"How many on the plane? Innocent people? What virus?"

"Four hundred trained terrorists, I think. No innocents. Smallpox."

"Jesus, that's the scourge," Hawke said, pushing the accelerator to the floorboard. The Hagglund crested the top of the incline. To Hawke's enormous relief, the three Black Widows were waiting just as he'd left them.

"I was worried they might have destroyed our planes," he said to Ichi as he raced across the snow towards them. The sumo looked at him and smiled.

"You are not supposed to be alive."

"I suppose not," Hawke said, braking the ATV to a stop. He wished Ichi good luck and leapt out, running for his glider, organizing their escape as he ran. It had taken four minutes to reach the snowfield. Quick leapt off the roof of the cab and landed in the soft snow.

"Tommy, let's roll. We've got less than eight minutes till bombs away. You guys know the drill. Mario and Ferg rig the poles for the snatch. You and Gidwitz keep the ambassador as comfortable as you can until we're ready to get him into my plane. Gidwitz goes with you. My new friend Ichi-san will ride in *Widowmaker*. You guys'll have to remove the middle seat to make room. Ditto my plane for Kelly. Move it!"

Hawke slid the canopy back and climbed into his pilot's seat. There was a thin coating of frost on his instrument panel. He was thankful no snowfall had accumulated on his long slender wings. He lit up *Hawkeye*'s radio and thumbed the mike. His first order of business was getting his men the hell off this mountain. Behind him, the middle seat was being removed. The mission read-out on the panel ticked down to four minutes.

"*Gabriel, Gabriel,* this is *Hawkeye,*" he radioed the surveillance plane circling above him. "Come back."

"Roger, *Hawkeye,* this is *Gabriel.* Shaving it a little close today, aren't you, Captain?"

"We have the hostage, *Gabriel.* Alive, barely. Have emergency medical and trauma standing by to receive us. I am rigging the snatch poles for our extraction now," Hawke said. "Poles and snatch wires will be up in under two minutes, so I want three Navy STOLs lined up with their hooks down and ready to grab us, over."

"Uh, roger that, *Hawkeye,* if you look to your right, you'll see them coming up the valley now." Three of the four prop-driven planes that had delivered the gliders would now retrieve the survivors. A tailhook on each Navy STOL would snag a wire strung between two telescoping fiberglass poles mounted in the snow ahead of each plane. That wire was connected to an eyebolt at the nose of each glider. This glider snatch had been perfected by Navy pilots in the Pacific in 1944. It usually worked.

The last set of poles went up and he saw Ferg race for his plane.

Two minutes. Quick raced by, giving him a thumbs-up. The poles were all rigged and the crews were loading up. The Blue Mountain Boys were almost ready for extraction.

"Appreciate that, *Gabriel,* I need an immediate scrambled patch to the White House now. I repeat, this is Code Red FLASH-traffic emergency, over."

"Uh, roger, we'll put you through, *Hawkeye,*" the E2-C pilot said, all the banter gone now. "Stand by, over."

Fifteen seconds later, after Brick Kelly had been carefully lowered and strapped on his back inside the newly created cockpit space, Hawke was talking to the president of the United States. He thumbed a switch to the right of his altimeter and the canopy cover closed silently over his head. Another toggle switch turned on the heat.

"Good work, *Hawkeye*," Jack McAtee said, "I'm monitoring your traffic with the boys upstairs. You need to get those damn planes out of there now."

"Working on it, Mr. President. We got Brick. I also have vital information—"

"You got to bin Wazir?" Hawke could hear the desperate edge of hope in the president's voice. "What did you get?"

"Sir, bin Wazir blew a British Airways 747 out of the sky about twenty minutes ago. I saw it happen. Don't know point of origin, but she was out over the Pacific, inbound to Los Angeles—"

The president cut him off, and Hawke could hear him barking orders to his staff. One minute. Christ!

The first Navy STOL roared ten feet over his head, snagged his wire, and the Black Widow glider lifted off, accelerating from zero to one hundred and twenty miles an hour in one second. *Hawkeye* and her tug flew straight up the crevasse and out into clear air. He looked back and down. *FlyBaby* and *Widowmaker* were airborne too, their tow planes climbing out fast.

Seconds later, his glider was rocked by the shock waves of massive explosions below. The B-52s, mere glints of silver above, had opened their bomb bays. American Tomahawk missiles, having flown all the way from the *Nimitz* Battle Group, were slamming into the mountain fortress, pulverizing it. The mountain peaks, where he'd been moments earlier, now disappeared in a massive cloud of ice, rock, and debris climbing into the sky. It looked like a volcano blowing its top. But his little flock, now down to three, had made it out just in time.

"Go ahead, *Hawkeye*," the president said. "I've got

you on speaker. We're all here in the Situation Room. What we know is, there was an explosion aboard a British Air carrier, but the plane is still apparently inbound."

"Yes, sir, there may be another inbound aircraft carrying four hundred tangos infected with—"

"*Another* plane?"

"Affirmative, sir. You have an airplane inbound to Los Angeles that is not what it appears to be."

"What about the goddamn Pigskins, Alex? Where are they?"

"I asked bin Wazir if the bombs were already inside the U.S. His reply, holy warriors now carry death to America. A scourge far more lethal than the atom. Quote, 'Ten million Americans will die today—an angel of death will descend.'"

"Carrying how, Alex? How the hell were the warriors carrying the cargo? Angel of death? What in God's name—"

"I know this sounds crazy, sir, but I saw it. When the British flight blew—"

"You *saw* the British plane go down?"

"Affirmative. Live feed on a monitor."

"You *assume* it was a live feed."

"Affirmative, sir, an assumption. When it blew, bin Wazir said, quote, 'Another plane, identical, now takes its place.' I have that confirmed through one source. That's all I've got, sir."

"An *identical* plane? To the British flight?"

"That's what he said, sir, confirmed by my source. Bin Wazir told me that in one hour, America as we know it will cease to exist."

"Jesus Christ—hold on, Alex—get Davis at NAS

Miramar to scramble every goddamn F-15 and F-16 fighter he's got, now! Alex, repeat, he said one hour?"

"Yes, sir. That was 1400 hours. Exactly twenty-eight minutes ago."

"Thirty-two minutes left."

"Aye, sir."

Hawke could hear a good deal of heated discussion at the other end. When the president returned, his voice was calm but edged with steel.

"This *second* inbound 747 you spoke of, *Hawkeye*. Would you characterize that as *hard* information, over?"

There was a long pause before Alex Hawke replied.

"Negative, sir, I could not go that far. Strike that, *would* not go that far."

"God help us."

"Yes, sir."

CHAPTER
FIFTY-EIGHT

Flight 00

Naturally, he was a little nervous, Johnny Adare reassured himself, wiping the sweat from his palms on his trousers. Hell, you got a suitcase bulging with a couple of million pounds cash in the back of the bus. Your passenger manifest includes four hundred zoned-out zombies, and you've got one royally pissed-off pilot back there somewhere, too. You got LSD or Ecstasy or God knows what in your oxygen system, and, plus, you got a lunatic Indian snake charmer sitting in the left-hand seat shooting a goddamn movie.

And that was all before the really bad part started.

"British 77 heavy," a voice suddenly crackled over his headphones. "This is L.A. Center, good afternoon."

He looked over at the doctor and tried to pull himself together. He'd been dreading this part. How to pull it off, meaning land this plane at LAX without a hitch and walk away a millionaire. The main thing was to stay cool and act normally.

The doc nodded "okay," go ahead. Adare thumbed the mike.

"L.A. Center, British 77 heavy at three-five-oh,

good afternoon," Adare said, and thank God he now actually remembered what real pilots sounded like.

"Speedbird 77 heavy . . . hold on, sir . . . uh, roger . . . turn right to a heading of one-four-oh and . . . uh . . . stand by."

"Speedbird 77, roger!"

"Excellent, Johnny!" Soong said, all excited. "Perfect! Just like that. Keep it up and we are good!" It was a few minutes before the tower came back.

"Uh, Speedbird 77 heavy, sorry about that. I have you, radar contact, one-sixteen northwest of Los Angeles. Descend now and maintain flight level one-niner-zero . . . L.A. Center."

"Descend and maintain one-niner-zero, Speedbird 77 heavy."

Another long silence. Johnny watched Soong with his camera. Soon, he'd be getting a good shot of the hazy California coastline in the far distance. Malibu down there somewhere. Man, the stories old Johnny could tell about Malibu nights—

"Uh . . . Speedbird 77 heavy, give me your fuel remaining and souls on board."

"Stand by, L.A. . . ." he said, looking at Soong.

"Tell him . . . okay . . . tell him 367 passengers," the doctor said, running his finger down the last passenger manifest he'd downloaded from British Air. He had all the documents spread out on his lap. Crew names and everything. He was prepared for this, had to give the little bugger credit.

"77 heavy, this is Center. I need the number of souls on board and fuel remaining . . ."

"Los Angeles, we have 367 souls on board, and 20,000 pounds remaining."

"Stand by, 77 . . ."

"Some kind of a problem, Center?"

"Speedbird 77, confirm you are squawking two-five-zero-six . . ."

"Squawking two-five-zero-six, L.A. Center."

"Captain, could I have your name?"

"Center, certainly . . . may we ask why . . . what the hell?"

Dr. Soong looked over at him, exasperated. "Just tell him! Simon Breckenridge. Jesus Christ, Johnny. Don't lose it now."

"Los Angeles Center, British 77 heavy, this is Captain Simon Breckenridge. Some kind of a problem, L.A. Center?"

Another long silence.

"Speedbird 77 heavy, this is L.A. Center . . . uh, affirmative. Affirmative, some kind of a problem, sir. I will need your personal company I.D. number, over."

"Stand by, L.A. . . ."

He looked at Soong who was feverishly going through the reams of paperwork.

"Damn! This ain't working, Doc! They smell something."

Soong put a hand on his shoulder, trying to reassure him.

"Don't do this, Johnny! We're so close! I feed you everything you need to land this plane! No question we can't answer. Walk away. Rich, rich, rich! All we need is you to stay calm. Okay? You see? Deep breath, that's it. Here's your ID number! Now. Read it to him but ask him why first. This is most unusual, you're resenting this question, okay?"

"L.A., Speedbird 77 heavy . . . right, this is Captain

Simon Breckenridge, company ident alpha–four–four–
x-ray–seven, over."

"Roger, 77 heavy . . . that's company ident
alpha–four–four–x-ray–seven, sir."

"That's affirmative, L.A. Can I ask why
you . . . uh—"

"Uh, okay, thank you, Captain. Sorry. Please come to
heading zero-three-zero, contact SoCal Approach on
one-two-five point two and have a good afternoon,
Speedbird 77 heavy."

"One-two-five point two, Speedbird, good day!"

Johnny sat back in the seat and rubbed his face with
both hands. Then he looked over at the little doctor
and both of them laughed out loud. They'd done it!

The president shook his head and rubbed his bloodshot
eyes. His family was safe deep inside a mountain somewhere in West Virginia. He wished he could say the
same for the other couple of hundred million souls
he'd sworn to protect. Could the Constitution survive
this attack? Could democracy? Jesus. He hadn't slept
much in a week and he was not one of those guys, and
there were some in Washington, who could get away
with it.

There was one thing that terrified the president of
the United States right now, and it scared him more
than anything else. Bad advice.

"What do you think, Warren?" he asked his vice
president, Warren Baker.

"I think Hawke's got bad information, sir. Period.
You heard that pilot. Why, he—"

"Steve?"

Steve Thompson, his national security advisor,

looked at him for a long beat, then nodded his head. "I agree with Warren, Mr. President, look, you've got a foreign carrier properly transponding his assigned squawk, correctly identifying himself absolutely as the assigned company pilot to that squawk, and now we got an outbound American Airlines captain in visual contact saying it's got the same damn tail number as the British Air plane that left Singapore roughly twelve hours ago."

"That British Air pilot. He sound to you like he had a gun to his head?"

"He absolutely did not, Mr. President," Thompson said. "Rock solid."

"No," Baker agreed. "No coercion in that voice."

"Holy Mother of God," the president said. "Get the British prime minister on the line. And patch me through to *Hawkeye*." A Marine bird colonel waved at him and he picked up the blinking phone.

"*Hawkeye*, we got a little problem here," the president said.

"Yes, sir," Alex Hawke replied.

"Airplane now approaching LAX is a Boeing 747-400ER, tail number matches the one BA confirms as having departed Singapore at 0700 hours this morning. Passenger count is identical. Squawk code identical. Pilot identifies himself as Captain Simon Breckenridge, exactly the man who should be sitting in the left-hand seat according to the BA spokesman in London, and has correctly given his company identification number. Any ideas?"

"Yes, sir. Shoot him down."

CHAPTER FIFTY-NINE

The White House

"Shoot down a civilian airliner with a few hundred people aboard. Based on your best guess as to what the hell is actually going on here."

"It's not a guess, sir."

"I've known you a long time, Alex."

"Yes, sir."

"We're not on speaker. Just you and me. Haven't got a lot of time here. You told me yourself that what you had, you would not, or could not, characterize as hard information, correct?"

"That's correct, sir."

"You saw an aircraft explode, but it was on a monitor."

"Yes, sir."

"Could have been a tape. Could have been digitally altered in some way."

"Could have been, yes, sir."

"This information about an alleged second 747 carrying terrorists you received directly from bin Wazir himself."

"Yes, sir."

"Confirmed by a secondary source."

"Yes, sir."

"Reliable? Who the hell is it?"

"He's a sumo wrestler, sir."

"Alex, listen. Unless you've got something, anything you're not telling me, and I mean right this second, I'm going to authorize the FAA to let that airplane land in Los Angeles, you got me?"

"Mr. President, the man flying that plane is not who he says he is. Nor is that airplane what it appears, no doubt unquestionably in many people's eyes, to be."

"How do you know that?"

"My gut."

"Your gut. Well, that's hardly enough to go on now, is it? Shoot down a planeload of people. Alex, you know I'm sorry as hell about Tex Patterson. Goddamn it. Tex was one of my closest friends. But you did a fine job of getting Brick Kelly out of that goddamn place alive, helluva job, and I want to personally—"

"His mother, sir."

"His mother?"

"His mother. Or, his wife or his girlfriend. Doesn't matter, as long as they're close. We could patch them through right to the pilot. Have them ask him a few intimate—"

"Goddamn right we could! Good thinking! Jesus Christ! Stay with me—I want you to hear the whole thing—hey, Karen, you still got British Airways on the line? Tell 'em you want personnel, now! Call the FAA and tell them to buy time. Put that plane in a traffic hold—Alex, you still there?"

"Yes, sir."

"Okay, we've got BA chief of personnel on, go ahead, Alex, this is your baby."

"Hello?" Hawke said.

"This is Patrick O'Dea speaking, sir, how may we be of service?"

"Mr. O'Dea, Alex Hawke speaking, there's a problem with one of your pilots. Simon Breckenridge. I'd like to speak immediately to his wife. Or closest relative. And I need you to ring straight through—"

"It's the middle of the night here, sir! We—"

"The president of the United States is also on the line, Mr. O'Dea. This is a crisis situation—"

"Yeah, this is President McAtee in Washington, Mr. O'Dea. I'd appreciate it if you'd just put us through to Captain Breckenridge's closest relative."

"Certainly, Mr. President, I, uh, I'm just looking—ah, here we are, his wife, yes, a Mrs. Marjorie Breckenridge living in Hay-on-Wye. I'll put you through to her straightaway, Mr. President."

There was a faint screeching tone, during which the president said to Hawke, "We'll take it from here, Alex. I'll keep this line open and . . . however this plays out, good work and God bless, *Hawkeye*."

A ring, and then a woman answered, "Hullo?"

"Mrs. Breckenridge? This is Jack McAtee, president of the United States calling."

"Very funny," the woman's voice again. "If you call this number again, I shall call the police. They can trace you, you know. Good-bye and don't ever—"

"Wait! Don't hang up! It's about your husband, Simon!"

Navy F/A18-E Super Hornets suddenly swarmed around the inbound 747 like angry bees. Upstairs, F-117A Stealth fighters from Miramar were standing by. Johnny Adare was on the radio now, talking to the

tower, trying desperately to stay calm. Soong was filming the fighters, but he wasn't very calm either. It was
almost worth it to see the little bastard sweat.

"Squawk two-five-zero-six, climb and maintain
flight level one-niner-zero," L.A. said.

"Climb and maintain one-niner-zero, Speedbird 77
heavy . . . Uh, what exactly is the problem, L.A.
Approach?"

"We're trying to work that out, sir. Captain, I have
an urgent call for you. I'm patching it through to you
now."

"What?" Johnny Adare said. "What are you talking—"

"Simon? Simon, what's going on?" a woman's voice
asked him. Johnny grabbed at Soong's shirt, pulling
him closer. Then he had his hand around his throat,
shaking him like a ragdoll.

"They've got a fucking woman on the phone now
fucking wants to talk to me!" Adare hissed in his ear.
"You got some fucking ideas how to handle this part,
you bleeding little shit?"

"Stay cool, Johnny, just talk to her—whatever she
wants to hear."

"Simon," the woman said, "you don't sound like
yourself. Are you all right, love? They won't tell me
what this is about. They want me to—to ask you our
children's names, dear."

"Children's names?" Adare said, his voice rising
involuntarily.

"Yes, dear. The children's names—"

"Well, there's little Simon. And, of course—"

"Oh, dear God! Are you quite all right, dear? Has

someone got a gun? Tell me what's wrong! I can't stand this. I can't—"

"Yes, I'm fine. What's the matter? I don't—"

"For God's sakes, Simon, we don't *have* any children anymore! That lorry came round the bend and—oh, my God! This is not my husband! You are not my husband, do you hear me, whoever you are? God damn all of you! Is this some kind of sick joke?"

Hawke heard a sharp clack over the radio as the receiver in a small town in Wales was slammed down.

"God damn it!" the president screamed at his staff. "You all hear that? Jesus Christ!"

Somebody, somewhere, then said, "Go ahead, Mr. President. The Navy link is back up. Top Hat fighter squadron can hear you loud and clear now." The president got back on the radio.

"Top Hat Squadron leader, Top Hat Squadron leader. This is your commander-in-chief speaking. Do you copy?"

"Yes, sir, I read you loud and clear, sir. I am required to ask for your mission code, sir."

"That's correct. This is *Warhorse*, son. Whisky Alpha Romeo. I repeat, this is *Warhorse*, Whisky Alpha Romeo."

"Uh, roger, *Warhorse*, this is *Gunfighter*, over. Sir."

"I want your squadron to arm your weapons, *Gunfighter*."

"Armed, sir. That's affirmative."

"I want you boys to escort that British Air flight to the ground. I want him to land now. L.A. Tower is halting all traffic within a radius of twenty miles and clearing all runways. Put him on the ground, son. Do it right—"

Hawke heard this exchange and immediately thumbed his mike, interrupting the president.

"*Warhorse, Warhorse,* break. This is *Hawkeye,* over.*"

"Yeah, go ahead, *Hawkeye.*"

"Sir, I strongly reco taking this bird out in the desert. Edwards Air Force Base is the closest. Over."

"Copy. Hell, he's right, *Gunfighter,*" the president said. "You fellas copy that? Take him to Edwards. I'll get the reception party organized, over."

"Roger, *Warhorse,* we copy that. Top Hat will force a landing at Edwards. Uh, sir, we may encounter resistance—he, uh, is not responding at this time, sir. How far may we go, sir, over."

There was a long pause, and then the president spoke, all weariness gone from his voice.

"What's your name, *Gunfighter?*"

"My name is Captain Wiley Reynolds Jr., Mr. President."

"Captain Reynolds, I authorize you to do absolutely whatever it takes to protect your country. *Gunfighter.* Acknowledge."

"Whatever it takes, sir. Over."

CHAPTER SIXTY

Flight 00

Adare watched in stunned disbelief as four American Navy F/A-18E Super Hornets positioned themselves directly fore and aft of his airplane. And, there were two more right on his bloody wingtips, maybe a foot of separation to port and starboard. He could fucking well read the serial numbers on the bright yellow–tipped air-to-air missiles tucked up under their wings.

Five hundred feet above him was another squadron of fighters, Hornets from down at Miramar. His repeated calls to the tower in the last three or four minutes had gone unanswered. How the living hell, he wondered then, did he get himself into this bloody mess? Oh, yeah. The doctor and his money. Soong was begging him to just put the plane down. The Navy fighters scared the bejesus out of the little guy. Not Johnny Adare, however. He still felt safe.

"You think I'm putting this thing down at an Air Force base? That's suicide! We're out of here. No bloody way in hell they will shoot down an unarmed civilian carrier! We'll go to Mexico, I don't know, Alaska—"

"Johnny, calm down. Not to worry, okay? I can talk us out of this. It's the only way out, now. Give me the radio."

"Talk us out of it? You are wholly insane, man. I thought this whole thing was going to be a walk in the park! We land, let all the zombies disembark. They go blow up a few nuclear reactors or what have you while we walk away rich. Now—"

"Listen. They will shoot, Johnny. That 9/11 plane that went down in Pennsylvania? If it had not crashed, the president had ordered them to shoot it down before it took out the White House. I know this."

"Jesus Christ," Adare said, and then he heard a squawk in his headphones.

"Speedbird, I am the Navy F-18 Hornet riding on your starboard wingtip. Captain Wiley Reynolds, Top Hat Squadron leader, U.S. Navy. I say again, you are ordered to initiate descent and land your aircraft immediately at Edwards Air Force Base. If you maintain current altitude and continue to disregard this order, I am authorized to take offensive measures against you. I repeat, descend and land your aircraft on Edwards runway two-niner at once. Over."

"He means it!" Soong shouted. "He'll shoot! Oh, my God!" Khalid was shouting at him too, pounding on the cockpit door again. Johnny couldn't hear what he was saying out there, but he had a pretty good idea.

"Fuck you, Navy," Johnny Adare said.

"Hey, *Gunfighter,* am I hearing things?" another Top Hat pilot said. "I think the man just said something impolite. Over."

"British Airways, I say again, this is the U.S. Navy Super Hornet on your starboard wing. I am rapidly running out of patience with you. You familiar with the AIM-9 Sidewinder missiles you see under my wings, sir? If you do not want to see one or two headed up your tailpipe, I strongly advise you to begin your descent immediately. Follow us down."

Johnny looked again at his fuel indicators and felt his whole life running out of gas. There was no way he'd make it even to Mexico, much less that old WWII airstrip up in the Aleutians he'd been thinking about. Christ. Only half an hour ago, he'd been dreaming about that first dry martini tonight in the Polo Lounge. Fuck.

He now had the hollow feeling of someone whose worst nightmare had come true. All of his plans and dreams of the future, his role as the dashing pilot who retired to his little pub in his little corner of Ireland—it was rumored about town that he was very rich—all of this was finished. His future now was, what, years of imprisonment? Maybe even execution. Yeah, they shot guys for this shit now. His daughter, Caitlin, had MS. He'd never see her again.

"We'll follow them down," Johnny told Soong finally. "But I don't want to hear another fucking word out of you, understand?"

"Johnny—"

"And don't call me Johnny!"

There was a beeping noise as he reached over and disengaged the autopilot. Then he raised the speed brake and eased the controls forward to initiate his descent. A fiery orange haze hung over the Mojave Desert and the Sierra Madre mountain range beyond. Like flying into hell, he thought, but maybe he could still find a way out. Put down on one of those desert highways or even—

"Speedbird 77 heavy, L.A. Approach, contact arrivals one-three-three point eight. You are cleared to land on runway two-five left, over."

"British 77 heavy, yeah, thanks, L.A. I don't think we'll be needing that runway after all. Seems we've been diverted to Edwards Air Force Base."

"Uh, roger, 77, this is L.A. Approach. Have a good afternoon, sir."

"You bet, L.A. Good day."

"Good job, Speedbird, this is *Gunfighter*. About time you came to your senses. We'll peel off and give you a little flying room, sir."

The Navy jets did just that. About thirty fucking feet of flying room on all four sides. And more bleeding squadrons upstairs. The Yanks were acting like he was trying to blow up their whole bloody country. But then, maybe he was. He didn't really know everything Poison Ivy and the Pasha had planned really, now did he?

Johnny called the hostesses and got Fiona on the intercom. She was slightly hysterical, more than slightly, but he didn't really have the time to calm her down. He told her to get everybody strapped in, they'd be landing somewhere in a few minutes. He didn't tell her he didn't have a clue exactly what was waiting for them down there.

Four Super Hornets rode the big airplane all the way down. The Top Hat squadron pilots, who'd heard the entire radio exchange, all had fairly itchy trigger fingers. Whoever this bastard was, he'd blown a civilian airliner out of the sky to get here. The big plane and its many escorts came in out of the west, down over the blue Pacific idly lapping at the California beaches, through the orange haze that blanketed the city of Los Angeles and the San Fernando Valley. They flew on, out over the

Mojave Desert, some ninety miles north of the city. Johnny Adare got his gear down when they told him to. Five minutes later, he was looking at the sprawl that was Edwards Air Force Base. With a whole lot of interested parties looking on, Flight 00 from Suva Island finally touched down on runway two-niner.

Flashing blue and red lights lined both sides of the runway. A squadron of recently scrambled Edwards AFB F-117A Stealth fighters roared overhead in the opposite direction, looking like a flock of evil black wizards. Emergency fire equipment, HAZMAT, and military vehicles raced across the field. Then, maybe a third of the way down the runway, Adare saw an Abrams M1A2 main battle tank squadron, flanked in a V-formation, throwing up a huge cloud of dust as they rumbled straight towards his plane.

"Tanks! Good Christ!" Adare shouted. "They've got the whole fucking army waiting down here! You still think you can talk your way out of this?"

"Yes," Soong said quietly. He held up something that looked like a shiny football and smiled. Johnny didn't have time for his or anybody else's bullshit anymore.

He shoved his throttles right to the firewall and the big jet roared forward down the runway toward the oncoming tank squadron. He rotated, and his gear cleared the turrets of the lead tanks by maybe ten feet.

"I don't know about you, but this ain't my idea of retirement, Doc. Fuck it."

Fifteen minutes later, while Johnny Adare was circling low over downtown Los Angeles at about two thousand feet, Hawke and the president, half a world apart, were engaged in a very urgent and private conversation.

"We're about a New York minute from Armageddon, here, Alex. He now claims he's got a nuclear device aboard that plane."

"You want my advice, Mr. President?"

"Yes, Alex, by God, I certainly do."

Every minute or so his loop meant Adare was flying directly into the setting sun and it was killing his eyes. He was bloody well exhausted now. He just wanted to go to sleep. Doctor Soong had ceased his wailing and was balled up into the fetal position in the left-hand seat, cradling the small football-shaped nuclear device in his hands, his finger curled around the ignition switch.

"They won't do it, Johnny. I'm telling you. They won't shoot. They just won't risk a catastrophic radioactive explosion over this city. We'll think of something. Yes, yes, a little time to think is all we need."

"You lied to me, you little bastard. You told me you didn't load any fooking nukes aboard. Too unstable, you said. Christ."

"I am a congenital liar. It is something I cannot help."

"Jesus. I don't—we can't keep this bluff up. We're just about running out of fuel here. I'll have to ditch the goddamn thing pretty soon."

"It's not a bluff!" Soong said, his black eyes gleaming. "Never a bluff, Johnny, when you hold precisely the cards you say you hold. Look! You see that tall group of buildings? Near the golf course? It's called Century City. Take us down there. Excellent. High-target opportunity."

"What the fuck," Adare said wearily.

Johnny descended to a slow elliptical pattern about a thousand feet above the gleaming complex of office towers. He could see traffic backed up at the stoplights along two major intersecting boulevards. Rush hour. The light was pretty now. Kind of a rosy gold. There was a lush green golf course just beyond a thick hedge along one of the boulevards. Another world, fifty yards away from all the cars. People just going about their lives. Playing golf on one side of the hedge. Headed home on the other. Going to the cinema. Having a pint at the local pub. Kissing a pretty girl in a dark corner.

He heard a noise in his headphones.

"How long you want to play this game, Speedbird?" the Navy Super Hornet pilot now said. At first, when he'd bolted on the runway, the guy he called Navy had been extremely pissed. That's when Soong got on the radio. And, now that they all knew about Soong's Pigskin, and all the other suitcase nukes they were apparently carrying in the belly of the plane, Navy and everybody else had calmed way down. Or, at least Navy had lowered the decibel level over the radio.

Nice guy, Navy, Johnny thought. Name was Reynolds. Sounded like a guy you wouldn't mind having a few pops with. Adare banked the big plane and descended five hundred feet. The shouting and screaming in the back of the bus had died down. Probably praying back there, Johnny imagined.

"How much longer you plan to dick around up here, Cap?" Navy said.

"How long you got, Navy?" Johnny asked him.

"Oh, we never close."

"Well, I guess we just—hey! What are you doing with that thing? I don't—don't want to—don't—"

"You're breaking up, Cap. What did you—"

Muffled sounds and a high-pitched noise were coming from the cockpit. What they heard was the sound of Adare seizing the crazed doctor by the scruff of his scrawny neck. Soong had pushed a series of buttons on the device and it was now emitting a high keening sound. He slammed the Indian's head repeatedly against the windscreen, not stopping until the glass was smeared with bright red blood. Poison Ivy was screaming now, begging Johnny to stop.

Finally, knowing he was fast losing consciousness, Soong attempted to detonate the nuclear device. But, in order to do so, he slightly shifted his death grip on the trigger mechanism. In that infinite fraction of a second, Johnny Adare seized the device and snatched it from Soong's grasp, breaking the man's wrist in the doing. Soong howled in fresh pain and lunged for his creation, but Adare sent him flying back into the pilot's seat with the back of his left hand.

Captain Wiley Reynolds, like everyone else overhearing the life-or-death drama in the 747 cockpit, held his breath for what seemed an eternity.

"Is the president still on the line?" they finally heard a voice say. It was the pilot, Adare.

"I am," Jack McAtee said.

"I, uh, I don't want to do this—shut the fuck up! I'm talking to the president—I don't want to do this, sir. Kill all those innocent people down there."

"No, you definitely do not want to do that."

"Is there some, uh, arrangement we could make?"

"You mean, some kind of immunity?"

"That's correct."

"We could talk about that. I would need your

absolute assurance that the man in your cockpit has disarmed his device."

"He doesn't have it anymore. I took it away from him. I made him disarm . . . I don't think it's armed any longer."

There was a pause as everyone drew a collective breath. Finally, the president spoke.

"I won't negotiate with terrorists, son. As long as you are in my country's sovereign airspace, you are a terrorist. Get twelve miles out over the Pacific, we can have a little talk."

"Yeah. Okay. Listen, thanks a lot, sir."

"You are doing the right thing. That's all I can say."

"Hey, Navy?" Adare said, after a moment.

"Yeah, Cap."

"Can you guys give me a little breathing room here?"

"Yeah, will do. You'll want to climb now to five thousand and go to heading two-seven-zero, Cap. I say again, climb and maintain five thousand, heading two-seven-zero. Over."

The squadron of Super Hornets closest to the big airliner gave the target a thousand more yards fore and aft. Reynolds and his wingman over on the 747's port side peeled away, decelerated, and tucked in behind flight 77.

"Climbing through one, going to five, heading two-seven-zero, Navy," Adare said, watching the Hornet on his starboard wing arc away and disappear aft of his line of sight. A moment later, his radio crackled again.

"Roger, Cap, this is *Gunfighter,* standing by. I'll be right behind you. This would not be a good time to get cute."

A long minute of silence passed.

"*Hawkeye,* you still standing by?" the president finally said, going private with Hawke and the Navy pilot Reynolds.

"That's affirmative, sir," Hawke said.

"It's nut-cutting time, Alex. Four hundred souls. Talk to me."

"I stand by my original assessment, Mr. President," Hawke said. "No innocents aboard that airplane."

"You copy what *Hawkeye* says, *Gunfighter?*"

"Aye, aye, copy that, sir, that's affirm."

"Okay, then *Gunfighter,* this is *Warhorse.* God help us all. I order you to do your duty, son."

"Copy that, *Warhorse.* Understood. *Gunfighter* will execute as ordered, sir. Over."

The infrared system of the AIM-9X Sidewinder air-to-air missile permits the pilot to launch his heat-seeking missiles and then take evasive action while the missile homes in on the exhaust of the target. Once launched, the missiles travel at supersonic speeds. Infrared sensors and a conical scanner in the nose cone track the target. Reflected lasers tell the missile when it has reached optimum destructive range and trigger the warhead.

Captain Wiley Reynolds thumbed the switch that armed the Sidewinders below his wings. A keening warning signal filled the Super Hornet's cockpit. He could now fire at will. He took a long hard look at the British Airways plane silhouetted in the setting sun.

Even as his right hand moved to activate the fire control system, his gut was having trouble accepting the signals his rational mind was sending. Distorted reality. He felt just like some poor GI wandering alone in a dusty village, encountering a woman in heavy robes with a baby in her arms.

The president had nailed it. It was nut-cutting time.

It's not a baby, goddamn it, it's a bomb, his mind said.

Captain Reynolds pulled the trigger. The missile streaked away trailing a thin stream of white smoke.

"Hey, Navy, we twelve miles out yet?" Adare said, a raspy catch in his voice. The glare of the setting sun off the Pacific was making his eyes water and he wiped them furiously with the back of his hand.

"Getting close, Cap."

"Ever get over to Ireland?"

"Someday. Hear it's a beautiful country."

"So bloody *green*, mate. It's like a dream."

"Yeah."

"Round of Guinness on me whenever you do, Navy."

"Appreciate the offer, Cap."

"Hey, listen—"

EPILOGUE

Islamorada

They sat together on the sand, about twenty yards from the tide line, watching the orange ball of the sun go down. The woman was arranging a small mound of seashells next to her, prizes from the afternoon. The sun was still hot, but a breeze was rising gently and you could smell the cool of late October that had been hiding in the heat all day. The tide was receding, leaving the firm wet sand to the seagulls. Creamy masses of cumulus clouds lay on the far horizon, and there were thin feathers of cirrus against the high western sky.

"Either the bonefish are getting smarter, or I'm getting stupider," the man said, staring into the setting sun and saying exactly what was on his mind.

A look of deep satisfaction appeared around the woman's eyes. The Florida Keys, just as she'd hoped, were working their magic on both of them. Just the fact that the man had gotten to this sunshine state of mind was enough to make the woman smile and run her fingers through his thick black hair, still damp from their recent swim.

"Bones are the smartest fish in the world," Conch said. "Don't be so hard on yourself, baby. Anyway, comparisons are odious."

Alex Hawke laughed and lay back on the sand, hands clasped behind his head. He closed his eyes against the sun and his mouth relaxed into its normally bemused half-smile. The sand beneath him was still warm. The beer in his hand was still cold. It had been a good day.

"Place is lousy with bougainvillea this time of year," Conch said through a yawn, tracing the nasty purple weal on Hawke's ribcage. His broken ribs were healing slowly.

"Don't you hate it?" Hawke said.

The two of them had been here at Islamorada for almost a week, hiding from the world at Conch's little fishing place. "Shacking up," as Alex had put it, smiling down at her that first morning, waking up early in her bed. He said, "Never quite understood the term until just this moment."

It was a shack, and proud of it, but it was also right on the water, a small wooden structure on a sandy beach, hidden away in a half-moon cove of dense mangroves. Conch Shell was at the dead end of a twisting sandy lane that wound its way through the thick sea grape, ending about half a mile from the main road. White bougainvillea framed the front door, and the wild garden was aflame with tropical foliage, hibiscus and oleander.

When Alex had agreed to come down, she'd gone out and bought a second-hand flats boat to go with her island getaway, a sixteen-foot Backcountry Skiff. He loved bonefishing. And so they'd spent this morning, like every morning, poling across the gin-clear flats, chasing bones.

Even if they made sleepy love upon waking, they

were out on the water every morning by eight. At noon, Alex would crack open his first cold beer, a Kalik from the Bahamas, his longtime favorite. At one, they'd eat whatever Conch had packed in the basket that day. By three in the afternoon, after a swim and maybe a rum, they were ready to get out of the tropical sun. And so they did, emerging from the small bed again only when it was time to climb into Conch's battered old Jeep and race over to Lorelei's in time for the sunset celebration, the margaritas, and vintage Jimmy Buffett.

She lay back on the sand beside him. The rim of the orange ball would not touch the sea for another ten minutes. They'd decided to stay put tonight, order in some Chinese from Great Wall Taki-Outi. Their shoulders were touching; the saltwater was drying to a white frosting on their lips and cheeks and deeply tanned bodies.

Alex Hawke rested his right hand on her sun-warm thigh and said, "Happy?"

God.

Consuelo de los Reyes had lost her heart to this very man on this very island once long ago. No, that was wrong. She hadn't lost it. She had given it away. Grabbed him by his big shoulders on a beach not half a mile from here and said of her rapidly beating heart, "Here, Mister, you take this damned thing and put it in your pocket." And, now, finally, after many empty years of gradually reclaiming it, and then trying fiercely to protect it, here she was by his side on another beach, an accomplished historian trying desperately not to let history repeat itself.

"Nice day," he said softly.

"Another lousy day in paradise."

"Somebody's got to do it."

"Might as well be us, right?"

"Is Paris a city? Is my companion a woman of almost supernatural beauty and brilliance?"

"Almost?"

She rolled over to her side, propped her head in the palm of her hand and kissed his salty lips. He placed his hand firmly on the hill of her breast and kissed her back, hard, and somehow the sun set on the little cove without either of them seeing it. Later, they walked barefoot up the beach to the little house in the indigo dusk and he wrapped her in his arms before they stepped inside.

"No fishing tomorrow, dear girl. I've got a mission."

"Can I come?"

"Nope, secret."

"Oh."

"Nothing too dangerous. I'll be home for supper."

"You be careful out there, sailor."

He awoke during the night to the sound of a brief, hard rain on the tin roof. Conch moved her cool naked hip against him and he made love to her, slowly, with great affection, in the way of old lovers. He rose at dawn the next morning. To keep Sniper quiet while he showered and shaved, he tossed a handful of Cheezbits into her cage out on the screened porch. Then he slipped into his grey Bud 'n Mary's Marina T-shirt, a pair of faded khaki shorts, and his flip-flops, and left the house, easing the screen door shut behind him. Conch had been dead asleep, snoring lightly when he'd left the bed, and he'd broken his promise to wake her. She could use a few more hours, and so could he, he thought staring at his reflection in the mirror over the sink. Damned demon rum. Aptly named stuff, he felt like hell.

He cranked up the Jeep and nosed through the thick sea grape bushes into the deeply rutted sandy drive. It was going to be a scorcher and for once he wished Conch's old heap had a top. Pausing at the main highway, he flashed his headlights twice. Two DSS guys who were eating donuts in the black Suburban parked across from the hidden drive smiled at him. Conch's security details loved it down here, too, most of them fishing for bone or tarpon whenever they got a few hours free. The guy behind the wheel was Gidwitz. Hawke had made sure Ron landed this plum assignment as part of his recuperation. He deserved it after all he'd done up on the mountain. The Iceman.

He turned left and headed north on U.S. 1. The famous Overseas Highway was only two lanes all the way up the chain of Keys to the Turnpike and Miami. The locals still called it the Old Road. With traffic, it took him a little over two hours to reach the Miami airport. But he was standing at the security checkpoint when Stokely, wearing an XXXL white *guayabera* and a broad-brimmed straw hat, appeared in the midst of a gaggle of passengers. He wasn't hard to spot.

"Yeah, there he is," Stoke said, striding toward him with a huge white smile. "There is the man! Come here, boy, give old Stoke a hug." The two men embraced with great affection. Though they had spoken often on the telephone, it had been weeks since they'd seen each other. Hawke was still deeply moved by what his old friend had done for him down here in

Florida, very nearly losing his life in the doing. He'd tried to express his feelings about it on the phone many times and failed miserably.

"Hey, Stoke, damn it's good to see you," Hawke said, grabbing his carry-on and slinging it over his shoulder. "Thanks for coming, man. I appreciate it."

"Oh, hold up. I see. You think I came all the way down here to see you! Check out your skinny little white ass? You know I love you, brother, but, man, I got me a fine woman down here, now. Told you 'bout her."

"Fancha, right?"

"Fancha, that's right. Bona fide contender for the title! She's got her a nice little place out on Key Biscayne. Oh, yeah. It's all deluxe! Where's your car at? Sooner I'm done with you, sooner I go see her."

"You have any more luggage?"

"More than this? Who you think I am? You?"

"Right. Let's go."

"Look at you wearing them funky little flip-floppy sandals. Man, I thought you'd be in a tie at least, show some respect."

It took them an hour in the Jeep to reach the Ocean Reef Club in Key Largo. Hawke had hired a boat, a twenty-four-foot Captiva with twin Mercruiser 250s. The name, *Hurry-Cane,* was painted over the faded red "Key Largo" on her transom. The charter captain assured him she'd do forty knots with ease.

Hawke had stopped in Florida City on the way back down and bought them a bag of ice, cold beer, and Cuban sandwiches at the bait shop where he also gassed up.

Stoke climbed aboard the Captiva and cranked the engines. Hawke handed the food, beer and ice down to him, then a five to the kid for helping with the lines. Then he stepped down onto the boat himself and they shoved off, sliding through the shadows of the big yachts on their way out to the channel. Since Stoke knew where they were going, he did the driving.

The bay was flat calm. They rode mostly in silence, Stoke leaving him alone with his thoughts.

After a considerable time, as if reading his thoughts, Stoke said to him, "Listen, I don't want you to go giving me all the credit for this. Ross, either. We couldn't have gotten nowhere with finding this cat and running his ass down hadn't been for my man Ambrose Congreve of Scotland Yard."

Hawke smiled at this mention of his old friend. Congreve had taken a little farm in Tuscany for a few months and was blissfully happy there. "Yeah, Stoke. Ambrose Congreve. He's got himself a new dog and he's learning Italian."

"Italian? Man can't even speak English plain enough so most normal folks can understand him."

"He says the same about you, Stoke," Hawke grinned.

"You got to love him," Stoke laughed, and the two men lapsed once more into silence.

"Okay, this is it," Stoke said, easing the throttles after about another half an hour of running wide open across the mirrored bay. The boat came off plane and settled. They'd sped across Card Sound and up into lower Biscayne Bay. The sun was hot and Alex had taken off his sweat-drenched shirt. They'd passed an endless series of small mangrove cays to starboard, all of them looking exactly alike to him.

"Does it have a name?" he asked, staring at the small island.

"Yeah. Call it No Name Key. Really, that's the name."

Alex moved aft to stand beside Stoke at the console.

"Right here?" he said, trying to see it all in his head.

"Yeah. Right in here. He went in there first, in the Cigarette, and me and Ross followed him."

"Let's go."

On both sides of the water here, the bushes and shrubs were still blackened and twisted. The muddy banks were charcoal grey. Stoke stopped the boat. This had to be where the ammo explosion had blown Ross out of the water. Stoke looked at him. "You sure you still want to go ashore? Skeets eat you alive back in there."

"Yeah. C'mon, let's go."

"Awright, but like I say, it ain't much to see."

They found the little clearing.

"See that big tree over there? That's the one I told you about. Called a Gumbo Limbo. That's where he was waiting, up at the top there."

Alex started forward, but Stoke put a hand on his arm. "Let's go round behind it. You got to watch out. That's all quicksand all around here."

They approached the peeling reddish tree from behind. Hawke could see the whole thing now. Stoke up to his waist in the quicksand near the base of the tree, two bullets in him, thinking he was going to die all alone. Believing Ross was dead. His friend Hawke half a world away. And the man who'd murdered Vicky sitting right here, on the spot where Hawke was standing now, waiting for it to happen. Enjoying it— watching his friend here suffer and—

"Hey. You want me to wait in the boat, boss?" Stoke said, studying him carefully.

"If you don't mind, Stoke. Thanks. I'll only be a minute."

"Sure."

Hawke sat down under the Gumbo tree and stared at the quicksand grave of his wife's killer. There was no marker, of course, nothing to identify this spot. There would be no mourners at this graveside. Ever. Only two other men even knew it existed. Still, he had needed to see it. It had been necessary to come here, sit under this tree.

Vicky is buried beneath a tree. A tree she played in as a child. A beautiful old oak beside the Mississippi.

"You killed my wife," Hawke said softly. "One fine morning on the steps of a church. In her wedding dress. I would have found you sooner or later. I would have looked into your eyes as I killed you. You got lucky in a way, dead man. My friends got to you before I could."

He had no idea how long he sat there under the Gumbo tree on No Name Key, but, finally, it was long enough.

"It should have been me," he said aloud, getting to his feet.

He turned to walk away, paused, and looked back one last time. "But you're just as dead as if I'd done it myself," he said. "Dead is dead."

It was over.

An unmarked grave on an island with no name for the man with no eyes.

He went back to find Stoke and the *Hurry-Cane*. With any luck at all, they'd be back at the dock before the cold beer ran out.

*   *   *

Hawke found Conch sitting on the sand, her long legs stretched out, the foamy white froth lapping at her brown feet. He ran quickly through the soft sand down to the water. They could still make it to Lorelei's for the afterglow if they left right now.

"Hey, you," he said. He kissed the top of her head and collapsed in the sand beside her, staring at the fiery water and sky.

"Missed you," Conch said.

She took his hand.

"Well, I'm back."

"You know what, Hawke?" she said, kissing the palm of his hand.

"No idea. Tell me."

"I think maybe you just might be."

The blood-red sun dropped into the sea.

ATRIA BOOKS
PROUDLY PRESENTS

TSAR

TED BELL

Coming soon in hardcover
from Atria Books

Turn the page for a preview of
Tsar. . . .

PROLOGUE

October 1962

1

The end of the world was in plain sight: Missiles sprouted in the cane fields of Cuba, American and Soviet battleships squared off in the South Atlantic. America's young president, John Fitzgerald Kennedy, had had himself one hell of a week.

The Kremlin's angry salvos continued night and day, as events spun rapidly out of control. Bellicose communiqués volleyed and thundered between Moscow and Washington; frayed nerves snapped and sizzled like live wires at either end. Diplomacy was long past the tipping point and the old, tried-and-true Cold War rules of engagement no longer applied.

There were no rules, none at all, not now. Not since Russian premier Nikita Khrushchev had started declaring "We will bury you!" to Western ambassadors and banging his shoe on the table at the UN, and certainly not since Castro's imported Russian ICBMs had been discovered ninety miles from Miami.

The once rock-solid fortress of Camelot, the cherished, peaceful realm of the handsome young king and his beautiful queen, had begun to crumble and crack.

And through that ever-widening fissure, Jack Kennedy knew, lay a doorway straight to Hell.

Between them, the two major combatants had more than fifteen thousand nuclear warheads aimed at each other's throats. On the borders of Western Europe stood ninety Soviet divisions, ready to roll. America's army, navy, and Strategic Air Command bomber squadrons had gone, for the first time in history, to DEFCON 2. A heartbeat away from all-out war. And that's where things had stood all week.

Two helpless giants, afraid to breathe.

Until now.

On this rainy, late October afternoon in 1962, Jack Kennedy was well aware that global nuclear annihilation was no longer the stuff of nightmares, it was right around the corner.

It was closer than Christmas.

At the nightmare's vortex stood the embattled White House. Everyone who worked at 1600 Pennsylvania Avenue was struggling to function for one more hour, one more day, in an atmosphere of impending doom. On people's desks, the faces of cherished children, pets, and loved ones, many framed in crayon-colored popsicle sticks, never let them forget for an instant what they might, at any moment, lose forever.

The U.S. response time to a Cuba-based incoming Soviet missile attack was only thirty-five minutes. That gave a few lucky White House staffers and high-ranking generals seven minutes to dive into helicopters bound for the "Rock," a top-secret underground bunker carved inside a Maryland mountain.

Those remaining behind would just have to grab their pictures, shut their eyes, and dive under their desks, like the school kids in those pitiful Civil Defense ads on TV. The Desk. Against the Bomb. It was a sick joke.

Jack Kennedy ducked into a darkened West Wing alcove and popped two Percodans. His Addison's was acting up, his nerves were shot, and his back was killing him. But his brother Bobby was waiting for him in his last remaining sanctuary, the Oval Office, and he headed for the stairs.

Kennedy had just emerged from the Situation Room after yet another superheated briefing with his Joint Chiefs. The hawkish Pentagon brass wanted immediate, preemptive nuclear strikes deep within the heart of Russia. Kennedy wouldn't budge: his Cuban naval blockade, he insisted, was America's best hope of calling Khrushchev's bluff and averting all-out war.

Behind the closed doors of the Oval Office, Jack Kennedy paced before the crackling fire, his public face gone, his private one a rictus of worry and pain.

"You heard about this goddamn 'Redstick' business, Jack?" Bobby Kennedy asked his older brother.

"Hell, it's all they want to talk about down there. Now they've finally got the stick to beat me with, they are hell-bent to use it."

"Tell me, Jack."

"At the Russian convoy's current speed, the Pentagon calculates Soviet ships will arrive at our outer defensive perimeter in less than seventy-two hours. But, based on all this new intelligence we've been getting from British Naval Intelligence, the scales may have tipped dangerously in favor of Russia's submarine hunter-killers."

"Why?"

"The Russkies have some new kind of undersea acoustic technology called SOFAR, an advanced sonar-buoy code-named 'Redstick.' Apparently they can pick up our sub's screw signatures from a thousand miles away. Jesus, Bobby. If it's true, it means our blockade is full of holes. Worthless, just like the Chiefs have been telling me for days."

Bobby, his hands shoved deep in his pockets, his shoulders slumping with fatigue and anxiety, stood staring through the window at the sodden Rose Garden. He wasn't sure how much more bad news his brother could take. He put a smile on his face and turned toward Jack.

"Look. The Brits are on it. All we can do at the moment is being done."

"Any word from them? Christ, we've been waiting to hear something from that sub of theirs since dawn. Timely information from them is as rare as rocking-horse shit."

"Naval Intelligence London just called Defense. Their sub *Dreadnought* is steaming at flank speed, en route to pick up one of their top field agents in Scotland. A man named Hawke. Sub's ETA at Scarp Island in the Hebrides is 0600 GMT. Hawke will be inserted inside the Soviet's Arctic 'Redstick' base six hours later. If their man gets in and out alive, we'll know something definitive about Redstick's range parameters, acoustic sensitivity, and communication capabilities, and—"

"Fuck the acoustic sensitivity! I want to know how many of these damn things they've got and where the hell they're located! If they're anywhere near our theatre of operations, I want to know how fast we can take them out."

"The Brits say we'll have that intelligence in twelve hours."

"Twelve? Bobby, goddamn it, I need this information *now*. If they've deployed these fucking Redsticks in the South Atlantic, it affects every single defensive operation Admiral Dennison's submarine forces are conducting down there."

"Apparently, Hawke is the best they've got, Jack. If anything can be done, he can do it."

"Well, I hope to God they're right," Kennedy said, collapsing into his favorite wooden rocker, the one with the cane seat and yellow canvas covering the wooden back.

Kennedy, rocking as he stared into the fire, desperately tried to come to grips with the fact that he was suddenly entrusting the fate of the whole damn world to some goddamn Englishman he'd never even heard of.

"Hawke?" Jack Kennedy said rubbing his reddened eyes and staring up at Bobby.

"Who the living hell is Hawke?"

2

He had a rifle slung on his back and a single bullet burning a hole in his pocket.

His name was Hawke.

He was a hard-hearted warrior in a Cold War suddenly gone piping hot. Killing time before a mission pick-up, he was stalking a giant red stag across the island of Scarp's rain-swept moors. The Monarch of Shalloch had eluded him for years. But Hawke's trigger finger was itching so severely, he thought this might be the day man and beast had their final reckoning.

Marching along the seaside cliff, head high, Hawke

himself was like a stag in a state of high alert. The year was 1962 and he was twenty-seven years old, already an old man in Naval Intelligence. After many long months patrolling these very waters aboard a Royal Navy destroyer, searching for Russian submarines, he'd personally felt the menace and reach of Soviet power. Always aching to strike back, it looked as if he might now have a sporting chance to spill some bright red Russian blood.

He'd arrived on the godforsaken island of Scarp two days ahead of his scheduled submarine pickup, travel arrangements courtesy of the Royal Navy. His mission, Operation Redstick, was so highly classified, he wouldn't be briefed until he was aboard *Dreadnought* and headed north of the Arctic Circle. There, on a Norwegian island called Svalbard, was some kind of secret Russian listening post. That's all he knew.

He could guess the rest. It would be his job, he imagined, to find out what the hell the post was all about and then destroy it. Getting out alive would not be mentioned in his brief. But that would be the tricky bit, all right.

Sod it all. He wasn't dead yet, and he still had a few hours left until his pickup. The Monarch, a great red stag, was out there somewhere on the moors or the cliff below. The single bullet in Hawke's pocket had his name engraved on it. He began a careful descent of the cliff face. It was bitterly cold. A fog was rolling in from the sea. Visibility: not good.

Suddenly, amidst the cries of gulls and terns, an odd sound made him look up. Bloody hell, it had sounded like the crack of a high-powered rifle!

Another stalker, tracking the Monarch of Shalloch? Impossible. This miserable island was inhabited only by sheep, crofters, and farmers. They would hardly be out stalking on a god-awful day like—

Christ! The bastard fired again. And this time there was no mistaking his target. Hawke ducked behind a rocky outcropping and waited, forcing his heart rate slow to normal. Another round whistled just above his head. And another.

He caught a glint of sunlight up above, probably reflected off the shooter's binoculars. The man was climbing. Hawke's own position was dangerously exposed. He looked around frantically for cover. Should the man climb even a few feet higher, he'd be completely unprotected. That thicket of trees on the ledge below now looked very good.

Hawke bolted from the now worthless protection of rock and leapt into space. Landing on the ledge on his feet, he went into a tuck and rolled inside the trees. A hundred feet below, the cold and fog-bound sea crashed against ageless rocks.

Five more shots rang out, rounds ripping into the thicket of birch above his head, shredding leaves and branches, debris raining down. Firing blindly now, the shooter knew he was the one exposed for the moment.

Hawke removed the single red-tipped cartridge from his pocket, inserted it into the breech, and shot the bolt.

He took a deep breath and held it, slowing his mind and body down. He was a trained sniper. He knew how to do this. He knew the distance to the target, about 190 yards, the angle of incidence approximately 37 degrees, humidity 100 percent, wind three-to-six miles per hour from his left at 45 degrees. One bullet, one shot. You got the kill or you did not.

Stags, of course, could not shoot back if you missed.

Hawke tucked the stock deep into his shoulder and welded his cheek to it. He a put his eye to the scope, and set his aim, bisecting the target's form with the crosshairs. His finger closed, adding precisely a pound and a half's worth of pressure to the trigger, not an ounce more. Keep it light . . . deep breath now . . . release it halfway . . . wait for it.

The crosshairs bisected the target's face. That's precisely where he aimed to shoot him. Right in the face. Into his eyes. Shoot him in a part of the skull that will cause irrevocable, instantaneous death.

He fired.

The round cooked off, his single bullet found its mark.

His stalker lay facedown, a pool of dark blood forming under what remained of his head. He was dressed for the hunt, a well-used oiled coat, twills. Hawke looked at his boots and saw they were identical to his own, custom made at Lobb's of St. James. An Englishman? He fished inside the dead chap's trouser pockets. A few quid, an American Zippo lighter, a book of matches from the Savoy Grill with a London phone number scrawled inside in a feminine hand.

Inside the old Barbour jacket pockets, nothing but ammunition and a tourist map of the Outer Hebrides, recently purchased. He pulled off the boots and used his hunting knife to pry off the heels. Inside the left boot heel, a hollowed-out space had been professionally created.

Opening the small oilskin packet stuffed inside, Hawke found a thin leather billfold bearing the familiar "sword and shield" pin of the KGB. He knew its meaning well enough: the shield to defend the glorious

Revolution, the sword to smite its foes. Inside the wallet were papers in Cyrillic, clearly issued by the Committee for State Security, popularly known as the KGB.

Also inside the wallet, a not unflattering photograph of Hawke himself taken recently at an outdoor café in Paris. The woman at the table with him was a pretty American actress from Louisiana. His beloved Kitty. Moments after this picture had been taken, he'd asked her to marry him.

Was this just an isolated assassination attempt, based on his past sins? Or, had the KGB penetrated Operation Redstick? If the latter, the mission was clearly compromised. The Russians on that frozen Arctic island would be waiting for him. Losing the element of surprise always made things a bit more dicey.

He stood there, looking at the dead Russian, an idea forming in his head. Whitehall could immediately put out a coded signal, on a channel the Russians regularly monitored.

"Sub arrived on station 0600 for pickup," the false signal would read. *"Two corpses found at site: British agent and KGB assassin both apparently killed during struggle. Mission compromised, operation aborted."*

Worth a shot, at any rate.

There was a collapsible spade inside the stalking pack on his back. He slipped out of the canvas shoulder straps, removed the shovel from the pack, and, his spirits lightened considerably, found himself whistling a bit of "A Nightingale Sang in Berkeley Square" as he plunged his spade again and again into the icy ground.

Sometimes a man just had to bury his past and bloody well get on with it.

CHAPTER ONE

Bermuda
Present Day

War and peace. In Alexander Hawke's experience, life usually boiled down to one or the other. Like his namesake late father, a hero much decorated for his daring Cold War exploits against the Soviets, Hawke greatly favored peace but was notoriously adept at war. Whenever and wherever in the world his rather exotic skill set was required, Alex Hawke gladly sallied forth. Cloak donned, dagger to hand, he would jubilantly enter and reenter the eternal fray.

He was thirty-three years old. A good age, by his accounts, not too young and not too old. A fine balance of youth and experience, if one could be so bold.

Alex Hawke, let it first be said, was a creature of radiant violence. Attack came naturally to him; the man was all fire. Shortly after his squalling birth, his very English father had declared to his equally American mother, "He seems to me, Kitty, a boy born with a heart ready for any fate. I only wonder what ballast will balance all that bloody sail."

Normally a cool, rather detached character, Alex Hawke's simmering blood could roil to a rapid boil at very short notice. Oddly enough, his true nature was not readily apparent to the casual observer. Someone who chanced to meet him, say, on an evening's stroll through Berkeley Square, would find him an amiable, even jolly chap. He might even be whistling a chirrupy tune about nightingales or somesuch. There was an easy grace about the man, a cheery nonchalance that put most people at their ease.

But it was Hawke's what-the-hell grin, a look so freighted with charm that no woman, and even few men, could resist, that made him who he was.

Hawke was noticeable. A big man with a heroic head, he stood well north of six feet and worked hard at a strict exercise regimen to keep himself extremely fit. His face was finely modeled, its character deeply etched by the myriad wonders and doubts of his inner experience.

His glacial blue eyes were brilliant, and the play of his expression had a flashing range, from the merriment and charm with which he charged his daily conversation, to a profound earnestness. His demeanor could quickly assume a tragic and powerful look which could make even a trivial topic suddenly assume new and enlightening importance.

He had a full head of rather untamable jet-black hair, a high, clear brow, and a straight, imperious nose. Below it was a strong chin and a well-sculpted mouth with just a hint of cruelty at the corners.

Picture a hale fellow well met whom men wanted to stand a drink and whom women much preferred horizontal.

He'd been dozing on a pristine Bermuda beach for the better part of an hour. It was a hot day, a day that was shot blue all through. The fluttering eyelids and the thin smile on Hawke's salt-parched lips belied the rather exotic dream he was having. Suddenly, some noise from above, perhaps the dolphinlike clicking of a long-tailed Bermuda Petrel, startled him from his reverie. He cracked one eye, then the other, smiling at the fleeting memory of sexual bliss still imprinted on the back of his mind.

Erotic images, fleshy nymphs of pink and creamy white, fled quickly as he raised up his head and peered alertly at the brightness of the real world through two fiercely narrowed blue eyes. Just inside the reef line, a white sail shivered and flipped to leeward. As he watched the graceful little Bermuda sloop, the sail turned to windward again and from across the water he distinctly heard the ruffle and snap of canvas.

No question about this time and place in his life, he thought, gazing at the gently lapping surf: my blue heaven.

Here on this sunlit mid-Atlantic isle, peace abounded. These, finally, were the "blue days" he had longed for. His most recent "red" period, a rather dodgy affair involving a madman named Papa Top and armies of Hezbollah *jihadistas* deep in the Amazon, was mercifully fading from memory. Every new blue day pushed those fearful memories deeper into the depths of his consciousness and for that he was truly grateful.

He rolled over easily onto his back. The sugary sand, like pinkish talc, was warm beneath his bare skin. Must have drifted off after his most recent swim. Hmm. He linked his hands behind his still-damp head and breathed deeply, the fresh salt air filling his lungs.

The sun was still high in the azure blue Bermuda sky.

He lifted his arm to gaze lazily at his dive watch. It

was just after two o'clock in the afternoon. A smile flitted across his lips as he contemplated the remainder of the day's schedule. He had nothing on this evening save a quiet dinner with his closest friend, Ambrose Congreve, and his fiancée, Diana Mars, at eight. He licked the dried salt from his lips, closed his eyes, and let the sun take his naked body.

His refuge was a small cove of crystalline turquoise water. Wavelets slid up and over dappled pinkish sand before retreating to regroup and charge once more. This tiny bay, perhaps a hundred yards across at its mouth, was invisible from the coast road. The South Road, as it was called, had been carved into the jagged coral and limestone centuries earlier and extended all the way along the coast to Somerset and the Royal Naval Dockyard.

Fringed with flourishing green sea grape, Hawke's little crescent of paradise was indistinguishable from countless coves just like it stretching east and west along the southern coast of Bermuda. The only access was from the sea. After months of visiting the cove undisturbed, he'd begun to think of the spot as his own. He'd nicknamed it "No-Name Bay."

Hawke had chosen Bermuda carefully. He saw it as an ideal spot to nurse his wounds and heal his battered psyche. Situated in the mid-Atlantic, roughly equidistant between his twin capitals of London and Washington, Bermuda was quaintly civilized, featured balmy weather, a happy-go-lucky population, and, it was somewhere few of his acquaintances, friend or foe, would ever think to look for him.

In the year prior, his bout of nasty scrapes in the Amazon jungles had included skirmishes with various tropical fevers that had nearly taken his life. But, after six idyllic months of marinating in this tropic sea and air, he concluded that he'd never felt better in his life. Even with a modest daily intake of Mr. Gosling's elixir, called by the natives "black rum," he had somehow gotten his six-foot-plus frame down to his fighting weight of 180. He now had a deepwater tan and a flat belly and he felt just fine. In his early thirties, he felt twenty if a day.

Hawke had taken refuge in a small, somewhat dilapidated, beach cottage. The old house, originally a sugar mill, was perched, some might say precariously, above the sea a few miles west of his current location. He had gotten into the very healthy habit of swimming to this isolated beach every day. Three miles twice daily was not excessive and not a bad addition to his normal workout routine, which included a few hundred sit-ups and pull-ups, not to mention serious weight-training.

His privacy thus assured, his habit at his private beach was to shed his swimsuit once he'd arrived. He'd made a ritual of stripping it off and hanging it on a nearby mangrove branch. Then, a few hours sunning *au naturel,* as our French cousins would have it. He was normally a modest man, but the luxuriant feeling of cool air and sunlight on parts not normally exposed was too delightful to be denied. He'd gotten so accustomed to this new regime, the merest idea of wearing trunks here would seem superfluous, ridiculous even. And—what?

He stared with disbelieving eyes.

What the bloody hell was *that*?